PETER RUFF

and the Double Four

E. Phillips Oppenheim

Peter Ruff and the Double Four

E. Phillips Oppenheim

© 1st World Library, 2006
PO Box 2211
Fairfield, IA 52556
www.1stworldlibrary.com
First Edition

LCCN: 2007921185

Softcover ISBN: 978-1-4218-4122-9
Hardcover ISBN: 978-1-4218-4121-2
eBook ISBN: 978-1-4218-4123-6

Purchase *"Peter Ruff and the Double Four"*
as a traditional bound book at:
www.1stWorldLibrary.com/purchase.asp?ISBN=978-1-4218-4122-9

1st World Library is a literary, educational organization
dedicated to:

- Creating a free internet library of downloadable ebooks

- Hosting writing competitions and offering book
  publishing scholarships.

Interested in more 1st World Library books?
contact: literacy@1stworldlibrary.com
Check us out at: www.1stworldlibrary.com

CONTENTS

BOOK ONE

BOOK TWO

BOOK ONE

CHAPTER I

INTRODUCING MR. PETER RUFF

There was nothing about the supper party on that particular Sunday evening in November at Daisy Villa, Green Street, Streatham, which seemed to indicate in any way that one of the most interesting careers connected with the world history of crime was to owe its very existence to the disaster which befell that little gathering. The villa was the residence and also - to his credit – the unmortgaged property of Mr. David Barnes, a struggling but fairly prosperous coal merchant of excellent character, some means, and Methodist proclivities. His habit of sitting without his coat when carving, although deprecated by his wife and daughter on account of the genteel aspirations of the latter, was a not unusual one in the neighbourhood; and coupled with the proximity of a cold joint of beef, his seat at the head of the table, and a carving knife and fork grasped in his hands, established clearly the fact of his position in the household, which a somewhat weak physiognomy might otherwise have led the casual observer to doubt. Opposite him, at the other end of the table, sat his wife, Mrs. Barnes, a somewhat voluminous lady with a high colour, a black satin frock, and many ornaments. On her left the son of the house, eighteen years old, of moderate stature, somewhat pimply, with the fashion of the moment reflected in his pink tie with white spots, drawn through a gold ring, and curving outwards to seek obscurity underneath a dazzling waistcoat. A white tube-rose in his buttonhole might have been intended as a sort of compliment to the occasion, or an indication of his intention to take a walk after supper in the fashionable purlieus of the neighbourhood. Facing him sat his sister - a fluffy-haired, blue-eyed young lady, pretty in her way, but chiefly noticeable for a peculiar sort of self-consciousness blended with self-satisfaction, and possessed only at a certain period in their lives by young ladies of her age. It was almost the air of the cat in whose interior reposes the missing canary, except that in this instance the canary obviously existed in the person of the young man who sat at her side, introduced formally to the household for the first time. That young man's name was - at the moment - Mr. Spencer Fitzgerald.

It seems idle to attempt any description of a person who, in the past, had secured a certain amount of fame under a varying personality; and who, in the future, was to become more than ever notorious under a far less aristocratic pseudonym than that by which he was at present known to the inhabitants of Daisy Villa. There are photographs of him in New York and Paris, St. Petersburg and Chicago, Vienna and Cape Town, but there are no two pictures which present to the casual observer the slightest likeness to one another. To allude to him by the name under which he had won some part, at least, of the affections of Miss Maud Barnes, Mr. Spencer Fitzgerald, as he sat there, a suitor on probation for her hand, was a young man of modest and genteel appearance. He wore a blue serge suit - a little underdressed for the occasion, perhaps; but his tie and collar were neat; his gold-rimmed spectacles - if a little disapproved of by Maud on account of the air of steadiness which they imparted - suggested excellent son-in-lawlike qualities to Mr. and Mrs. Barnes. He had the promise of a fair moustache, but his complexion generally was colourless. His features, except for a certain regularity, were undistinguished. His speech was modest and correct. His manner varied with his company. To-night it had been pronounced, by excellent judges - genteel.

The conversation consisted - naturally enough, under the circumstances - of a course of subtle and judicious pumping, tactfully prompted, for the most part, by Mrs. Barnes. Such,

E. Phillips Oppenheim

for instance, as the following:

"Talking about Marie Corelli's new book reminds me, Mr. Fitzgerald - your occupation is connected with books, is it not?" his prospective mother-in-law enquired, artlessly.

Mr. Fitzgerald bowed assent.

"I am cashier at Howell & Wilson's in Cheapside," he said. "We sell a great many books there - as many, I should think, as any retail establishment in London."

"Indeed!" Mrs. Barnes purred. "Very interesting work, I am sure. So nice and intellectual, too; for, of course, you must be looking inside them sometimes."

"I know the place well," Mr. Adolphus Barnes, Junior, announced condescendingly, - "pass it every day on my way to lunch."

"So much nicer," Mrs. Barnes continued, "than any of the ordinary businesses - grocery or drapery, or anything of that sort."

Miss Maud elevated her eyebrows slightly. Was it likely that she would have looked with eyes of favour upon a young man engaged in any of these inferior occupations?

"There's money in books, too," Mr. Barnes declared with sudden inspiration. His prospective son-in-law turned towards him deferentially.

"You are right, sir," he admitted. "There is money in them. There's money for those who write, and there's money for those who sell. My occupation," he continued, with a modest little cough, "brings me often into touch with publishers, travellers and clerks, so I am, as it were, behind the scenes to some extent. I can assure you," he continued, looking from Mr. Barnes to his wife, and finally transfixing Mr. Adolphus -

"I can assure you that the money paid by some firms of publishers to a few well-known authors - I will mention no names - as advances against royalties, is something stupendous!"

"Ah!" Mr. Barnes murmured, solemnly shaking his head.

"Marie Corelli, I expect, and that Hall Caine," remarked young Adolphus.

"Seems easy enough to write a book, too," Mrs. Barnes said. "Why, I declare that some of those we get from the library - we subscribe to a library, Mr. Fitzgerald - are just as simple and straightforward that a child might have written them. No plot whatsoever, no murders or mysteries or anything of that sort - just stories about people like ourselves. I don't see how they can pay people for writing stories about people just like those one meets every day!"

"I always say," Maud intervened, "that Spencer means to write a book some day. He has quite the literary air, hasn't he, mother?"

"Indeed he has!" Mrs. Barnes declared, with an appreciative glance at the gold-rimmed spectacles.

Mr. Fitzgerald modestly disclaimed any literary aspirations.

"The thing is a gift, after all," he declared, generously. "I can keep accounts, and earn a fair salary at it, but if I attempted fiction I should soon be up a tree."

Mr. Barnes nodded his approval of such sentiments.

"Every one to his trade, I say," he remarked. "What sort of salaries do they pay now in the book trade?" he asked guilelessly.

"Very fair," Mr. Fitzgerald admitted candidly, - "very fair indeed."

E. Phillips Oppenheim

"When I was your age," Mr. Barnes said reflectively, "I was getting - let me see - forty-two shillings a week. Pretty good pay, too, for those days."

Mr. Fitzgerald admitted the fact.

"Of course," he said apologetically, "salaries are a little higher now all round. Mr. Howell has been very kind to me, - in fact I have had two raises this year. I am getting four pounds ten now."

"Four pounds ten per week?" Mrs. Barnes exclaimed, laying down her knife and fork.

"Certainly," Mr. Fitzgerald answered. "After Christmas, I have some reason to believe that it may be five pounds."

Mr. Barnes whistled softly, and looked at the young man with a new respect.

"I told you that - Mr. - that Spencer was doing pretty well, Mother," Maud simpered, looking down at her plate.

"Any one to support?" her father asked, transferring a pickle from the fork to his mouth.

"No one," Mr. Fitzgerald answered. "In fact, I may say that I have some small expectations. I haven't done badly, either, out of the few investments I have made from time to time."

"Saved a bit of money, eh?" Mr. Barnes enquired genially.

"I have a matter of four hundred pounds put by," Mr. Fitzgerald admitted modestly, "besides a few sticks of furniture. I never cared much about lodging-house things, so I furnished a couple of rooms myself some time ago."

Mrs. Barnes rose slowly to her feet.

"You are quite sure you won't have a small piece more of beef?" she enquired anxiously.

"Just a morsel?" Mr. Barnes asked, tapping the joint insinuatingly with his carving knife.

"No, I thank you!" Mr. Fitzgerald declared firmly. "I have done excellently."

"Then if you will put the joint on the sideboard, Adolphus," Mrs. Barnes directed, "Maud and I will change the plates. We always let the girl go out on Sundays, Mr. Fitzgerald," she explained, turning to their guest. "It's very awkward, of course, but they seem to expect it."

"Quite natural, I'm sure," Mr. Fitzgerald murmured, watching Maud's light movements with admiring eyes. "I like to see ladies interested in domestic work."

"There's one thing I will say for Maud," her proud mother declared, plumping down a dish of jelly upon the table, "she does know what's what in keeping house, and even if she hasn't to scrape and save as I did when David and I were first married, economy is a great thing when you're young. I have always said so, and I stick to it."

"Quite right, Mother," Mr. Barnes declared.

"If instead of sitting there," Mrs. Barnes continued in high good humour, "you were to get a bottle of that port wine out of the cellarette, we might drink Mr. Fitzgerald's health, being as it's his first visit."

Mr. Barnes rose to his feet with alacrity. "For a woman with sound ideas," he declared, "commend me to your mother!"

Maud, having finished her duties, resumed her place by the side of the guest of the evening. Their hands met under the tablecloth for a moment. To the girl, the pleasure of such a proceeding was natural enough, but Fitzgerald asked himself for the fiftieth time why on earth he, who, notwithstanding his present modest exterior, was a young man of some experience, should from such primitive love-making derive a rapture which nothing else in life afforded him. He was, at that moment, content with his future, - a future which he had absolutely and finally decided upon. He was content with his father-in-law and his mother-in-law, with Daisy Villa, and the prospect of a Daisy Villa for himself, - content, even, with Adolphus! But for Mr. Spencer Fitzgerald, these things were not to be! The awakening was even then at hand.

The dining room of Daisy Villa fronted the street, and was removed from it only a few feet. Consequently, the footsteps of passers-by upon the flagged pavement were clearly distinguishable. It was just at the moment when Mrs. Barnes was inserting a few fresh almonds into a somewhat precarious tipsy cake, and Mr. Barnes was engaged with the decanting of the port, that two pairs of footsteps, considerably heavier than those of the ordinary promenader, paused outside and finally stopped. The gate creaked. Mr. Barnes looked up.

"Hullo!" he exclaimed. "What's that? Visitors?"

They all listened. The front-door bell rang. Adolphus, in response to a gesture from his mother, rose sulkily to his feet.

"Job I hate!" he muttered as he left the room.

The rest of the family, full of the small curiosity of people of their class, were intent upon listening for voices outside. The demeanour of Mr. Spencer Fitzgerald, therefore, escaped their notice. It is doubtful, in any case, whether their perceptions would have been sufficiently keen to have enabled them to trace the workings of emotion in the countenance of a person so magnificently endowed by Providence with the art of subterfuge. Mr. Spencer Fitzgerald seemed simply to have stiffened in acute and earnest attention. It was only for a moment that he hesitated. His unfailing inspiration told him the truth!

His course of action was simple, - he rose to his feet and strolled to the window.

"Some people who have lost their way in the fog, perhaps," he remarked. "What a night!"

He laid his hand upon the sash - simultaneously there was a rush of cold air into the room, a half-angry, half-frightened exclamation from Adolphus in the passage, a scream from Miss Maud - and no Mr. Spencer Fitzgerald! No one had time to be more than blankly astonished. The door was opened, and a police inspector, in very nice dark braided uniform and a peaked cap, stood in the doorway.

Mr. Barnes dropped the port, and Mrs. Barnes, emulating her daughter's example, screamed. The inspector, as though conscious of the draught, moved rapidly toward the window.

"You had a visitor here, Mr. Barnes," he said quickly - "a Mr. Spencer Fitzgerald. Where is he?"

There was no one who could answer! Mr. Barnes was speechless between the shock of the spilt port and the appearance of a couple of uniformed policemen in his dining room. John Dory, the detective, he knew well enough in his private capacity, but in his uniform, and attended by policemen, he presented a new and startling appearance! Mrs. Barnes was in hysterics, and Maud was gazing like a creature turned to stone at the open window, through which little puffs of fog were already drifting into the room. Adolphus, with an air of bewilderment, was standing with his mouth and eyes wider open than they had ever been in his life. And as for the honoured guest of these admirable inhabitants of Daisy Villa, there was not the slightest doubt but that Mr. Spencer Fitzgerald had disappeared through the window!

Fitzgerald's expedition was nearly at an end. Soon he paused,

E. Phillips Oppenheim

crossed the road to a block of flats, ascended to the eighth floor by an automatic lift, and rang the bell at a door which bore simply the number II. A trim parlourmaid opened it after a few minutes' delay.

"Is Miss Emerson at home?" he asked.

"Miss Emerson is in," the maid admitted, with some hesitation, "but I am not sure that she will see any one to-night."

"I have a message for her," Fitzgerald said.

"Will you give me your name, sir, please?" the maid asked.

An inner door was suddenly opened. A slim girl, looking taller than she really was by reason of the rug upon which she stood, looked out into the hall - a girl with masses of brown hair loosely coiled on her head, with pale face and strange eyes. She opened her lips as though to call to her visitor by name, and as suddenly closed them again. There was not much expression in her face, but there was enough to show that his visit was not unwelcome.

"You!" she exclaimed. "Come in! Please come in at once!"

Fitzgerald obeyed the invitation of the girl whom he had come to visit. She had retreated a little into the room, but the door was no sooner closed than she held out her hands.

"Peter!" she exclaimed. "Peter, you have come to me at last!"

Her lips were a little parted; her eyes were bright with pleasure; her whole expression was one of absolute delight. Fitzgerald frowned, as though he found her welcome a little too enthusiastic for his taste.

"Violet," he said, "please don't look at me as though I were a prodigal sheep. If you do, I shall be sorry that I came."

Her hands fell to her side, the pleasure died out of her face - only her eyes still questioned him. Fitzgerald carefully laid his hat on a vacant chair.

"Something has happened?" she said. "Tell me that all that madness is over - that you are yourself again!"

"So far as regards my engagement with Messrs. Howell & Wilson," he said, despondently, "you are right. As regards - Miss Barnes, there has been no direct misunderstanding between us, but I am afraid, for the present, that I must consider that - well, in abeyance."

"That is something!" she exclaimed, drawing a little breath of relief. "Sit down, Peter. Will you have something to eat? I finished dinner an hour ago, but -"

"Thank you," Fitzgerald interrupted, "I supped - extremely well in Streatham!"

"In Streatham!" she repeated. "Why, how did you get there? The fog is awful."

"Fogs do not trouble me," Fitzgerald answered. "I walked. I could have done it as well blindfold. I will take a whisky and soda, if I may."

She led him to an easy-chair.

"I will mix it myself," she said.

Without being remarkably good-looking, she was certainly a pleasant and attractive-looking young woman. Her cheeks were a little pale; her hair - perfectly natural - was a wonderful deep shade of soft brown. Her eyes were long and narrow - almost Oriental in shape - and they seemed in some queer way to match the room; he could have sworn that in the firelight they flashed green. Her body and limbs, notwithstanding her extreme slightness, were graceful, perhaps, but with the grace

E. Phillips Oppenheim

of the tigress. She wore a green silk dressing jacket, pulled together with a belt of lizard skin, and her neck was bare. Her skirt was of some thin black material. She was obviously in deshabille, and yet there was something neat and trim about the smaller details of her toilette.

"Go on, please, Peter," she begged. "You are keeping me in suspense."

"There isn't much to tell," he answered. "It's over - that's all."

She drew a sharp breath through her teeth.

"You are not going to marry that girl - that bourgeois doll in Streatham?"

Fitzgerald sat up in his chair.

"Look here," he said, seriously, "don't you call her names. If I'm not going to marry her, it isn't my fault. She is the only girl I have ever wanted, and probably - most probably - she will be the only one I ever shall want. That's honest, isn't it?"

The girl winced.

"Yes," she said, "it is honest!"

"I should have married her," the young man continued, "and I should have been happy. I had my eye on a villa - not too near her parents - and I saw my way to a little increase of salary. I should have taken to gardening, to walks in the Park, with an occasional theatre, and I should have thoroughly enjoyed a fortnight every summer at Skegness or Sutton-on-Sea. We should have saved a little money. I should have gone to church regularly, and if possible I should have filled some minor public offices. You may call this bourgeois - it was my idea of happiness."

"Was!" she murmured.

"Is still," he declared, sharply, "but I shall never attain to it. To-night I had to leave Maud - to leave the supper table of Daisy Villa - through the window!"

She looked at him in amazement.

"The police," he explained. "That brute Dory was at the bottom of it."

"But surely," she murmured, "you told me that you had a bona-fide situation -"

"So I had," he declared, "and I was a fool not to be content with it. It was my habit of taking long country walks, and their rotten auditing, which undid me! You understand that this was all before I met Maud? Since the day I spoke to her, I turned over a new leaf. I have left the night work alone, and I repaid every penny of the firm's money which they could ever have possibly found out about. There was only that one little affair of mine down at Sudbury."

"Tell me what you are going to do?" she whispered.

"I have no alternative," he answered. "The law has kicked me out from the respectable places. The law shall pay!"

She looked at him with glowing eyes.

"Have you any plans?" she asked, softly.

"I have," he answered. "I have considered the subject from a good many points of view, and I have decided to start in business for myself as a private detective."

She raised her eyebrows.

"My dear Peter!" she murmured. "Couldn't you be a little more original?"

"That is only what I am going to call myself," he answered. "I may tell you that I am going to strike out on somewhat new lines."

"Please explain," she begged.

He recrossed his knees and made himself a little more comfortable.

"The weak part of every great robbery, however successful," he began, "is the great wastage in value which invariably results. For jewels which cost - say five thousand pounds, and to procure which the artist has to risk his life as well as his liberty, he has to consider himself lucky if he clears eight hundred. For the Hermitage rubies, for instance, where I nearly had to shoot a man dead, I realized rather less than four hundred pounds. It doesn't pay."

"Go on," she begged.

"I am not clear," he continued, "how far this class of business will attract me at all, but I do not propose, in any case, to enter into any transactions on my own account. I shall work for other people, and for cash down. Your experience of life, Violet, has been fairly large. Have you not sometimes come into contact with people driven into a situation from which they would willingly commit any crime to escape if they dared? It is not with them a question of money at all - it is simply a matter of ignorance. They do not know how to commit a crime. They have had no experience, and if they attempt it, they know perfectly well that they are likely to blunder. A person thoroughly experienced in the ways of criminals - a person of genius like myself - would have, without a doubt, an immense clientele, if only he dared put up his signboard. Literally, I cannot do that. Actually, I mean to do so! I shall be willing to accept contracts either to help nervous people out of an undesirable crisis; or, on the other hand, to measure my wits against the wits of Scotland Yard, and to discover the criminals whom they have failed to secure. I shall make my own bargains, and I shall be paid in cash. I shall take on nothing that I am not certain about."

"But your clients?" she asked, curiously. "How will you come into contact with them?"

He smiled.

"I am not afraid of business being slack," he said. "The world is full of fools."

"You cannot live outside the law, Peter," she objected. "You are clever, I know, but they are not all fools at Scotland Yard."

"You forget," he reminded her, "that there will be a perfectly legitimate side to my profession. The other sort of case I shall only accept if I can see my way clear to make a success of it. Needless to say, I shall have to refuse the majority that are offered to me."

She came a little nearer to him.

"In any case," she said, with a little sigh, "you have given up that foolish, bourgeois life of yours?"

He looked down into her face, and his eyes were cold.

"Violet," he said, "this is no time for misunderstandings. I should like you to know that apart from one young lady, who possesses my whole affection -"

"All of it?" she pleaded.

"All!" he declared emphatically. "She will doubtless be faithless to me - under the circumstances, I cannot blame her - but so far as I am concerned, I have no affection whatever for any one else."

She crept back to her place.

"I could be so useful to you," she murmured.

"You could and you shall, if you will be sensible," he answered.

"Tell me how?" she begged.

He was silent for a moment.

"Are you acting now?" he asked.

"I am understudying Molly," she answered, "and I have a very small part at the Globe."

He nodded.

"There is no reason to interfere with that," he said, "in fact, I wish you to continue your connection with the profession. It brings you into touch with the class of people among whom I am likely to find clients."

"Go on, please," she begged.

"On two conditions - or rather one," he said, "you can, if you like, become my secretary and partner - and find the money we shall require to make a start."

"Conditions?" she asked.

"You must understand, once and for all," he said, "that I will not be made love to, and that I can treat you only as a working; companion. My name will be Peter Ruff, and yours Miss Brown. You will have to dress like a secretary, and behave like one. Sometimes there will be plenty of work for you, and sometimes there will be none at all. Sometimes you will be bored to death, and sometimes there will be excitement. I do not wish to make you vain, but I may add, especially as you are aware of my personal feelings toward you, that you are the only person in the world to whom I would make this offer."

She sighed gently.

"Tell me, Peter," she asked, "when do you mean to start this new enterprise?"

"Not for six months - perhaps a year," he answered. "I must go to Paris - perhaps Vienna. I might even have to go to New York. There are certain associations with which I must come into touch - certain information I must become possessed of."

"Peter," she said, "I like your scheme, but there is just one thing. Such men as you should be the brains of great enterprises. Don't you understand what I mean? It shouldn't be you who does the actual thing which brings you within the power of the law. I am not over-scrupulous, you know. I hate wrongdoing, but I have never been able to treat as equal criminals the poor man who steals for a living, and the rich financier who robs right and left out of sheer greed. I agree with you that crime is not an absolute thing. The circumstances connected with every action in life determine its morality or immorality. But, Peter, it isn't worth while to go outside the law!"

He nodded.

"You are a sensible girl," he said, "I have always thought that. We'll talk over my cases together, if they seem to run a little too close to the line."

"Very well, Peter," she said, "I accept."

E. Phillips Oppenheim

CHAPTER II

A NEW CAREER

About twelve months after the interrupted festivities at Daisy Villa, that particular neighbourhood was again the scene of some rejoicing. Standing before the residence of Mr. Barnes were three carriages, drawn in each case by a pair of grey horses. The coachmen and their steeds were similarly adorned with white rosettes. It would have been an insult to the intelligence of the most youthful of the loungers-by to have informed them that a wedding was projected.

At the neighbouring church all was ready. The clerk stood at the door, the red drugget was down, the usual little crowd were standing all agog upon the pavement. There was one unusual feature of the proceedings: Instead of a solitary policeman, there were at least a dozen who kept clear the entrance to the church. Their presence greatly puzzled a little old gentleman who had joined the throng of sightseers. He pushed himself to the front and touched one of them upon the shoulder.

"Mr. Policeman," he said, "will you tell me why there are so many of you to keep such a small crowd in order?"

"Bridegroom's a member of the force, sir, for one reason," the man answered good-humouredly.

"And the other?" the old gentleman persisted.

The policeman behaved as though he had not heard - a proceeding which his natural stolidity rendered easy. The little old gentleman, however, was not so easily put off. He tapped the man once more upon the shoulder.

"And the other reason, Mr. Policeman?" he asked insinuatingly.

"Not allowed to talk about that, sir," was the somewhat gruff reply.

The little old gentleman moved away, a trifle hurt. He was a very nicely dressed old gentleman indeed, and everything about him seemed to savour of prosperity. But he was certainly garrulous. An obviously invited guest was standing upon the edge of the pavement stroking a pair of lavender kid gloves. The little old gentleman sidled up to him.

"I beg your pardon, sir," he said, raising his hat. "I am just back from Australia - haven't seen a wedding in England for fifty years. Do you think that they would let me into the church?"

The invited guest looked down at his questioner and approved of him. Furthermore, he seemed exceedingly glad to be interrupted in his somewhat nervous task of waiting for the wedding party.

"Certainly, sir," he replied cheerfully. "Come along in with me, and I'll find you a seat."

Down the scarlet drugget they went - the big best man with the red hands and the lavender kid gloves and the opulent-looking old gentleman with the gold-rimmed spectacles and the handsome walking stick.

"Dear me, this is very interesting!" the latter remarked. "Is it the custom, sir, always, may I ask, in this country, to have so many policemen at a wedding?"

The big man looked downward and shook his head.

"Special reason," he said mysteriously. "Fact is, young lady was engaged once to a very bad character - a burglar whom the police have been wanting for years. He had to leave the country, but he has written her once or twice since in a mysterious sort of way - wanted her to be true to him, and all that sort of thing. Dory - that's the bridegroom - has got a sort of an idea that he may turn up to-day."

"This is very exciting - very!" the little old gentleman remarked. "Reminds me of our younger days out in Australia."

"You sit down here," the best man directed, ushering his companion into an empty pew. "I must get back again outside, or I shall have the bridegroom arriving."

"Good-day to you, sir, and many thanks!" the little old gentleman said politely.

Soon the bridegroom arrived - a smart young officer, well thought of at Scotland Yard, well set up, wearing a long tail coat a lilac and white tie, and shaking in every limb. He walked up the aisle accompanied by the best man, and the little old gentleman from Australia watched him genially from behind those gold-rimmed glasses. And, then, scarcely was he at the altar rails when through the open church door one heard the sounds of horses' feet, one heard a rustle, the murmur of voices, caught a glimpse of a waiting group arranging themselves finally in the porch of the church. Maud, on the arm of her father, came slowly up the aisle. The little old gentleman turned his head as though this was something upon which he feared to look. He saw nothing of Mr. Barnes, in a new coat, with tuberose and spray of maidenhair in his coat, and exceedingly tight patent leather boots on his feet; he saw nothing of Mrs. Barnes, clad in a gown of the lightest magenta, with a bonnet smothered with violets.

It was in the vestry that the only untoward incident of that highly successful wedding took place. The ceremony was over! Bride, bridegroom and parents trooped in. And when the register was opened, one witness had already signed! In the clear, precise writing his name stood out upon the virgin page -

Spencer Fitzgerald

The bridegroom swore, the bride nearly collapsed. The clerk pressed into the hands of the latter an envelope.

"From the little old gentleman," he announced, "who was fussing round the church this morning."

Mrs. Dory tore it open and gave a cry of delight. A diamond cross, worth all the rest of her presents put together, flashed soft lights from a background of dull velvet. Her husband had looked over her shoulder, and with a scowl seized the morocco case and threw it far from him.

It was the only disturbing incident of a highly successful function!

At precisely the same moment when the wedding guests were seated around the hospitable board of Daisy Villa, a celebration of a somewhat different nature was taking place in the more aristocratic neighbourhood of Curzon Street. Here, however, the little party was a much smaller one, and the innocent gaiety of the gathering at Daisy Villa was entirely lacking. The luncheon table around which the four men were seated presented all the unlovely signs of a meal where self-restraint had been abandoned - where conviviality has passed the bounds of licence. Edibles were represented only by a single dish of fruit; the tablecloth, stained with wine and cigar ash, seemed crowded with every sort of bottle and every sort of glass. A magnum of champagne, empty, another half full, stood in the middle of the table; whisky, brandy, liqueurs of various sorts were all represented; glasses - some full, some empty, some filled with cigar ash and cigarette stumps - an ugly sight!

E. Phillips Oppenheim

The guest in chief arose. Short, thick-set, red-faced, with bulbous eyes, and veins about his temples which just now were unpleasantly prominent, he seemed, indeed, a very fitting person to have been the recipient of such hospitality. He stood clutching a little at the tablecloth and swaying upon his feet. He spoke as a drunken man, but such words as he pronounced clearly showed him to be possessed of a voice naturally thick and raspy. It was obvious that he was a person of entirely different class from his three companions.

"G - gentlemen," he said, "I must be off. I thank you very much for this - hospitality. Honoured, I'm sure, to have sat down in such - such company. Good afternoon, all!"

He lurched a little toward the door, but his neighbour at the table - who was also his host - caught hold of his coat tail and pulled him back into his chair.

"No hurry, Masters," he said. "One more liqueur, eh? It's a raw afternoon."

"N - not another drop, Sir Richard!" the man declared. "Not another drop to drink. I am very much obliged to you all, but I must be off. Must be off," he repeated, making another effort to rise.

His host held him by the arm. The man resented it - he showed signs of anger.

"D - n it all! I - I'm not a prisoner, am I?" he exclaimed angrily. "Tell you I've got - appointment - club. Can't you see it's past five o'clock?"

"That's all right, Masters," the man whom he had addressed as Sir Richard declared soothingly. "We want just a word with you on business first, before you go - Colonel Dickinson, Lord Merries and myself."

Masters shook his head.

"See you to-morrow," he declared. "No time to talk business now. Let me go!"

He made another attempt to rise, which his host also prevented.

"Masters, don't be a fool!" the latter said firmly. "You've got to hear what we want to say to you. Sit down and listen."

Masters relapsed sullenly into his chair. His little eyes seemed to creep closer to one another. So they wanted to talk business! Perhaps it was for that reason that they had bidden him sit at their table - had entertained him so well! The very thought cleared his brain.

"Go on," he said shortly.

Sir Richard lit a cigarette and leaned further back in his chair. He was a man apparently about fifty years of age - tall, well dressed, with good features, save for his mouth, which resembled more than anything a rat trap. He was perfectly bald, and he had the air of a man who was a careful liver. His eyes were bright, almost beadlike; his fingers long and a trifle over-manicured. One would have judged him to be what he was - a man of fashion and a patron of the turf.

"Masters," he said, "we are all old friends here. We want to speak to you plainly. We three have had a try, as you know - Merries, Dickinson and myself - to make the coup of our lives. We failed, and we're up against it hard."

"Very hard, indeed," Lord Merries murmured softly.

"Deuced hard!" Colonel Dickinson echoed.

Masters was sitting tight, breathing a little hard, looking fixedly at his host.

"Take my own case first," the latter continued. "I am Sir

E. Phillips Oppenheim

Richard Dyson, ninth baronet, with estates in Wiltshire and Scotland, and a town house in Cleveland Place. I belong to the proper clubs for a man in my position, and, somehow or other - we won't say how - I have managed to pay my way. There isn't an acre of my property that isn't mortgaged for more than its value. My town house - well, it doesn't belong to me at all! I have twenty-six thousand pounds to pay you on Monday. To save my life, I could not raise twenty-six thousand farthings! So much for me."

The man Masters ground his teeth.

"So much for you!" he muttered.

"Take the case next," Sir Richard continued, "of my friend Merries here. Merries is an Earl, it is true, but he never had a penny to bless himself with. He's tried acting, reporting, marrying - anything to make an honest living. So far, I am afraid we must consider Lord Merries as something of a failure, eh?"

"A rotten failure, I should say," that young nobleman declared gloomily.

"Lord Merries is, to put it briefly, financially unsound," Sir Richard declared.

"What is the amount of your debt to Mr. Masters, Jim?"

"Eleven thousand two hundred pounds," Lord Merries answered.

"And we may take it, I presume, for granted that you have not that sum, nor anything like it, at your disposal?" Sir Richard asked.

"Not a fiver!" Lord Merries declared with emphasis.

"We come now, Mr. Masters, to our friend Colonel

Dickinson," Sir Richard continued. "Colonel Dickinson is, perhaps, in a more favourable situation than any of us. He has a small but regular income, and he has expectations which it is not possible to mortgage fully. At the same time, it will be many years before they can - er - fructify. He is, therefore, with us in this somewhat unpleasant predicament in which we find ourselves."

"Cut it short," Masters growled. "I'm sick of so much talk. What's it all mean?"

"It means simply this, Mr. Masters," Sir Richard said, "we want you to take six months' bills for our indebtedness to you."

Masters rose to his feet. His thick lips were drawn a little apart. He had the appearance of a savage and discontented animal.

"So that's why I've been asked here and fed up with wine and stuff, eh?" he exclaimed thickly. "Well, my answer to you is soon given. NO! I'll take bills from no man! My terms are cash on settling day - cash to pay or cash to receive. I'll have no other!"

Sir Richard rose also to his feet.

"Mr. Masters, I beg of you to be reasonable," he said. "You will do yourself no good by adopting this attitude. Facts are facts. We haven't got a thousand pounds between us."

"I've heard that sort of a tale before," Masters answered, with a sneer. "Job Masters is too old a bird to be caught by such chaff. I'll take my risks, gentlemen. I'll take my risks."

He moved toward the door. No one spoke a word. The silence as he crossed the room seemed a little ominous. He looked over his shoulder. They were all three standing in their places, looking at him. A vague sense of uneasiness disturbed his equanimity.

E. Phillips Oppenheim

"No offence, gents," he said, "and good afternoon!"

Still no reply. He reached the door and turned the handle. The door was fast. He shook it - gently at first, and then violently. Suddenly he realized that it was locked. He turned sharply around.

"What game's this?" he exclaimed, fiercely. "Let me out!"

They stood in their places without movement. There was something a little ominous in their silence. Masters was fast becoming a sober man.

"Let me out of here," he exclaimed, "or I'll break the door down!"

Sir Richard Dyson came slowly towards him. There was something in his appearance which terrified Masters. He raised his fist to strike the door. He was a fighting man, but he felt a sudden sense of impotence.

"Mr. Masters," Sir Richard said suavely, "the truth is that we cannot afford to let you go - unless you agree to do what we have asked. You see we really have not the money or any way of raising it - and the inconvenience of being posted you have yourself very ably pointed out. Change your mind, Mr. Masters. Take those bills. We'll do our best to meet them."

"I'll do nothing of the sort," Masters answered, striking the door fiercely with his clenched fist. "I'll have cash - nothing but the cash!"

There was a dull, sickening thud, and the bookmaker went over like a shot rabbit. His legs twitched for a moment - a little moan that was scarcely audible broke from his lips. Then he lay quite still. Sir Richard bent over him with the life preserver still in his hand.

"I've done it!" he muttered, hoarsely. "One blow! Thank

Heaven, he didn't want another! His skull was as soft as pudding! Ugh!"

He turned away. The man who lay stretched upon the floor was an ugly sight. His two companions, cowering over the table, were not much better. Dyson's trembling fingers went out for the brandy decanter. Half of what he poured out was spilled upon the tablecloth. The rest he drank from a tumbler, neat.

"It's nervous work, this, you fellows," he said, hoarsely.

"It's hellish!" Dickinson answered. "Let's have some air in the room. By God, it's close!"

He sank back into his chair, white to the lips. Dyson looked at him sharply.

"Look here," he exclaimed, "I hold you both to our bargain! I was to be the one he attacked and who struck the blow - in self-defence! Remember that - it was in self-defence! I've done it! I've done my share! I hope to God I'll forget it some day. Andrew, you know your task. Be a man, and get to work!"

Dickinson rose to his feet unsteadily. "Yes!" he said. "What was it? I have forgotten, for the moment, but I am ready."

"You must get his betting book from his pocket," Sir Richard directed. "Then you must help Merries downstairs with him, and into the car. Merries is - to get rid of him."

Merries shivered. His hand, too, went out for the brandy.

"To get rid of him," he muttered. "It sounds easy!"

"It is easy," Sir Richard declared. "You have only to keep your nerve, and the thing is done. No one will see him inside the car, in that motoring coat and glasses. You can drive some-where out into the country and leave him."

"Leave him!" Merries repeated, trembling. "Leave him - yes!"

Neither of the two men moved.

"I must do more than my share, I suppose," Sir Richard declared contemptuously. "Come!"

They dragged the man's body on to a chair, wrapped a huge coat around him, tied a motoring cap under his chin, fixed goggles over his eyes. Sir Richard strolled into the hall and opened the front door. He stood there for a moment, looking up and down the street. When he gave the signal they dragged him out, supported between them, across the pavement, into the car. Ugh! His attitude was so natural as to be absolutely ghastly. Merries started the car and sprang into the driver's seat. There were people in the Square now, but the figure reclining in the dark, cushioned interior looked perfectly natural.

"So long, Jimmy," Sir Richard called out. "See you this evening."

"Right O!" Merries replied, with a brave effort.

Peter Ruff, summoned by telephone from his sitting room, slipped down the stairs like a cat - noiseless, swift. The voice which had summoned him had been the voice of his secretary - a voice almost unrecognisable - a voice shaken with fear. Fear? No, it had been terror!

On the landing below, exactly underneath the room from which he had descended, there was a door upon which his name was written upon a small brass plate - Mr. Peter Ruff. He opened and closed it behind him with a swift movement which he had practised in his idle moments. He found himself looking in upon a curious scene.

Miss Brown, with the radiance of her hair effectually

concealed, in plain black skirt and simple blouse - the ideal secretary - had risen from the seat in front of her typewriter, and was standing facing the door through which he had entered, with a small revolver - which he had given her for a birthday present only the day before - clasped in her outstretched hand. The object of her solicitude was, it seemed to Peter Ruff, the most pitiful-looking object upon which he had ever looked. The hours had dwelt with Merries as the years with some people, and worse. He had lost his cap; his hair hung over his forehead in wild confusion; his eyes were red, bloodshot, and absolutely aflame with the terrors through which he had lived - underneath them the black marks might have been traced with a charcoal pencil. His cheeks were livid save for one burning spot. His clothes, too, were in disorder - the starch had gone from his collar, his tie hung loosely outside his waistcoat. He was cowering back against the wall. And between him and the girl, stretched upon the floor, was the body of a man in a huge motor coat, a limp, inert mass which neither moved nor seemed to have any sign of life. No wonder that Peter Ruff looked around his office, whose serenity had been so tragically disturbed, with an air of mild surprise.

"Dear me," he exclaimed, "something seems to have happened! My dear Violet, you can put that revolver away. I have secured the door."

Her hand fell to her side. She gave a little shiver of relief. Peter Ruff nodded.

"That is more comfortable," he declared. "Now, perhaps, you will explain -"

"That young man," she interrupted, "or lunatic - whatever he calls himself - burst in here a few minutes ago, dragging - that!" She pointed to the motionless figure upon the floor. "If I had not stopped him, he would have bolted off without a word of explanation."

E. Phillips Oppenheim

Peter Ruff, with his back against the door, shook his head gravely.

"My dear Lord Merries," he said, "my office is not a mortuary."

Merries gasped.

"You know me, then?" he muttered, hoarsely.

"Of course," Ruff answered. "It is my profession to know everybody. Go and sit down upon that easy-chair, and drink the brandy and soda which Miss Brown is about to mix for you. That's right."

Merries staggered across the room and half fell into an easy-chair. He leaned over the side with his face buried in his hands, unable still to face the horror which lay upon the floor. A few seconds later, the tumbler of brandy and soda was in his hands. He drank it like a man who drains fresh life into his veins.

"Perhaps now," Peter Ruff suggested, pointing to the motion-less figure, "you can give me some explanation as to this!"

Merries looked away from him all the time he was speaking. His voice was thick and nervous.

"There were three of us lunching together," he began - "four in all. There was a dispute, and this man threatened us. After-wards there was a fight. It fell to my lot to take him away, and I can't get rid of him! I can't get rid of him!" he repeated, with something that sounded like a sob.

"I still do not see," Peter Ruff argued, "why you should have brought him here and deposited him upon my perfectly new carpet."

"You are Peter Ruff," Merries declared. "'Crime Investigator and Private Detective,' you call yourself. You are used to this sort of thing. You will know what to do with it. It is part of your business."

"I can assure you," Peter Ruff answered, "that you are under a delusion as to the details of my profession. I am Peter Ruff," he admitted, "and I call myself a crime investigator - in fact, I am the only one worth speaking of in the world. But I certainly deny that I am used to having dead bodies deposited upon my carpet, and that I make a habit of disposing of them - especially gratis."

Merries tore open his coat.

"Listen," he said, his voice shaking hysterically, "I must get rid of it or go mad. For two hours I have been driving about in a motor car with - it for a passenger. I drove to a quiet spot and I tried to lift it out - a policeman rode up! I tried again, a man rushed by on a motor cycle, and turned to look at me! I tried a few minutes later - the policeman came back! It was always the same. The night seemed to have eyes. I was watched everywhere. The - the face began to mock me. I'll swear that I heard it chuckle once!"

Peter Ruff moved a little further away.

"I don't think I'll have anything to do with it," he declared. "I don't like your description at all."

"It'll be all right with you," Merries declared eagerly. "It's my nerves, that's all. You see, I was there - when the accident happened. See here," he added, tearing a pocketbook from his coat, "I have three hundred and seventy pounds saved up in case I had to bolt. I'll keep seventy - three hundred for you - to dispose of it!"

Ruff leaned over the motionless body, looked into its face, and nodded.

E. Phillips Oppenheim

"Masters, the bookmaker," he remarked. "H'm! I did hear that he had a lot of money coming to him over the Cambridgeshire."

Merries shuddered.

"May I go?" he pleaded. "There's the three hundred on the table. For God's sake, let me go!"

Peter Ruff nodded.

"I wish you'd saved a little more," he said. "However -"

He turned the lock and Merries rushed out of the room. Ruff looked across the room towards his secretary.

"Ring up 1535 Central," he ordered, sharply.

Peter Ruff had descended from his apartments on the top floor of the building, in a new brown suit with which he was violently displeased, to meet a caller.

"I am sorry to intrude - Mr. Ruff, I believe it is?" Sir Richard Dyson said, a little irritably - "but I have not a great deal of time to spare -"

"Most natural!" Peter Ruff declared. "Pray take a chair, Sir Richard. You want to know, of course, about Lord Merries and poor Masters."

Sir Richard stared at his questioner, for a moment, without speech. Once more the fear which he had succeeded in banishing for a while, shone in his eyes - revealed itself in his white face.

"Try the easy-chair, Sir Richard," Ruff continued, pleasantly. "Leave your hat and cane on the table there, and make yourself comfortable. I should like to understand exactly what you have come to me for."

Sir Richard moved his head toward Miss Brown.

"My business with you," he said, "is more than ordinarily private. I have the honour of knowing Miss -"

"Miss Brown," Peter interrupted quickly. "In these offices, this young lady's name is Miss Violet Brown."

Sir Richard shrugged his shoulders.

"It is of no importance," he said, "only, as you may understand, my business with you scarcely requires the presence of a third party, even one with the discretion which I am sure Miss - Brown possesses."

"In these matters," Ruff answered, "my secretary does not exist apart from myself. Her presence is necessary. She takes down in shorthand notes of our conversation. I have a shocking memory, and there are always points which I forget. At the conclusion of our business, whatever it may be, these notes are destroyed. I could not work without them, however."

Sir Richard glanced a little doubtfully at the long, slim back of the girl who sat with her face turned away from him. "Of course," he began, "if you make yourself personally responsible for her discretion -"

"I am willing to do so," Ruff interrupted, brusquely. "I guarantee it. Go on, please."

"I do not know, of course, where you got your information from," Sir Richard began, "but it is perfectly true that I have come here to consult you upon a matter in which the two people whose names you have mentioned are concerned. The disappearance of Job Masters is, of course, common talk; but I cannot tell what has led you to associate with it the temporary absence of Lord Merries from this country."

"Let me ask you this question," Ruff said. "How are you

affected by the disappearance of Masters?"

"Indirectly, it has caused me a great deal of inconvenience," Sir Richard declared.

"Facts, please," murmured Peter.

"It has been rumoured," Sir Richard admitted, "that I owed Masters a large sum of money which I could not pay."

"Anything else?"

"It has also been rumoured," Sir Richard continued, "that he was seen to enter my house that day, and that he remained there until late in the afternoon."

"Did he?" asked Ruff.

"Certainly not," Sir Richard answered.

Peter Ruff yawned for a moment, but covered the indiscretion with his hand.

"Respecting this inconvenience," he said, "which you admit that the disappearance of Job Masters has caused you, what is its tangible side?"

Sir Richard drew his chair a little nearer to the table where Ruff was sitting. His voice dropped almost to a whisper.

"It seems absurd," he said, "and yet, what I tell you is the truth. I have been followed about - shadowed, in fact - for several days. Men, even in my own social circle, seem to hold aloof from me. It is as though," he continued slowly, "people were beginning to suspect me of being connected in some way with the man's disappearance."

Ruff, who had been making figures with a pencil on the edge of his blotting paper, suddenly turned round. His eyes flashed with a new light as they became fixed upon his companion's.

"And are you not?" he asked, calmly. Sir Richard bore himself well. For a moment he had shrunk back. Then he half rose to his feet.

"Mr. Ruff!" he said. "I must protest -"

"Stop!"

Peter Ruff used no violent gesture. Only his forefinger tapped the desk in front of him. His voice was as smooth as velvet.

"Tell me as much or as little as you please, Sir Richard," he said, "but let that little or that much be the truth! On those terms only I may be able to help you. You do not go to your physician and expect him to prescribe to you while you conceal your symptoms, or to your lawyer for advice and tell him half the truth. I am not asking for your confidence. I simply tell you that you are wasting your time and mine if you choose to withhold it."

Sir Richard was silent. He recognized a new quality in the man - but the truth was an awful thing to tell! He considered - then told.

Ruff briskly asked two questions. "In alluding to your heavy settlement with Masters, you said just now that you could not have paid him - then."

"Quite so," Sir Richard admitted. "That is the rotten part of the whole affair. Four days later a wonderful double came off - one in which we were all interested, and one which not one of us expected. We've drawn a considerable amount already from one or two bookies, and I believe even Masters owes us a bit now."

"Thank you," Ruff said. "I think that I know everything now. My fee is five hundred guineas."

Sir Richard looked at him.

"What?" he exclaimed.

"Five hundred guineas," Ruff repeated.

"For a consultation?" Sir Richard asked.

Peter Ruff shook his head.

"More than that," he said. "You are a brave man in your way, Sir Richard Dyson, but you are going about now shivering under a load of fear. It sits like a devil incarnate upon your shoulders. It poisons the air wherever you go. Write your cheque, Sir Richard, and you can leave that little black devil in my wastebasket. You are under my protection. Nothing will happen to you."

Sir Richard sat like a man mesmerised. The little man with the amiable expression and the badly fitting suit was leaning back in his chair, his finger tips pressed together, waiting.

"Nothing will happen!" Sir Richard repeated, incredulously.

"Certainly not. I guarantee you against any inconvenience which might arise to you from this recent unfortunate affair. Isn't that all you want?"

"It's all I want, certainly," Sir Richard declared, "but I must understand a little how you propose to secure my immunity."

Ruff shook his head.

"I have my own methods," he said. "I can help only those who trust me."

Sir Richard drew a cheque book from his pocket. "I don't know why I should believe in you," he said, as he wrote the cheque.

"But you do," Peter Ruff said, smiling. "Fortunately for you, you do!"

It was not so easy to impart a similar confidence into the breast of Colonel Dickinson, with whom Sir Richard dined that night tete-a-tete. Dickinson was inclined to think that Sir Richard ad been "had."

"You've paid a ridiculous fee," he argued, "and all that you have in return is the fellow's promise to see you through. It isn't like you to part with money so easily, Richard. Did he hypnotise you?"

"I don't think so," Sir Richard answered. "I wasn't conscious of it."

"What sort of a fellow is he?" Dickinson asked.

Sir Richard looked reflectively into his glass.

"He's a vulgar sort of little Johnny," he said. "Looks as though he were always dressed in new clothes and couldn't get used to them."

Three men entered the room. Two remained in the background. John Dory came forward towards the table.

"Sir Richard Dyson," he said, gravely, "I have come upon an unpleasant errand."

"Go on," Sir Richard said, fingering something hard inside pocket of his coat.

"I have a warrant for your arrest," Dory continued, "in connection with the disappearance of Job Masters on Saturday, the 10th of November last. I will read the terms of the warrant, if you choose. It is my duty to warn you that anything you may now say can be used in evidence against you. This gentleman, I believe, is Colonel Dickinson?"

E. Phillips Oppenheim

"That is my name, sir," Dickinson answered, with unexpected fortitude.

"I regret to say," the detective continued, "that I have also a warrant for your arrest in connection with the same matter."

Sir Richard had hold of the butt end of his revolver then. Like grisly phantoms, the thoughts chased one another through his brain. Should he shoot and end it - pass into black nothingness - escape disgrace, but die like a rat in a corner? His finger was upon the trigger. Then suddenly his heart gave a great leap. He raised his head as though listening. Something flashed in his eyes - something that was almost like hope. There was no mistaking that voice which he had heard in the hall! He made a great rally.

"I can only conclude," he said, turning to the detective, "that you have made some absurd blunder. If you really possess the warrants you speak of, however, Colonel Dickinson and I will accompany you wherever you choose."

Then the door opened and Peter Ruff walked in, followed by Job Masters, whose head was still bandaged, and who seemed to have lost a little flesh and a lot of colour. Peter Ruff looked round apologetically. He seemed surprised not to find Sir Richard Dyson and Colonel Dickinson alone. He seemed more than ever surprised to recognize Dory.

"I trust," he said smoothly, "that our visit is not inopportune. Sir Richard Dyson, I believe?" he continued, bowing - "my friend, Mr. Masters here, has consulted me as to the loss of a betting book, and we ventured to call to ask you, sir, if by any chance on his recent visit to your house -"

"God in Heaven, it's Masters!" Dyson exclaimed. "It's Job Masters!"

"That's me, sir," Masters admitted. "Mr. Ruff thought you

might be able to help me find that book."

Sir Richard swayed upon his feet. Then the blood rushed once more through his veins.

"Your book's here in my cabinet, safe enough," he said. "You left it here after our luncheon that day. Where on earth have you been to, man?" he continued. "We want some money from you over Myopia."

"I'll pay all right, sir," Masters answered. "Fact is, after our luncheon party I'm afraid I got a bit fuddled. I don't seem to remember much."

He sat down a little heavily. Peter Ruff hastened to the table and took up a glass.

"You will excuse me if I give him a little brandy, won't you, sir?" he said. "He's really not quite fit for getting about yet, but he was worrying about his book."

"Give him all the brandy he can drink," Sir Richard answered.

The detective's face had been a study. He knew Masters well enough by sight - there was no doubt about his identity! His teeth came together with an angry little click. He had made a mistake! It was a thing which would be remembered against him forever! It was as bad as his failure to arrest that young man at Daisy Villa.

"Your visit, Masters," Sir Richard said, with a curious smile at the corners of his lips, "is, in some respects, a little opportune. About that little matter we were speaking of," he continued, turning towards the detective.

"We have only to offer you our apologies, Sir Richard," Dory answered.

Then he crossed the room and confronted Peter Ruff.

E. Phillips Oppenheim

"Do I understand, sir, that your name is Ruff - Peter Ruff?" he asked.

"That is my name, sir," Peter Ruff admitted, pleasantly "Yours I believe, is Dory. We are likely to come across one another now and then, I suppose. Glad to know you."

The detective stood quite still, and there was no geniality in his face.

"I wonder - have we ever met before?" he asked, without removing his eyes from the other's face. Peter Ruff smiled.

"Not professionally, at any rate," he answered. "I know that Scotland Yard you don't think much of us small fry, but we find out things sometimes!"

"Why didn't you contradict all those rumours as to his disappearance?" the detective asked, pointing to where Job Masters was contentedly sipping his brandy and water.

"I was acting for my client, and in my own interests," replied Peter. "It was surely no part of my duty to save you gentlemen at Scotland Yard from hunting up mare's nests!"

John Dory went out, followed by his men. Sir Richard took Peter Ruff by the arm, and, leading him to the sideboard, mixed him a drink.

"Peter Ruff," he said, "you're a clever scoundrel, but you've earned your five hundred guineas. Hang it, you're welcome to them! Is there anything else I can do for you?"

Peter Ruff raised his glass and set it down again. Once more he eyed with admiration his client's well-turned out figure.

"You might give me a letter to your tailors, Sir Richard," he begged.

Sir Richard laughed outright - it was some time since he had laughed!

"You shall have it, Peter Ruff," he declared, raising his glass - "and here's to you!"

E. Phillips Oppenheim

CHAPTER III

VINCENT CAWDOR, COMMISSION AGENT

For the second time since their new association, Peter Ruff had surprised that look upon his secretary's face. This time he wheeled around in his chair and addressed her.

"My dear Violet," he said, "be frank with me. What is wrong?"

Miss Brown turned to face her employer. Save for a greater demureness of expression and the extreme simplicity of her attire, she had changed very little since she had given up her life of comparative luxury to become Peter Ruff's secretary. There was a sort of personal elegance which clung to her, notwithstanding her strenuous attempts to dress for her part, except for which she looked precisely as a private secretary and typist should look. She even wore a black bow at the back of her hair.

"I have not complained, have I?" she asked.

"Do not waste time," Peter Ruff said, coldly. "Proceed."

"I have not enough to do," she said. "I do not understand why you refuse so many cases."

Peter Ruff nodded.

"I did not bring my talents into this business," he said, "to watch flirting wives, to ascertain the haunts of gay husbands, or to detect the pilferings of servants."

"Anything is better than sitting still," she protested.

"I do not agree with you," Peter Ruff said. "I like sitting still very much indeed - one has time to think. Is there anything else?"

"Shall I really go on?" she asked.

"By all means," he answered.

"I have idea," she continued, "that you are subordinating your general interests to your secret enmity - to one man. You are waiting until you can find another case in which you are pitted against him."

"Sometimes," Peter Ruff said, "your intelligence surprises me!"

"I came to you," she continued, looking at him earnestly, "for two reasons. The personal one I will not touch upon. The other was my love of excitement. I have tried many things in life, as you know, Peter, but I have seemed to carry always with me the heritage of weariness. I thought that my position here would help me to fight against it."

"You have seen me bring a corpse to life," Peter Ruff reminded her, a little aggrieved.

She smiled.

"It was a month ago," she reminded him.

"I can't do that sort of thing every day," he declared.

"Naturally," she answered; "but you have refused four cases within the last five days."

E. Phillips Oppenheim

Peter Ruff whistled softly to himself for several moments.

"Seen anything of our new neighbour in the flat above?" he asked, with apparent irrelevance.

Miss Brown looked across at him with upraised eyebrows.

"I have been in the lift with him twice," she answered.

"Fancy his appearance?" Ruff asked, casually.

"Not in the least!" Violet answered. "I thought him a vulgar, offensive person!"

Peter Ruff chuckled. He seemed immensely delighted.

"Mr. Vincent Cawdor he calls himself, I believe," he remarked.

"I have no idea," Miss Brown declared. The subject did not appeal to her.

"His name is on a small copper plate just over the letter-box," Ruff said. "Rather neat idea, by the bye. He calls himself a commission agent, I believe."

Violet was suddenly interested. She realized, after all, that Mr. Vincent Cawdor might be a person of some importance.

"What is a commission agent?" she asked.

Peter Ruff shook his head.

"It might mean anything," he declared. "Never trust any one who is not a little more explicit as to his profession. I am afraid that this Mr. Vincent Cawdor, for instance, is a bad lot."

"I am sure he is," Miss Brown declared.

"Looks after a pretty girl, coughs in the lift - all that sort of thing, eh?" Peter Ruff asked.

She nodded.

"Disgusting!" she exclaimed, with emphasis.

Peter Ruff sighed, and glanced at the clock. The existence of Mr. Vincent Cawdor seemed to pass out of his mind.

"It is nearly one o'clock," he said. "Where do you usually lunch, Violet?"

"It depends upon my appetite," she answered, carelessly. "Most often at an A B C."

"To-day," Peter Ruff said, "you will be extravagant - at my expense."

"I had a poor breakfast," Miss Brown remarked, complacently.

"You will leave at once," Peter Ruff said, "and you will go to the French Cafe at the Milan. Get a table facing the courtyard, and towards the hotel side of the room. Keep your eyes open and tell me exactly what you see."

She looked at him with parted lips. Her eyes were full of eager questioning.

"Mere skirmishing," Peter Ruff continued, "but I think - yes, I think that it may lead to something."

"Whom am I to watch?" she asked.

"Any one who looks interesting," Peter Ruff answered. "For instance, if this person Vincent Cawdor should be about."

"He would recognize me!" she declared.

Peter Ruff shrugged his shoulders.

"One must hold the candle," he remarked.

"I decline to flirt with him," she declared. "Nothing would induce me to be pleasant to such an odious creature."

"He will be too busy to attempt anything of the sort. Of course he may not be there. It may be the merest fancy on my part. At any rate, you may rely upon it that he will not make any overtures in a public place like the Milan. Mr. Vincent Cawdor may be a curious sort of person, but I do not fancy that he is a fool!"

"Very well," Miss Brown said, "I will go."

"Be back soon after three," Peter Ruff said. "I am going up to my room to do my exercises."

"And afterwards?" she asked.

"I shall have my lunch sent in," he answered. "Don't hurry back, though. I shall not expect you till a quarter past three."

It was a few minutes past that time when Miss Brown returned. Peter Ruff was sitting at his desk, looking as though he had never moved. He was absorbed by a book of patterns sent in by his new tailor, and he only glanced up when she entered the room.

"Violet," he said, earnestly, "come in and sit down. I want to consult you. There is a new material here - a sort of mouse-coloured cheviot. I wonder whether it would suit me?"

Violet was looking very handsome and a little flushed. She raised her veil and came over to his side.

"Put that stupid book away, Peter," she said. "I want to tell you about the Milan."

He leaned back in his chair.

"Ah!" he said. "I had forgotten! Was Mr. Vincent Cawdor there?"

"Yes!" she answered, still a little breathless. "There was some one else there, too, in whom you are still more interested."

He nodded.

"Go on," he said.

"Mr. Vincent Cawdor," she continued, "came in alone. He looked just as objectionable as ever, and he stared at me till I nearly threw my wine glass at him."

"He did not speak to you?" Peter Ruff asked.

"I was afraid that he was going to," Miss Brown said, "but fortunately he met a friend who came to his table and lunched with him."

"A friend," Ruff remarked. "Good! What was he like?"

"Fair, slight, Teutonic," Miss Brown answered. "He wore thick spectacles, and his moustache was positively yellow."

Ruff nodded.

"Go on," he said.

"Towards the end of luncheon," she continued, "an American came up to them."

"An American?" Peter Ruff interrupted. "How do you know that?"

Miss Brown smiled.

"He was clean-shaven and he wore neat clothes," she said. "He talked with an accent you could have cut with a knife and he had a Baedeker sticking out of his pocket. After luncheon, they all three went away to the smoking room."

Peter Ruff nodded.

"Anything else?" he asked.

The girl smiled triumphantly.

"Yes!" she declared. "There was something else - something which I think you will find interesting. At the next table to me there was a man - alone. Can you guess who he was?"

"John Dory," Ruff said, calmly.

The girl was disappointed.

"You knew!" she exclaimed.

"My dear Violet," he said, "I did not send you there on a fool's errand."

"There is something doing, then?" she exclaimed.

"There is likely," he answered, grimly, "to be a great deal doing!"

The two men who stood upon the hill, and Peter Ruff, who lay upon his stomach behind a huge boulder, looked upon a new thing.

Far down in the valley from out of a black shed - the only sign of man's handiwork for many miles - it came - something grey at first, moving slowly as though being pushed down a slight incline, then afloat in the air, gathering speed - something between a torpedo with wings and a great prehistoric insect. Now and then it described strange circles, but mostly it came towards them as swift and as true as an arrow shot from a bow. The two men looked at one another - the shorter, to whose cheeks the Cumberland winds had brought no trace of colour, gave vent to a hoarse exclamation.

"He's done it!" he growled.

"Wait!" the other answered.

Over their heads the thing wheeled, and seemed to stand still in the air. The beating of the engine was so faint that Peter Ruff from behind the boulder, could hear all that was said. A man leaned out from his seat - a man with wan cheeks but blazing eyes.

"Listen," he said. "Take your glasses. There - due north - can you see a steeple?"

The men turned their field glasses in the direction toward which the other pointed. "Yes!" they answered. "It is sixteen miles, as the crow flies, to Barnham Church - thirty-two miles there and back. Wait!"

He swung round, dived till he seemed about to touch the hillside, then soared upwards and straight away. Peter Ruff took out his watch. The other two men gazed with fascinated eyes after the disappearing speck.

"If he does it -" the shorter one muttered.

"He will do it!" the other answered.

He was back again before their eyes were weary of watching. Peter Ruff, from behind the boulder, closed his watch. Thirty-two miles in less than half an hour! The youth leaned from his seat.

"Is it enough?" he asked, hoarsely.

"It is enough!" the two men answered together. "We will come down."

The youth touched a lever and the machine glided down towards the valley, falling all the while with the effortless grace a parachute. The shed from which his machine had issued was midway down a slope, with a short length of rails which ran, apparently, through it. The machine seemed to hover for several moments above the building, then descended slowly on to the rails and disappeared in the shed. The two men were already half-way down the hill. Peter Ruff rose from behind the boulder, stretched himself with a sense of immense relief, and lit a pipe. As yet he dared not descend. He simply changed his hiding place for a spot which enabled him to command a view of the handful of cottages at the back of the hill. He had plenty to think about. It was a wonderful thing - this - which he had seen!

The youth, meanwhile, was drinking deep of the poisonous cup. He walked between the two men - his cheeks were flushed, his eyes on fire.

"If all the world to-day had seen what we have seen," the older man was saying, "there would be no more talk of Wilbur Wrights or Farmans. Those men are babies, playing with their toys."

"Mine is the ideal principle," the youth declared. "No one else has thought of it, no one else has made use of it. Yet all the time I am afraid - it is so simple."

"Sell quick, then," the fair-headed man advised. "By to-morrow night I can promise you fifty thousand pounds."

The youth stopped. He drew a deep breath.

"I shall sell," he declared. "I need money. I want to live. Fifty thousand pounds is enough. Eleven weary months I have slept and toiled there in the shed."

"It is finished," the older man declared. "To-night you shall come with us to London. To-morrow night your pockets shall be full of gold. It will be a change for you."

The youth sobbed.

"God knows it will," he muttered. "I haven't two shillings in the world, and I owe for my last petrol."

The two men laughed heartily. The elder took a little bundle of notes from his pocket and handed them to the boy.

"Come," he said, "not for another moment shall you feel as poor as that. Money will have no value for you in the future. The fifty thousand pounds will only be a start. After that, you will get royalties. If I had it, I would give you a quarter of a million now for your plans; I know that I can get you more."

The youth laughed hysterically. They entered the tiny inn and drank home-made wine - the best they could get. Then a great car drew up outside, and the older - the clean-shaven man, who looked like an American - hurried out, and dragging a hamper from beneath the seat returned with a gold-foiled bottle in his hand.

"Come," he said, "a toast! We have one bottle left - one bottle of the best!"

"Champagne!" the youth cried eagerly, holding out his hand.

"The only wine for the conquerors," the other declared, pouring it out into the thick tumblers. "Drink, all of you, to the Franklin Flying Machine, to the millions she will earn - to to-morrow night!"

The youth drained his glass, watched it replenished, and drained it again. Then they went out to the car.

"There is one thing yet to be done," he said. "Wait here for me."

They waited whilst he climbed up toward the shed. The two men watched him. A little group of rustics stood open-mouthed around the great car. Then there was a little shout. From above their heads came the sound of a great explosion - red flames were leaping up from that black barn to the sky. The two men looked at one another. They rushed to the hill and met the youth descending.

"What the -"

He stopped them.

"I dared not leave it here," he explained. "It would have been madness. I am perfectly certain that I have been watched during the last few days. I can build another in a week. I have the plans in my pocket for every part."

The older man wiped the perspiration from his forehead.

"You are sure - that you have the plans?" he asked.

The youth struck himself on the chest.

"They are here," he answered, "every one of them!"

"Perhaps you are right, then," the other man answered. "It gave me a turn, though. You are sure that you can make it again in the time you say?"

"Of course!" the youth answered, impatiently. "Besides, the thing is so simple. It speaks for itself."

They climbed into the car, and in a few minutes were rushing away southwards.

"To-morrow night - to-morrow night it all begins!" the youth continued. "I must start with ready-made clothes. I'll get the best I can, eat the best I can, drink wine, go to the music halls. To-morrow night."

His speech ended in a wail - a strange, half-stifled cry which rang out with a chill, ghostly sound upon the black silence. His face was covered with a wet towel, a ghastly odor was in his nostrils, his lips refused to utter any further sound. He lay back among the cushions, senseless. The car slowed down.

"Get the papers, quick!" the elder man muttered, opening the youth's coat. "Here they are! Catch hold, Dick! My God! What's that?"

He shook from head to foot. The little fair man looked at him with contempt.

"A sheep bell on the moor," he said. "Are you sure you have everything?"

"Yes!" the other muttered.

They both stood up and raised the prostrate form between them. Below them were the black waters of the lake.

"Over with him!" the younger said. "Quick!"

Once more his companion shrank away.

"Listen!" he muttered, hoarsely.

They both held their breaths. From somewhere along the road behind came a faint sound like the beating of an engine.

"It's a car!" the elder man exclaimed. "Quick! Over with him!"

They lifted the body of the boy, whose lips were white and speechless now, and threw him into the water. With a great splash he disappeared. They watched for a moment. Only the ripples flowed away from the place where he had sunk. They jumped back to their seats.

"There's something close behind," the older man muttered.

E. Phillips Oppenheim

"Get on! Fast! Fast!"

The younger man hesitated.

"Perhaps," he said slowly, "it would be better to wait and see who it is coming up behind. Our young friend there is safe. The current has him, and the tarn is bottomless."

There was a moment's indecision - a moment which was to count for much in the lives of three men. Then the elder one's counsels prevailed. They crept away down the hill, smoothly and noiselessly. Behind them, the faint throbbing grew less and less distinct. Soon they heard it no more. They drove into the dawn and through the long day.

Side by side on one of the big leather couches in the small smoking room of the Milan Hotel, Mr. James P. Rounceby and his friend Mr. Richard Marnstam sat whispering together. It was nearly two o clock, and they were alone in the room. Some of the lights had been turned out. The roar of life in the streets without had ceased. It was an uneasy hour for those whose consciences were not wholly at rest!

The two men were in evening dress - Rounceby in dinner coat and black tie, as befitted his role of travelling American. The glasses in front of them were only half-filled, and had remained so for the last hour. Their conversation had been nervous and spasmodic. It was obvious that they were waiting for some one.

Three o'clock struck by the little timepiece on the mantel shelf. A little exclamation of a profane nature broke from Rounceby's lips. He leaned toward his companion.

"Say," he muttered, in a rather thick undertone, "how about this fellow Vincent Cawdor? You haven't any doubts about him, I suppose? He's on the square, all right, eh?"

Marnstam wet his lips nervously.

"Cawdor's all right," he said. "I had it direct from headquarters at Paris. What are you uneasy about, eh?"

Rounceby pointed towards the clock.

"Do you see the time?" he asked.

"He said he'd be late," Marnstam answered.

Rounceby put his hand to his forehead and found it moist.

"It's been a silly game, all along," he muttered. "We'd better have brought the young ass up here and jostled him!"

"Not so easy," Marnstam answered. "These young fools have a way of turning obstinate. He'd have chucked us, sure. Anyhow, he's safer where he is."

They relapsed once more into silence. A storm of rain beat upon the window. Rounceby glanced up. It was as black out there as were the waters of that silent tarn! The man shivered as the thought struck him. Marnstam, who had no nerves, twirled his moustache and watched his companion with wonder.

"You look as though you saw a ghost," he remarked.

"Perhaps I do!" Rounceby growled.

"You had better finish your drink, my dear fellow," Marnstam advised. "Afterwards -"

Suddenly he stiffened into attention. He laid his hand upon his companion's knee.

"Listen!" he said. "There is some one coming."

They leaned a little forward. The swing doors were opened. A girl's musical laugh rang out from the corridor. Tall and elegant, with her black lace skirt trailing upon the floor, her left hand resting upon the shoulder of the man into whose ear she was whispering, and whom she led straight to one of the writing tables, Miss Violet Brown swept into the room. On her right, and nearest to the two men, was Mr. Vincent Cawdor.

"Now you can go and talk to your friends!" she exclaimed, lightly. "I am going to make Victor listen to me."

Cawdor left his two companions and sank on to the couch by Rounceby's side. The young man, with his opera hat still on his head, and the light overcoat which he had been carrying on the floor by his side, was seated before the writing table with his back to them. Miss Brown was leaning over him, with her hand upon the back of his chair. They were out of hearing of the other three men.

"Well, Rounceby, my friend," Mr. Vincent Cawdor remarked, cheerfully, "you're having a late sitting, eh?"

"We've been waiting for you, you fool!" Rounceby answered. "What on earth are you thinking about, bringing a crowd like this about with you, eh?"

Cawdor smiled, reassuringly.

"Don't you worry," he said, in a lower tone. "I know my way in and out of the ropes here better than you can teach me. A big hotel like this is the safest and the most dangerous place in the world - just how you choose to make it. You've got to bluff 'em all the time. That's why I brought the young lady - particular friend of mine - real nice girl, too!"

"And the young man?" Rounceby asked, suspiciously.

Cawdor grew more serious.

"That's Captain Lowther," he said softly - "private secretary to Colonel Dean, who's the chief of the aeronaut department at

Aldershot. He has a draft in his pocket for twenty thousand pounds. It is yours if he is satisfied with the plans."

"Twenty thousand pounds!" Marnstam said, thoughtfully. "It is very little - very little indeed for the risks which we have run!"

Cawdor moved his place and sat between the men. He laid a hand upon Marnstam's shoulder - another on Rounceby's knee.

"My dear friends," he said, impressively, "if you could have built a model, or conducted these negotiations in the usual way, you might have asked a million. As it is, I think I am the only man in England who could have dealt with this matter - so satisfactorily."

Rounceby glanced suspiciously at the young man to whom Miss Brown was still devoting the whole of her attention.

"Why don't he come out and talk like a man?" he asked. "What's the idea of his sitting over there with his back to us?"

"I want him never to see your faces - to deal only with me," Cawdor explained. "Remember that he is in an official position. The money he is going to part with is secret service money."

The two men were beginning to be more reassured. Rounceby slowly produced a roll of oilskin from his pocket.

"He'll look at them as he sits there," he insisted. "There must be no copying or making notes, mind."

Cawdor smiled in a superior fashion.

"My dear fellow," he said, "you are dealing with the emissary of a government - not one of your own sort."

Rounceby glanced at his companion, who nodded. Then he handed over the plans.

"Tell him to look sharp," he said. "It's not so late but that there may be people in here yet."

Cawdor crossed the room with the plans, and laid them down before the writing table. Rounceby rose to his feet and lit a cigar. Marnstam walked to the further window and back again. They stood side by side. Rounceby's whole frame seemed to have stiffened with some new emotion.

"There's something wrong, Jim," Marnstam whispered softly in his ear. "You've got the old lady in your pocket?"

"Yes!" Rounceby answered thickly, "and, by Heavens, I'm going to use it!"

"Don't shoot unless it's the worst," Marnstam counselled. "I shall go out of that window, into the tree, and run for the river. But bluff first, Jim - bluff for your life!"

There were swinging doors leading into the room from the hotel side, and a small door exactly opposite which led to the residential part of the place. Both of these doors were opened at precisely the same moment. Through the former stepped two strong looking men in long overcoats, and with the unmistakable appearance of policemen in plain clothes. Through the latter came John Dory! He walked straight up to the two men. It spoke volumes for his courage that, knowing their characters and believing them to be in desperate straits, he came unarmed.

"Gentlemen," he said, "I hold warrants for your arrest. I will not trouble you with your aliases. You are known to-day, I believe, as James Rounceby and Richard Marnstam. Will you come quietly?"

Marnstam's expression was one of bland and beautiful surprise.

"My dear sir," he said, edging, however, a little toward the window - "you must be joking! What is the charge?"

"You are charged with the wilful murder of a young man named Victor Franklin," answered Dory. "His body was recovered from Longthorp Tarn this afternoon. You had better say nothing. Also with the theft of certain papers known to have been in his possession."

Now it is possible that at this precise moment Marnstam would have made his spring for the window and Rounceby his running fight for liberty. The hands of both men were upon their revolvers, and John Dory's life was a thing of no account. But at this juncture a thing happened. There were in the room the two policemen guarding the swing doors, and behind them the pale faces of a couple of night porters looking anxiously in. Vincent Cawdor and Miss Brown were standing side by side, a little in the background, and the young man who had been their companion had risen also to his feet. As though with some intention of intervening, he moved a step forward, almost in line with Dory. Rounceby saw him, and a new fear gripped him by the heart. He shrank back, his fingers relaxed their hold of his weapon, the sweat was hot upon his forehead. Marnstam, though he seemed for a moment stupefied, realised the miracle which had happened and struck boldly for his own.

"If this is a joke," he said, "it strikes me as being a particularly bad one. I should like to know, sir, how you dare to come into this room and charge me and my friend - Mr. Rounceby - with being concerned in the murder of a young man who is even now actually standing by your side."

John Dory started back. He looked with something like apprehension at the youth to whom Marnstam pointed.

"My name is Victor Franklin," that young man declared. "What's all this about?"

E. Phillips Oppenheim

Dory felt the ground give beneath his feet. Nevertheless, he set his teeth and fought for his hand.

"You say that your name is Victor Franklin?" he asked.

"Certainly!"

"You are the inventor of a flying machine?"

"I am."

"You were in Westmoreland with these two men a few days go?"

"I was," the young man admitted.

"You left the village of Scawton in a motor car with them?"

"Yes! We quarrelled on the way, and parted."

"You were robbed of nothing?"

Victor Franklin smiled.

"Certainly not," he answered. "I had nothing worth stealing except my plans, and they are in my pocket now."

There was a few moments' intense silence. Dory wheeled suddenly round, and looked to where Mr. Vincent Cawdor had been standing.

"Where is Mr. Cawdor?" he asked, sharply.

"The gentleman with the grey moustache left a few seconds ago," one of the men at the door said. Dory was very pale.

"Gentlemen," he said, "I have to offer you my apologies. I have apparently been deceived by some false information. The charge is withdrawn."

He turned on his heel and left the room. The two policemen followed him.

"Keep them under observation," Dory ordered shortly, "but I am afraid this fellow Cawdor has sold me."

He found a hansom outside, and sprang into it.

"Number 27, Southampton Row," he ordered.

Rounceby and his partner were alone in the little smoking room. The former was almost inarticulate. The night porter brought them brandy, and both men drank.

"We've got to get to the bottom of this, Marnstam," Mr. Rounceby muttered.

Mr. Marnstam was thinking.

"Do you remember that sound through the darkness," he said - "the beating of an engine way back on the road?"

"What of it?" Rounceby demanded.

"It was a motor bicycle," Marnstam said quietly. "I thought so at the time."

"Supposing some one followed us and pulled him out," Rounceby said, hoarsely, "why are we treated like this? I tell you we've been made fools of! We've been treated like children - not even to be punished! We'll have the truth somehow out of that devil Cawdor! Come!"

They made their way to the courtyard and found a cab.

"Number 27, Southampton Row!" they ordered.

They reached their destination some time before Dory, whose horse fell down in the Strand, and who had to walk. They

E. Phillips Oppenheim

ascended to the fourth floor of the building and rang the bell of Vincent Cawdor's room - no answer. They plied the knocker - no result. Rounceby peered through the keyhole.

"He hasn't come home yet," he remarked. "There is no light anywhere in the place."

The door of a flat across the passage was quietly opened. Mr. Peter Ruff, in a neat black smoking suit and slippers, and holding a pipe in his hand, looked out.

"Excuse me, gentlemen," he said, "but I do not think that Mr. Cawdor is in. He went out early this evening, and I have not heard him return."

The two men turned away.

"We are much obliged to you, sir," Mr. Marnstam said.

"Can I give him any message?" Peter Ruff asked, politely. "We generally see something of one another in the morning."

"You can tell him -" Rounceby began.

"No message, thanks!" Marnstam interrupted. "We shall probably run across him ourselves to-morrow."

John Dory was nearly a quarter of an hour late. After his third useless summons, Mr. Peter Ruff presented himself again.

"I am afraid," he said, "you will not find my neighbour at home. There have been several people enquiring for him to-night, without any result."

John Dory came slowly across the landing.

"Good evening, Mr. Ruff!" he said.

"Why, it's Mr. Dory!" Peter Ruff declared. "Come in, do, and have a drink."

John Dory accepted the invitation, and his eyes were busy in that little sitting room during the few minutes which it took his host to mix that whisky and soda.

"Nothing wrong with our friend opposite, I hope?" Peter Ruff asked, jerking his head across the landing.

"I hope not, Mr. Ruff," John Dory said. "No doubt in the morning he will be able to explain everything. I must say that I should like to see him to-night, though."

"He may turn up yet," Peter Ruff remarked, cheerfully. "He's like myself - a late bird."

"I fear not," Dory answered, drily. "Nice rooms you have here, sir. Just a sitting room and bedroom, eh?"

Peter Ruff stood up and threw open the door of the inner apartment.

"That's so," he answered. "Care to have a look round?"

The detective did look round, and pretty thoroughly. As soon as he was sure that there was no one concealed upon the premises, he drank his whisky and soda and went.

"I'll look in again to see Cawdor," he remarked - "to-morrow, perhaps, or the next day."

"I'll let him know if I see him about," Peter Ruff declared. "Sorry the lift's stopped. Three steps to the left and straight on. Good-night!"

Miss Brown arrived early the following morning, and was disposed to be inquisitive.

"I should like to know," she said, "exactly what has become of

Mr. Vincent Cawdor."

Peter Ruff took her upstairs. There was a little mound of ashes in the grate.

She nodded.

"I imagined that," she said. "But why did you send me out to watch yourself?"

"My dear Violet," Peter Ruff answered, "there is no man in the world to-day who is my equal in the art of disguising himself. At the same time, I wanted to know whether I could deceive you. I wanted to be quite sure that my study of Mr. Vincent Cawdor was a safe one. I took those rooms in his name and in his own person. I do not think that it occurred even to our friend John Dory to connect us in his mind."

"Very well," she went on. "Now tell me, please, what took you up to Westmoreland?"

"I followed Rounceby and Marnstam," he answered, "I knew them when I was abroad, studying crime - I could tell you a good deal about both those men if it were worth while - and I knew, when they hired a big motor car and engaged a crook to drive it, that they were worth following. I saw the trial of the flying machine, and when they started off with young Franklin, I followed on a motor bicycle. I fished him out of the tarn where they left him for dead, brought him on to London, and made my own terms with him."

"What about the body which was found in the Longthorp Tarn?" she asked.

"I had that telegram sent myself," Peter Ruff answered.

She looked at him severely.

"You went out of your way to make a fool of John Dory!" she

said, frowning at him.

"That I admit," he answered.

"It seems to me," she continued, "that that, after all, has been the chief object of the whole affair. I do not see that we - that is the firm - profit in the least."

Peter Ruff chuckled.

"We've got a fourth share in the Franklin Flying Machine," he answered, "and I'm hanged if I'd sell it for a hundred thousand pounds."

"You've taken advantage of that young man's gratitude," she declared.

Peter Ruff shook his head.

"I earned the money," he answered.

CHAPTER IV

THE INDISCRETION OF LETTY SHAW

Amidst a storm of whispered criticisms, the general opinion was that Letty Shaw was a silly little fool who ought to have known better. When she had entered the restaurant a few minutes before midnight, followed by Austen Abbott, every one looked to see a third person following them. No third person, however, appeared. Gustav himself conducted them to a small table laid for two, covered with pink roses, and handed his fair client the menu of a specially ordered supper. There was no gainsaying the fact that Letty and her escort proposed supping alone!

The Cafe at the Milan was, without doubt, the fashionable rendezvous of the moment for those ladies connected with the stage who, after their performance, had not the time or the inclination to make the conventional toilet demanded by the larger restaurants. Letty Shaw, being one of the principal ornaments of the musical comedy stage, was well known to every one in the room. There was scarcely a person there who within the last fortnight had not found an opportunity of congratulating her upon her engagement to Captain the Honourable Brian Sotherst. Sotherst was rich, and one of the most popular young men about town. Letty Shaw, although she had had one or two harmless flirtations, was well known as a self-respecting and hard-working young actress who loved her work, and against whom no one had ever had a word to say. Consequently, the shock was all the greater when, within a fortnight of her engagement, she was thus to be seen openly supping alone with the most notorious woman hunter about town - a man of bad reputation, a man, too, towards whom Sotherst was known to have a special aversion. Nothing but a break with Sotherst or a fit of temporary insanity seemed to explain, even inadequately, the situation.

Her best friend - the friend who knew her and believed in her - rose to her feet and came sailing down the room. She nodded gaily to Abbott, whom she hated, and whom she had not recognized for years, and laid her hand upon Letty's arm.

"Where's Brian?" she asked.

Letty shrugged her shoulders - it was not altogether a natural gesture.

"On duty to-night," she answered.

Her best friend paused for a moment.

"Come over and join our party, both of you," she said. "Dicky Pennell's here and Gracie Marsh - just landed. They'd love to meet you."

Letty shook her head slowly. There was a look in her face which even her best friend did not understand.

"I'm afraid that we can't do that," she said. "I am Mr. Abbott's guest."

"And to-night," Austen Abbott intervened, looking up at the woman who stood between them, "I am not disposed to share Miss Shaw with anybody."

Her best friend could do no more than shake her head and go away. The two were left alone for the rest of the evening. When they departed together, people who knew felt that a whiff of tragedy had passed through the room. Nobody understood - or pretended to understand. Even before her engagement, Letty had never been known to sup alone with a man. That she should do so now, and with this particular man, was preposterous!

"Something will come of it," her best friend murmured, sadly, as she watched Austen Abbott help his companion on with her cloak.

Something did!

Peter Ruff rose at his accustomed time the following morning, and attired himself, if possible, with more than his usual care. He wore the grey suit which he had carefully put out the night before, but he hesitated long between the rival appeals of a red tie with white spots and a plain mauve one. He finally chose the latter, finding that it harmonised more satisfactorily with his socks, and after a final survey of himself in the looking-glass, he entered the next room, where his coffee was set out upon a small round table near the fire, together with his letters and newspapers.

Peter Ruff was, after all, like the rest of us, a creature of habit. He made an invariable rule of glancing through the news-papers before he paid any regard at all to his letters or his breakfast. In the absence of anything of a particularly sensa-tional character, he then opened his letters in leisurely fashion, and went back afterwards to the newspaper as he finished his meal. This morning, however, both his breakfast and letters remained for some time untouched. The first paragraph which caught his eye as he shook open the Daily Telegraph was sufficiently absorbing. There it was in great black type:

TERRIBLE TRAGEDY IN THE FLAT OF A WELL-KNOWN ACTRESS!

AUSTEN ABBOTT SHOT DEAD!
ARREST OF CAPTAIN SOTHERST

Beyond the inevitable shock which is always associated with the taking of life, and the unusual position of the people concerned in it, there was little in the brief account of the incident to excite the imagination. A policeman on the pavement outside the flat in which Miss Shaw and her mother lived fancied that he heard, about two o'clock in the morning, the report of a revolver shot. As nothing further transpired, and as the sound was very indistinct, he did not at once enter the building, but kept it, so far as possible, under observation. About twenty minutes later, a young gentleman in evening dress came out into the street, and the policeman noticed at once that he was carrying a small revolver, which he attempted to conceal. The constable thereupon whistled for his sergeant, and accompanied by the young gentleman - who made no effort to escape - ascended to Miss Shaw's rooms, where the body of Austen Abbott was discovered lying upon the threshold of the sitting room with a small bullet mark through the forehead. The inmates of the house were aroused and a doctor sent for. The deceased man was identified as Austen Abbott - a well-known actor - and the man under arrest gave his name at once as Captain the Honourable Brian Sotherst. Peter Ruff sighed as he laid down the paper. The case seemed to him perfectly clear, and his sympathies were altogether with the young officer who had taken the law into his own hands. He knew nothing of Miss Letty Shaw, and, consequently, did her, perhaps, less than justice in his thoughts. Of Austen Abbott, on the other hand, he knew a great deal - and nothing of good. It was absurd, after all, that any one should be punished for killing such a brute!

He descended, a few minutes later, to his office, and found Miss Brown busy arranging a bowl of violets upon his desk.

"Isn't it horrible?" she cried, as he entered, carrying a bundle of papers under his arm. "I never have had such a shock!"

"Do you know any of them, then?" Peter Ruff asked, straightening his tie in the mirror.

"Of course!" she answered. "Why, I was in the same company as Letty Shaw for a year. I was at the Milan, too, last night. Letty was there having supper alone with Austen Abbott. We all said that there'd be trouble, but of course we never dreamed of this! Isn't there any chance for him, Peter? Can't he get off?"

Peter Ruff shook his head.

"I'm afraid not," he answered. "They may be able to bring evidence of a quarrel and reduce it to manslaughter, but what you've just told me about this supper party makes it all the worse. It will come out in the evidence, of course."

"Captain Sotherst is such a dear," Miss Brown declared, "and so good-looking! And as for that brute Austen Abbott, he ought to have been shot long ago!"

Peter Ruff seated himself before his desk and hitched up his trousers at the knees.

"No doubt you are right, Violet," he said, "but people go about these things so foolishly. To me it is simply exasperating to reflect how little use is made of persons such as myself, whose profession in life it is to arrange these little matters. Take the present case, for example. Captain Sotherst had only to lay these facts before me, and Austen Abbott was a ruined man. I could have arranged the affair for him in half-a-dozen different ways. Whereas now it must be a life for a life - the life of an honest young English gentleman for that of a creature who should have been kicked out of the world as vermin!... I have some letters give you, Violet, if you please."

She swung round in her chair reluctantly.

"I can't help thinking of that poor young fellow," she said, with a sigh.

"Sentiment after office hours, if you please!" said Peter.

Then there came a knock at the door.

His visitor lifted her veil, and Peter Ruff recognized her immediately.

"What can I do for you, Lady Mary?" he asked.

She saw the recognition in his eyes even before he spoke, and wondered at it.

"You know me?" she exclaimed.

"I know most people," he answered, drily; "it is part of my profession."

"Tell me - you are Mr. Peter Ruff," she said, "the famous specialist in the detection of crime? You know that Brian Sotherst is my brother?"

"Yes," he said, "I know it! I am sorry - very sorry, indeed."

He handed her a chair. She seated herself with a little tightening of the lips.

"I want more than sympathy from you, Mr. Ruff," she warned him. "I want your help."

"It is my profession," he admitted, "but your brother's case makes intervention difficult, does it not?"

"You mean -" she began.

"Your brother himself does not deny his guilt, I understand."

"He has not denied it," she answered - "very likely he will not do so before the magistrate - but neither has he admitted it. Mr. Ruff, you are such a clever man. Can't you see the truth?"

Peter Ruff looked at her steadily for several moments.

"Lady Mary," he said, "I can see what you are going to suggest. You are going on the assumption that Austen Abbott was shot by Letty Shaw and that your brother is taking the thing on his shoulders."

"I am sure of it!" she declared. "The girl did it herself, beyond a doubt. Brian would never have shot any one. He might have horsewhipped him, perhaps - even beaten him to death - but shot him in cold blood - never!"

"The provocation -" Ruff began.

"There was no provocation," she interrupted. "He was engaged to the girl, and of course we hated it, but she was an honest little thing, and devoted to him."

"Doubtless," Ruff admitted. "But all the same, as you will hear before the magistrates, or at the inquest, she was having supper alone with Austen Abbott that night at the Milan."

Lady Mary's eyes flashed.

"I don't believe it!" she declared.

"It is nevertheless true," Peter Ruff assured her. "There is no shadow of doubt about it."

Lady Mary was staggered. For a few moment she seemed struggling to rearrange her thoughts.

"You see," Ruff continued, "the fact that Miss Shaw was willing to sup with Austen Abbott tete-a-tete renders it more improbable that she should shoot him in her sitting room, an hour or so later, and then go calmly up to her mother's room as though nothing had happened."

Lady Mary had lost some of her confidence, but she was

not daunted.

"Even if we have been deceived in the girl," she said, thoughtfully - "even if she were disposed to flirt with other men - even then there might be a stronger motive than ever for her wishing to get rid of Abbott. He may have become jealous, and threatened her."

"It is, of course, possible," Ruff assented, politely. "Your theory would, at any rate, account for your brother's present attitude."

She looked at him steadfastly.

"You believe, then," she said, "that my brother shot Austen Abbott?"

"I do," he admitted frankly. "So does every man or woman of common sense in London. On the facts as they are stated in the newspapers, with the addition of which I have told you, no other conclusion is possible."

Lady Mary rose.

"Then I may as well go," she said tearfully.

"Not at all," Peter Ruff declared. "Listen. This is a matter of business with me. I say that on the facts as they are known, your brother's guilt appears indubitable. I do not say that there may not be other facts in the background which alter the state of affairs. If you wish me to search for them, engage me, and I will do my best."

"Isn't that what I am here for?" the girl exclaimed.

"Very well," Peter Ruff said. "My services are at your disposal."

"You will do your best - more than your best, won't you?" she

E. Phillips Oppenheim

begged. "Remember that he is my brother - my favourite brother!"

"I will do what can be done," Peter Ruff promised. "Please sit down at that desk and write me two letters of Introduction."

She drew off her gloves and prepared to obey him.

"To whom?" she asked.

"To the solicitors who are defending your brother," he said, "and to Miss Letty Shaw."

"You mean to go and see her?" Lady Mary asked, doubtfully.

"Naturally," Peter Ruff answered. "If your supposition is correct, she might easily give herself away under a little subtle cross-examination. It is my business to know how to ask people questions in such a way that if they do not speak the truth their words give some indication of it. If she is innocent I shall know that I have to make my effort in another direction."

"What other direction can there be?" Lady Mary asked dismally.

Peter Ruff said nothing. He was too kind-hearted to kindle false hopes.

"It's a hopeless case, of course," Miss Brown remarked, after Lady Mary had departed.

"I'm afraid so," Peter Ruff answered. "Still I must earn my money. Please get some one to take you to supper to-night at the Milan, and see if you can pick up any scandal."

"About Letty?" she asked.

"About either of them," he answered. "Particularly I should like to know if any explanation has cropped up of her supping alone with Austen Abbott."

"I don't see why you can't take me yourself," she remarked. "You are on the side of the law this time, at any rate."

"I will," he answered, after a moment's hesitation. "I will call for you at eleven o'clock to-night."

He rose and closed his desk emphatically.

"You are going out?" she asked.

"I am going to see Miss Letty Shaw," he answered.

He took a taxicab to the flats, and found a handful of curious people still gazing up at the third floor. The parlourmaid who answered his summons was absolutely certain that Miss Shaw would not see him. He persuaded her, after some difficulty, to take in his letter while he waited in the hall. When she returned, she showed him into a small sitting room and pulled down the blinds.

"Miss Shaw will see you, sir, for a few minutes," she announced, in a subdued tone. "Poor dear young lady," she continued, "she has been crying her eyes out all the morning."

"No wonder," Peter Ruff said, sympathetically. "It's a terrible business, this!"

"One of the nicest young men as ever walked," the girl declared, firmly. "As for that brute, he deserved all he's got, and more!"

Peter Ruff was left alone for nearly a quarter of an hour. Then the door was softly opened and Letty Shaw entered. There was no doubt whatever about her suffering. Ruff, who had seen her only lately at the theatre, was shocked. Under her eyes were blacker lines than her pencil had ever traced. Not only was she ghastly pale, but her face seemed wan and shrunken. She spoke to him the moment she entered, leaning with on hand upon the sideboard.

"Lady Mary writes that you want to help us," she said. "How can you? How is it possible?"

Even her voice had gone. She spoke hoarsely, and as though short of breath. Her eyes searched his face feverishly. It seemed cruelty not to answer her at once, and Peter Ruff was not a cruel man. Nevertheless, he remained silent, and it seemed to her that his eyes were like points of fire upon her face.

"What is the matter?" she cried, with breaking voice. "What have you come for? Why don't you speak to me?"

"Madam," Peter Ruff said, "I should like to help you, and I will do what I can. But in order that I may do so, it is necessary that you should answer me two questions - truthfully!"

Her eyes grew wider. It was the face of a terrified child.

"Why not?" she exclaimed. "What have I to conceal?"

Peter Ruff's expression never changed. There was nothing about him, as he stood there with his hands behind him, his head thrown a little forward, in the least inspiring - nothing calculated to terrify the most timid person. Yet the girl looked at him with the eyes of a frightened bird.

"Remember, then," he continued, smoothly, "that what you say to me is sacred. You and I are alone without witnesses or eavesdroppers. Was it Brian Sotherst who shot Abbott - or was it you?"

She gave a little cry. Her hands clasped the sides of her head in horror.

"I!" she exclaimed, "I! God help me!"

He waited. In a moment she looked up.

"You cannot believe that," she said, with a calmness for which he was scarcely prepared. "It is absurd. I left the room by the inner door as he took up his hat to step out into the hall."

"Incidentally," he asked - "this is not my other question, mind - why did you not let him out yourself?"

"We had disagreed," she answered, curtly.

Peter Ruff bent his head in assent.

"I see," he remarked. "You had disagreed. Abbott probably hoped that you would relent, so he waited for a few minutes. Brian Sotherst, who had escaped from his engagement in time, he thought, to come and wish you good night, must have walked in and found him there. By the bye, how would Captain Sotherst get in?"

"He had a key," the girl answered. "My mother lives here with me, and we have only one maid. It was more convenient. I gave him one washed in gold for a birthday present only a few days ago."

"Thank you," Peter Ruff said. "The revolver, I understand, was your property?"

She nodded.

"It was a present from Brian," she said. "He gave it to me in a joke, and I had it on the table with some other curiosities."

"The first question," Peter Ruff said, "is disposed of. May I proceed to the second?"

The girl moistened her lips.

"Yes!" she answered.

"Why did you sup alone with Austen Abbott last night?"

She shrank a little away.

"Why should I not?" she asked.

"You have been on the stage, my dear Miss Shaw," Peter Ruff continued, "for between four and five years. During the whole of that time, it has been your very wise habit to join supper parties, of course, when the company was agreeable to you, but to sup alone with no man! Am I not right?"

"You seem to know a great deal about me," she faltered.

"Am I not right?" he repeated.

"Yes!"

"You break your rule for the first time," Peter Ruff continued, "in favour of a man of notoriously bad character, a few weeks after the announcement of your engagement to an honourable young English gentleman. You know very well the construction likely to be put upon your behaviour - you, of all people, would be the most likely to appreciate the risk you ran. Why did you run it? In other words, I repeat my question. Why did you sup alone with Austen Abbott last night?"

All this time she had been standing. She came a little forward now, and threw herself into an easy-chair.

"It doesn't help!" she exclaimed. "All this doesn't help!"

"Nor can I help you, then," Peter Ruff said, stretching out his hand for his hat.

She waved to him to put it down.

"I will tell you," she said. "It has nothing to do with the case, but since you ask, you shall know. There is a dear little girl in our company - Fluffy Dean we all call her - only eighteen years old. We all love her, she is so sweet, and just like I was when I first went on the stage, only much nicer. She is very pretty, she has no money, and she is such an affectionate little dear that although she is as good as gold, we are all terrified for her sake whenever she makes acquaintances. Several of us who are most interested made a sort of covenant. We all took it in turns to look after her, and try to see that she did not meet any one she shouldn't. Yet, for all our precautions, Austen Abbott got hold of her and turned her silly little head. He was a man of experience, and she was only a child. She wouldn't listen to us - she wouldn't hear a word against him. I took what seemed to me to be the only chance. I went to him myself - I begged for mercy, I begged him to spare the child. I swore that if - anything happened to her, I would start a crusade against him, I would pledge my word that he should be cut by every decent man and woman on the stage! He listened to what I had to say and at first he only smiled. When I had finished, he made me an offer. He said that if I would sup with him alone at the Milan, and permit him to escort me home afterwards, he would spare the child. One further condition he made - that I was to tell no one why I did it. It was the man's brutal vanity! I made the promise, but I break it now. You have asked me and I have told you. I went through with the supper, although I hated it. I let him come in for a drink as though he had been a friend. Then he tried to make love to me. I took the opportunity of telling him exactly what I thought of him. Then I showed him the door, and left him. Afterwards - afterwards - Brian came in! They must have met upon the very threshold!"

Peter Ruff took up his hat.

"Thank you!" he said.

"You see," she continued, drearily, "that it all has very little to do with the case. I meant to keep it to myself, because, of course, apart from anything else, apart from Brian's meeting him coming out of my rooms, it supplies an additional cause for anger on Brian's part."

"I see," he answered. "I am much obliged to you, Miss Shaw. Believe me that you have my sincere sympathy!"

Peter Ruff's farewell words were unheard. Letty had fallen forward in her chair, her head buried in her hands.

Peter Ruff went to Berkeley Square and found Lady Mary waiting for him. Sir William Trencham, the great solicitor, was with her. Lady Mary introduced the two men. All the time she was anxiously watching Ruff's face.

"Mr. Ruff has been to see Miss Shaw," she explained to Sir William. "Mr. Ruff, tell me quickly," she continued, with her hand upon his shoulder, "did she say anything? Did you find anything out?"

He shook his head.

"No!" he said. "I found nothing out!"

"You don't think, then," Lady Mary gasped, "that there is any chance - of getting her to confess - that she did it herself?"

"Why should she have done it herself?" Peter Ruff asked. "She admits that the man tried to make love to her. She simply left him. She was in her own home, with her mother and servant within call. There was no struggle in the room - we know that. There was no necessity for any."

"Have you made any other enquiries?" Lady Mary asked.

"The few which I have made," Peter Ruff answered gravely, "point all in the same direction. I ascertained at the Milan that your brother called there late last night, and that he heard Miss Shaw had been supping alone with Austen Abbott. He followed them home. I have ascertained, too, that he had a key to Miss Shaw's flat. He apparently met Austen Abbott upon the threshold."

Lady Mary covered her face with her hands. She seemed to read in Ruff's words the verdict of the two men - the verdict of common sense. Nevertheless, he made one more request before leaving.

"I should like to see Captain Sotherst, if you can get me an order," he said to Sir William.

"You can go with me to-morrow morning," the lawyer answered. "The proceedings this morning, of course, were simply formal. Until after the inquest it will be easy to arrange an interview."

Lady Mary looked up quickly.

"There is still something in your mind, then?" she asked. "You think that there is a bare chance?"

"There is always the hundredth chance!" Peter Ruff replied.

Peter Ruff and Miss Brown supped at the Milan that night as they had arranged, but it was not a cheerful evening. Brian Sotherst had been very popular among Letty Shaw's little circle of friends, and the general feeling was one of horror and consternation at this thing which had befallen him. Austen Abbot, too, was known to all of them, and although a good many of the men - and even the women - were outspoken enough to declare at once that it served him right, nevertheless, the shock of death - death without a second's warning - had a paralysing effect even upon those who were his severest critics. Violet Brown spoke to a few of her friends - introduced Peter Ruff here and there - but nothing was said which could throw in any way even the glimmerings of a new light upon the tragedy. It all seemed too hopelessly and fatally obvious.

About twenty minutes before closing time, the habitues of the place were provided with something in the nature of a

E. Phillips Oppenheim

sensation. A little party entered who seemed altogether free from the general air of gloom. Foremost among them was a very young and exceedingly pretty girl, with light golden hair waved in front of her forehead, deep blue eyes, and the slight, airy figure of a child. She was accompanied by another young woman, whose appearance was a little too obvious to be prepossessing, and three or four young men - dark, clean-shaven, dressed with the irritating exactness of their class - young stockbrokers or boys about town. Miss Brown's eyes grew very wide open.

"What a little beast!" she exclaimed.

"Who?" Peter Ruff asked.

"That pretty girl there," she answered - "Fluffy Dean her name is. She is Letty Shaw's protege, and she wouldn't have dreamed of allowing her to come out with a crowd like that. Tonight, of all nights," she continued, indignantly, "when Letty is away!"

Peter Ruff was interested.

"So that is Miss Fluffy Dean," he remarked, looking at her curiously. "She seems a little excited."

"She's a horrid little wretch!" Miss Brown declared. "I hope that some one will tell Letty, and that she will drop her now. A girl who would do such a thing as that when Letty is in such trouble isn't worth taking care of! Just listen to them all!"

They were certainly becoming a little boisterous. A magnum of champagne was being opened. Fluffy Dean's cheeks were already flushed, and her eyes glittering. Every one at the table was talking a great deal and drinking toasts.

"This is the end of Fluffy Dean," Violet Brown said, severely. "I hate to be uncharitable, but it serves her right."

Peter Ruff paid his bill.

"Let us go," he said.

In the taxicab, on their way back to Miss Brown's rooms, Ruff was unusually silent, but just before he said good night to her - on the pavement, in fact, outside her front door - he asked a question.

"Violet," he said, "would you like to play detective for an hour or two?"

She looked at him in some surprise.

"You know I always like to help in anything that's going," she said.

"Letty Shaw was an Australian, wasn't she?" he asked.

"Yes."

"She was born there, and lived there till she was nearly eighteen - is that true?" he asked again.

"Quite true," Miss Brown answered.

"You know the offices of the P.& O. line of steamers in Pall Mall?" he asked.

She nodded.

"Well?"

"Get a sailing list to Australia - there should be a boat going Thursday. Present yourself as a prospective passenger. See how many young women alone there are going out, and ask their names. Incidentally put in a little spare time watching the office."

She looked at him with parted lips and wide-open eyes.

E. Phillips Oppenheim

"Do you think -" she began.

He shook her hand warmly and stepped back into the taxicab.

"Good night!" he said. "No questions, please. I shan't expect you at the office at the usual time to-morrow, at any rate. Telephone or run around if you've anything to tell me."

The taxicab disappeared round the corner of the street. Miss Brown was standing still upon the pavement with the latchkey in her hand.

It was afternoon before the inquest on the body of Austen Abbott, and there was gathered together in Letty Shaw's parlor a curiously assorted little group of people. There was Miss Shaw herself - or rather what seemed to be the ghost of herself - and her mother; Lady Mary and Sir William Trencham; Peter Ruff and Violet Brown - and Mr. John Dory. The eyes of all of them were fixed upon Peter Ruff, who was the latest arrival. He stood in the middle of the room, calmly taking off his gloves, and glancing complacently down at his well-creased trousers.

"Lady Mary," he said, "and Miss Shaw, I know that you are both anxious for me to explain why I ask you to meet me here this afternoon, and why I also requested my friend Mr. Dory from Scotland Yard, who has charge of the case against Captain Sotherst, to be present. I will tell you."

Mr. Dory nodded, a little impatiently.

"Unless you have something very definite to say," he remarked, "I think it would be as well to postpone any general discussion of this matter until after the inquest. I must warn you that so far as I, personally, am concerned, I must absolutely decline to allude to the subject at all. It would be most unprofessional."

"I have something definite to say," Peter Ruff declared, mildly.

Lady Mary's eyes flashed with hope - Letty Shaw leaned forward in her chair with white, drawn face.

"Let it be understood," Peter Ruff said, with a slight note of gravity creeping into his tone, "that I am here solely as the agent of Lady Mary Sotherst. I am paid and employed by her. My sole object is on her behalf, therefore, to discover proof of the innocence of Captain Sotherst. I take it, however," he added, turning towards the drooping figure in the easy-chair, "that Miss Shaw is as anxious to have the truth known."

"Of course! Of course!" she murmured.

"In France," Peter Ruff continued, "there is a somewhat curious custom, which, despite a certain theatricality, yet has its points. The scene of a crime is visited, and its events, so far as may be, reconstructed. Let us suppose for a moment that we are now engaged upon something of the sort."

Letty Shaw shrank back in her chair. Her thin white fingers were gripping its sides. Her eyes seemed to look upon terrible things.

"It is too - awful!" she faltered.

"Madam," Peter Ruff said, firmly, "we seek the truth. Be so good as to humour me in this. Dory, will you go to the front door, stand upon the mat - so? You are Captain Sotherst - you have just entered. I am Austen Abbott. You, Miss Shaw, have just ordered me from the room. You see, I move toward the door. I open it - so. Miss Shaw," he added, turning swiftly towards her, "once more will you assure me that every one who was in the flat that night, with the exception of your domestic servant, is present now?"

"Yes," she murmured.

"Good! Then who," he asked, suddenly pointing to a door on the left - "who is in that room?"

They had all crowded after him to the threshold - thronging around him as he stood face to face with John Dory. His finger never wavered - it was pointing steadily towards that closed door a few feet to the left. Suddenly Letty Shaw rushed past them with a loud shriek.

"You shall not go in!" she cried. "What business is it of his?"

She stood with her back to the door, her arms outstretched like a cross. Her cheeks were livid. Her eyes seemed starting from her head.

Peter Ruff and John Dory laid their hands upon the girl's wrists. She clung to her place frantically. She was dragged from it, screaming. Peter Ruff, as was his right, entered first. Almost immediately he turned round, and his face was very grave.

"Something has happened in here, I am afraid," he said. "Please come in quietly."

On the bed lay Fluffy Dean, fully dressed - motionless. One hand hung down toward the floor - from the lifeless fingers a little phial had slipped. The room was full of trunks addressed to -

MISS SMITH,
Passenger to Melborne.
S.S. Caroline.

Peter Ruff moved over toward the bed and took up a piece of paper, upon which were scribbled a few lines in pencil.

"I think," he said, "that I must read these aloud. You all have a right to hear them."

No one spoke. He continued:

Forgive me, Letty, but I cannot go to Australia. They would only bring me back. When I remember that awful moment, my brain burns - I feel that I am going mad! Some day I should do this - better now. Give my love to the girls.

FLUFFY.

They sent for a doctor, and John Dory rang up Scotland Yard. Letty Shaw had fainted, and had been carried to her room. While they waited about in strange, half-benumbed excitement, Peter Ruff once more spoke to them.

"The reconstruction is easy enough now," he remarked. "The partition between this sitting room and that little bedroom is only an artificial one - something almost as flimsy as a screen. You see," he continued, tapping with his knuckles, "you can almost put your hand through it. If you look a little lower down, you will see where an opening has been made. Fluffy Dean was being taken care of by Miss Shaw - staying with her here, even. Miss Dean hears her lover's voice in this room - hears him pleading with Miss Shaw on he night of the murder. She has been sent home early from the theatre, and it is just possible that she saw or had been told that Austen Abbott had fetched Miss Shaw after the performance and had taken her to supper. She was mad with anger and jealousy. The revolver was there upon the table, with a silver box of cartridges. She possessed herself of it and waited in her room. What she heard proved, at least, her lover's infidelity. She stood there at her door, waiting. When Austen Abbott comes out, she shoots, throws the revolver at him, closes her door, and goes off into a faint. Perhaps she hears footsteps - a key in the door. At any rate, Captain Sotherst arrives a few minutes later. He finds, half in the hall, half on the threshold of the sitting room, Austen Abbott dead, and Miss Shaw's revolver by the side of him. If he had been a wise young man, he would have aroused the household. Why he did not do so, we can perhaps guess. He put two and two together a little too quickly. It is certain that he believed that the dead man had been shot by his fiancee. His first thought was to get rid of the revolver. At any rate, he walked down to the street with it in his hand, and was

E. Phillips Oppenheim

promptly arrested by the policeman who had heard the shot. Naturally he refused to plead, because he believed that Miss Shaw had killed the man, probably in self-defence. She, at first, believed her lover guilty, and when afterwards Fluffy Dean confessed, she, with feminine lack of common sense, was trying to get the girl out of the country before telling the truth. A visit of hers to the office of the steamship company gave me the clue I required."

Lady Mary grasped both his hands.

"And Scotland Yard," she exclaimed, with a withering glance at Dory, "have done their best to hang my brother!"

Peter Ruff raised his eyebrows.

"Dear Lady Mary," he said, "remember that it is the business of Scotland Yard to find a man guilty. It is mine, when I am employed for that purpose, to find him innocent. You must not be too hard upon my friend Mr. Dory. He and I seem to come up against each other a little too often, as it is."

"A little too often!" John Dory repeated, softly. "But one cannot tell. Don't believe, Lady Mary," he added, "that we ever want to kill an innocent man."

"It is your profession, though," she answered, "to find criminals - and his," she added, touching Peter Ruff on the shoulder, "to look for the truth."

Peter Ruff bowed low - the compliment pleased him.

CHAPTER V

DELILAH FROM STREATHAM

It was a favourite theory with Peter Ruff that the morning papers received very insufficient consideration from the majority of the British public. A glance at the headlines and a few of the spiciest paragraphs, a vague look at the leading article, and the sheets were thrown away to make room for more interesting literature. It was not so with Peter Ruff. Novels he very seldom read - he did not, in fact, appreciate the necessity for their existence. The whole epitome of modern life was, he argued, to be found among the columns of the daily press. The police news, perhaps, was his favourite study, but he did not neglect the advertisements. It followed, therefore, as a matter of course, that the appeal of "M" in the personal column of the Daily Mail was read by him on the morning of its appearance - read not once only nor twice - it was a paragraph which had its own peculiar interest for him.

Mr. Spencer Fitzgerald, if still in England, is requested to communicate with "M," at Vagali's Library, Cook's Alley, Ledham Street, Soho.

Peter Ruff laid the paper down upon his desk and looked steadily at a box of India-rubber bands. Almost his fingers, as he parted with the newspaper, had seemed to be shaking. His eyes were certainly set in an unusually retrospective stare. Who was this who sought to probe his past, to renew an acquaintance with a dead personality? "M" could be but one person! What did she want of him? Was it possible that, after all, a little flame of sentiment had been kept alight in her bosom, too - that in the quiet moments her thoughts had turned towards him as his had so often done to her? Then a sudden idea - an ugly thought - drove the tenderness from his face. She was no longer Maud Barnes - she was Mrs. John Dory, and John Dory was his enemy! Could there be treachery lurking beneath those simple lines? Things had not gone well with John Dory lately. Somehow or other, his cases seemed to have crumpled into dust. He was no longer held in the same esteem at headquarters. Yet could even John Dory stoop to such means as these?

He turned in his chair.

"Miss Brown," he said, "please take your pencil."

"I am quite ready, sir," she answered.

He marked the advertisement with a ring and passed it to her.

"Reply to that as follows," he said:

DEAR SIR:

I notice in the Daily Mail of this morning that you are enquiring through the "personal" column for the whereabouts of Mr. Spencer Fitzgerald. That gentleman has been a client of mine, and I have been in occasional communication with him. If you will inform me of the nature of your business, I may, perhaps, be able to put you in touch with Mr. Fitzgerald. You will understand, however, that, under the circumstances, I shall require proofs of your good faith.

Truly yours,
PETER RUFF.

Miss Brown glanced through the advertisement and closed her

notebook with a little snap.

"Did you say - 'Dear Sir'?" she asked.

"Certainly!" Peter Ruff answered.

"And you really mean," she continued, with obvious disapproval, "that I am to send this?"

"I do not usually waste my time," Peter Ruff reminded her, mildly, "by giving you down communications destined for the waste-paper basket."

She turned unwillingly to her machine.

"Mr. Fitzgerald is very much better where he is," she remarked.

"That depends," he answered.

She adjusted a sheet of paper into her typewriter.

"Who do you suppose 'M' is?" she asked.

"With your assistance," Peter Ruff remarked, a little sarcastically - "with your very kind assistance - I propose to find out!"

Miss Brown sniffed, and banged at the keys of her typewriter.

"That coal-dealer's girl from Streatham!" she murmured to herself....

A few politely worded letters were exchanged. "M" declined to reveal her identity, but made an appointment to visit Mr. Ruff at his office. The morning she was expected, he wore an entirely new suit of clothes and was palpably nervous. Miss Brown, who had arrived a little late, sat with her back turned upon him, and ignored even his usual morning greeting. The atmosphere of the office was decidedly chilly! Fortunately, the expected visitor arrived early.

Peter Ruff rose to receive his former sweetheart with an agitation perforce concealed, yet to him poignant indeed. For it was indeed Maud who entered the room and came towards him with carefully studied embarrassment and half doubtfully extended hand. He did not see the cheap millinery, the slightly more developed figure, the passing of that insipid prettiness which had once charmed him into the bloom of an over-early maturity. His eyes were blinded with that sort of masculine chivalry - the heritage only of fools and very clever men - which takes no note of such things. It was Miss Brown who, from her place in a corner of the room, ran over the cheap attractions of this unwelcome visitor with an expression of scornful wonder - who understood the tinsel of her jewellery, the cheap shoddiness of her ready-made gown; who appreciated, with merciless judgment, her mincing speech, her cheap, flirtatious method.

Maud, with a diffidence not altogether assumed, had accepted the chair which Peter Ruff had placed for her, and sat fidgeting, for a moment, with the imitation gold purse which she was carrying.

"I am sure, Mr. Ruff," she said, looking demurely into her lap, "I ought not to have come here. I feel terribly guilty. It's such an uncomfortable sort of position, too, isn't it?"

"I am sorry that you find it so," Peter Ruff said. "If there is anything I can do -"

"You are very kind," she murmured, half raising her eyes to his and dropping them again, "but, you see, we are perfect strangers to one another. You don't know me at all, do you? And I have only heard of you through the newspapers. You might think all sorts of things about my coming here to make enquiries about a gentleman."

"I can assure you," Peter Ruff said, sincerely, "that you need have no fears - no fears at all. Just speak to me quite frankly. Mr. Fitzgerald was a friend of yours, was he not?"

Maud simpered.

"He was more than that," she answered, looking down. "We were engaged to be married."

Peter Ruff sighed.

"I knew all about it," he declared. "Fitzgerald used to tell me everything."

"You were his friend?" she asked, looking him in the face.

"I was," Peter Ruff answered fervently, "his best friend! No one was more grieved than I about that - little mistake."

She sighed.

"In some ways," she remarked softly, "you remind me of him."

"You could scarcely say anything," Peter Ruff murmured "which would give me more pleasure. I am flattered."

She shook her head.

"It isn't flattery," she said, "it's the truth. You may be a few years older, and Spencer had a very nice moustache, which you haven't, but you are really not unlike. Mr. Ruff, do tell me where he is!"

Peter Ruff coughed.

"You must remember," he said, "that Mr. Fitzgerald's absence was caused by events of a somewhat unfortunate character."

"I know all about it," she answered, with a little sigh.

"You can appreciate the fact, therefore," Peter Ruff continued, "that as his friend and well-wisher I can scarcely disclose his whereabouts without his permission. Will you tell me exactly why you want to meet him again?"

She blushed - looked down and up again - betrayed, in fact, all the signs of confusion which might have been expected from her.

"Must I tell you that?" she asked.

"You are married, are you not?" Peter Ruff asked, looking down at her wedding ring.

She bit her lip with vexation. What a fool she had been not to take it off!

"Yes! Well, no - that is to say -"

"Never mind," Peter Ruff interrupted. "Please don't think that I want to cross-examine you. I only asked these questions because I have a sincere regard for Fitzgerald. I know how fond he was of you, and I cannot see what there is to be gained, from his point of view, by reopening old wounds."

"I suppose, then," she remarked, looking at him in such a manner that Miss Brown had to cover her mouth with her hands to prevent her screaming out - "I suppose you are one of those who think it a crime for a woman who is married even to want to see, for a few moments, an old sweetheart?"

"On the contrary," Peter Ruff answered, "as a bachelor, I have no convictions of any sort upon the subject."

She sighed.

"I am glad of that," she said.

"I am to understand, then," Peter Ruff remarked, "that your reason for wishing to meet Mr. Fitzgerald again is purely a sentimental one?"

"I am afraid it is," she murmured; "I have thought of him so often lately. He was such a dear!" she declared, with enthusiasm.

"I have never been sufficiently thankful," she continued, "that he got away that night. At the time, I was very angry, but often since then I have wished that I could have passed out with him into the fog and been lost - but I mustn't talk like this! Please don't misunderstand me, Mr. Ruff. I am happily married - quite happily married!"

Peter Ruff sighed.

"My friend Fitzgerald," he remarked, "will be glad to hear that."

Maud fidgeted. It was not quite the effect she had intended to produce!

"Of course," she remarked, looking away with a pensive air, "one has regrets."

"Regrets!" Peter Ruff murmured.

"Mr. Dory is not well off," she continued, "and I am afraid that I am very fond of life and going about, and everything is so expensive nowadays. Then I don't like his profession. I think it is hateful to be always trying to catch people and put them in prison - don't you, Mr. Ruff?"

Peter Ruff smiled.

"Naturally," he answered. "Your husband and I work from the opposite poles of life. He is always seeking to make criminals of the people whom I am always trying to prove worthy members of society."

"How noble!" Maud exclaimed, clasping her hands and looking up at him. "So much more remunerative, too, I should think," she added, after a moment's pause.

"Naturally," Peter Ruff admitted. "A private individual will pay more to escape from the clutches of the law than the law will to secure its victims. Scotland Yard expects them to come into its arms automatically - regards them as a perquisite of its existence."

"I wish my husband were in your profession, Mr. Ruff," Maud said, with a sidelong glance of her blue eyes which she had always found so effective upon her various admirers. "I am sure that I should be a great deal fonder of him."

Peter Ruff leaned forward in his chair. He, too, had expressive eyes at times.

"Madam," he said - and stopped. But Maud blushed, all the same.

She looked down into her lap.

"We are forgetting Mr. Fitzgerald," she murmured.

Peter Ruff glanced up at the clock.

"It is a long story," he said. "Are you in a hurry, Mrs. Dory?

"Not at all," she assured him, "unless you want to close you office, or anything. It must be nearly one o'clock."

"I wonder," he asked, "if you would do me the honour of lunching with me? We might go to the Prince's or the Carlton - whichever you prefer. I will promise to talk about Mr. Fitzgerald all the time."

"Oh, I couldn't!" Maud declared, with a little gasp. "At least - well, I'm sure I don't know!"

"You have no engagement for luncheon?" Peter Ruff asked quietly.

"Oh, no!" she answered; "but, you see, we live so quietly. I have never been to one of those places. I'd love to go - but if we were seen! Wouldn't people talk?"

Peter Ruff smiled. Just the same dear, modest little thing!

"I can assure you," he said, "that nothing whatever could be said against our lunching together. People are not so strict nowadays, you know, and a married lady has always a great deal of latitude."

She looked up at him with a dazzling smile.

"I'd simply love to go to Prince's!" she declared.

"Cat!" Miss Brown murmured, as Peter Ruff and his client left the room together.

Peter Ruff returned from his luncheon in no very jubilant state of mind. For some time he sat in his easy-chair, with his legs crossed and his finger tips pressed close together, looking steadily into space. Contrary to his usual custom, he did not smoke. Miss Brown watched him from behind her machine.

"Disenchanted?" she asked calmly.

Peter Ruff did not reply for several moments.

"I am afraid," he admitted, hesitatingly, "that marriage with John Dory has - well, not had a beneficial effect. She allowed me, for instance, to hold her hand in the cab! Maud would never have permitted a stranger to take such a liberty in the old days."

Miss Brown smiled curiously.

"Is that all?" she asked.

Peter Ruff felt that he was in the confessional.

"She certainly did seem," he admitted, "to enjoy her champagne a great deal, and she talked about her dull life at home a little more, perhaps, than was discreet to one who was presumably a stranger. She was curious, too, about dining out. Poor little girl, though. Just fancy, John Dory has never taken her anywhere but to Lyons' or an A B C, and the pit of a theatre!"

"Which evening is it to be?" Miss Brown asked.

"Something was said about Thursday," Peter Ruff admitted.

"And her husband?" Miss Brown enquired.

"He happens to be in Glasgow for a few days," Peter Ruff answered.

Miss Brown looked at her employer steadily. She addressed him by his Christian name, which was a thing she very seldom did in office hours.

"Peter," she said, "are you going to let that woman make a fool of you?"

He raised his eyebrows.

"Go on," he said; "say anything you want to - only, if you please, don't speak disrespectfully of Maud."

"Hasn't it ever occurred to you at all," Miss Brown continued, rising to her feet, "that this Maud, or whatever you want to call her, may be playing a low-down game of her husband's? He hates you, and he has vague suspicions. Can't you see that he is probably making use of your infatuation for his common, middle-class little wife, to try and get you to give yourself away? Can't you see it, Peter? You are not going to tell me that you are so blind as all that!"

"I must admit," he answered with a sigh, "that, although I

think you go altogether too far, some suspicion of the sort has interfered with my perfect enjoyment of the morning."

Miss Brown drew a little breath of relief. After all, then, his folly was not so consummate as it had seemed!

"What are you going to do about it, then?" she asked.

Peter Ruff coughed - he seemed in an unusually amenable frame of mind, and submitted to cross-examination without murmur.

"The subject of Mr. Spencer Fitzgerald," he remarked, "seemed, somehow or other, to drop into the background during our luncheon. I propose, therefore, to continue to offer to Mrs. John Dory my most respectful admiration. If she accepts my friendship, and is satisfied with it, so much the better. I must admit that it would give me a great deal of pleasure to be her occasional companion - at such times when her husband happens to be in Glasgow!"

"And supposing," Miss Brown asked, "that this is not all she wants - supposing, for instance, that she persists in her desire for information concerning Mr. Spencer Fitzgerald?"

"Then," Peter Ruff admitted, "I'm afraid that I must conclude that her unchivalrous clod of a husband has indeed stooped to make a fool of her."

"And in that case," Miss Brown demanded, "what shall you do?"

"I was just thinking that out," Peter Ruff said mildly, "when you spoke...."

The friendship of Peter Ruff with the wife of his enemy certainly appeared to progress in most satisfactory fashion. The dinner and visit to the theatre duly took place. Mr. Ruff was afterwards permitted to offer a slight supper and to accompany

E. Phillips Oppenheim

his fair companion a portion of the way home in a taxicab. She made several half-hearted attempts to return to the subject of Spencer Fitzgerald, but her companion had been able on each occasion to avoid the subject. Whether or not she was the victim of her husband's guile, there was no question about the reality of her enjoyment during the evening. Ruff, when he remembered the flash of her eyes across the table, the touch of her fingers in the taxi, was almost content to believe her false to her truant lover. If only she had not been married to John Dory, he realised, with a little sigh, that he might have taught her to forget that such a person existed as Spencer Fitzgerald, might have induced her to become Mrs. Peter Ruff!

On their next meeting, however, Peter Ruff was forced to realise that his secretary's instinct had not misled her. It was, alas, no personal and sentimental regrets for her former lover which had brought the fair Maud to his office. The pleasures of her evening - they dined at Romano's and had a box at the Empire - were insufficient this time to keep her from recurring continually to the subject of her vanished lover. He tried strategy - jealousy amongst other things.

"Supposing," he said, as they sat quite close to one another in the box during the interval, "supposing I were to induce our friend to come to London - I imagine he would be fairly safe now if he kept out of your husband's way - what would happen to me?"

"You!" she murmured, glancing at him from behind her fan and then dropping her eyes.

"Certainly - me!" he continued. "Don't you think that I should be doing myself a very ill turn if I brought you two together? I have very few friends, and I cannot afford to lose one. I am quite sure that you still care for him."

She shook her head.

"Not a scrap!" she declared.

"Then why did you put that advertisement in the paper?" Ruff asked, with smooth but swift directness.

She was not quick enough to parry his question. He read the truth in her disconcerted face. Knowing it now for a certainty, he hastened to her aid.

"Forgive me," he said, looking away. "I should not have asked that question - it is not my business. I will write to Fitzgerald. I will tell him that you want to see him, and that I think it would be safe for him to come to London."

Maud recovered herself quickly. She thanked him with her eyes as well as her words.

"And you needn't be jealous, really," she whispered behind her fan. "I only want to see him once for a few minutes - to ask a question. After that, I don't care what becomes of him."

A poor sort of Delilah, really, with her flushed face, her too elaborately coiffured hair with its ugly ornament, her ready-made evening dress with its cheap attempts at smartness, her cleaned gloves, indifferent shoes. But Peter Ruff thought otherwise.

"You mean that, after I have found him for you, you will still come out with me again sometimes?" he asked wistfully.

"Of course!" she answered. "Whenever I can without John knowing," she added, with an unpleasant little laugh. "If you only knew how I loved the music and the theatres, and this sort of life! What a good time your wife would have, Mr. Ruff!" she added archly.

It was no joking matter with him. He had to remember that he was, in effect, her tool, that she was making use of him, willing to betray her former lover at her husband's bidding. It was enough to make him, on his side, burn for revenge! Yet he put the thought away from him with a shiver. She was still the woman he had loved - she was still sacred to him! That night he pleaded an engagement, and sent her home in a taxicab alone.

John Dory, waiting patiently at home for his wife's return, felt a certain uneasiness when she swept into their little sitting room in all her cheap splendour, with flushed cheeks - an obvious air of satisfaction with herself and disdain for her immediate surroundings. John Dory was a commonplace looking man - the absence of his collar, and his somewhat shabby carpet slippers, did not improve his appearance. He had neglected to shave, and he was drinking beer. At headquarters he was not considered quite the smart young officer which he had once shown signs of becoming. He looked at his wife with darkening face, and his wife, on her part, thought of Peter Ruff in his immaculate evening clothes.

"Well," he remarked, grumblingly, "you seem to find a good deal of pleasure in this gadding about!"

She threw her soiled fan on the table.

"If I do," she answered, "you are not the one to sit there and reproach me with it, are you?"

"It's gone far enough, anyway," John Dory said. "It's gone further than I meant it to go. Understand me, Maud - it's finished! I'll find your old sweetheart for myself."

She laughed heartily.

"You needn't trouble," she answered, with a little toss of the head. "I am not such a fool as you seem to think me. Mr. Ruff has made an appointment with him."

There was a change in John Dory's face. The man's eyes were bright - they almost glittered.

"You mean that your friend Mr. Ruff is going to produce

Spencer Fitzgerald?" he exclaimed.

"He has promised to," she answered. "John," she declared, throwing herself into an easy-chair, "I feel horrid about it. I wonder what Mr. Ruff will think when he knows!"

"You can feel how you like," John Dory answered bluntly, "so long as I get the handcuffs on Spencer Fitzgerald's wrists!"

She shuddered. She looked at her husband with distaste.

"Don't talk about it!" she begged sharply. "It makes me feel the meanest creature that ever crawled. I can't help feeling, too, that Mr. Ruff will think me a wretch - quite the gentleman he's been all the time! I never knew any one half so nice!"

John Dory set down his empty glass.

"I wonder," he said, looking at her thoughtfully, "what made him take such a fancy to you! Rather sudden, wasn't it, eh?"

Maud tossed her head.

"I don't see anything so wonderful about that," she declared.

"Listen to me, Maud," her husband said, rising to his feet. "You aren't a fool - not quite. You've spent some time with Peter Ruff. How much - think carefully - how much does he remind you of Spencer Fitzgerald?"

"Not at all," she answered promptly. "Why, he is years older, and though Spencer was quite the gentleman, there's something about Mr. Ruff, and the way he dresses and knows his way about - well, you can tell he's been a gentleman all his life."

John Dory's face fell.

"Think again," he said.

She shook her head.

"Can't see any likeness," she declared. "He did remind me a little of him just at first, though," she added, reflectively - "little things he said, and sort of mannerisms. I've sort of lost sight of them the last few times, though."

"When is this meeting with Fitzgerald to come off?" John Dory asked abruptly.

She did not answer him at once. A low, triumphant smile had parted her lips.

"To-morrow night," she said; "he is to meet me in Mr. Ruff's office."

"At what time?" John Dory asked.

"At eight o'clock," she answered. "Mr. Ruff is keeping his office open late on purpose. Spencer thinks that afterwards he is going to take me out to dinner."

"You are sure of this?" John Dory asked eagerly. "You are sure that the man Ruff does not suspect you? You believe he means that you shall meet Fitzgerald?"

"I am sure of it," she answered. "He is even a little jealous," she continued, with an affected laugh. "He told me - well, never mind!"

"He told you what?" John Dory asked.

She laughed.

"Never you mind," she said. "I have done what you asked me anyway. If Mr. Ruff had not found me an agreeable companion he would not have bothered about getting Spencer to meet me. And now he's done it," she added, "I do believe he's a little jealous."

John Dory glared, but he said nothing. It seemed to him that his hour of revenge was close at hand!

It was the first occasion upon which words of this sort had passed between Peter Ruff and his secretary. There was no denying the fact that Miss Violet Brown was in a passion. It was an hour past the time at which she usually left the office. For an hour she had pleaded, and Peter Ruff remained unmoved.

"You are a fool!" she cried to him at last. "I am a fool, too, that I have ever wasted my thoughts and time upon you. Why can't I make you see? In every other way, heaven knows, you are clever enough! And yet there comes this vulgar, commonplace, tawdry little woman from heaven knows where, and makes such a fool of you that you are willing to fling away your career - to hold your wrists out for John Dory's handcuffs!"

"My dear Violet," Peter Ruff answered deprecatingly, "you really worry me - you do indeed!"

"Not half so much as you worry me," she declared. "Look at the time. It's already past seven. At eight o'clock Mrs. Dory - your Maud - is coming in here hoping to find her old sweetheart."

"Why not?" he murmured.

"Why not, indeed?" Miss Brown answered angrily. "Don't you know - can't you believe - that close on her heels will come her husband - that Mr. Spencer Fitzgerald, if ever he comes to life in this room, will leave it between two policemen?"

Peter Ruff sighed.

"What a pessimist you are, my dear Violet!" he said.

She came up to him and laid her hands upon his shoulders.

"Peter," she said, "I will tell you something - I must! I am fond of you, Peter. I always have been. Don't make me miserable if there is no need for it. Tell me honestly - do you really believe in this woman?"

He removed her hands gently, and raised them to his lips.

"My dear girl," he said, "I believe in every one until I find them out. I look upon suspicion as a vice. But, at the same time," he added, "there are always certain precautions which one takes."

"What precautions can you take?" she cried. "Can you sit there and make yourself invisible? John Dory is not a fool. The moment he is in this room with the door closed behind him, it is the end."

"We must hope not," Peter Ruff said cheerfully. "There are other things which may happen, you know."

She turned away from him a little drearily.

"You do not mind if I stay?" she said. "I am not working to-night. Perhaps, later on, I may be of use!"

"As you will," he answered. "You will excuse me for a little time, won't you? I have some preparations to make."

She turned her head away from him. He left the room and ascended the stairs to his own apartments.

Eight o'clock was striking from St. Martin's Church when the door of Peter Ruff's office was softly opened and closed again. A man in a slouch hat and overcoat entered, and after feeling along the wall for a moment, turned up the electric light. Violet Brown rose from her place with a little sob. She stretched out her hand to him.

"Peter!" she cried. "Peter!"

"My name," the newcomer said calmly, "is Mr. Spencer Fitzgerald."

"Oh, listen to me!" she begged. "There is still time, if you hurry. Think how many clever men before you have been deceived by the woman in whom they trusted. Please, please go! Hurry upstairs and put those things away."

"Madam," the newcomer said, "I am much obliged to you for your interest, but I think that you are making a mistake. I have come here to meet -"

He stopped short. There was a soft knocking at the door. A stifled scream broke from Violet Brown's lips.

"It is too late!" she cried. "Peter! Peter!"

She sank into her chair and covered her face with her hands. The door was opened and Maud came in. When she saw who it was who sat in Peter Ruff's place, she gave a little cry. Perhaps after all, she had not believed that this thing would happen.

"Spencer!" she cried, "Spencer! Have you really come back?"

He held out his hands.

"You are glad to see me?" he asked.

She came slowly forward. The man rose from his place and came towards her with outstretched hands. Then through the door came John Dory, and one caught a glimpse of others behind him.

"If my wife is not glad to see you, Mr. Spencer Fitzgerald," he aid, in a tone from which he vainly tried to keep the note of triumph, "I can assure you that I am. You slipped away from me cleverly at Daisy Villa, but this time I think you will not find it so easy."

Maud shrank back, and her husband took her place. But Mr. Spencer Fitzgerald looked upon them both as one who looks upon figures in a dream. Miss Brown rose hurriedly from her seat. She came over to him and thrust her arm through his.

"Peter," she said, taking his hand in hers, "don't shoot. It isn't worth while. You should have listened to me."

The little man in the gold-rimmed spectacles looked at her, looked at Mr. John Dory, looked at the woman who was shrinking back now against the wall.

"Really," he said, "this is the most extraordinary situation in which I ever found myself!"

"We will help you to realise it," John Dory cried, and the triumph in his tone had swelled into a deeper note. "I came here to arrest Mr. Fitzgerald, but I hear this young lady call you 'Peter.' Perhaps this may be the solution -"

The little man struck the table with the flat of his hand.

"Come," he said, "this is getting a bit too thick. First of all - you," he said, turning to Miss Brown - "my name is not Peter, and I have no idea of shooting anybody. As for that lady against the wall, I don't know her - never saw her before in my life. As for you," he added, turning to John Dory, "you talk about arresting me - what for?"

Mr. John Dory smiled.

"There is an old warrant," he said, "which I have in my pocket, but I fancy that there are a few little things since then which we may have to enquire into."

"This beats me!" the little man declared. "Who do you think

I am?"

"Mr. Spencer Fitzgerald, to start with," John Dory said. "It seems to me not impossible that we may find another pseudonym for you."

"You can find as many as you like," the little man answered testily, "but my name is James Fitzgerald, and I am an actor employed at the Shaftesbury Theatre, as I can prove with the utmost ease. I never called myself Spencer; nor, to my knowledge, was I ever called by such a name. Nor, as I remarked before, have I ever seen any one of you three people before with the exception of Miss Brown here, whom I have seen on the stage."

John Dory grunted.

"It was Mr. Spencer Fitzgerald," he said, "a clerk in Howell & Wilson's bookshop, who leapt out of the window of Daisy Villa two years ago. It may be Mr. James Fitzgerald now. Gentlemen of your profession have a knack of changing their names."

"My profession's as good as yours, anyway!" the little man exclaimed. "We aren't all fools in it! My friend Mr. Peter Ruff said to me that there was a young lady whom I used to know who was anxious to meet me again, and would I step around here about eight o'clock. Here I am, and all I can say is, if that's the young lady, I never saw her before in my life."

There was a moment's breathless silence. Then the door was softly opened. Violet Brown went staggering back like a woman who sees a ghost. She bit her lips till the blood came. It was Peter Ruff who stood looking in upon them - Peter Ruff, carefully dressed in evening clothes, his silk hat at exactly the correct angle, his coat and white kid gloves upon his arm.

"Dear me," he said, "you don't seem to be getting on very well! Mr. Dory," he added, with a note of surprise in his tone, "this is indeed an unexpected pleasure!"

The man who stood by the desk turned to him. The others were stricken dumb.

"Look here," he said, "there's some mistake. You told me to come here at eight o'clock to meet a young lady whom I used to know. Well, I never saw her before in my life," he added, pointing to Maud. "There's a man there who wants to arrest me - Lord knows what for! And here's Miss Brown, whom I have seen at the theatre several times but who never condescended to speak to me before, telling me not to shoot! What's it all about, Ruff? Is it a practical joke?"

Peter Ruff laid down his coat and hat, and sat upon the table with his hands in his pockets.

"Is it possible," he said, "that I have made a mistake? Isn't your second name Spencer?"

The man shook his head.

"My name is James Fitzgerald," he said. "I haven't missed a day at the Shaftesbury Theatre for three years, as you can find out by going round the corner. I never called myself Spencer, I was never clerk in a bookshop, and I never saw that lady before in my life."

Maud came out from her place against the wall, and leaned eagerly forward. John Dory turned his head slowly towards his wife. A sickening fear had arisen in his heart - gripped him by the throat. Fooled once more, and by Peter Ruff!

"It isn't Spencer!" Maud said huskily. "Mr. Ruff," she added, turning to him, "you know very well that this is not the Mr. Spencer Fitzgerald whom you promised to bring here to-night - Mr. Spencer Fitzgerald to whom I was once engaged."

Peter Ruff pointed to the figure of her husband.

"Madam," he said, "my invitation did not include your husband."

John Dory took a step forward, and laid his hands upon the shoulders of the man who called himself Mr. James Fitzgerald. He looked into his face long and carefully. Then he turned away, and, gripping his wife by the arm, he passed out of the room. The door slammed behind him. The sound of heavy footsteps was heard descending to the floor below.

Violet Brown crossed the room to where Peter Ruff was still sitting with a queer look upon his face, and, gripping him by the shoulders, shook him.

"How dare you!" she exclaimed. "How dare you! Do you know that I have nearly cried my eyes out?"

Peter Ruff came back from the world into which, for the moment, his thoughts had taken him.

"Violet," he said, "you have known me for some years. You have been my secretary for some months. If you choose still to take me for a fool, I cannot help it."

"But," she exclaimed, pointing to Mr. James Fitzgerald -

Peter Ruff nodded.

"I have been practising on him for some time," he said, with an air of self-satisfaction.

"A thin, mobile face, you see, and plenty of experience in the art of making up. It is astonishing what one can do if one tries."

Mr. James Fitzgerald picked up his hat and coat.

"It was worth more than five quid," he growled; "when I saw the handcuffs in that fellow's hand, I felt a cold shiver go down

E. Phillips Oppenheim

my spine."

Peter Ruff counted out two banknotes and passed them to his confederate.

"You have earned the money," he said. "Go and spend it. Perhaps, Violet," he added, turning towards her, "I have been a little inconsiderate. Come and have dinner with me, and forget it."

She drew a little sigh.

"You are sure," she murmured, "that you wouldn't rather take Maud?"

CHAPTER VI

THE LITTLE LADY FROM SERVIA

Westward sped the little electric brougham, driven without regard to police regulations or any rule of the road: silent and swift, wholly regardless of other vehicles - as though, indeed, its occupants were assuming to themselves the rights of Royalty. Inside, Peter Ruff, a little breathless, was leaning forward, tying his white cravat with the aid of the little polished mirror set in the middle of the dark green cushions. At his right hand was Lady Mary, watching his proceedings with an air of agonised impatience.

"Let me tell you -" she begged.

"Kindly wait till I have tied this and put my studs in," Peter Ruff interrupted. "It is impossible for me to arrive at a ball in this condition, and I cannot give my whole attention to more than one thing at a time."

"We shall be there in five minutes!" she exclaimed. "What is the good, unless you understand, of your coming at all?"

Peter Ruff surveyed his tie critically. Fortunately, it pleased him. He began to press the studs into their places with firm fingers. Around them surged the traffic of Piccadilly; in front, the gleaming arc of lights around Hyde Park Corner. They had several narrow escapes. Once the brougham swayed danger-ously as they cut in on the wrong side of an island lamp-post.

A policeman shouted after them, another held up his hand - the driver of the brougham took no notice.

"I am ready," Peter Ruff said, quietly.

"My younger brother - Maurice," she began, breathlessly - "you've never met him, I know, but you've heard me speak of him. He is private secretary to Sir James Wentley -"

"Minister for Foreign Affairs?" Ruff asked, swiftly.

"Yes! Maurice wants to go in for the Diplomatic Service. He is a dear, and so clever!"

"Is it Maurice who is in trouble?" Peter Ruff asked. "Why didn't he come himself?"

"I am trying to explain," Lady Mary protested. "This afternoon he had an important paper to turn into cipher and hand over to the Prime Minister at the Duchess of Montford's dance to-night. The Prime Minister will arrive in a motor car from the country at about two o'clock, and the first thing he will ask for will be that paper. It has been stolen!"

"At what time did your brother finish copying it, and when did he discover its loss?" Ruff asked, with a slight air of weariness. These preliminary enquiries always bored him.

"He finished it in his own rooms at half-past seven," Lady Mary answered. "He discovered its loss at eleven o'clock - directly he had arrived at the ball."

"Why didn't he come to me himself?" Peter Ruff asked. "I like to have these particulars at first hand."

"He is in attendance upon Sir James at the ball," Lady Mary answered. "There is trouble in the East, as you know, and Sir James is expecting dispatches to-night. Maurice is not allowed to leave."

"Has he told Sir James yet?"

"He had not when I left," Lady Mary answered. "If he is forced to do so, it will be ruin! Mr. Ruff, you must help us Maurice is such a dear, but a mistake like this, at the very beginning of his career, would be fatal. Here we are. That is my brother waiting just inside the hall."

A young man came up to them in the vestibule. He was somewhat pale, but otherwise perfectly self-possessed. From the shine of his glossy black hair to the tips of his patent boots he was, in appearance, everything that a young Englishman of birth and athletic tastes could hope to be. Peter Ruff liked the look of him. He waited for no introduction, but laid his hand at once upon the young man's shoulder.

"Between seven-thirty and arriving here," he said, drawing him on one side - "quick! Tell me, whom did you see? What opportunities were there of stealing the paper, and by whom?"

"I finished it at five and twenty past seven," the young man said, "sealed it in an official envelope, and stood it up on my desk by the side of my coat and hat and muffler, which my servant had laid there, ready for me to put on. My bedroom opens out from my sitting room. While I was dressing, two men called for me - Paul Jermyn and Count von Hern. They walked through to my bedroom first, and then sat together in the sitting room until I came out. The door was wide open, and we talked all the time."

"They called accidentally?" Peter Ruff asked.

"No - by appointment," the young man replied. "We were all coming on here to the dance, and we had agreed to dine together first at the Savoy."

"You say that you left the paper on your desk with your coat and hat?" Peter Ruff asked. "Was it there when you came out?"

"Apparently so," the young man answered. "It seemed to be standing in exactly the same place as where I had left it. I put it into my breast pocket, and it was only when I arrived here that I found the envelope seemed lighter, I went off by myself and tore it open. There was nothing inside but half a newspaper!"

"What about the envelope?" Peter Ruff asked. "That must have been the same sort of one as you had used or you would have noticed it?"

"It was," the Honorable Maurice answered.

"It was a sort which you kept in your room?"

"Yes!" the young man admitted.

"The packet was changed, then, by some one in your room, or some one who had access to it," Peter Ruff said. "How about your servant?"

"It was his evening off. I let him put out my things and go at seven o'clock."

"You must tell me the nature of the contents of the packet," Peter Ruff declared. "Don't hesitate. You must do it. Remember the alternative."

The young man did hesitate for several moments, but a glance into his sister's appealing face decided him.

"It was our official reply to a secret communication from Russia respecting - a certain matter in the Balkans."

Peter Ruff nodded.

"Where is Count von Hern?" he asked abruptly.

"Inside, dancing."

"I must use a telephone at once," Peter Ruff said. "Ask one of the servants here where I can find one."

Peter Ruff was conducted to a gloomy waiting room, on the table of which stood a small telephone instrument. He closed the door, but he was absent for only a few minutes. When he rejoined Lady Mary and her brother they were talking together in agitated whispers. The latter turned towards him at once.

"Do you mean that you suspect Count von Hern?" he asked, doubtfully. "He is a friend of the Danish Minister's, and every one says that he's such a good chap. He doesn't seem to take the slightest interest in politics - spends nearly all his time hunting or playing polo."

"I don't suspect any one," Peter Ruff answered. "I only know that Count von Hern is an Austrian spy, and that he took your paper! Has he been out of your sight at all since you rejoined him in the sitting room? I mean to say - had he any opportunity of leaving you during the time you were dining together, or did he make any calls en route, either on the way to the Savoy or from the Savoy here?"

The young man shook his head.

"He has not been out of my sight for a second."

"Who is the other man - Jermyn?" Peter Ruff asked. "I never heard of him."

"An American - cousin of the Duchess. He could not have had the slightest interest in the affair."

"Please take me into the ballroom," Peter Ruff said to Lady Mary. "Your brother had better not come with us. I want to be as near the Count von Hern as possible."

They passed into the crowded rooms, unnoticed, purposely avoiding the little space where the Duchess was still receiving

E. Phillips Oppenheim

the late comers among her guests. They found progress difficult, and Lady Mary felt her heart sink as she glanced at the little jewelled watch which hung from her wrist. Suddenly Peter Ruff came to a standstill.

"Don't look for a moment," he said, "but tell me as soon as you can- who is that tall young man, like a Goliath, talking to the little dark woman? You see whom I mean?"

Lady Mary nodded, and they passed on. In a moment or two she answered him.

"How strange that you should ask!" she whispered in his ear. "That is Mr. Jermyn."

They were on the outskirts now of the ballroom itself. One of Lady Mary's partners came up with an open programme and a face full of reproach.

"Do please forgive me, Captain Henderson," Lady Mary begged. "I have hurt my foot, and I am not dancing any more."

"But surely I was to take you in to supper?" the young officer protested, good-humouredly. "Don't tell me that you are going to cut that?"

"I am going to cut everything to-night with everybody," Lady Mary said. "Please forgive me. Come to tea to-morrow and I'll explain."

The young man bowed, and, with a curious glance at Ruff, accepted his dismissal. Another partner was simply waved away.

"Please turn round and come back," Peter Ruff said. "I want to see those two again."

"But we haven't found Count von Hern yet," she protested.

"Surely that is more important, is it not? I believe that I saw him dancing just now - there, with the tall girl in yellow."

"Never mind about him, for the moment," Ruff answered. "Walk down this corridor with me. Do you mind talking all the time, please? It will sound more natural, and I want to listen."

The young American and his partner had found a more retired seat now, about three quarters of the way down the pillared vestibule which bordered the ballroom. He was bending over his companion with an air of unmistakable devotion, but it was she who talked. She seemed, indeed, to have a good deal to say to him. The slim white fingers of one hand played all the time with a string of magnificent pearls. Her dark, soft eyes - black as aloes and absolutely un-English - flashed into his. A delightful smile hovered at the corners of her lips. All the time she was talking and he was listening. Lady Mary and her partner passed by unnoticed. At the end of the vestibule they turned and retraced their steps. Peter Ruff was very quiet - he had caught a few of those rapid words. But the woman's foreign accent had troubled him.

"If only she would speak in her own language!" he muttered.

Lady Mary's hand suddenly tightened upon his arm.

"Look!" she exclaimed. "That is Count von Hern!"

A tall, fair young man, very exact in his dress, very stiff in his carriage, with a not unpleasant face, was standing talking to Jermyn and his companion. Jermyn, who apparently found the intrusion an annoyance, was listening to the conversation between the two, with a frown upon his face and a general attitude of irritation. As Lady Mary and her escort drew near, the reason for the young American's annoyance became clearer - his two companions were talking softly, but with great animation, in a foreign language, which it was obvious that he did not understand. Peter Ruff's elbow pressed against his

E. Phillips Oppenheim

partner's arm, and their pace slackened. He ventured, even, to pause for a moment, looking into the ballroom as though in search of some one, and he had by no means the appearance of a man likely to understand Hungarian. Then, to Lady Mary's surprise, he touched the Count von Hern on the shoulder and addressed him.

"I beg your pardon, sir," he said, "but I fancy that we accidentally exchanged programmes, a few minutes ago, at the buffet. I have lost mine and picked up one which does not belong to me. As we were standing side by side, it is possibly yours."

"I believe not, sir," he answered, with that pleasant smile which had gone such a long way toward winning him the reputation of being "a good fellow" amongst a fairly large circle of friends. "I believe at any rate," he added, glancing at his programme, "that this is my own. You mistake me, probably, for some one else."

Peter Ruff, without saying a word, was actor enough to suggest that he was unconvinced. The Count good-humouredly held out his programme.

"You shall see for yourself," he remarked. "That is not yours, is it? Besides, I have not been to the buffet at all this evening."

Peter Ruff cast a swift glance down the programme which the Count had handed him. Then he apologised profusely.

"I was mistaken," he admitted. "I am very sorry."

The Count bowed.

"It is of no consequence, sir," he said, and resumed his conversation.

Peter Ruff passed on with Lady Mary. At a safe distance, she glanced at him enquiringly.

"It was his programme I wanted to see," Peter Ruff explained. "It is as I thought. He has had four dances with the Countess -"

"Who is she?" Lady Mary asked, quickly.

"The little dark lady with whom he is talking now," Peter Ruff continued. "He seems, too, to be going early. He has no dances reserved after the twelfth. We will go downstairs at once, if you please. I must speak to your brother."

"Have you been able to think of anything?" she asked, anxiously. "Is there any chance at all, do you think?"

"I believe so," Peter Ruff answered. "It is most interesting. Don't be too sanguine, though. The odds are against us, and the time is very short. Is the driver of your electric brougham to be trusted?"

"Absolutely," she assured him. "He is an old servant."

"Will you lend him to me?" Peter Ruff asked, "and tell him that he is to obey my instructions absolutely?"

"Of course," she answered. "You are going away, then?"

Peter Ruff nodded. He was a little sparing of words just then. The thoughts were chasing one another through his brain. He was listening, too, for the sweep of a dress behind.

"Is there nothing I can do?" Lady Mary begged, eagerly.

Peter Ruff shook his head. In the distance he saw the Honourable Maurice come quickly toward them. With a firm but imperceptible gesture he waved him away.

"Don't let your brother speak to me," he said. "We can't tell who is behind. What time did you say the Prime Minister was expected?"

"At two o'clock," Lady Mary said, anxiously.

Peter Ruff glanced at his watch. It was already half an hour past midnight.

"Very well," he said, "I will do what I can. If my theory is wrong, it will be nothing. If I am right - well, there is a chance, anyhow. In the meantime -"

"In the meantime?" she repeated, breathlessly.

"Take your brother back to the ballroom," Peter Ruff directed. "Make him dance - dance yourself. Don't give yourselves away by looking anxious. When the time is short - say at a quarter to two - he can come down here and wait for me."

"If you don't come!" she exclaimed.

"Then we shall have lost," Peter Ruff said, calmly. "If you don't see me again to-night, you had better read the newspapers carefully for the next few days."

"You are going to do something dangerous!" she protested.

"There is danger in interfering at all in such a matter as this," he answered, "but you must remember that it is not only my profession - it is my hobby. Remember, too," he added, with a smile, "that I do not often lose!"

For twenty minutes Peter Ruff sat in the remote corner of Lady Mary's electric brougham, drawn up at the other side of the Square, and waited. At last he pressed a button. They glided off. Before them was a large, closed motor car. They started in discreet chase.

Fortunately, however, the chase was not a long one. The car which Peter Ruff had been following was drawn up before a plain, solid-looking house, unlit and of gloomy appearance. The little lady with the wonderful eyes was already halfway up the flagged steps. Hastily lifting the flap and looking behind as they passed, her pursuer saw her open the door with a latchkey, and disappear. Peter Ruff pulled the check-string and descended. For several moments he stood and observed the house into which the lady whom he had been following had disappeared. Then he turned to the driver.

"I want you to watch that house," he said, "never to take your eyes off it. When I reappear from it, if I do at all, I shall probably be in a hurry. Directly you see me be on your box ready to start. A good deal may depend upon our getting away quickly."

"Very good, sir," the man answered. "How long am I to wait here for you?"

Peter Ruff's lips twisted into a curious little smile.

"Until two o'clock," he answered. "If I am not out by then, you needn't bother any more about me. You can return and tell your mistress exactly what has happened."

"Hadn't I better come and try and get you out, sir?" the man asked. "Begging your pardon, but her Ladyship told me that there might be queer doings. I'm a bit useful in a scrap, sir," he added. "I do a bit of sparring regularly."

Peter Ruff shook his head.

"If there's any scrap at all," he said, "you had better be out of it. Do as I have said."

The motor car had turned round and disappeared now, and in a few moments Peter Ruff stood before the door of the house into which the little lady had disappeared. The problem of entrance was already solved for him. The door had been left unlatched; only a footstool had been placed against it inside. Peter Ruff, without hesitation, pushed the door softly open and entered, replaced the footstool in its former position, and stood with his back to the wall, in the darkest corner of the hall, looking around him -listening intently. Nearly opposite the door of a room stood ajar. It was apparently lit up, but there was no sound of any one moving inside. Upstairs, in one of the rooms on the first floor, he could hear light footsteps - a woman's voice humming a song. He listened to the first few bars, and understanding became easier. Those first few bars were the opening ones of the Servian national anthem!

With an effort, Peter Ruff concentrated his thoughts upon the immediate present. The little lady was upstairs. The servants had apparently retired for the night. He crept up to the half-open door and peered in. The room, as he had hoped to find it, was empty, but Madame's easy-chair was drawn up to the fire, and some coffee stood upon the hob. Stealthily Peter Ruff crept in and glanced around, seeking for a hiding place. A movement upstairs hastened his decision. He pushed aside the massive curtains which separated this from a connecting room. He had scarcely done so when light footsteps were heard descending the stairs.

Peter Ruff found his hiding place all that could have been desired. This secondary room itself was almost in darkness, but he was just able to appreciate the comforting fact that it possessed a separate exit into the hall. Through the folds of the curtain he had a complete view of the further apartment. The little lady had changed her gown of stiff white satin for one of flimsier material, and, seated in the easy-chair, she was busy pouring herself out some coffee. She took a cigarette from a silver box, and lighting it, curled herself up in the chair and composed herself as though to listen. To her as well as to Peter Ruff, as he crouched in his hiding place, the moments seemed to pass slowly enough. Yet, as he realised afterward, it could not have been ten minutes before she sat upright in a listening attitude. There was some one coming! Peter Ruff, too, heard a man's firm footsteps come up the flagged stones.

The little lady sprang to her feet.

"Paul!" she exclaimed.

Paul Jermyn came slowly to meet her. He seemed a little out of breath. His tie was all disarranged and his collar unfastened.

The little lady, however, noticed none of these things. She looked only into his face.

"Have you got it?" she asked, eagerly.

He thrust his hand into his breast-coat pocket, and held an envelope out toward her.

"Sure!" he answered. "I promised!"

She gave a little sob, and with the packet in her hand came running straight toward the spot where Peter Ruff was hiding.

He shrank back as far as possible. She stopped just short of the curtain, opened the drawer of a table which stood there, and slipped the packet in. Then she came back once more to where Paul Jermyn was standing.

"My friend!" she cried, holding out her hands - "my dear, dear friend! Shall I ever be able to thank you enough?"

"Why, if you try," he answered, smiling, "I think that you could!"

She laid her hand upon his arm - a little caressing, foreign gesture.

"Tell me," she said, "how did you manage it?"

"We left the dance together," Jermyn said. "I could see that he wanted to get rid of me, but I offered to take him in my motor car. I told the man to choose some back streets, and while we were passing through one of them, I took Von Hern by the throat. We had a struggle, of course, but I got the paper."

"What did you do with Von Hern?" she asked.

"I left him on his doorstep," the young American answered. "He wasn't really hurt, but he was only half conscious. I don't think he'll bother any one to-night."

"You dear, brave man!" she murmured. "Paul, what am I to say to you?"

He laughed.

"That's what I'm here to ask," he declared. "You wouldn't give me my answer at the ball. Perhaps you'll give it me now?"

They sprang apart. Ruff felt his nerves stiffen - felt himself constrained to hold even his breath as he widened a little the crack in the curtains. This was no stealthy entrance. The door had been flung open. Von Hern, his dress in wild disorder, pale as a ghost, and with a great bloodstain upon his cheek, stood confronting them.

"When you have done with your love-making," he called out, "I'll trouble you to restore my property!"

The electric light gleamed upon a small revolver which flashed out toward the young American. Paul Jermyn never hesitated for a moment. He seized the chair by his side and flung it at Von Hern. There was a shot, the crash of the falling chair, a cry from Jermyn, who never hesitated, however, in his rush. The two men closed. A second shot went harmlessly to the ceiling. The little lady stole away - stole softly across the room toward the table. She opened the drawer. Suddenly the blood in her veins was frozen into fear. From nowhere, it seemed to her, came a hand which held her wrists like iron!

"Madam," Peter Ruff whispered from behind the curtain, "I am sorry to deprive you of it, but this is stolen property."

Her screams rang through the room. Even the two men

released one another.

"It is gone! It is gone!" she cried. "Some one was hiding in the room! Quick!"

She sprang into the hall. The two men followed her. The front door was slammed. They heard flying footsteps outside. Von Hern was out first, clearing the little flight of steps in one bound. Across the road he saw a flying figure. A level stream of fire poured from his hand - twice, three times. But Peter Ruff never faltered. Round the corner he tore. The man had kept his word - the brougham was already moving slowly.

"Jump in, sir," the man cried. "Throw yourself in. Never mind about the door."

They heard the shouts behind. Peter Ruff did as he was bid, and sat upon the floor, raising himself gradually to the seat when they had turned another corner. Then he put his head out of the window.

"Back to the Duchess of Montford's!" he ordered.

The latest of the guests had ceased to arrive - a few were already departing. It was an idle time, however, with the servants who loitered in the vestibules of Montford House, and they looked with curiosity upon this strange guest who arrived at five minutes to two, limping a little, and holding his left arm in his right hand. One footman on the threshold nearly addressed him, but the words were taken out of his mouth when he saw Lady Mary and her brother - the Honorable Maurice Sotherst - hasten forward to greet him.

Peter Ruff smiled upon them benignly.

"You can take the paper out of my breast-coat pocket," he said.

The young man's fingers gripped it. Through Lady Mary's great thankfulness, however, the sudden fear came shivering.

"You are hurt!" she whispered. "There is blood on your sleeve."

"Just a graze," Peter Ruff answered. "Von Hern wasn't much good at a running target. Back to the ballroom, young man," he added. "Don't you see who's coming?"

The Prime Minister came up the tented way into Montford House. He, too, wondered a little at the man whom he met on his way out, holding his left arm, and looking more as though he had emerged from a street fight than from the Duchess of Montford's ball. Peter Ruff went home smiling.

CHAPTER VII

THE DEMAND OF THE DOUBLE-FOUR

It was about this time that Peter Ruff found among his letters one morning a highly-scented little missive, addressed to him in a handwriting with which he had once been familiar. He looked at it for several moments before opening it. Even as the paper cutter slid through the top of the envelope, he felt that he had already divined the nature of its contents.

FRIVOLITY THEATRE
March 10th

MY DEAR Mr. RUFF:

I expect that you will be surprised to hear from me again, but I do hope that you will not be annoyed. I know that I behaved very horridly a little time ago, but it was not altogether my fault, and I have been more sorry for it than I can tell you - in fact, John and I have never been the same since, and for the present, at any rate, I have left him and gone on the stage. A lady whom I knew got me a place in the chorus here, and so far I like it immensely.

Won't you come and meet me after the show to-morrow night, and I will tell you all about it? I should like so much to see you again.

MAUD.

Peter Ruff placed this letter in his breast-coat pocket, and withheld it from his secretary's notice. He felt, however, very little pleasure at the invitation it conveyed. He hesitated for some time, in fact, whether to accept it or not. Finally, after his modest dinner that evening, he bought a stall for the Frivolity and watched the piece. The girl he had come to see was there in the second row of the chorus, but she certainly did not look her best in the somewhat scant costume required by the part. She showed no signs whatever of any special ability - neither her dancing nor her singing seemed to entitle her to any consideration. She carried herself with a certain amount of self-consciousness, and her eyes seemed perpetually fixed upon the occupants of the stalls. Peter Ruff laid down his glasses with something between a sigh and a groan. There was something to him inexpressibly sad in the sight of his old sweetheart so transformed, so utterly changed from the prim, somewhat genteel young person who had accepted his modest advances with such ladylike diffidence. She seemed, indeed, to have lost those very gifts which had first attracted him. Nevertheless, he kept his appointment at the stage-door.

She was among the first to come out, and she greeted him warmly - almost noisily. With her new profession, she seemed to have adopted a different and certainly more flamboyant deportment.

"I thought you'd come to-night," she declared, with an arch look. "I felt certain I saw you in the stalls. You are going to take me to supper, aren't you? Shall we go to the Milan?"

Peter Ruff assented without enthusiasm, handed her into a hansom, and took his place beside her. She wore a very large hat, untidily put on; some of the paint seemed still to be upon her face; her voice, too, seemed to have become louder, and her manner more assertive. There were obvious indications that she no longer considered brandy and soda an unladylike beverage. Peter Ruff was not pleased with himself or proud of his companion.

"You'll take some wine?" he suggested, after he had ordered, with a few hints from her, a somewhat extensive supper.

"Champagne," she answered, decidedly. "I've got quite used to it, nowadays," she went on. "I could laugh to think how strange it tasted when you first took me out."

"Tell me," Peter Ruff said, "why you have left your husband?"

She laughed.

"Because he was dull and because he was cross," she answered, "and because the life down at Streatham was simply intolerable. I think it was a little your fault, too," she said, making eyes; at him across the table. "You gave me a taste of what life was like outside Streatham, and I never forgot it."

Peter Ruff did not respond - he led the conversation, indeed, into other channels. On the whole, the supper was scarcely a success. Maud, who was growing to consider herself something of a Bohemian, and who certainly looked for some touch of sentiment on the part of her old admirer, was annoyed by the quiet deference with which he treated her. She reproached him with it once, bluntly.

"Say," she exclaimed, "you don't seem to want to be so friendly as you did! You haven't forgiven me yet, I suppose?"

Peter Ruff shook his head.

"It is not that," he said, "but I think that you have scarcely done a wise thing in leaving your husband. I cannot think that this life on the stage is good for you."

She laughed, scornfully.

"Well," she said, "I never thought to have you preaching at me!"

They finished their supper. Maud accepted a cigarette and did her best to change her companion's mood. She only alluded once more to her husband.

"I don't see how I could have stayed with him, anyhow," she said. "You know, he's been put back - he only gets two pounds fifteen a week now. He couldn't expect me to live upon that."

"Put back?" Peter Ruff repeated.

She nodded.

"He seemed to have a lot of bad luck this last year," she said. "All his cases went wrong, and they don't think so much of him at Scotland Yard as they did. I am not sure that he hasn't begun to drink a little."

"I am sorry to hear it," Peter Ruff said, gravely.

"I don't see why you should be," she answered, bluntly. "He was no friend of yours, nor isn't now. He may not be so dangerous as he was, but if ever you come across him, you take my tip and be careful. He means to do you a mischief some day, if he can. I am not sure," she added, "that he doesn't believe that it was partly your fault about my leaving home."

"I should be sorry for him to think that," Peter Ruff answered. "While we are upon the subject, can't you tell me exactly why your husband dislikes me so?"

"For one thing, because you have been up against him in several of his cases, and have always won."

"And for the other?"

"Well," she said, doubtfully, "he seems to connect you in his mind, somehow, with a boy who was in love with me once - Mr. Spencer Fitzgerald - you know who I mean."

Ruff nodded.

"He still has that in his mind, has he?" he remarked.

"Oh, he's mad!" she declared. "However, don't let us talk about him any more."

The lights were being put out. Peter Ruff paid his bill and they rose together.

"Come down to the fiat for an hour or so," she begged, taking his arm. "I have a dear little place with another girl - Carrie Pearce. I'll sing to you, if you like. Come down and have one drink, anyhow."

Peter Ruff shook his head firmly.

"I am sorry," he said, "but you must excuse me. In some ways, I am very old-fashioned," he added. "I never sit up late, and I hate music."

"Just drive as far as the door with me, then," she begged.

Peter Ruff shook his head.

"You must excuse me," he said, handing her into the hansom. "And, Maud," he added - "if I may call you so - take my advice: give it up - go back to your husband and stick to him - you'll be better off in the long run."

She would have answered him scornfully, but there was something impressive in the crisp, clear words - in his expression, too, as he looked into her eyes. She threw herself back in a corner of the cab with an affected little laugh, and turned her head away from him.

Peter Ruff walked back into the cloak-room for his coat and hat, and sighed softly to himself. It was the end of the one sentimental episode of his life!

It had been the study of Peter Ruff's life, so far as possible, to maintain under all circumstances an equable temperament, to refuse to recognize the meaning of the word "nerves," and to be guided in all his actions by that profound common sense which was one of his natural gifts. Yet there were times when, like any other ordinary person, he suffered acutely from presentiments. He left his rooms, for instance, at five o'clock on the afternoon of the day following his supper with Maud, suffering from a sense of depression for which he found it altogether impossible to account. It was true that the letter which he had in his pocket, the appointment which he was on his way to keep, were both of them probable sources of embarrassment and annoyance, if not of danger. He was being invited, without the option of refusal, to enter upon some risky undertaking which would yield him neither fee nor reward. Yet his common sense told him that it was part of the game. In Paris, he had looked upon his admittance into the order of the "Double-Four" as one of the stepping-stones to success in his career. Through them he had gained knowledge which he could have acquired in no other way. Through them, for instance, he had acquired the information that Madame la Comtesse de Pilitz was a Servian patriot and a friend of the Crown Prince; and that the Count von Hern, posing in England as a sportsman and an idler, was a highly paid and dangerous Austrian spy. There had been other occasions, too, upon which they had come to his aid. Now they had made an appeal to him - an appeal which must be obeyed. His time - perhaps, even, his safety - must be placed entirely at their disposal. It was only an ordinary return a thing expected of him - a thing which he dared not refuse. Yet he knew very well what he could not explain to them - that the whole success of his life depended so absolutely upon his remaining free from any suspicion of wrong-doing, that he had received his summons with something like dismay, and proceeded to obey it with unaccustomed reluctance.

He drove to Cirey's cafe in Regent Street, where he dismissed the driver of his hansom and strolled in with the air of an habitue. He selected a corner table, ordered some refreshment, and asked for a box of dominoes. The place was fairly well filled. A few women were sitting about; a sprinkling of Frenchmen were taking their aperitif; here and there a man of affairs, on his way from the city, had called in for a glass of vermouth. Peter Ruff looked them over, recognizing the type - recognizing, even, some of their faces. Apparently, the person whom he was to meet had not yet arrived.

He lit a cigarette and smoked slowly. Presently the door opened and a woman entered in a long fur coat, a large hat, and a thick veil. She raised it to glance around, disclosing the unnaturally pale face and dark, swollen eyes of a certain type of Frenchwoman. She seemed to notice no one in particular. Her eyes traveled over Peter Ruff without any sign of interest. Nevertheless, she took a seat somewhere near his and ordered some vermouth from the waiter, whom she addressed by name. When she had been served and the waiter had departed, she looked curiously at the dominoes which stood before her neighbor.

"Monsieur plays dominoes, perhaps?" she remarked, taking one of them into her fingers and examining it. "A very interesting game!"

Peter Ruff showed her a domino which he had been covering with his hand - it was a double four. She nodded, and moved from her seat to one immediately next him.

"I had not imagined," Peter Ruff said, "that it was a lady whom I was to meet."

"Monsieur is not disappointed, I trust?" she said, smiling. "If I talk banalities, Monsieur must pardon it. Both the waiters here are spies, and there are always people who watch. Monsieur is ready to do us a service?"

"To the limits of my ability," Peter Ruff answered. "Madame will remember that we are not in Paris; that our police system, if not so wonderful as yours, is still a closer and a more present thing. They have not the brains at Scotland Yard, but they are persistent - hard to escape."

"Do I not know it?" the woman said. "It is through them that we send for you. One of us is in danger."

"Do I know him?" Peter Ruff asked.

"It is doubtful," she answered. "Monsieur's stay in Paris was so brief. If Monsieur will recognize his name - it is Jean Lemaitre himself."

Peter Ruff started slightly.

"I thought," he said, with some hesitation, "that Lemaitre did not visit this country."

"He came well disguised," the woman answered. "It was thought to be safe. Nevertheless, it was a foolish thing. They have tracked him down from hotel to apartments, till he lives now in the back room of a wretched little cafe in Soho. Even from there we cannot get him away - the whole district is watched by spies. We need help."

"For a genius like Lemaitre," Peter Ruff said, thoughtfully, "to have even thought of Soho, was foolish. He should have gone to Hampstead or Balham. It is easy to fool our police if you know how. On the other hand, they hang on to the scent like leeches when once they are on the trail. How many warrants are there out against Jean in this country?"

"Better not ask that," the woman said, grimly. "You remember the raid on a private house in the Holloway Road, two years ago, when two policemen were shot and a spy was stabbed? Jean was in that - it is sufficient!"

"Are any plans made at all?" Peter Ruff asked.

"But naturally," the woman answered. "There is a motor car,

even now, of sixty-horse-power, stands ready at a garage in Putney. If Jean can once reach it, he can reach the coast. At a certain spot near Southampton there is a small steamer waiting. After that, everything is easy."

"My task, then," Peter Ruff said, thoughtfully, "is to take Jean Lemaitre from this cafe in Soho, as far as Putney, and get him a fair start?"

"It is enough," she answered. "There is a cordon of spies around the district. Every day they seem to chose in upon us. They search the houses, one by one. Only last night, the Hotel de Netherlands - a miserable little place on the other side of the street - was suddenly surrounded by policemen and every room ransacked. It may be our turn to-night."

"In one hour's time," Peter Ruff said, glancing at his watch, "I shall present myself as a doctor at the cafe. Tell me the address. Tell me what to say which will insure my admission to Jean Lemaitre!"

"The cafe," she answered, "is called the Hotel de Flandres. You enter the restaurant and you walk to the desk. There you find always Monsieur Antoine. You say to him simply - 'The Double-Four!' He will answer that he understands, and he will conduct you at once to Lemaitre."

Ruff nodded.

"In the meantime," he said, "let it be understood in the cafe - if there is any one who is not in the secret - that one of the waiters is sick. I shall come to attend him."

She nodded thoughtfully.

"As well that way as any other," she answered. "Monsieur is very kind. A bientot!"

She shook hands and they parted. Peter Ruff drove back to his rooms, rang up an adjoining garage for a small covered car such as are usually let out to medical men, and commenced to pack a small black bag with the outfit necessary for his purpose. Now that he was actually immersed in his work, the sense of depression had passed away. The keen stimulus of danger had quickened his blood. He knew very well that the woman had not exaggerated. There was no man more wanted by the French or the English police than the man who had sought his aid, and the district in which he had taken shelter was, in some respects, the very worst for his purpose. Nevertheless, Peter Ruff, who believed, at the bottom of his heart, in his star, went on with his preparations feeling morally certain that Jean Lemaitre would sleep on the following night in his native land.

At precisely the hour agreed upon, a small motor brougham pulled up outside the door of the Hotel de Flandres and its occupant - whom ninety-nine men out of a hundred would at once, unhesitatingly, have declared to be a doctor in moderate practice - pushed open the swing doors of the restaurant and made his way to the desk. He was of medium height; he wore a frock-coat - a little frayed; gray trousers which had not been recently pressed; and thick boots.

"I understand that one of your waiters requires my attendance," he said, in a tone not unduly raised but still fairly audible. "I am Dr. Gilette."

"Dr. Gilette," Antoine repeated, slowly.

"And number Double-Four," the doctor murmured.

Antoine descended from his desk.

"But certainly, Monsieur!" he said. "The poor fellow declares that he suffers. If he is really ill, he must go. It sounds brutal, but what can one do? We have so few rooms here, and so much business. Monsieur will come this way?"

Antoine led the way from the cafe into a very smelly region of narrow passages and steep stairs.

"It is to be arranged?" Antoine whispered, as they ascended.

"Without a doubt," the doctor answered. "Were there spies in the cafe?"

"Two," Antoine answered.

The doctor nodded, and said no more. He mounted to the third story. Antoine led him through a small sitting-room and knocked four times upon the door of an inner room. It suddenly was opened. A man - unshaven, terrified, with that nameless fear in his face which one sees reflected in the expression of some trapped animal - stood there looking out at them.

"'Double-Four'!" the doctor said, softly. "Go back into the room, please. Antoine will kindly leave us."

"Who are you?" the man gasped.

"'Double-Four'!" the doctor answered. "Obey me, and be quick for your life! Strip!"

The man obeyed.

Barely twenty minutes later, the doctor - still carrying his bag - descended the stairs. He entered the cafe from a somewhat remote door. Antoine hurried to meet him, and walked by his side through the place. He asked many questions, but the doctor contented himself with shaking his head. Almost in silence he left Antoine, who conducted him even to the door of his motor. The proprietor of the cafe watched the brougham disappear, and then returned to his desk, sighing heavily.

A man who had been sipping a liqueur dose at hand, laid down his paper.

E. Phillips Oppenheim

"One of your waiters ill, did I understand?" he asked. Monsieur Antoine was at once eloquent. It was the ill-fortune which had dogged him for the last four months! The man had been taken ill there in the restaurant. He was a Gascon - spoke no English - and had just arrived. It was not possible for him to be removed at the moment, so he had been carried to an empty bedroom. Then had come the doctor and forbidden his removal. Now for a week he had lain there and several of his other voyageurs had departed. One did not know how these things got about, but they spoke of infection. The doctor, who had just left - Dr. Gilette of Russell Square, a most famous physician - had assured him that there was no infection - no fear of any. But what did it matter - that? People were so hard to convince. Monsieur would like a cigar? But certainly! There were here some of the best.

Antoine undid the cabinet and opened a box of Havanas. John Dory selected one and called for another liqueur.

"You have trouble often with your waiters, I dare say," he remarked. "They tell me that all Frenchmen who break the law in their own country, find their way, sooner or later, to these parts. You have to take them without characters, I suppose?"

Antoine lifted his shoulders.

"But what could one do?" he exclaimed. "Characters, they were easy enough to write - but were they worth the paper they were written on? Indeed no!"

"Not only your waiters," Dory continued, "but those who stay in the hotels round here have sometimes an evil name."

Antoine shrugged his shoulders.

"For myself," he said, "I am particular. We have but a few rooms, but we are careful to whom we let them."

"Do you keep a visitors' book?"

"But no, Monsieur!" Antoine protested. "For why the necessity? There are so few who come to stay for more than the night - just now scarcely any one at all."

There entered, at that moment, a tall, thin man dressed in dark clothes, who walked with his hands in his overcoat pockets, as though it were a habit. He came straight to Dory and handed him a piece of paper.

John Dory glanced it through and rose to his feet. A gleam of satisfaction lit his eyes.

"Monsieur Antoine," he said, "I am sorry to cause you any inconvenience, but here is my card. I am a detective officer from Scotland Yard, and I have received information which compels me with your permission, to examine at once the sleeping apartments in your hotel."

Antoine was fiercely indignant.

"But, Monsieur!" he exclaimed. "I do not understand! Examine my rooms? But it is impossible! Who dares to say that I harbor criminals?"

"I have information upon which I can rely," John Dory answered, firmly. "This comes from a man who is no friend of mine, but he is well-known. You can read for yourself what he says."

Monsieur Antoine, with trembling fingers, took the piece of paper from John Dory's hands. It was addressed to -

Mr. JOHN DORY, DETECTIVE:

If you wish to find Jean Lemaitre, search in the upper rooms of the Hotel de Flandres. I have certain information that he is to be found there.

PETER RUFF.

E. Phillips Oppenheim

"Never," Antoine declared, "will I suffer such an indignity!"

Dory raised a police whistle to his lips.

"You are foolish," he said. "Already there is a cordon of men about the place. If you refuse to conduct me upstairs I shall at once place you under arrest."

Antoine, white with fear, poured himself out a liqueur of brandy.

"Well, well," he said, "what must be done, then! Come!"

He led the way out into that smelly network of passages, up the stairs to the first floor. Room after room he threw open and begged Dory to examine. Some of them were garishly furnished with gilt mirrors, cheap lace curtains tied back with blue ribbons. Others were dark, miserable holes, into which the fresh air seemed never to have penetrated. On the third floor they reached the little sitting-room, which bore more traces of occupation than some of the rooms below. Antoine would have passed on, but Dory stopped him.

"There is a door there," he said. "We will try that."

"It is the sick waiter who lies within," Antoine protested. "Monsieur can hear him groan."

There was, indeed, something which sounded like a groan to be heard, but Dory was obstinate.

"If he is so ill," he demanded, "how is he able to lock the door on the inside? Monsieur Antoine, that door must be opened."

Antoine knocked at it softly.

"Francois," he said, "there is another doctor here who would see you. Let us in."

There was no answer, Antoine turned to his companion with a little shrug of the shoulders, as one who would say - "I have done my best. What would you have?"

Dory put his shoulder to the door.

"Listen," he shouted through the keyhole, "Mr. Sick Waiter, or whoever you are, if you do not unlock this door, I am coming in!"

"I have no key," said a faint voice. "I am locked in. Please break open the door."

"But that is not the Voice of Francois!" Antoine exclaimed, in amazement.

"We'll soon see who it is," Dory answered.

He charged at the door fiercely. At the third assault it gave way.They found themselves in a small back bedroom, and stretched on the floor, very pale, and apparently only half-conscious, lay Peter Ruff. There was a strong smell of chloroform about. John Dory threw open the window. His fingers trembled a little. It was like Fate - this! At the end of every unsuccessful effort there was this man - Peter Ruff!

"What the devil are you doing here?" he asked.

Peter Ruff groaned.

"Help me up," he begged, "and give me a little brandy."

Antoine set him in an easy-chair and rang the bell furiously.

"It will come directly!" he exclaimed. "But who are you?"

Peter Ruff waited for the brandy. When he had sipped it, he drew a little breath as though of relief.

E. Phillips Oppenheim

"I heard," he said, speaking still with an evident effort, "that Lemaitre was here. I had secret information. I thought at first that I would let you know - I sent you a note early this morning. Afterwards, I discovered that there was a reward, and I determined to track him down myself. He was in here hiding as a sick waiter. I do not think," Peter Ruff added, "that Monsieur Antoine had any idea. I presented myself as representing a charitable society, and I was shown here to visit him. He was too clever, though, was Jean Lemaitre - too quick for me."

"You were a fool to come alone!" John Dory said. "Don't you know the man's record? How long ago did he leave?"

"About ten minutes," Peter Ruff answered. "You must have missed him somewhere as you came up. I crawled to the window and I watched him go. He left the restaurant by the side entrance, and took a taxicab at the corner there. It went northward toward New Oxford Street."

Dory turned on his heel - they heard him descending the stairs. Peter Ruff rose to his feet.

"I am afraid," he said, as he plunged his head into a basin of water, and came into the middle of the room rubbing it vigorously with a small towel, "I am afraid that our friend John Dory will get to dislike me soon! He passed out unnoticed, eh, Antoine?"

Antoine's face wore a look of great relief.

"There was not a soul who looked," he said. "We passed under the nose of the gentleman from Scotland Yard. He sat there reading his paper; and he had no idea. I watched Jean step into the motor. Even by now he is well on his way southwards. Twice he changes from motor to train, and back. They will never trace him."

Peter Ruff, who was looking amazingly better, sipped a further glass of liqueur. Together he and Antoine descended to the street.

"Mind," Peter Ruff whispered, "I consider that accounts are squared between me and 'Double-Four' now. Let them know that. This sort of thing isn't in my line."

"For an amateur," Antoine said, bowing low, "Monsieur commands my heartfelt congratulations!"

CHAPTER VIII

Mrs. BOGNOR'S STAR BOARDER

In these days, the duties of Miss Brown as Peter Ruff's secretary had become multifarious. Together with the transcribing of a vast number of notes concerning cases, some of which he undertook and some of which he refused, she had also to keep his cash book, a note of his investments and a record of his social engagements. Notwithstanding all these demands upon her time, however, there were occasions when she found herself, of necessity, idle. In one of these she broached the subject which had often been in her mind. They were alone, and not expecting callers. Consequently, she sat upon the hearthrug and addressed her employer by his Christian name.

"Peter," she said softly, "do you remember the night when you came through the fog and burst into my little flat?"

"Quite well," he answered, "but it is a subject to which I prefer that you do not allude."

"I will be careful," she answered. "I only spoke of it for this reason. Before you left, when we were sitting together, you sketched out the career which you proposed for yourself. In many respects, I suppose, you have been highly successful, but I wonder if it has ever occurred to you that your work has not proceeded upon the lines which you first indicated?"

He nodded.

"I think I know what you mean," he said. "Go on."

"That night," she murmured softly, "you spoke as a hunted man; you spoke as one at war with Society; you spoke as one who proposes almost a campaign against it. When you took your rooms here and called yourself Peter Ruff, it was rather in your mind to aid the criminal than to detect the crime. Fate seems to have decreed otherwise. Why, I wonder?"

"Things have gone that way," Peter Ruff remarked.

"I will tell you why," she continued. "It is because, at the bottom of your heart, there lurks a strong and unconquerable desire for respectability. In your heart you are on the side of the law and established things. You do not like crime; you do not like criminals. You do not like the idea of associating with them. You prefer the company of law-abiding people, even though their ways be narrow. It was part of that sentiment, Peter, which led you to fall in love with a coal-merchant's daughter. I can see that you will end your days in the halo of respectability."

Peter Ruff was a little thoughtful. He scratched his chin and contemplated the tip of his faultless patent boot. Self-analysis interested him, and he recognized the truth of the girl's words.

"You know, I am rather like that," he admitted. "When I see a family party, I envy them. When I hear of a man who has brothers and sisters and aunts and cousins, and gives family dinner-parties to family friends, I envy him. I do not care about the loose ends of life. I do not care about restaurant life, and ladies who transfer their regards with the same facility that they change their toilettes. You have very admirable powers of observation, Violet. You see me, I believe, as I really am."

"That being so," she remarked, "what are you going to say to Sir Richard Dyson?"

Peter Ruff was frank.

"Upon my soul," he answered, "I don't know!"

"You'll have to make up your mind very soon," she reminded him. "He is coming here at twelve o'clock."

Peter Ruff nodded.

"I shall wait until I hear what he has to say," he remarked.

"His letter gave you a pretty clear hint," Violet said, "that it was something outside the law."

"The law has many outposts," Peter Ruff said. "One can thread one's way in and out, if one knows the ropes. I don't like the man, but he introduced me to his tailor. I have never had any clothes like those he has made me."

She sighed.

"You are a vain little person," she said.

"You are an impertinent young woman!" he answered. "Get back to your work. Don't you hear the lift stop?"

She rose reluctantly, and resumed her place in front of her desk.

"If it's risky," she whispered, leaning round towards him, "don't you take it on. I've heard one or two things about Sir Richard lately."

Peter Ruff nodded. He, too, quitted his easy-chair, and took up a bundle of papers which lay upon his desk. There was a sharp tap at the door.

"Come in!" he said.

Sir Richard Dyson entered. He was dressed quietly, but with the perfect taste which was obviously an instinct with him, and he wore a big bunch of violets in his buttonhole. Nevertheless, the spring sunshine seemed to find out the lines in his face. His eyes were baggy - he had aged even within the last few months.

"Well, Mr. Ruff," he said, shaking hands, "how goes it?"

"I am very well, Sir Richard," Peter Ruff answered. "Please take a chair."

Sir Richard took the easy-chair, and discovering a box of cigarettes upon the table, helped himself. Then his eyes fell upon Miss Brown.

"Can't do without your secretary?" he remarked.

"Impossible!" Peter Ruff answered. "As I told you before, I am her guarantee that what you say to me, or before her, is spoken as though to the dead."

Sir Richard nodded.

"Just as well," he remarked, "for I am going to talk about a man who I wish were dead!"

"There are few of us," Peter Ruff said, "who have not our enemies."

"Have you any experience of blackmailers?" Sir Richard asked.

"In my profession," Peter Ruff answered, "I have come across such persons."

"I have come to see you about one," Sir Richard proceeded. "Many years ago, there was a fellow in my regiment who went to the bad - never mind his name. He passes to-day as Ted Jones - that name will do as well as another. I am not," Sir

E. Phillips Oppenheim

Richard continued, "a good-natured man, but some devilish impulse prompted me to help that fellow. I gave him money three or four times. Somehow, I don't think it's a very good thing to give a man money. He doesn't value it - it comes too easily. He spends it and wants more."

"There's a good deal of truth in what you say, Sir Richard," Peter Ruff admitted.

"Our friend, for instance, wanted more," Sir Richard continued. "He came to me for it almost as a matter of course. I refused. He came again; I lost my temper and punched his head. Then his little game began."

Peter Ruff nodded.

"He had something to work upon, I suppose?" he remarked.

"Most certainly he had," Sir Richard admitted. "If ever I achieved sufficient distinction in any branch of life to make it necessary that my biography should be written, I promise you that you would find it in many places a little highly colored. In other words, Mr. Ruff, I have not always adhered to the paths of righteousness."

A faint smile flickered across Peter Ruff's face.

"Sir Richard," he said, "your candor is admirable."

"There was one time," Sir Richard continued, "when I was really on my last legs. It was just before I came into the baronetcy. I had borrowed every penny I could borrow. I was even hard put to it for a meal. I went to Paris, and I called myself by another man's name. I got introduced to a somewhat exclusive club there. My assumed name was a good one - it was the name, in fact, of a relative whom I somewhat resembled. I was accepted without question. I played cards, and I lost somewhere about eighteen thousand francs."

"A sum," Peter Ruff remarked, "which you probably found it inconvenient to pay."

"There was only one course," Sir Richard continued, "and I took it. I went back the next night and gave checks for the amount of my indebtedness - checks which had no more chance of being met than if I were to draw to-night upon the Bank of England for a million pounds. I went back, however, with another resolve. I was considered to have discharged my liabilities, and we played again. I rose a winner of something like sixty thousand francs. But I played to win, Mr. Ruff! Do you know what that means?"

"You cheated!" Peter Ruff said, in an undertone.

"Quite true," Sir Richard admitted. "I cheated! There was a scandal, and I disappeared. I had the money, and though my checks for the eighteen thousand francs were met, there was a considerable balance in my pocket when I escaped out of France. There was enough to take me out to America - big game shooting in the far West. No one ever associated me with the impostor who had robbed these young French noblemen - no one, that is to say, except the person who passes by the name of Teddy Jones."

"How did he get to know?" Peter Ruff asked.

"The story wouldn't interest you," Sir Richard answered. "He was in Paris at the time - we came across one another twice. He heard the scandal, and put two and two together. I shipped him off to Australia when I came into the title. He has come back. Lately, I can tell you, he has pretty well drained me dry. He has become a regular parasite a cold-blooded leech. He doesn't get drunk now. He looks after his health. I believe he even saves his, money. There's scarcely a week I don't hear from him. He keeps me a pauper. He has brought me at last to that state when I feel that there must be an ending!"

"You have come to seek my help," Peter Ruff said, slowly.

"From what you say about this man, I presume that he is not to be frightened?"

"Not for a single moment," Sir Richard answered. "The law has no terrors for him. He is as slippery as an eel. He has his story pat. He even has his witnesses ready. I can assure you that Mr. Teddy Jones isn't by any means an ordinary sort of person."

"He is not to be bluffed," Peter Ruff said, slowly; "he is not to be bribed. What remains?"

"I have come here," Sir Richard said, "for your advice, Mr. Ruff."

"The blackmailer," Peter Ruff said, "is a criminal."

"He is a scoundrel!" Sir Richard assented.

"He is not fit to live," Peter Ruff repeated.

"He contaminates the world with every breath he draws!" Sir Richard assented.

"Perhaps," Peter Ruff said, "you had better give me his address, and the name he goes under."

"He lives at a boarding-house in Russell Street, Bloomsbury," Sir Richard said. "It is Mrs. Bognor's boarding-house. She calls it, I believe, the 'American Home from Home.' The number is 17."

"A boarding-house," Peter Ruff repeated, thoughtfully. "Makes it a little hard to get at him privately, doesn't it?"

"Fling him a bait and he will come to you," Sir Richard answered. "He is an adventurer pure and simple, though perhaps you wouldn't believe it to look at him now. He has grown fat on the money he has wrung from me."

"You had better leave the matter in my hands for a few days," Peter Ruff said. "I will have a talk with this gentleman and see whether he is really so unmanageable. If he is, there is, of course, only one way, and for that way, Sir Richard, you would have to pay a little high."

"If I were to hear to-morrow," Sir Richard said quietly, "that Teddy Jones was dead, I would give five thousand pounds to the man who brought me the information!"

Peter Ruff nodded.

"It would be worth that," he said - "quite! I will drop you a line in the course of the next few days."

Sir Richard took up his hat, lit another of Peter Ruff's cigarettes, and departed. They heard the rattle of the lift as it descended. Then Miss Brown turned round in her chair.

"Don't you do it, Peter!" she said solemnly. "The time has gone by for that sort of thing. The man may be unfit to live, but you don't need to risk as much as that for a matter of five thousand pounds."

Peter Ruff nodded.

"Quite right," he said; "quite right, Violet. At the same time, five thousand pounds is an excellent sum. We must see what can be done."

Peter Ruff's method of seeing what could be done was at first the very obvious one of seeking to discover any incidents in the past of the person known as Teddy Jones likely to reflect present discredit upon him if brought to light. From the first, it was quite clear that the career of this gentleman had been far from immaculate. His researches proved, beyond a doubt, that the gentleman in question had resorted, during the last ten or fifteen years, to many and very questionable methods of obtaining a living. At the same time, there was nothing which

E. Phillips Oppenheim

Peter Ruff felt that the man might not brazen out. His present mode of life seemed - on the surface, at any rate - to be beyond reproach. There was only one association which was distinctly questionable, and it was in this one direction, therefore, that Peter Ruff concentrated himself. The case, for some reason, interested him so much that he took a close and personal interest in it, and he was rewarded one day by discovering this enemy of Sir Richard's sitting, toward five o'clock in the afternoon, in a cafe in Regent Street, engrossed in conversation with a person whom Peter Ruff knew to be a very black sheep indeed - a man who had been tried for murder, and concerning whom there were still many unpleasant rumors. From behind his paper in a corner of the cafe, Peter Ruff watched these two men. Teddy Jones - or Major Edward Jones, as it seemed he was now called - was a person whose appearance no longer suggested the poverty against which he had been struggling most of his life. He was well dressed and tolerably well turned out. His face was a little puffy, and he had put on flesh during these days of his ease. His eyes, too, had a somewhat furtive expression, although his general deportment was one of braggadocio. Peter Ruff, quick always in his likes or dislikes, found the man repulsive from the start. He felt that he would have a genuine pleasure, apart from the matter of the five thousand pounds, in accelerating Major Jones's departure from a world which he certainly did not adorn.

The two men conducted their conversation in a subdued tone, which made it quite impossible for Peter Ruff, in his somewhat distant corner, to overhear a single word of it. It was obvious, however, that they were not on the best of terms. Major Jones's companion was protesting, and apparently without success, against some course of action or speech of his companions. The conversation, on the other hand, never reached a quarrel, and the two men left the place together apparently on ordinary terms of friendliness. Peter Ruff at once quitted his seat and crossed the room toward the spot where they had been sitting. He dived under the table and picked up a newspaper - it was the only clue left to him as to the nature of their conversation. More than once, Major Jones who had, soon after their arrival, sent a waiter for it, had pointed to a certain paragraph as though to give weight to his statements. Peter Ruff had noticed the exact position of that paragraph. He smoothed out the paper and found it at once. It was an account of the murder of a wealthy old woman, living on the outskirts of a country village not far from London. Peter Ruff's face did not change as he called for another vermouth and read the description, slowly. Yet he was aware that he had possibly stumbled across the very thing for which he had searched so urgently! The particulars of the murder he already knew well, as at one time he had felt inclined to aid the police in their so far fruitless investigations. He therefore skipped the description of the tragedy, and devoted his attention to the last paragraph, toward which he fancied that the finger of Major Jones had been chiefly directed. It was a list of the stolen property, which consisted of jewelry, gold and notes to a very considerable amount. With the waiter's permission, he annexed the paper, cut out the list of articles with a sharp penknife, and placed it in his pocketbook before he left the cafe.

In the course of some of the smaller cases with which Peter Ruff had been from time to time connected, he had more than once come into contact with the authorities at Scotland Yard, and he had several acquaintances there - not including Mr. John Dory - to whom, at times, he had given valuable information. For the first time, he now sought some return for his many courtesies. He drove straight from the cafe to the office of the Chief of the Criminal Investigation Department. The questions he asked there were only two, but they were promptly and courteously answered. Peter Ruff left the building and drove back to his rooms in a somewhat congratulatory frame of mind. After all, it was chance which was the chief factor in the solution of so many of these cases! Often he had won less success after months of untiring effort than he had gained during that few minutes in the cafe in Regent Street.

Peter Ruff became an inmate of that very select boarding-house carried on by Mrs. Bognor at number 17 Russell Street,

E. Phillips Oppenheim

Bloomsbury. He arrived with a steamer trunk, an elaborate traveling-bag and a dressing-case; took the best vacant room in the house, and dressed for dinner. Mrs. Bognor looked upon him as a valuable addition to her clientele, and introduced him freely to her other guests. Among these was Major Edward Jones. Major Jones sat at Mrs. Bognor's right hand, and was evidently the show guest of the boarding-house. Peter Ruff, without the least desire to attack his position, sat upon her left and monopolized the conversation. On the third night it turned, by chance, upon precious stones. Peter Ruff drew a little chamois leather bag from his pocket.

"I am afraid," he said, "that my tastes are peculiar. I have been in the East, and I have seen very many precious stones in their uncut state. To my mind, there is nothing to be compared with opals. These are a few I brought home from India. Perhaps you would like to look at them, Mrs. Bognor."

They were passed round, amidst a little chorus of admiration.

"The large one with the blue fire," Peter Ruff remarked, "is, I think, remarkably beautiful. I have never seen a stone quite like it."

"It is wonderful!" murmured the young lady who was sitting at Major Jones's right hand. "What a fortunate man you are, Mr. Ruff, to have such a collection of treasures!"

Peter Ruff bowed across the table. Major Jones, who was beginning to feel that his position as show guest was in danger, thrust his hand into his waistcoat pocket and produced a lady's ring, in which was set a single opal.

"Very pretty stones," he remarked carelessly, "but I can't say I am very fond of them. Here's one that belonged to my sister, and my grandmother before her. I have it in my pocket because I was thinking of having the stone reset and making a present of it to a friend of mine."

Peter Ruff's popularity waned - he had said nothing about making a present to any one of even the most insignificant of his opals! And the one which Major Jones now handed round was certainly a magnificent stone. Peter Ruff examined it with the rest, and under the pretext of studying the setting, gazed steadfastly at the inside through his eyeglass. Major Jones, from the other side of the table, frowned, and held out his hand for the ring.

"A very beautiful stone indeed!" Peter Ruff declared, passing it across the tablecloth. "Really, I do not think that there is one in my little collection to be compared with it. Have you many treasures like this, Major Jones?"

"Oh, a few!" the Major answered carelessly, "family heirlooms, most of them."

"You will have to give me the ring, Major Jones," the young lady on his right remarked archly. "It's bad luck, you know, to give it to any one who is not born in October, and my birthday is on the twelfth."

"My dear Miss Levey," Major Jones answered, whispering in her ear, "more unlikely things have happened than that I should beg your acceptance of this little trifle."

"Sooner or later," Peter Ruff said genially, "I should like to have a little conversation with you, Major. I fancy that we ought to be able to find plenty of subjects of common interest."

"Delighted, I'm sure!" the latter answered, utterly unsuspicious. "Shall we go into the smoking-room now, or would you rather play a rubber first?"

"If it is all the same to you," Peter Ruff said, "I think we will have a cigar first. There will be plenty of time for bridge afterwards."

"May I offer you a cigar, sir?" Major Jones inquired, passing across a well-filled case.

Peter Ruff sighed.

"I am afraid, Major," he said, "that there is scarcely time. You see, I have a warrant in my pocket for your arrest, and I am afraid that by the time we got to the station -"

Major Jones leaned forward in his chair. He gripped the sides tightly with both hands. His eyes seemed to be protruding from his head.

"For my what?" he exclaimed, in a tone of horror.

"For your arrest," Peter Ruff explained calmly. "Surely you must have been expecting it! During all these years you must have grown used to expecting it at every moment!"

Major Jones collapsed. He looked at Ruff as one might look at a man who has taken leave of his senses. Yet underneath it all was the coward's fear!

"What are you talking about, man?" he exclaimed. "What do you mean? Lower your voice, for heaven's sake! Consider my position here! Some one might overhear! If this is a joke, let me tell you that it's a d-d foolish one!"

Peter Ruff raised his eyebrows.

"I do not wish," he said, "to create a disturbance - my manner of coming here should have assured you of that. At the same time, business is business. I hold a warrant for your arrest, and I am forced to execute it."

"Do you mean that you are a detective, then?" Major Jones demanded.

He was a big man, but his voice seemed to have grown very

small indeed.

"Naturally," Peter Ruff answered. "I should not come here without authority."

"What is the charge?" the other man faltered.

"Blackmail," Peter Ruff said slowly. "The information against you is lodged by Sir Richard Dyson."

It seemed to Peter Ruff, who was watching his companion closely, that a wave of relief passed over the face of the man who sat cowering in his chair. He certainly drew a little gasp - stretched out his hands, as though to thrust the shadow of some fear from him. His voice, when he spoke, was stronger. Some faint show of courage was returning to him.

"There is some ridiculous mistake," he declared. "Let us talk this over like sensible men, Mr. Ruff. If you will wait until I have spoken to Sir Richard, I can promise you that the warrant shall be withdrawn, and that you shall not be the loser."

"I am afraid it is too late for anything of that sort," Peter Ruff said. "Sir Richard's patience has been completely exhausted by your repeated demands."

"He never told me so," Major Jones whined. "I quite thought that he was always glad to help an old friend. As a matter of fact, I had not meant to ask him for anything else. The last few hundreds I had from him was to have closed the thing up. It was the end."

Peter Ruff shook his head.

"No," he said, "it was not the end! It never would have been the end! Sir Richard sought my advice, and I gave it him without hesitation. Sooner or later, I told him, he would have to adopt different measures. I convinced him. I represent those measures!"

E. Phillips Oppenheim

"But the matter can be arranged," Major Jones insisted, with a little shudder, "I am perfectly certain it can be arranged. Mr. Ruff, you are not an ordinary police officer - I am sure of that. Give me a chance of having an interview with Sir Richard before anything more is done. I will satisfy him, I promise you that. Why, if we leave the place together like this, every one here will get to know about it!"

"Be reasonable," Peter Ruff answered. "Of course everyone will get to know about it! Blackmailing cases always excite a considerable amount of interest. Your photograph will probably be in the Daily Mirror tomorrow or the next day. In the meantime, I must trouble you to pay your respects to Mrs. Bognor and to come with me."

"To Sir Richard's house?" Major Jones asked, eagerly.

"To the police-stations," Peter Ruff answered.

Major Jones did not rise. He sat for a few moments with his head buried in his hands.

"Mr. Ruff," he said hoarsely, "listen to me. I have been fortunate lately in some investments. I am not so poor as I was. I have my check-book in my pocket, and a larger balance in the bank now than I have ever had before. If I write you a check for, say, a hundred - no, two! - five!" he cried, desperately, watching Peter Ruff's unchanging face - "five hundred pounds, will you come round with me to Sir Richard's house in a hansom at once?"

Peter Ruff shook his head.

"Five thousand pounds would not buy your liberty from me, Major Jones," he said.

The man became abject.

"Have pity, then," he pleaded. "My health is not good - I

couldn't stand imprisonment. Think of what it means to a man of my age suddenly to leave everything worth having in life just because he may have imposed a little on the generosity of a friend! Think how you would feel, and be merciful!"

Peter Ruff shook his head slowly. His face was immovable, but there was a look in his eyes from which the other man shrank.

"Major Jones," he said, "you ask me be merciful. You appeal to my pity. For such as you I have no pity, nor have I ever shown any mercy. You know very well, and I know, that when once the hand of the law touches your shoulder, it will not be only a charge o blackmail which the police will bring against you!"

"There is nothing else - nothing else!" he cried. "Take half my fortune, Mr. Ruff. Let me get away. Give me a chance - just a sporting chance!"

"I wonder," Peter Ruff said, "what chance that poor old lady in Weston had? No, I am not saying you murdered her. You never had the pluck. Your confederate did that, and you handled the booty. What were the initials inside that ring you showed us to-night, Major Jones?"

"Let me go to my bedroom," he said, in a strange, far-away tone. "You can come with me and stand outside."

Peter Ruff assented.

"To save scandal," he said, "yes!"

Three flights of stairs they climbed. When at last they reached the door, the trembling man made one last appeal.

"Mr. Ruff," he said, "have a little mercy. Give me an hour's start - just a chance for my life!"

Peter Ruff pushed him in the door.

E. Phillips Oppenheim

"I am not a hard man," he said, "but I keep my mercy for men!"

He took the key from the inside of the door, locked it, and with the key in his pocket descended to the drawing room. The young lady who had sat on Major Jones's right was singing a ballad. Suddenly she paused in the middle of her song. The four people who were playing bridge looked up. Mrs. Bognor screamed.

"What was that?" she asked quickly.

"It sounded," Peter Ruff said, "very much like revolver shot."

"I see," Sir Richard remarked, with a queer look in his eyes, as he handed over a roll of notes to Peter Ruff, "the jury brought it in 'Suicide'! What I can't understand is -"

"Don't try," Peter Ruff interrupted briskly. "It isn't in the bond that you should understand."

Sir Richard helped himself to a drink. A great burden had passed from his shoulders, but he was not feeling at his best that morning. He could scarcely keep his eyes from Peter Ruff.

"Ruff," he said, "I have known you some time, and I have known you to be a square man. I have known you to do good-natured actions. I came to you in desperation but I scarcely expected this!"

Peter Ruff emptied his own tumbler and took up his hat.

"Sir Richard," he said, "you are like a good many other people. Now that the thing is done, you shrink from the thought of it. You even wonder how I could have planned to bring about the death of this man. Listen, Sir Richard. Pity for the deserving, or for those who have in them one single quality, one single grain, of good, is a sentiment which deserves respect. Pity for vermin, who crawl about the world leaving a poisonous trail upon everything they touch, is a false and unnatural sentiment. For every hopelessly corrupt man who is induced to quit this life there is a more deserving one, somewhere or other, for whom the world is a better place."

"So that, after all, you are a philanthropist, Mr. Ruff," Sir Richard said, with a forced smile.

Peter Ruff shook his head.

"A philosopher," he answered, buttoning up his notes.

E. Phillips Oppenheim

CHAPTER IX

THE PERFIDY OF MISS BROWN

Peter Ruff came down to his office with a single letter in his hand, bearing a French postmark. He returned his secretary's morning greeting a little absently, and seated himself at his desk.

"Violet," he asked, "have you ever been to Paris?"

She looked at him compassionately.

"More times than you, I think, Peter," she answered.

He nodded.

"That," he exclaimed, "is very possible! Could you get ready to leave by the two-twenty this afternoon?"

"What, alone?" she exclaimed.

"No - with me," he answered.

She shut down her desk with a bang.

"Of course I can!" she exclaimed. "What a spree!"

Then she caught sight of a certain expression on Peter Ruff's face, and she looked at him wonderingly.

"Is anything wrong, Peter?" she asked.

"No," he answered, "I cannot say that anything is wrong. I have had an invitation to present myself before a certain society in Paris of which you have some indirect knowledge. What the summons means I cannot say."

"Yet you go?" she exclaimed.

"I go," he answered. "I have no choice. If I waited here twenty-four hours, I should hear of it."

"They can have nothing against you," she said. "On the contrary, the only time they have appealed for your aid, you gave it - very valuable aid it must have been, too."

Peter Ruff nodded.

"I cannot see," he admitted, "what they can have against me. And yet, somehow, the wording of my invitation seemed to me a little ominous. Perhaps," he added, walking to the window and standing looking out for a moment, "I have a liver this morning. I am depressed. Violet, what does it mean when you are depressed?"

"Shall you wear your gray clothes for traveling?" she asked, a little irrelevantly.

"I have not made up my mind," Peter Ruff answered. "I thought of wearing my brown, with a brown overcoat. What do you suggest?"

"I like you in brown," she answered, simply. "I should change, if I were you."

He smiled faintly.

"I believe," he said, "that you have a sort of superstition that as I change my clothes I change my humors."

"Should I be so very far wrong?" she asked. "Don't think that I am laughing at you, Peter. The greatest men in the world have had their foibles."

Peter Ruff frowned.

"We shall be away for several days," he said. "Be sure that you take some wraps. It will be cold, crossing."

"Are you going to close the office altogether?" she asked.

Peter Ruff nodded.

"Put up a notice," he said - "'Back on Friday.' Pack up your books and take them round to the Bank before you leave. The lift man will call you a taxi-cab."

He watched her preparations with a sort of gloomy calm.

"I wish you'd tell me what is the matter with you?" she asked, as she turned to follow her belongings.

"I do not know," Peter Ruff said. "I, suppose I am suffering from what you would call presentiments. Be at Charing-Cross punctually."

"Why do you go at all?" she asked. "These people are of no further use to you. Only the other day, you were saying that you should not accept any more outside cases."

"I must go," Peter Ruff answered. "I am not afraid of many things, but I should be afraid of disobeying this letter."

They had a comfortable journey down, a cool, bright crossing, and found their places duly reserved for them in the French train. Miss Brown, in her neat traveling clothes and furs, was conscious of looking her best, and she did all that was possible to entertain her traveling companion. But Peter Ruff seemed like a man who labors under some sense of apprehension. He had faced death more than once during the last few years - faced it without flinching, and with a certain cool disregard which can only come from the highest sort of courage. Yet he knew, when he read over again in the train that brief summons which he was on his way to obey, that he had passed under the shadow of some new and indefinable fear. He was perfectly well aware, too, that both on the steamer and on the French train he was carefully shadowed. This fact, however, did not surprise him. He even went out of his way to enter into conversation with one of the two men whose furtive glances into their compartment and whose constant proximity had first attracted his attention. The man was civil but vague. Nevertheless, when they took their places in the dining-car, they found the two men at the next table. Peter Ruff pointed them out to his companion.

"'Double-Fours'!" he whispered. "Don't you feel like a criminal?"

She laughed, and they took no more notice of the men. But as the train drew near Paris, he felt some return of the depression which had troubled him during the earlier part of the day. He felt a sense of comfort in his companion's presence which was a thing utterly strange to him. On the other hand, he was conscious of a certain regret that he had brought her with him into an adventure of which he could not foresee the end.

The lights of Paris flashed around them - the train was gradually slackening speed. Peter Ruff, with a sigh, began to collect their belongings.

"Violet," he said, "I ought not to have brought you." Something in his voice puzzled her. There had been every few times, during all the years she had known him, when she had been able to detect anything approaching sentiment in his tone - and those few times had been when he had spoken of another woman.

"Why not?" she asked, eagerly.

E. Phillips Oppenheim

Peter Ruff looked out into the blackness, through the glittering arc of lights, and perhaps for once he suffered his fancy to build for him visions of things that were not of earth. If so, however, it was a moment which swiftly passed. His reply was in a tone as matter of fact as his usual speech.

"Because," he said, "I do not exactly see the end of my present expedition - I do not understand its object."

"You have some apprehension?" she asked.

"None at all," he answered. "Why should I? There is an unwritten bargain," he added, a little more slowly, "to which I subscribed with our friends here, and I have certainly kept it. In fact, the balance is on my side. There is nothing for me to fear."

The train crept into the Gare du Nord, and they passed through the usual routine of the Customs House. Then, in an omnibus, they rumbled slowly over the cobblestones, through the region of barely lit streets and untidy cafes, down the Rue Lafayette, across the famous Square and into the Rue de Rivoli.

"Our movements," Peter Ruff remarked dryly, "are too well known for us to attempt to conceal them. We may as well stop at one of the large hotels. It will be more cheerful for you while I am away."

They engaged rooms at the Continental. Miss Brown, whose apartments were in the wing of the hotel overlooking the gardens, ascended at once to her room. Peter Ruff, who had chosen a small suite on the other side, went into the bar for a whiskey and soda. A man touched him on the elbow.

"For Monsieur," he murmured, and vanished.

Peter Ruff turned and opened the note. It bore a faint perfume, it had a coronet upon the flap of the envelope, and it was written in a delicate feminine handwriting.

DEAR Mr. RUFF:

If you are not too tired with your journey, will you call soon after one o'clock to meet some old friends?

BLANCHE DE MAUPASSIM.

Peter Ruff drank his whiskey and soda, went up to his rooms, and made a careful toilet. Then he sent a page up for Violet, who came down within a few minutes. She was dressed with apparent simplicity in a high-necked gown, a large hat, and a single rope of pearls. In place of the usual gold purse, she carried a small white satin bag, exquisitely hand-painted. Everything about her bespoke that elegant restraint so much a feature of the Parisian woman of fashion herself. Peter Ruff, who had told her to prepare for supping out, was at first struck by the simplicity of her attire. Afterwards, he came to appreciate its perfection.

They went to the Cafe de Paris, where they were the first arrivals. People, however, began to stream in before they had finished their meal, and Peter Ruff, comparing his companion's appearance with the more flamboyant charms of these ladies from the Opera and the theatres, began to understand the numerous glances of admiration which the impressionable Frenchmen so often turned in their direction. There was between them, toward the end of the meal, something which amounted almost to nervousness.

"You are going to keep your appointment to-night, Peter?" his companion asked.

Peter Ruff nodded.

"As soon as I have taken you home," he said. "I shall probably return late, so we will breakfast here to-morrow morning, if you like, at half-past twelve. I will send a note to your room

E. Phillips Oppenheim

when I am ready."

She looked him in the eyes.

"Peter," she said, "supposing that note doesn't come!"

He shrugged his shoulders.

"My dear Violet," he said, "you and I - or rather I, for you are not concerned in this - live a life which is a little different from the lives of most of the people around us. The million pay their taxes, and they expect police protection in times of danger. For me there is no such resource. My life has its own splendid compensations. I have weapons with which to fight any ordinary danger. What I want to explain to you is this - that if you hear no more of me, you can do nothing. If that note does not come to you in the morning, you can do nothing. Wait here for three days, and after that go back to England. You will find a letter on your desk, telling you there exactly what to do."

"You have something in your mind," she said, "of which you have not told me."

"I have nothing," he answered, firmly. "Upon my honor, I know of no possible cause of offense which our friends could have against me. Their summons is, I will admit, somewhat extraordinary, but I go to obey it absolutely without fear. You can sleep well, Violet. We lunch here to-morrow, without a doubt."

They drove back to the hotel almost in silence. Violet was looking fixedly out of the window of the taxicab, as though interested in watching the crowds upon the street. Peter Ruff appeared to be absorbed in his own thoughts. Yet perhaps they were both of them nearer to one another than either surmised. Their parting in the hall of the Continental Hotel was unemotional enough. For a moment Peter Ruff had hesitated while her hand had lain in his. He had opened his lips as though he had something to say. Her eyes grew suddenly softer - seemed to seek his as though begging for those unspoken words. But Peter Ruff did not say them then.

"I shall be back all right," he said. "Good night, Violet! Sleep well!"

He turned back towards the waiting taxicab.

"Number 16, Rue de St. Quintaine," he told the man. It was not a long ride. In less than a quarter of an hour, Peter Ruff presented himself before a handsome white house in a quiet, aristocratic-looking street. At his summons, the postern door flew open, and a man-servant in plain livery stood at the second entrance.

"Madame la Marquise?" Peter Ruff asked.

The man bowed in silence, and took the visitor's hat and overcoat. He passed along a spacious hall and into a delightfully furnished reception room, where an old lady with gray hair sat in the midst of a little circle of men. Peter Ruff stood, for a moment, upon the threshold, looking around him. She held out her hands.

"It is Monsieur Peter Ruff, is it not? At last, then, I am gratified. I have wished for so long to see one who has become so famous."

Peter Ruff took her hands in his and raised them gallantly to his lips.

"Madame," he said, "this is a pleasure indeed. At my last visit here, you were in Italy."

"I grow old," she answered. "I leave Paris but little now. Where one has lived, one should at least be content to die."

"Madame speaks a philosophy," Peter Ruff answered, "which

as yet she has no need to learn."

The old lady turned to a man who stood upon her right:

"And this from an Englishman!" she exclaimed.

There were others who took Peter Ruff by the hand then. The servants were handing round coffee in little Sevres cups. On the sideboard was a choice of liqueurs and bottles of wine. Peter Ruff found himself hospitably entertained with both small talk and refreshments. But every now and then his eyes wandered back to where Madame sat in her chair, her hair as white as snow - beautiful still, in spite of the cruel mouth and the narrow eyes.

"She is wonderful!" he murmured to a man who stood by his side.

"She is eighty-six," was the answer in a whisper, "and she knows everything."

As the clock struck two, a tall footman entered the room and wheeled Madame's chair away. Several of the guests left at the same time. Ruff, when the door was closed, counted those who remained. As he had imagined would be the case, he found that there were eight.

A tall, gray-bearded man, who from the first had attached himself to Ruff, and who seemed to act as a sort of master of ceremonies, now approached him once more and laid his hand upon his shoulder.

"Mon ami," he said, "we will now discuss, if it pleases you, the little matter concerning which we took the liberty of asking you to favor us with a visit."

"What, here?" Peter Ruff asked, in some surprise.

His friend, who had introduced himself as Monsieur de

Founcelles, smiled.

"But why not?" he asked. "Ah, but I think I understand!" he added, almost immediately. "You are English, Monsieur Peter Ruff, and in some respects you have not moved with the times. Confess, now, that your idea of a secret society is a collection of strangely attired men who meet in a cellar, and build subterranean passages in case of surprise. In Paris, I think, we have gone beyond that sort of thing. We of the 'Double-Four' have no headquarters save the drawing-room of Madame; no hiding-places whatsoever; no meeting-places save the fashionable cafes or our own reception rooms. The police follow us - what can they discover? - nothing! What is there to discover? - nothing! Our lives are lived before the eyes of all Paris. There is never any suspicion of mystery about any of our movements. We have our hobbies, and we indulge in them. Monsieur the Marquis de Sogrange here is a great sportsman. Monsieur le Comte owns many racehorses. I myself am an authority on pictures, and own a collection which I have bequeathed to the State. Paris knows us well as men of fashion and mark - Paris does not guess that we have perfected an organization so wonderful that the whole criminal world pays toll to us."

"Dear me," Peter Ruff said, "this is very interesting!"

"We have a trained army at our disposal," Monsieur de Founcelles continued, "who numerically, as well as in intelligence, outnumber the whole force of gendarmes in Paris. No criminal from any other country can settle down here and hope for success, unless he joins us. An exploit which is inspired by us cannot fail. Our agents may count on our protection, and receive it without question."

"I am bewildered," Peter Ruff said, frankly. "I do not understand how you gentlemen - whom one knows by name so well as patrons of sport and society, can spare the time for affairs of such importance."

Monsieur de Founcelles nodded.

"We have very valuable aid," he said. "There is below us - the 'Double-Four'- the eight gentlemen now present, an executive council composed of five of the shrewdest men in France. They take their orders from us. We plan, and they obey. We have imagination, and special sources of knowledge. They have the most perfect machinery for carrying out our schemes that it is possible to imagine. I do not wish to boast, Mr. Ruff, but if I take a directory of Paris and place after any man's name, whatever his standing or estate, a black cross, that man dies before seven days have passed. You buy your evening paper - a man has committed suicide! You read of a letter found by his side: an unfortunate love affair - a tale of jealousy or reckless speculation. Mr. Ruff, the majority of these explanations are false. They are invented and arranged for by us. This year alone, five men in Paris, of position, have been found dead, and accounted, for excellent reasons, suicides. In each one of these cases, Monsieur Ruff, although not a soul has a suspicion of it, the removal of these men was arranged for by the' Double-Four.'"

"I trust," Peter Ruff said, "that it may never be my ill-fortune to incur the displeasure of so marvelous an association."

"On the contrary, Monsieur Ruff," the other answered, "the attention of the association has been directed towards certain incidents of your career in a most favorable manner. We have spoken of you often lately, Mr. Ruff, between ourselves. We arrive now at the object for which we begged the honor of your visit. It is to offer you the Presidency of our Executive Council."

Peter Ruff had thought of many things, but he had not thought of this! He gasped, recovered himself, and realized at once the dangers of the position in which he stood.

"The Council of Five!" he said thoughtfully.

"Precisely," Monsieur de Founcelles replied. "The salary - forgive me for giving such prominence to a matter which you doubtless consider of secondary importance - is ten thousand pounds a year, with a residence here and in London - also servants."

"It is princely!" Peter Ruff declared. "I cannot imagine, Monsieur, how you could have believed me capable of filling such a position."

"There is not much about you, Mr. Ruff, which we do not know," Monsieur de Founcelles answered. "There are points about your career which we have marked with admiration. Your work over here was rapid and comprehensive. We know all about your checkmating the Count von Hern and the Comtesse de Pilitz. We have appealed to you for aid once only - your response was prompt and brilliant. You have all the qualifications we desire. You are still young, physically you are sound, you speak all languages, and you are unmarried."

"I am what?" Peter Ruff asked, with a start.

"A bachelor," Monsieur de Founcelles answered. "We who have made crime and its detection a life-long study, have reduced many matters concerning it to almost mathematical exactitude. Of one thing we have become absolutely convinced - it is that the great majority of cases in which the police triumph are due to the treachery of women. The criminal who steers clear of the other sex escapes a greater danger than the detectives who dog his heels. It is for that reason that we choose only unmarried men for our executive council."

Peter Ruff made a gesture of despair. "And I am to be married in a month!" he exclaimed.

There was a murmur of dismay. If those other seven men had not once intervened, it was because the conduct of the affair had been voted into the hands of Monsieur de Founcelles, and there was little which he had left unsaid. Nevertheless, they

E. Phillips Oppenheim

had formed a little circle around the two men. Every word passing between them had been listened to eagerly. Gestures and murmured exclamations had been frequent enough. There arose now a chorus of voices which their leader had some difficulty in silencing.

"It must be arranged!"

"But it is impossible - this!"

"Monsieur Ruff amuses himself with us!"

"Gentlemen," Peter Ruff said, "I can assure you that I do nothing of the sort. The affair was arranged some months ago, and the young lady is even now in Paris, purchasing her trousseau."

Monsieur de Founcelles, with a wave of the hand, commanded silence. There was probably a way out. In any case, one must be found.

"Monsieur Ruff," he said, "putting aside, for one moment, your sense of honor, which of course forbids you even to consider the possibility of breaking your word - supposing that the young lady herself should withdraw -"

"You don't know Miss Brown!" Peter Ruff interrupted. "It is a pleasure to which I hope to attain," Monsieur de Founcelles declared, smoothly. "Let us consider once more my proposition. I take it for granted that, apart from this threatened complication, you find it agreeable?"

"I am deeply honored by it," Peter Ruff declared.

"Well, that being so," Monsieur de Founcelles said, more cheerfully, "we must see whether we cannot help you. Tell me, who is this fortunate young lady - this Miss Brown?"

"She is a young person of good birth and some means," Peter

Ruff declared. "She is, in a small way, an actress; she has also been my secretary from the first." Monsieur de Founcelles nodded his head thoughtfully.

"Ah!" he said. "She knows your secrets, then, I presume?"

"She does," Peter Ruff assented. "She knows a great deal!"

"A young person to be conciliated by all means," Monsieur de Founcelles declared. "Well, we must see. When, Monsieur Ruff, may I have the opportunity of making the acquaintance of this young lady?"

"To-morrow morning, or rather this morning, if you will," Peter Ruff answered. "We are taking breakfast together at the cafe de Paris. It will give me great pleasure if you will join us."

"On the contrary," Monsieur de Founcelles declared, "I must beg of you slightly to alter your plans. I will ask you and Mademoiselle to do me the honor of breakfasting at the Ritz with the Marquis de Sogrange and myself, at the same hour. We shall find there more opportunity for a short discussion."

"I am entirely at your service," Peter Ruff answered. There were signs now of a breaking-up of the little party.

"We must all regret, dear Monsieur Ruff," Monsieur de Founcelles said, as he made his adieux, "this temporary obstruction to the consummation of our hopes. Let us pray that Mademoiselle will not be unreasonable."

"You are very kind," Peter Ruff murmured.

Peter Ruff drove through the gray dawn to his hotel, in the splendid automobile of Monsieur de Founcelles, whose homeward route lay in that direction. It was four o'clock when he accepted his key from a sleepy-looking clerk, and turned towards the staircase. The hotel was wrapped in semi-gloom. Sweepers and cleaners were at work. The palms had been turned out into the courtyard. Dust sheets lay over the furniture. One person only, save himself and the untidy-looking servants, was astir. From a distant corner which commanded the entrance, he saw Violet stealing away to the corridor which led to her part of the hotel. She had sat there all through the night to see him come in - to be assured of his safety! Peter Ruff stared after her disappearing figure as one might have watched a ghost.

The luncheon-party was a great success. Peter Ruff was human enough to be proud of his companion - proud of her smartness, which was indubitable even here, surrounded as they were by Frenchwomen of the best class; proud of her accent, of the admiration which she obviously excited in the two Frenchmen. His earlier enjoyment of the meal was a little clouded from the fact that he felt himself utterly outshone in the matter of general appearance. No tailor had ever suggested to him a coat so daring and yet so perfect as that which adorned the person of the Marquis de Sogrange. The deep violet of his tie was a shade unknown in Bond Street - inimitable - a true education in color. They had the bearing, too, these Frenchmen! He watched Monsieur de Founcelles bending over Violet, and he was suddenly conscious of a wholly new sensation. He did not recognize - could not even classify it. He only knew that it was not altogether pleasant, and that it set the warm blood tingling through his veins.

It was not until they were sitting out in the winter garden, taking their coffee and liqueurs, that the object of their meeting was referred to. Then Monsieur de Founcelles drew Violet a little away from the others, and the Marquis, with a meaning smile, took Peter Ruff's arm and led him on one side. Monsieur de Founcelles wasted no words at all.

"Mademoiselle," he said, "Monsieur Ruff has doubtless told you that last night I made him the offer of a great position among us."

She looked at him with twinkling eyes.

"Go on, please," she said.

"I offered him a position of great dignity - of great responsibility," Monsieur de Founcelles continued. "I cannot explain to you its exact nature, but it is in connection with the most wonderful organization of its sort which the world has ever known."

"The 'Double-Four,'" she murmured.

"Attached to the post is a princely salary and but one condition," Monsieur de Founcelles said, watching the girl's face. "The condition is that Mr. Ruff remains a bachelor."

Violet nodded.

"Peter's told me all this," she remarked. "He wants me to give him up."

Monsieur de Founcelles drew a little closer to his companion. There was a peculiar smile upon his lips.

"My dear young lady," he said softly, "forgive me if I point out to you that with your appearance and gifts a marriage with our excellent friend is surely not the summit of your ambitions! Here in Paris, I promise you, here - we can do much better than that for you. You have not, perhaps, a dot? Good! That is our affair. Give up our friend here, and we deposit in any bank you like to name the sum of two hundred and fifty thousand francs."

"Two hundred and fifty thousand francs!" Violet repeated, slowly.

Monsieur de Founcelles nodded.

"It is enough?" he asked.

She shook her head.

E. Phillips Oppenheim

"It is not enough," she answered.

Monsieur de Founcelles raised his eyebrows.

"We do not bargain," he said coldly, and money is not the chief thing in the world. It is for you, then, to name a sum."

"Monsieur de Founcelles," she said, "can you tell me the amount of the national debt of France?"

"Somewhere about nine hundred million francs, I believe," he answered.

She nodded.

"That is exactly my price," she declared.

"For giving up Peter Ruff?" he gasped.

She looked at her employer thoughtfully.

"He doesn't look worth it, does he?" she said, with a queer little smile. "I happen to care for him, though - that's all."

Monsieur de Founcelles shrugged his shoulders. He knew men and women, and for the present he accepted defeat. He sighed heavily,

"I congratulate our friend, and I envy him," he said. "If ever you should change your mind, Mademoiselle -"

"It is our privilege, isn't it?" she remarked, with a brilliant smile. "If I do, I shall certainly let you know."

On the way home, Peter Ruff was genial - Miss Brown silent. He had escaped from a difficult position, and his sense of gratitude toward his companion was strong. He showed her many little attentions on the voyage which sometimes escaped him. From Dover, they had a carriage to themselves.

"Peter," Miss Brown said, after he had made her comfortable, "when is it to be?"

"When is what to be?" he asked, puzzled.

"Our marriage," she answered, looking at him for a moment in most bewildering fashion and then suddenly dropping her eyes.

Peter Ruff returned her gaze in blank amazement.

"What do you mean, Violet?" he exclaimed.

"Just what I say," she answered, composedly. "When are we going to be married?"

Peter Ruff frowned.

"What nonsense!" he said. "We are not going to be married. You know that quite well."

"Oh, no, I don't!" she declared, smiling at him in a heavenly fashion. "At your request I have told Monsieur de Founcelles that we were engaged. Incidentally, I have refused two hundred and fifty thousand francs and, I believe, an admirer, for your sake. I declared that I was going to marry you, and I must keep my word."

Peter Ruff began to feel giddy.

"Look here, Violet," he said, "you know very well that we arranged all that between ourselves."

"Arranged all that?" she repeated, with a little laugh. "Perhaps we did. You asked me to marry you, and you posed as my fiancee. You kept it up just as long as you - it suits me to keep it up a little longer."

"Do you mean to say - do you seriously mean that you expect

me to marry you?" he asked, aghast.

"I do," she admitted. "I have meant you to for some time, Peter!"

She was very alluring, and Peter Ruff hesitated. She held out her hands and leaned towards him. Her muff fell to the floor. She had raised her veil, and a faint perfume of violets stole into the carriage. Her lips were a little parted, her eyes were saying unutterable things.

"You don't want me to sue you, do you, Peter?" she murmured.

Peter Ruff sighed - and yielded.

CHAPTER X

WONDERFUL JOHN DORY

The woman who had been Peter Ruff's first love had fallen upon evil days. Her prettiness was on the wane - powder and rouge, late hours, and excesses of many kinds, had played havoc with it, even in these few months. Her clothes were showy but cheap. Her boots themselves, unclean and down at heel, told the story. She stood upon the threshold of Peter Ruff's office, and looked half defiantly, half doubtfully at Violet, who was its sole occupant.

"Can I do anything for you?" the latter asked, noticing the woman's hesitation.

"I want to see Mr. Ruff," the visitor said.

"Mr. Ruff is out at present," Violet answered.

"When will he be in?"

"I cannot tell you," Violet said. "Perhaps you had better leave a message. Or will you call again? Mr. Ruff is very uncertain in his movements."

Maud sank into a chair.

"I'll wait," she declared.

"I am not sure," Violet remarked, raising her eyebrows, "whether that will be convenient. There may be other clients in. Mr. Ruff himself may not be back for several hours."

"Are you his secretary?" Maud asked, without moving.

"I am his secretary and also his wife," Violet declared. The woman raised herself a little in her chair.

"Some people have all the luck," she muttered. "It's only a few months ago that Mr. Ruff was glad enough to take me out. You remember when I used to come here?"

"I remember," Violet assented.

"I was all right then," the woman continued, "and now - now I'm down and out," she added, with a little sob. "You see what I am like. You look as though you didn't care to have me in the office, and I don't wonder at it. You look as though you were afraid I'd come to beg, and you are right - I have come to beg."

"I am sure Mr. Ruff will do what he can for you," Violet said, "although -"

"I see you know all about it," Maud interrupted, with a hard little laugh. "I came once to wheedle information out of him. I came to try and betray the only man who ever really cared for me. Mr. Ruff was too clever, and I am thankful for it. I have been as big a fool as a woman can be, but I am paying - oh, I am paying for it right enough!"

She swayed in her chair, and Violet was only just in time to catch her. She led the fainting woman to an inner room, made her comfortable upon a sofa, and sent out for some food and a bottle of wine. Down in the street below, John Dory, who had tracked his wife to the building, was walking away with face as black as night. He knew that Maud had lost her position, that she was in need of money - almost penniless. He had waited to see to whom she would turn, hoping - poor fool as he called himself - that she would come back to him. And it was his enemy to whom she had gone! He had seen her enter the building; he knew that she had not left it. In the morning they brought him another report - she was still within. It was the end, this, he told himself! There must be a settlement between him and Peter Ruff!

Mr. John Dory, who had arrived at Clenarvon Court in a four-wheel cab from the nearest railway station, was ushered by the butler to the door of one of the rooms on the ground floor, overlooking the Park. A policeman was there on guard - a policeman by his attitude and salute, although he was in plain clothes. John Dory nodded, and turned to the butler.

"You see, the man knows me," he said. "Here is my card. I am John Dory from Scotland Yard. I want to have a few words with the sergeant."

The butler hesitated.

"Our orders are very strict, sir," he said. "I am afraid that I cannot allow you to enter the room without a special permit from his lordship. You see, we have had no advice of your coming."

John Dory nodded.

"Quite right," he answered. "If every one were to obey his orders as literally, there would be fewer robberies. However, you see that this man recognizes me."

The butler turned toward an elderly gentleman in a pink coat and riding-breeches, who had just descended into the hall.

"His lordship is here," he said. "He will give you permission, without a doubt. There is a gentleman from Scotland Yard, your lordship," he explained, "who wishes to enter the morning-room to speak with the sergeant."

E. Phillips Oppenheim

"Inspector John Dory, at your lordship's service," saluting. "I have been sent down from town to help in this little business."

Lord Clenarvon smiled.

"I should have thought that, under the circumstances," he said, "two of you would have been enough. Still, it is not for me to complain. Pray go in and speak to the sergeant. You will find him inside. Rather dull work for him, I'm afraid, and quite unnecessary."

"I am not so sure, your lordship," Dory answered. "The Clenarvon diamonds are known all over the world, and I suppose there isn't a thieves' den in Europe that does not know that they will remain here exposed with your daughter's other wedding presents."

Lord Clenarvon smiled once more and shrugged his shoulders. He was a man who had unbounded faith in his fellow-creatures.

"I suppose," he said, "it is the penalty one has to pay for historical possessions. Go in and talk to the sergeant, by all means, Mr. Dory. I hope that Graves will succeed in making you comfortable during your stay here."

John Dory was accordingly admitted into the room which was so jealously guarded. At first sight, it possessed a somewhat singular appearance. The windows had every one of them been boarded up, and the electric lights consequently fully turned on. A long table stood in the middle of the apartment, serving as support for a long glass showcase, open at the top. Within this, from end to end, stretched the presents which a large circle of acquaintances were presenting to one of the most popular young women in society, on the occasion of her approaching marriage to the Duke of Rochester. In the middle, the wonderful Clenarvon diamonds, set in the form of a tiara, flashed strange lights into the somberly lit apartment. At the end of the table a police sergeant was sitting, with a little pile of newspapers and illustrated journals before him. He rose to his feet with alacrity at his superior's entrance.

"Good morning, Saunders," John Dory said. "I see you've got it pretty snug in here."

"Pretty well, thank you, sir," Saunders answered. "Is there anything stirring?"

John Dory looked behind to be sure that the door was closed. Then he stopped for a moment to gaze at the wonderful diamonds, and finally sat on the table by his subordinate's side.

"Not exactly that, Saunders," he said. "To tell you the truth, I came down here because of that list of guests you sent me up."

Saunders smiled.

"I think I can guess the name you singled out, sir," he said.

"It was Peter Ruff, of course," Dory said. "What is he doing here in the house, under his own name, and as a guest?"

"I have asked no questions, sir," Saunders answered. "I under-lined the name in case it might seem worth your while to make inquiries."

John Dory nodded.

"Nothing has happened, of course?" he asked.

"Nothing," Saunders answered. "You see, with the windows all boarded up, there is practically only the ordinary door to guard, so we feel fairly secure."

"No one hanging about?" the detective asked. "Mr. Ruff himself, for instance, hasn't been trying to make your acquaintance?"

"No sign of it, sir," the man answered. "I saw him pass through the hall yesterday afternoon, as I went off duty, and he was in riding clothes all splashed with mud. I think he has been hunting every day."

John Dory muttered something between his lips, and turned on his heel.

"How many men have you here, Saunders?" he asked.

"Only two, sir, beside myself," the man replied.

The detective went round the boarded windows, examining the work carefully until he reached the door.

"I am going to see if I can have a word with his lordship," he said.

He caught Lord Clenarvon in the act of mounting his horse in the great courtyard.

"What is it, Mr. Dory?" the Earl asked, stooping down.

"There is one name, your lordship, among your list of guests, concerning which I wish to have a word with you," the detective said - "the name of Mr. Peter Ruff."

"Don't know anything about him," Lord Clenarvon answered, cheerfully. "You must see my daughter, Lady Mary. It was she who sent him his invitation. Seems a decent little fellow, and rides as well as the best. You'll find Lady Mary about somewhere, if you'd like to ask her."

Lord Clenarvon hurried off, with a little farewell wave of his crop, and John Dory returned into the house to make inquiries respecting Lady Mary. In a very few minutes he was shown into her presence. She smiled at him cheerfully.

"Another detective!" she exclaimed. "I am sure I ought to feel quite safe now. What can I do for you, Mr. Dory?"

"I have had a list of the guests sent to me," Dory answered, "in which I notice the name of Mr. Peter Ruff."

Lady Mary nodded.

"Well?" she asked.

"I have just spoken to his lordship," the detective continued, "and he referred me to you."

"Do you want to know all about Mr. Ruff?" Lady Mary asked, smiling.

"If your ladyship will pardon my saying so, I think that neither you nor any one else could tell me that. What I wished to say was that I understood that we at Scotland Yard were placed in charge of your jewels until after the wedding. Mr. Peter Ruff is, as you may be aware, a private detective himself."

"I understand perfectly," Lady Mary said. "I can assure you, Mr. Dory, that Mr. Ruff is here entirely as a personal and very valued friend of my own. On two occasions he has rendered very signal service to my family - services which I am quite unable to requite."

"In that case, your ladyship, there is nothing more to be said. I conceive it, however, to be my duty to tell you that in our opinion - the opinion of Scotland Yard- there are things about the career of Mr. Peter Ruff which need explanation. He is a person whom we seldom let altogether out of our sight."

Lady Mary laughed frankly.

"My dear Mr. Dory," she said, "this is one of the cases, then, in which I can assure you that I know more than Scotland Yard. There is no person in the world in whom I have more confidence, and with more reason, than Mr. Peter Ruff."

John Dory bowed.

"I thank your ladyship," he said. "I trust that your confidence will never be misplaced. May I ask one more question?"

"Certainly," Lady Mary replied, "so long as you make no insinuations whatever against my friend."

"I should be very sorry to do so," John Dory declared. "I simplywish to know whether Mr. Ruff has any instructions from you with reference to the care of your jewels?"

"Certainly not," Lady Mary replied, decidedly. "Mr. Ruff is here entirely as my guest. He has been in the room with the rest of us, to look at them, and it was he, by the bye, who discovered a much more satisfactory way of boarding the windows. Anything else, Mr. Dory?"

"I thank your ladyship, nothing!" the detective answered. "With your permission, I propose to remain here until after the ceremony."

"Just as you like, of course," Lady Mary said. "I hope you will be comfortable."

John Dory bowed, and returned to confer with his sergeant. Afterwards, finding the morning still fine, he took his hat and went for a walk in the park.

As a matter of fact, this, in some respects the most remarkable of the adventures which had ever befallen Mr. Peter Ruff, came to him by accident. Lady Mary had read the announcement of his marriage in the paper, had driven at once to his office with a magnificent present, and insisted upon his coming with his wife to the party which was assembling at Clenarvon Court in honor of her own approaching wedding. Peter Ruff had taken few holidays of late years, and for several days had thoroughly enjoyed himself. The matter of the Clenarvon jewels he considered, perhaps, with a slight professional interest; but so far as he could see, the precautions for guarding them were so adequate that the subject did not remain in his memory. He had, however, a very distinct and disagreeable shock when, on the night of John Dory's appearance, he recognized among a few newly-arrived guests the Marquis de Sogrange. He took the opportunity, as soon as possible, of withdrawing his wife from a little circle among whom they had been talking, to a more retired corner of the room. She saw at once that something had happened to disturb him.

"Violet," he said, "don't look behind now -"

"I recognized him at once," she interrupted. "It is the Marquis de Sogrange."

Peter Ruff nodded.

"It will be best for you," he said, "not to notice him. Of course, his presence here may be accidental. He has a perfect right to enter any society he chooses. At the same time, I am uneasy."

She understood in a moment.

"The Clenarvon diamonds!" she whispered. He nodded.

"It is just the sort of affair which would appeal to the 'Double-Four,'" he said. "They are worth anything up to a quarter of a million, and it is an enterprise which could scarcely be attempted except by some one in a peculiar position. Violet, if I were not sure that he had seen me, I should leave the house this minute."

"Why?" she asked, wonderingly.

"Don't you understand," Peter Ruff continued, softly, "that I myself am still what they call a corresponding member of the 'Double-Four,' and they have a right to appeal to me for help in this country, as I have a right to appeal to them for help or information in France? We have both made use of one another, to some extent. No doubt, if the Marquis has any scheme in his mind, he would look upon me as a valuable ally."

She turned slowly pale.

"Peter," she said, "you wouldn't dream - you wouldn't dare to be so foolish?"

He shook his head firmly.

"My dear girl," he said, "we talked that all out long ago. A few years since, I felt that I had been treated badly, that I was an alien, and that the hand of the law was against me. I talked wildly then, perhaps. When I put up my sign and sat down for clients, I meant to cheat the law, if I could. Things have changed, Violet. I want nothing of that sort. I have kept my hands clean and I mean to do so. Why, years ago," he continued, "when I was feeling at my wildest, these very jewels were within my grasp one foggy night, and I never touched them."

"What would happen if you refused to help?"

"I do not know," Peter Ruff answered. "The conditions are a little severe. But, after all, there are no hard and fast rules. It rests with the Marquis himself to shrug his shoulders and appreciate my position. Perhaps he may not even exchange a word with me. Here is Lord Sotherst coming to talk to you, and Captain Hamilton is waiting for me to tell him an address. Remember, don't recognize Sogrange."

Dinner that night was an unusually cheerful meal. Peter Ruff, who was an excellent raconteur, told many stories. The Marquis de Sogrange was perhaps the next successful in his efforts to entertain his neighbors. Violet found him upon her left hand, and although he showed not the slightest signs of having ever seen her before, they were very soon excellent friends. After dinner, Sogrange and Peter Ruff drifted together on their way to the billiard-room. Sogrange, however, continued to talk courteously of trifles until, having decided to watch the first game, they found themselves alone on the leather divan surrounding the room.

"This is an unexpected pleasure, my friend," Sogrange said, watching the ash of his cigar. "Professional?"

Peter Ruff shook his head. "Not in the least," he answered. "I have had the good fortune to render Lady Mary and her brother, at different times, services which they are pleased to value highly. We are here as ordinary guests - my wife and I." The Marquis sighed.

"Ah, that wife of yours, Ruff," he said. "She is charming, I admit, and you are a lucky man; but it was a price - a very great price to pay."

"You, perhaps, are ambitious, Marquis," Peter Ruff answered. "I have not done so badly. A little contents me."

Sogrange looked at him as though he were some strange creature.

"I see!" he murmured. "I see! With you, of course, the commercial side comes uppermost. Mr. Ruff, what do you suppose the income from my estate amounts to?" Peter Ruff shook his head. He did not even know that the Marquis was possessed of estates!

"Somewhere about seven millions of francs," Sogrange declared. "There are few men in Paris more extravagant than I, and I think that we Frenchmen know what extravagance means. But I cannot spend my income. Do you think that it is for the sake of gain that I have come across the Channel to add the Clenarvon diamonds to our coffers?"

Peter Ruff sat very still.

E. Phillips Oppenheim

"You mean that?" he said.

"Of course!" Sogrange answered. "Didn't you realize it directly you saw me? What is there, do you think, in a dull English house-party to attract a man like myself? Don't you understand that it is the gambler's instinct - the restless desire to be playing pitch-and-toss with fate, with honor, with life and death, if you will - that brings such as myself into the ranks of the 'Double-Four'? It is the weariness which kills, Peter Ruff. One must needs keep it from one's bones."

"Marquis," Peter Ruff answered, "I do not profess to understand you. I am not weary of life, in fact I love it. I am looking forward to the years when I have enough money - and it seems as though that time is not far off - when I can buy a little place in the country, and hunt a little and shoot a little, and live a simple out-of-door life. You see, Marquis, we are as far removed as the poles."

"Obviously!" Sogrange answered.

"Your confidence," Peter Ruff continued, "the confidence with which you have honored me, inspires me to make you one request. I am here, indeed, as a friend of the family. You will not ask me to help in any designs you may have against the Clenarvon jewels?"

Sogrange leaned back in his chair and laughed softly. His lips, when they parted from his white teeth, resolved themselves into lines which at that moment seemed to Peter Ruff more menacing than mirthful. Sogrange was, in many ways, a man of remarkable appearance.

"Oh, Peter Ruff," he said, "you are a bourgeois little person! You should have been the burgomaster in a little German town, or a French mayor with a chain about your neck. We will see. I make no promises. All that I insist upon, for the present, is that you do not leave this house-party without advising me - that is to say, if you are really looking forward to that pleasant life in the country, where you will hunt a little and shoot a little, and grow into the likeness of a vegetable. You, with your charming wife! Peter Ruff, you should be ashamed to talk like that! Come, I must play bridge with the Countess. I am engaged for a table."

The two men parted. Peter Ruff was uneasy. On his way from the room, Lord Sotherst insisted upon his joining a pool.

"Charming fellow, Sogrange," the latter remarked, as he chalked his cue. "He has been a great friend of the governor's - he and his father before him. Our families have intermarried once or twice."

"He seems very agreeable," Peter Ruff answered, devoting himself to the game.

The following night, being the last but one before the wedding itself, a large dinner-party had been arranged for, and the resources of even so princely a mansion as Clenarvon Court were strained to their utmost by the entertainment of something like one hundred guests in the great banqueting-hall. The meal was about half-way through when those who were not too entirely engrossed in conversation were startled by hearing a dull, rumbling sound, like the moving of a number of pieces of heavy furniture. People looked doubtfully at one another. Peter Ruff and the Marquis de Sogrange were among the first to spring to their feet.

"It's an explosion somewhere," the latter cried. "Sounds close at hand, too."

They made their way out into the hall. Exactly opposite now was the room in which the wedding presents had been placed, and where for days nothing had been seen but a closed door and a man on duty outside. The door now stood wide open, and in place of the single electric light which was left burning through the evening, the place seemed almost aflame.

E. Phillips Oppenheim

Ruff, Sogrange and Lord Sotherst were the first three to cross the threshold. They were met by a rush of cold wind. Opposite to them, two of the windows, with their boardings, had been blown away. Sergeant Saunders was still sitting in his usual place at the end of the table, his head bent upon his folded arms. The man who had been on duty outside was standing over him, white with horror. Far away in the distance, down the park, one could faintly hear the throbbing of an engine, and Peter Ruff, through the chasm, saw the lights of a great motor-car flashing in and out amongst the trees. The room itself - the whole glittering array of presents - seemed untouched. Only the great center-piece - the Clenarvon diamonds - had gone. Even as they stood there, the rest of the guests crowding into the open door, John Dory tore through, his face white with excitement. Peter Ruff's calm voice penetrated the din of tongues.

"Lord Sotherst," he said, "you have telephones in the keepers' lodges. There is a motor-car being driven southwards at full speed. Telephone down, and have your gates secured. Dory, I should keep every one out of the room. Some one must telephone for a doctor. I suppose your man has been hurt."

The guests were wild with curiosity, but Lord Clenarvon, with an insistent gesture, led the way back to the diningroom.

"Whatever has happened," he said, "the people who are in charge there know best how to deal with the situation. There is a detective from Scotland Yard and his subordinates, and a gentleman in whom I also have most implicit confidence. We will resume our dinner, if you please, ladies and gentlemen."

Unwillingly, the people were led away. John Dory was already in his great-coat, ready to spring into the powerful motor-car which had been ordered out from the garage. A doctor, who had been among the guests, was examining the man Saunders, who sat in that still, unnatural position at the head of the table.

"The poor fellow has been shot in the back of the head with

some peculiar implement," he said. "The bullet is very long - almost like a needle - and it seems to have penetrated very nearly to the base of the brain."

"Is he dead?" Peter Ruff asked.

The doctor shook his head.

"No!" he answered. "An inch higher up and he must have died at once. I want some of the men-servants to help me carry him to a bedroom, and plenty of hot water. Some one else must go for my instrument case."

Lord Sotherst took these things in charge, and John Dory turned to the man whom they had found standing over him.

"Tell us exactly what happened," he said, briefly.

"I was standing outside the door," the man answered. "I heard no sound inside - there was nothing to excite suspicion in any way. Suddenly there was this explosion. It took me, perhaps, thirty or forty seconds to get the key out of my pocket and unlock the door. When I entered, the side of the room was blown in like that, the diamonds were gone, Saunders was leaning forward just in the position he is in now, and there wasn't another soul in sight. Then you and the others came."

John Dory rushed from the room; they had brought him word that the car was waiting. At such a moment, he was ready even to forget his ancient enmity. He turned towards Peter Ruff, whose calm bearing somehow or other impressed even the detective with a sense of power.

"Will you come along?" he asked.

Peter Ruff shook his head.

"Thank you, Dory, no!" he said. "I am glad you have asked me, but I think you had better go alone."

A few seconds later, the pursuit was started. Saunders was carried out of the room, followed by the doctor. There remained only Peter Ruff and the man who had been on duty outside. Peter Ruff seated himself where Saunders had been sitting, and seemed to be closely examining the table all round for some moments. Once he took up something from between the pages of the book which the Sergeant had apparently been reading, and put it carefully into his own pocketbook. Then he leaned back in the chair, with his hands clasped behind his head and his eyes fixed upon the ceiling, as though thinking intently.

"Hastings," he said to the policeman, who all the time was pursuing a stream of garrulous, inconsequent remarks, "I wonder whether you'd step outside and see Mr. Richards, the butler. Ask him if he would be so good as to spare me a moment."

"I'll do it, sir," the man answered, with one more glance through the open space. "Lord!" he added, "they must have been in through there and out again like cats!"

"It was quick work, certainly," Peter Ruff answered, genially, "but then, an enterprise like this would, of course, only be attempted by experts."

Peter Ruff was not left alone long. Mr. Richards came hurrying in.

"This is a terrible business, sir!" he said. "His lordship has excused me from superintending the service of the dinner. Anything that I can do for you I am to give my whole attention to. These were my orders."

"Very good of you, Richards," Peter Ruff answered, "very thoughtful of his lordship. In the first place, then, I think, we will have the rest of this jewelry packed in cases at once. Not that anything further is likely to happen," he continued, "but still, it would be just as well out of the way. I will remain here and superintend this, if you will send a couple of careful servants. In the meantime, I want you to do something else for me."

"Certainly, sir," the man answered.

"I want a plan of the house," Peter Ruff said, "with the names of the guests who occupy this wing."

The butler nodded gravely.

"I can supply you with it very shortly, sir," he said. "There is no difficulty at all about the plan, as I have several in my room; but it will take me some minutes to pencil in the names."

Peter Ruff nodded.

"I will superintend things here until you return," he said.

"It is to be hoped, sir," the man said, as he retreated, "that the gentleman from Scotland Yard will catch the thieves. After all, they hadn't more than ten minutes' start, and our Daimler is a flyer."

"I'm sure I hope so," Peter Ruff answered, heartily.

But, alas! no such fortune was in store for Mr. John Dory. At daybreak he returned in a borrowed trap from a neighboring railway station.

"Our tires had been cut," he said, in reply to a storm of questions. "They began to go, one after the other, as soon as we had any speed on. We traced the car to Salisbury, and there isn't a village within forty miles that isn't looking out for it."

Peter Ruff, who had just returned from an early morning walk, nodded sympathetically.

E. Phillips Oppenheim

"Shall you be here all day, Mr. Dory?" he asked. "There's just a word or two I should like to have with you."

Dory turned away. He had forced himself, in the excitement of the moment, to speak to his ancient enemy, but in this hour of his humility the man's presence was distasteful to him.

"I am not sure," he said, shortly. "It depends on how things may turn out."

The daily life at Clenarvon Court proceeded exactly as usual. Breakfast was served early, as there was to be big day's shoot. The Marquis de Sogrange and Peter Ruff smoked their cigarettes together afterwards in the great hall. Then it was that Peter Ruff took the plunge.

"Marquis," he said, "I should like to know exactly how I stand with you - the 'Double-Four,' that is to say - supposing I range myself for an hour or so on the side of the law?"

Sogrange smiled.

"You amuse yourself, Mr. Ruff," he remarked genially.

"Not in the least," Peter Ruff answered. "I am serious."

Sogrange watched the blue cigarette smoke come down his nose.

"My dear friend," he said, "I am no amateur at this game. When I choose to play it, I am not afraid of Scotland Yard. I am not afraid," he concluded, with a little bow, "even of you!"

"Do you ever bet, Marquis?" Peter Ruff asked.

"Twenty-five thousand francs," Sogrange said, smiling, "that your efforts to aid Mr. John Dory are unavailing."

Peter Ruff entered the amount in his pocketbook. "It is a

bargain," he declared. "Our bet, I presume, carries immunity for me?"

"By all means," Sogrange answered, with a little bow.

The Marquis beckoned to Lord Sotherst, who was crossing the hall.

"My dear fellow," he said, "do tell me the name of your hatter in London. Delions failed me at the last moment, and I have not a hat fit for the ceremony to-morrow."

"I'll lend you half-a-dozen, if you can wear them," Lord Sotherst answered, smiling. "The governor's sure to have plenty, too."

Sogrange touched his head with a smile.

"Alas!" he said. "My head is small, even for a Frenchman's. Imagine me - otherwise, I trust, suitably attired - walking to the church to-morrow in a hat which came to my ears!"

Lord Sotherst laughed.

"Scotts will do you all right," he said. "You can telephone."

"I shall send my man up," Sogrange determined. "He can bring me back a selection. Tell me, at what hour is the first drive this morning, and are the places drawn yet?"

"Come into the gun-room and we'll see," Lord Sotherst answered.

Peter Ruff made his way to the back quarters of the house. In a little sitting-room he found the man he sought, sitting alone. Peter Ruff closed the door behind him.

"John Dory," he said, "I have come to have a few words with you."

The detective rose to his feet. He was in no pleasant mood. Though the telephone wires had been flashing their news every few minutes, it seemed, indeed, as though the car which they had chased had vanished into space.

"What do you want to say to me?" he asked gruffly.

"I want, if I can," Peter Ruff said earnestly, "to do you a service."

Dory's eyes glittered.

"I think," he said, "that I can do without your services."

"Don't be foolish," Peter Ruff said. "You are harboring a grievance against me which is purely an imaginary one. Now listen to the facts. You employ your wife - which after all, Dory, I think, was not quite the straight thing - to try and track down a young man named Spencer Fitzgerald, who was formerly, in a small way, a client of mine. I find your wife an agreeable companion - we become friends. Then I discover her object, and know that I am being fooled. The end of that little episode you remember. But tell me why should you bear me ill-will for defending my friend and myself?"

The detective came slowly up to Peter Ruff. He took hold of the lapel of the other's coat with his left hand, and his right hand was clenched. But Peter Ruff did not falter.

"Listen to me," said Dory. "I will tell you what grudge I bear against you. It was your entertainment of my wife which gave her the taste for luxury and for gadding about. Mind, I don't blame you for that altogether, but there the fact remains. She left me. She went on the stage."

"Stop!" Peter Ruff said. "You must still hold me blameless. She wrote to me. I went out with her once. The only advice I gave her was to return to you. So far as I am concerned, I have treated her with the respect that I would have shown my own sister."

"You lie!" Dory cried, fiercely. "A month ago, I saw her come to your flat. I watched for hours. She did not leave it - she did not leave it all that night!"

"If you object to her visit," Peter Ruff said quietly, "it is my wife whom you must blame."

John Dory relaxed his hand and took a quick step backwards.

"Your wife?" he muttered.

"Exactly!" Peter Ruff answered. "Maud - Mrs. Dory - called to see me; she was ill - she had lost her situation - she was even, I believe, faint and hungry. I was not present. My wife talked to her and was sorry for her. While the two women were there together, your wife fainted. She was put to bed in our one spare room, and she has been shown every attention and care. Tell me, how long is it since you were at home?"

"Not for ten days," Dory answered, bitterly. "Why?"

"Because when you go back, you will find your wife there," Peter Ruff answered. "She has given up the stage. Her one desire is to settle down and repay you for the trouble she has caused you. You needn't believe me unless you like. Ask my wife. She is here. She will tell you."

Dory was overcome. He went back to his seat by the window, and he buried his face for a moment in his hands.

"Ruff," he said, "I don't deserve this. I've had bad times lately, though. Everything has gone against me. I think I have been a bit careless, with the troubles at home and that."

"Stop!" Peter Ruff insisted. "Now I come to the immediate object of my visit to you. You have had some bad luck at headquarters. I know of it. I am going to help you to reinstate yourself brilliantly. With that, let us shake hands and bury all the soreness that there may be between us."

John Dory stared at his visitor.

"Do you mean this?" he asked.

"I do," answered Peter. "Please do not think that I mean to make any reflection upon your skill. It is just a chance that I was able to see what you were not able to see. In an hour's time, you shall restore the Clenarvon diamonds to Lord Clenarvon. You shall take the reward which he has just offered, of a thousand pounds. And I promise you that the manner in which you shall recover the jewels shall be such that you will be famous for a long time to come."

"You are a wonderful man!" said Dory, hoarsely. "Do you mean, then, that the jewels were not with those men in the motor-car?"

"Of course not!" Peter Ruff answered. "But come along. The story will develop."

At half-past ten that morning, a motor-car turned out from the garage at Clenarvon Court, and made its way down the avenue. In it was a single passenger - the dark-faced Parisian valet of the Marquis de Sogrange. As the car left the avenue and struck into the main road, it was hailed by Peter Ruff and John Dory, who were walking together along the lane.

"Say, my man," Peter Ruff said, addressing the chauffeur, "are you going to the station?"

"Yes, sir!" the man answered. "I am taking down the Marquis de Sogrange's servant to catch the eleven o'clock train to town."

"You don't mind giving us a lift?" Peter Ruff asked, already opening the door.

"Certainly not, sir," the man answered, touching his hat.

Peter Ruff and John Dory stepped into the tonneau of the car. The man civilly lifted the hatbox from the seat, and made room for his enforced companions. Nevertheless, it was easy to see that he was not pleased.

"There's plenty of room here for three," Peter Ruff said, cheerfully, as they sat on either side of him. "Drive slowly, please, chauffeur. Now, Mr. Lemprise," Peter Ruff added, "we will trouble you to change places."

"What do you mean?" the man called out, suddenly pale as death.

He was held as though in a vice. John Dory's arm was through his on one side, and Peter Ruff's on the other. Apart from that, the muzzle of a revolver was pressed to his forehead.

"On second thoughts," Peter Ruff said, "I think we will keep you like this. Driver," he called out, "please return to the Court at once."

The man hesitated.

"You recognize the gentleman who is with me?" Peter Ruff said. "He is the detective from Scotland Yard. I have full authority from Lord Clenarvon over all his servants. Please do as I say."

The man hesitated no more. The car was backed and turned, the Frenchman struggling all the way like a wild cat. Once he tried to kick the hatbox into the road, but John Dory was too quick for him. So they drove up to the front door of the Court, to be welcomed with cries of astonishment from the whole of the shooting party, who were just starting. Foremost among them was Sogrange. They crowded around the car. Peter Ruff touched the hatbox with his foot.

"If we could trouble your Lordship," he said, "to open that hatbox, you will find something that will interest you. Mr. Dory has planned a little surprise for you, in which I have been permitted to help."

The women, who gathered that something was happening, came hastening out from the hall. They all crowded round Lord Clenarvon, who was cutting through the leather strap of the hatbox. Inside the silk hat which reposed there, were the Clenarvon diamonds. Monsieur le Marquis de Sogrange was one of the foremost to give vent to an exclamation of delight.

"Monsieur le Marquis," Peter Ruff said, "this should be a lesson to you, I hope, to have the characters of your servants more rigidly verified. Mr. Dory tells me that this man came into your employ at the last moment with a forged recommendation. He is, in effect, a dangerous thief."

"You amaze me!" Sogrange exclaimed.

"We are all interested in this affair," Peter Ruff said, "and my friend John Dory here is, perhaps, too modest properly to explain the matter. If you care to come with me, we can reconstruct, in a minute, the theft."

John Dory and Peter Ruff first of all handed over their captive, who was now calm and apparently resigned, to the two policemen who were still on duty in the Court. Afterwards, Peter Ruff led the way up one flight of stairs, and turned the handle of the door of an apartment exactly over the morning-room. It was the bedroom of the Marquis de Sogrange.

"Mr. Dory's chase in the motor-car," he said, "was, as you have doubtless gathered now, merely a blind. It was obvious to his intelligence that the blowing away of the window was merely a ruse to cover the real method of the theft. If you will allow me, I will show you how it was done."

The floor was of hardwood, covered with rugs. One of these,

near the fireplace, Peter Ruff brushed aside. The seventh square of hardwood from the mantelpiece had evidently been tampered with. With very little difficulty, he removed it.

"You see," he explained, "the ceiling of the room below is also of paneled wood. Having removed this, it is easy to lift the second one, especially as light screws have been driven in and string threaded about them. There is now a hole through which you can see into the room below. Has Dory returned? Ah, here he is!"

The detective came hurrying into the room, bearing in his hand a peculiar-shaped weapon, a handful of little darts like those which had been found in the wounded man's head, and an ordinary fishing-rod in a linen case.

"There is the weapon," Peter Ruff said, "which it was easy enough to fire from here upon the man who was leaning forward exactly below. Then here, you will see, is a somewhat peculiar instrument, which shows a great deal of ingenuity in its details."

He opened the linen case, which was, by the bye, secured by a padlock, and drew out what was, to all appearance, an ordinary fishing-rod, fitted at the end with something that looked like an iron hand. Peter Ruff dropped it through the hole until it reached the table, moved it backwards and forwards, and turned round with a smile.

"You see," he said, "the theft, after all, was very simple. Personally, I must admit that it took me a great deal by surprise, but my friend Mr. Dory has been on the right track from the first. I congratulate him most heartily."

Dory was a little overcome. Lady Mary shook him heartily by the hand, but as they trooped downstairs she stooped and whispered in Peter Ruff's ear.

E. Phillips Oppenheim

"I wonder how much of this was John Dory," she said, smiling.

Peter Ruff said nothing. The detective was already on the telephone, wiring his report to London. Every one was standing about in little knots, discussing this wonderful event. Sogrange sought Lord Clenarvon, and walked with him, arm in arm, down the stairs.

"I cannot tell you, Clenarvon," he said, "how sorry I am that I should have been the means of introducing a person like this to the house. I had the most excellent references from the Prince of Strelitz. No doubt they were forged. My own man was taken ill just before I left, and I had to bring some one."

"My dear Sogrange," Lord Clenarvon said, "don't think of it. What we must be thankful for is that we had so brilliant a detective in the house."

"As John Dory?" Sogrange remarked, with a smile. Lord Clenarvon nodded.

"Come," he said, "I don't see why we should lose a day's sport because the diamonds have been recovered. I always felt that they would turn up again some day or other. You are keen, I know, Sogrange."

"Rather!" the Marquis answered. "But excuse me for one moment. There is Mrs. Ruff looking charming there in the corner. I must have just a word with her."

He crossed the room and bowed before Violet.

"My dear lady," he said, "I have come to congratulate you. You have a clever husband - a little cleverer, even, than I thought. I have just had the misfortune to lose to him a bet of twenty-five thousand francs."

Violet smiled, a little uneasily.

"Peter doesn't gamble as a rule," she remarked.

Sogrange sighed.

"This, alas, was no gamble!" he said. "He was betting upon certainties, but he won. Will you tell him from me, when you see him, that although I have not the money in my pocket at the moment, I shall pay my debts. Tell him that we are as careful to do that in France as we are to keep our word!"

He bowed, and passed out with the shooting-party on to the terrace. Peter Ruff came up, a few minutes later, and his wife gave him the message.

"I did that man an injustice," Peter Ruff said with a sigh of relief. "I can't explain now, dear. I'll tell you all about it later in the day."

"There's nothing wrong, is there?" she asked him, pleadingly.

"On the contrary," Peter Ruff declared, "everything is right. I have made friends with Dory, and I have won a thousand pounds. When we leave here, I am going to look out for that little estate in the country. If you come out with the lunch, dear, I want you to watch that man Hamilton's coat. It's exactly what I should like to wear myself at my own shooting parties. See if you can make a sketch of it when he isn't looking."

Violet laughed.

"I'll try," she promised.

BOOK TWO

CHAPTER I

RECALLED BY THE DOUBLE-FOUR

It is the desire of Madame that you should join our circle here on Thursday evening next at ten o'clock.

The man looked up from the sheet of note-paper which he held in his hand, and gazed through the open French-windows before which he was standing. It was a very pleasant and very peaceful prospect. There was his croquet lawn, smooth-shaven, the hoops neatly arranged, the chalk-mark firm and distinct upon the boundary. Beyond, the tennis court, the flower gardens, and, to the left, the walled fruit garden. A little farther away was the paddock and orchard, and a little farther still, the farm, which for the last four years had been the joy of his life. His meadows were yellow with buttercups; a thin line of willows showed where the brook wound its lazy way through the bottom fields. It was a home, this, in which a man could well lead a peaceful life, could dream away his days to the music of the west wind, the gurgling stream, the song of birds, and the low murmuring of insects. Peter Ruff stood like a man turned to stone, for, even as he looked, these things passed away from before his eyes, the roar of the world beat in his ears - the world of intrigue, of crime, the world where the strong man hewed his way to power, and the weaklings fell like corn before the sickle.

"It is the desire of Madame!"

Peter Ruff clenched his fists as he stood there. It was a message from a world every memory of which had been deliberately crushed, a world, indeed, in which he had seemed no longer to hold any place. Scarcely yet of middle age, well-preserved, upright, with neat figure dressed in the conventional tweeds and gaiters of an English country gentleman, he not only had loved his life, but he looked the part. He was Peter Ruff, Esquire, of Aynesford Manor, in the county of Somerset. It could not be for him, this strange summons.

The rustle of a woman's soft draperies broke in upon his reverie. He turned around with his usual morning greeting upon his lips. If country life had agreed with Peter Ruff, it had transformed his wife. Her cheeks were no longer pale; the extreme slimness of her figure was no longer apparent. She was just a little more matronly, perhaps, but without doubt a most beautiful woman. She came smiling across the room - a dream of white muslin and pink ribbons.

"Another forage bill, my dear Peter?" she demanded, passing her arm through his. "Put it away and admire my new morning gown. It came straight from Paris, and you will have to pay a great deal of money for it."

He pulled himself together - he had no secrets from his wife.

"Listen," he said, and read aloud:

RUE DE ST. QUINTAINE.
PARIS.

DEAR Mr. RUFF,

It is a long time since we had the pleasure of a visit from you. It is the desire of Madame that you should join our circle here on Thursday evening next at ten o'clock.

SOGRANGE.

Violet was a little perplexed. She failed, somehow, to recognize the sinister note underlying those few sentences, "It sounds friendly enough," she remarked. "You are not obliged to go, of course,"

Peter Ruff smiled grimly.

"Yes, it sounds all right," he admitted.

"They won't expect you to take any notice of it, surely?" she continued. "When you bought this place, Peter, and left your London offices, you gave them definitely to understand that you had retired into private life, that all these things were finished with you."

"There are some things," Peter Ruff said, slowly, "which are never finished."

"But you resigned," she reminded him. "I remember your letter distinctly."

"From the Double-Four," he answered, "no resignation is recognized save death. I did what I could and they accepted my explanations, gracefully and without comment. Now that the time has come, however, when they think they need my help, you see they do not hesitate to claim it."

"You will not go, Peter? You will not think of going?" she begged.

He twisted the letter between his fingers and sat down to his breakfast.

"No," he said, "I shall not go."

That morning Peter Ruff spent upon his farm, looking over his stock, examining some new machinery, and talking crops with his bailiff. In the afternoon he played his customary round of golf. It was the sort of day which, as a rule, he found completely satisfactory, yet, somehow or other, a certain sense of weariness crept in upon him toward its close.

Two days later he received another letter. This time it was couched in different terms. On a square card, at the top of which was stamped a small coronet, he read as follows:

Madame de Maupassim at home, Saturday evening, May 2nd, at ten o'clock.

In small letters at the bottom left-hand corner were added the words:

To meet friends.

Peter Ruff put the card upon the fire and went out for a morning's rabbit shooting with his keeper. When he returned luncheon was ready, but Violet was absent. He rang the bell.

"Where is your mistress, Jane?" he asked the parlor-maid.

The girl had no idea. Mrs. Ruff had left for the village several hours before; since then she had not been seen. Peter Ruff ate his luncheon alone, and understood. The afternoon wore on, and at night he traveled up to London. He knew better than to waste time by purposeless inquiries. Instead he took the nine o'clock train the next morning to Paris.

It was a chamber of death into which he was ushered, dismal - yet, of its sort, unique, marvelous. The room itself might have been the sleeping apartment of an empress - lofty, with white paneled walls, adorned simply with gilded lines; with high windows, closely curtained now, so that neither sound nor the light of day might penetrate into the room. In the middle of the apartment upon a canopy bedside, which had once adorned a king's palace, lay Madame de Maupassim. Her face was already touched with the finger of death, yet her eyes were undimmed and her lips unquivering. Her hands, covered with rings, lay out before her upon the lace coverlid. Supported by many pillows, she was issuing her last instructions with the cold precision of the man of affairs who makes the necessary arrangements for a few days, absence from his business.

Peter Ruff, who had not even been allowed sufficient time to change his traveling clothes, was brought without hesitation to her bedside. She looked at him in silence for a moment, with a cold glitter in her eyes.

"You are four days late, Monsieur Peter Ruff," she remarked. "Why did you not obey your first summons?

"Madame," he answered, "I thought there must be a misunderstanding. Four years ago, I gave notice to the council that I had married and retired into private life. A country farmer is of no further use to the world."

The woman's thin lip curled.

"From death and the Double Four," she said, "there is no resignation which counts. You are as much our creature to-day, as I am the creature of the disease which is carrying me across the threshold of death."

Peter Ruff remained silent. The woman's words seemed full of dread significance. Besides, how was it possible to contradict the dying?

"It is upon the unwilling of the world," she continued, speaking slowly, yet with extraordinary distinctness, "that its greatest honors are often conferred. The name of my successor has been balloted for, secretly. It is you, Peter Ruff, who have been chosen."

This time he was silent because he was literally bereft of words. This woman was dying and fancying strange things! He looked from one to the other of the stern, pale faces of those who were gathered around her bedside. Seven of them there were - the same seven. At that moment their eyes were all focused upon him. Peter Ruff shrank back.

"Madame," he murmured, "this cannot be."

Her lips twitched as though she would have smiled. "What we have decided," she said, "we have decided. Nothing can alter that, not even the will of Mr. Peter Ruff."

"I have been out of the world for four years," Peter Ruff protested. "I have no longer ambitions, no longer any desire -"

"You lie!" the woman interrupted. "You lie or you do yourself an injustice. We gave you four years, and looking into your face, I think that it has been enough. I think that the weariness is there already. In any case, the charge which I lay upon you in these my last moments, is one which you can escape by death only."

A low murmur of voices from those others repeated her words.

"By death only!"

Peter Ruff opened his lips, but closed them again without speech. A wave of emotion seemed passing through the room. Something strange was happening. It was Death itself, which had come among them.

A morning journalist wrote of the death of Madame eloquently, and with feeling. She had been a broad-minded aristocrat, a woman of brilliant intellect and great friendships, a woman of whose inner life during the last ten or fifteen years little was known, yet who, in happier times, might well have played a great part in the history of her country.

Peter Ruff drove back from the cemetery with the Marquis de Sograange, and, for the first time since the death of Madame, serious subjects were spoken of.

"I have waited here patiently," he declared, " but there are

E. Phillips Oppenheim

limits. I want my wife."

Sogrange took him by the arm and led him into the library of the house in the Rue de St. Quintaine. The six men who were already there waiting rose to their feet.

"Gentlemen," the Marquis said, "is it your will that I should be spokesman?"

There was a murmur of assent. Then Sogrange turned toward his companion, and something new seemed to have crept into his manner - a solemn, almost a threatening note.

"Peter Ruff," he continued, "you have trifled with the one organization in this world which has never allowed liberties to be taken with it. Men who have done greater service than you have died, for the disobedience of a day. You have been treated leniently, according to the will of Madame. According to her will, and in deference to the position which you must now take up among us, we will treat you as no other has ever been treated by us. The Double-Four admits your leadership and claims you for its own."

"I am not prepared to discuss anything of the sort," Peter Ruff declared, doggedly, "until my wife is restored to me."

The Marquis smiled.

"The traditions of your race, Mr. Ruff," he said, "are easily manifest in you. Now hear our decision. Your wife shall be restored to you on the day when you take up this position to which you have become entitled. Sit down and listen."

Peter Ruff was a rebel at heart, but he felt the grip of iron.

"During these four years when you, my friend, have been growing turnips and shooting your game, events in the great world have marched, new powers have come into being, a new page of history has been opened. As everything which has good at the heart evolves toward the good, so we of the Double-Four have lifted our great enterprise onto a higher plane. The world of criminals is still at our beck and call, we still claim the right to draw the line between moral theft and immoral honesty, but to-day the Double-Four is concerned with greater things. Within the four walls of this room, within the hearing of these my brothers, whose fidelity is as sure as the stones of Paris, I tell you a great secret. The government of our country has craved for our aid and the aid of our organization. It is no longer the wealth of the world alone, which we may control, but the actual destinies of nations."

"What I suppose you mean to say is," Peter Ruff remarked, "that you've been going in for politics?"

"You put it crudely, my English bull-dog," Sogrange answered, "but you are right. We are occupied now by affairs of international importance. More than once, during the last few month, ours has been the hand which has changed the policy of an empire."

"Most interesting," Peter Ruff declared, "but so far as I, personally, am concerned -"

"Listen," interrupted the Marquis. "Not a hundred yards from the French Embassy, in London, there is waiting for you a house and servants no less magnificent than the Embassy itself. You will become the ambassador in London of the Double-Four, titular head of our association, a personage whose power is second to none in your great city. I do not address words of caution to you, my friend, because we have satisfied ourselves as to your character and capacity before we consented that you should occupy your present position. But I ask you to remember this. The will of Madame lives even beyond the grave. The spirit which animated her when alive breathes still in all of us. In London you will wield a great power. Use it for the common good. And, remember this - the Double-Four has never failed, the Double-Four never can fail."

"I am glad to hear you are so confident," Peter Ruff said. "Of course, if I have to take this thing on, I shall do my best, but if I might venture to allude, for a moment, to anything so trifling as my own domestic affairs, I am very anxious to know about my wife."

Sogrange smiled.

"You will find Mrs. Ruff awaiting you in London," he announced. "Your address is Porchester House, Porchester Square."

"When do I go there?" Peter Ruff asked.

"To-night," was the answer.

"And what do I do when I get there?" he persisted.

"For three days," the Marquis told him, "you will remain indoors, and give audience to whoever may come to you. At the end of that time, you will understand a little more of our purpose and our objects - perhaps, even, of our power."

"I see difficulties," Peter Ruff remarked. "There will be a good many people who will remember me when I had offices in Southampton Row. My name, you see, is uncommon."

Sogrange drew a document from the breast pocket of his coat.

"When you leave this house to-night," he proclaimed, "we bid good-by forever to Mr. Peter Ruff. You will find in this envelope the title deeds of a small property which is our gift to you. Henceforth you will be known by the name and title of your estates."

"Title!" Peter Ruff gasped.

"You will reappear in London," Sogrange continued, "as the Baron de Grost."

Peter Ruff shook his head.

"It won't do," he declared, "people will find me out."

"There is nothing to be found out," the Marquis went on, a little wearily. "Your country life has dulled your wits, Baron. The title and the name are justly yours - they go with the property. For the rest, the history of your family, and of your career up to the moment when you enter Porchester House to-night, will be inside this packet. You can peruse it upon the journey, and remember that we can, at all times, bring a hundred witnesses, if necessary, to prove that you are who you declare yourself to be. When you get to Charing-Cross, do not forget that it will be the carriage and servants of the Baron de Grost which await you."

Peter Ruff shrugged his shoulders.

"Well," he said, thoughtfully, "I suppose I shall get used to it."

"Naturally," Sogrange answered. "For the moment, we are passing through a quiet time, necessitated by the mortal illness of Madame. You will be able to spend the next few weeks in getting used to your new position. You will have a great many callers, inspired by us, who will see that you make the right acquaintances and that you join the right clubs. At the same time, let me warn you always to be ready. There is trouble brewing just now all over Europe. In one way or another, we may become involved at any moment. The whole machinery of our society will be explained to you by your secretary. You will find him already installed at Porchester House. A glass of wine, Baron, before you leave."

Peter Ruff glanced at the clock.

"There are my things to pack," he began -

Sogrange smiled.

"Your valet is already on the front seat of the automobile which is waiting," he remarked. "You will find him attentive and trustworthy. The clothes which you brought with you we have taken the liberty of dispensing with. You will find others in your trunk, and at Porchester House you can send for any tailor you choose. One toast, Baron. We drink to the Double-Four - to the great cause!"

There was a murmur of voices. Sogrange lifted once more his glass.

"May Peter Ruff rest in peace!" he said. "We drink to his ashes. We drink long life and prosperity to the Baron de Grost!"

CHAPTER II

PRINCE ALBERT'S CARD DEBTS

It was half past twelve, and every table at the Berkeley Bridge Club was occupied. On the threshold of the principal room a visitor, who was being shown around, was asking questions of the secretary.

"Is there any gambling here?" he inquired.

The secretary shrugged his shoulders.

"I am afraid that some of them go a little beyond the club points," he answered. "You see that table against the wall? They are playing shilling auction there."

The table near the wall was, perhaps, the most silent. The visitor looked at it last and most curiously.

"Who is the dissipated-looking boy playing there?" he asked.

"Prince Albert of Trent," the secretary answered.

"And who is the little man, rather like Napoleon, who sits in the easy-chair and watches?"

"The Baron de Grost."

"Never heard of him," the visitor declared.

E. Phillips Oppenheim

"He is a very rich financier who has recently blossomed out in London," the secretary said. "One sees him everywhere. He has a good-looking wife, who is playing in the other room."

"A good-looking wife," the visitor remarked, thoughtfully "But, yes! I thank you very much, Mr. Courtledge for showing me round. I will find my friends now."

He turned away, leaving Courtledge alone, for a minute or two, on the threshold of the card room. The secretary's attention was riveted upon the table near the wall, and the frown on his face deepened. Just as he was moving off, the Baron de Grost rose and joined him.

"They are playing a little high in here this evening," the latter remarked quietly.

Courtledge frowned.

"I wish I had been in the club when they started," he said, gloomily. "My task is all the more difficult now."

The Baron de Grost looked pensively, for a moment, at the cigarette which he was carrying.

"By the bye, Mr. Courtledge," he asked, with apparent irrelevance, "what was the name of the tall man with whom you were talking just now?"

"Count von Hern. He was brought in by one of the attaches at the German Embassy."

Baron de Grost passed his arm through the secretary's and led him a little way through the corridor.

"I thought I recognized our friend," he remarked. "His presence here this evening is quite interesting."

"Why this evening?"

Baron de Grost avoided the question.

"Mr. Courtledge," he said, "I think that you will allow me to ask you something without thinking me impertinent. You know that my wife and I have taken some interest in Prince Albert. It is on his account, is it not, that you look so gloomy to-night, as though you had an execution in front of you?"

Courtledge nodded.

"I am afraid," he announced, "that we have come to the end of our tether with that young man. It's a pity, too, for he isn't a bad sort, and it will do the club no good if it gets about. But he hasn't settled up for a fortnight, and the matter came before the committee this afternoon. He owes one man over seven hundred pounds."

The Baron de Grost listened gravely.

"Are you going to speak to him to-night?" he asked.

"I must. I am instructed by the committee to ask him not to come to the club again until he has discharged his obligations."

De Grost smoked thoughtfully for a few moments.

"Well," he said, "I suppose there is no getting out of it. Don't rub it in too thick, though. I mean to have a talk with the boy afterwards, and if I am satisfied with what he says, the money will be all right."

Courtledge raised his eyebrows.

"You know, of course, that he has a very small income and no expectations?"

"I know that," Baron de Grost answered. "At the same time, it is hard to forget that he really is a member of the royal house, even though the kingdom is a small one."

"Not only is the kingdom a small one," Courtledge remarked, "but there are something like five lives between him and the succession. However, it's very good-natured of you, Baron, to think of lending him a hand. I'll let him down as lightly as I can. You know him better than any one; I wonder if you could make an excuse to send him out of the room? I'd rather no one saw me talking to him."

"Quite easy," said the Baron. "I'll manage it."

The rubber was just finishing as De Grost re-entered the room. He touched the young man, who had been the subject of their conversation, upon the shoulder.

"My wife would like to speak to you for a moment," he said. "She is in the other room."

Prince Albert rose to his feet. He was looking very pale, and the ash-tray in front of him was littered with cigarette ends.

"I will go and pay my respects to the Baroness," he declared. "It will change my luck, perhaps. Au revoir!"

He passed out of the room and all eyes followed him.

"Has the Prince been losing again to-night?" the Baron asked.

One of the three men at the table shrugged his shoulders.

"He owes me about five hundred pounds," he said, "and to tell you the truth, I'd really rather not play any more. I don't mind high points, but his doubles are absurd."

"Why not break up the table?" the Baron suggested. "The boy can scarcely afford such stakes."

He strolled out of the room in time to meet the Prince, who was standing in the corridor. A glance at his face was sufficient - the secretary had spoken. He would have hurried off, but the

Baron intercepted him.

"You are leaving, Prince?" he asked.

"Yes!" was the somewhat curt reply.

"I will walk a little way with you, if I may," De Grost continued. "My wife brought Lady Brownloe, and the brougham only holds two comfortably."

Prince Albert made no reply. He seemed just then scarcely capable of speech. When they had reached the pavement, however, the Baron took his arm.

"My young friend," he inquired, "how much does it all amount to?"

The Prince turned towards him with darkening face.

"You knew, then," he demanded, "that Mr. Courtledge was going to speak to me of my debts?"

"I was sorry to hear that it had become necessary," the Baron answered. "You must not take it too seriously. You know very well that at a club like the Berkeley, which has such a varied membership, card debts must be settled on the spot."

"Mine will be settled before mid-day to-morrow," the young man declared, sullenly. "I am not sure that it may not be to-night."

De Grost was silent for a moment. They had turned into Piccadilly. He summoned a taxicab.

"Do you mind coming round to my house and talking to me, for a few minutes?" he asked.

The young man hesitated.

"I'll come round later on," he suggested. "I have a call to make first."

Da Grost held open the door of the taxicab.

"I want a talk with you," he said, "before you make that call."

"You speak as though you knew where I was going," the Prince remarked.

His companion made no reply, but the door of the taxicab was still open and his hand had fallen ever so slightly upon the other's shoulder. The Prince yielded to the stronger will. He stepped inside.

They drove in silence to Porchester Square. The Baron led the way through into his own private sanctum, and closed the door carefully. Cigars, cigarettes, whiskey and soda, and liqueurs were upon the sideboard.

"Help yourself, Prince," he begged, "and then, if you don't mind, I am going to ask you a somewhat impertinent question."

The Prince drank the greater part of a whiskey and soda and lit a cigarette. Then he set his tumbler down and frowned.

"Baron de Grost," he said, "you have been very kind to me since I have had the pleasure of your acquaintance. I hope you will not ask me any question that I cannot answer."

"On the contrary," his host declared, "the question which I shall ask will be one which it will be very much to your advantage to answer. I will put it as plainly as possible. You are going, as you admit yourself, to pay your card debts to-night or to-morrow morning, and you are certainly not going to pay them out of your income. Where is the money coming from?"

Albert of Trent seemed suddenly to remember that after all he was of royal descent. He drew himself up and bore himself, for a moment, as a Prince should.

"Baron de Grost," he said, "you pass the limits of friendship when you ask such a question. I take the liberty of wishing you good-night."

He moved towards the door. The Baron, however, was in the way - a strong, motionless figure, and his tone, when he spoke again, was convincing.

"Prince," he declared, "I speak in your own interests. You have not chosen to answer my question. Let me answer it for you. The money to pay your debts, and I know not how much besides, was to come from the Government of a country with whom none of your name or nationality should willingly have dealings."

The Prince started violently. The shock caused him to forget his new-found dignity.

"How, in the devil's name, do you know that?" he demanded.

"I know more," the Baron continued. "I know the consideration which you were to give for this money."

Then the Prince began plainly to show the terror which had crept into his heart - the terror and the shame. He looked at his host like a man dazed with hearing strange things.

"It comes to nothing," he said, in a hard, unnatural tone. "It is a foolish bargain, indeed. Between me and the throne are four lives. My promise is not worth the paper it is written upon. I shall never succeed."

"That, Prince, is probably where you are misinformed," the Baron replied. "You are just now in disgrace with your family, and you hear from them only what the newspapers choose to tell."

E. Phillips Oppenheim

"Has anything been kept back from me?" the Prince asked.

"Tell me this first," De Grost insisted. "Am I not right in assuming that you have signed a solemn undertaking that, in the event of your succeeding to the throne of your country, you will use the whole of your influence towards concluding a treaty with a certain Power, one of the provisions of which is that that Power shall have free access to any one of your ports in the event of war with England?"

There was a moment's silence. The Prince clutched the back of the chair against which he was leaning.

"Supposing it were true?" he muttered. "It is, after all, an idle promise."

The Baron shook his head slowly.

"Prince," he said, "it is no such idle promise as it seems. The man who is seeking to trade upon your poverty knew more than he would tell you. You may have read in the newspapers that your two cousins are confined to the palace with slight colds. The truth has been kept quiet, but it is none the less known to a few of us. The so-called cold is really a virulent attack of diphtheria, and, according to to-night's reports, neither Prince Cyril nor Prince Henry are expected to live."

"Is this true?" the Prince gasped.

"It is true," his host declared. "My information can be relied upon."

The Prince sat down suddenly. He was looking whiter than ever, and very scared.

"Even then," he murmured, "there is John."

"You have been out of touch with your family for some months," De Grost reminded his visitor. "One or two of us, however, know what you, probably, will soon hear. Prince John has taken the vows and solemnly resigned, before the Archbishop, his heirship. He will be admitted into the Roman Catholic Church in a week or two, and will go straight to a monastery."

"It's likely enough," the Prince gasped. "He always wanted to be a monk."

"You see now," the Baron continued, "that your friend's generosity was not so wonderful a thing. Count von Hern was watching you to-night at the Bridge Club. He has gone home; he is waiting now to receive you. Apart from that, the man Nisch, with whom you have played so much, is a confederate of his, a political tout, not to say a spy."

"The brute!" Prince Albert muttered. "I am obliged to you, Baron, for having warned me," he added, rising slowly to his feet. "I shall sign nothing. There is another way."

De Grost shook his head.

"My young friend," he said, "there is another way, indeed, but not the way you have in your mind at this moment. I offer you an alternative. I will give you notes for the full amount you owe to-night, so that you can, if you will, go back to the club direct from here and pay everything - on one condition."

"Condition!"

"You must promise to put your hand to no document which the Count von Hern may place before you, and pledge your word that you have no further dealings with him."

"But why should you do this for me?" the Prince exclaimed. "I do not know that I shall ever be able to pay you."

"If you succeed to the throne, you will pay me," the Baron de Grost said. "If you do not succeed, remember that I am a rich

E. Phillips Oppenheim

man, and that I shall miss this money no more than the sixpence which you might throw to a crossing-sweeper."

The Prince was silent. His host unlocked a small cabinet and took from it a bundle of notes.

"Tell me the whole amount you owe," he insisted, "every penny, mind."

"Sixteen hundred pounds," was the broken reply.

De Grost counted a little roll and laid it upon the table.

"There are two thousand pounds," he said. "Listen, Prince. A name such as you bear carries with it certain obligations. Remember that, and try and shape your life accordingly. Take my advice - go back to your own country and find some useful occupation there, even if you only rejoin your regiment and wear its uniform. The time may come when your country will require you, for her work comes sooner or later to every man. You are leading a rotten life over here, a life which might have led to disaster and dishonor, a life, as you know, which might have ended in your rooms to-night with a small bullet hole in your forehead. Brave men do not die like that. Take up the money, please."

The Baron de Grost sent a cipher dispatch to Paris that night, and received an answer which pleased him.

"It is a small thing," he read, "but it is well done. Particulars of a matter of grave importance will reach you to-morrow." letter.

CHAPTER III

THE AMBASSADOR'S WIFE

Alone in his study, with fast-locked door, Peter, Baron de Grost, sat reading, word by word, with zealous care the despatch from Paris which had just been delivered into his hands. From the splendid suite of reception rooms which occupied the whole of the left-hand side of the hall came the faint sound of music. The street outside was filled with automobiles and carriages setting down their guests. Madame was receiving to-night a gathering of very distinguished men and women, and it was only for a few moments, and on very urgent business indeed, that her husband had dared to leave her side.

The room in which he sat was in darkness except for the single heavily shaded electric lamp which stood by his elbow. Nevertheless, there was sufficient illumination to show that Peter had achieved one, at least, of his ambitions. He was wearing court dress, with immaculate black silk stockings and diamond buckles upon his shoes. A red ribbon was in his buttonhole and a French order hung from his neck. His passion for clothes was certainly amply ministered to by the exigencies of his new position. Once more he read those last few words of this unexpectedly received despatch, read them with a frown upon his forehead and the light of trouble in his eyes. For three months he had done nothing but live the life of an ordinary man of fashion and wealth. His first task, for which, to tell the truth, he had been anxiously waiting, was here before him, and he found it little to his liking. Again, he read slowly to himself the last paragraph of Sogrange's.

As ever, dear friend, one of the greatest sayings which the men of my race have ever perpetrated once more justifies itself - "Cherchez la femme!" Of Monsieur we have no manner of doubt. We have tested him in every way. And to all appearance Madame should also be above suspicion. Yet those things of which I have spoken have happened. For two hours this morning I was closeted with Picon here. Very reluctantly he has placed the matter in my hands. I pass it on to you. It is your first undertaking, cher Baron, and I wish you bon fortune. A man of gallantry, as I know you are, you may regret that it should be a woman, and a beautiful woman, too, against whom the finger must be pointed. Yet, after all, the fates are strong and the task is yours.

SOGRANGE.

The music from the reception rooms grew louder and more insistent. Peter rose to his feet, and moving to the fireplace, struck a match and carefully destroyed the letter which he had been reading. Then he straightened himself, glanced for a moment at the mirror, and left the room to join his guests.

"Monsieur le Baron jests," the lady murmured.

The Baron de Grost shook his head.

"Indeed, no, Madame!" he answered earnestly. "France has offered us nothing more delightful in the whole history of our entente than the loan of yourself and your brilliant husband. Monsieur de Lamborne makes history among us politically, while Madame -"

The Baron sighed, and his companion leaned a little towards him; her dark eyes were full of sentimental regard.

"Yes?" she murmured. "Continue. It is my wish."

"I am the good friend of Monsieur de Lamborne," the Baron said, and in his tone there seemed to lurk some far-away touch of regret, "yet Madame knows that her conquests here have been many."

The Ambassador's wife fanned herself and remained silent for a moment, a faint smile playing at the corners of her full, curving lips. She was, indeed, a very beautiful woman - elegant, a Parisienne to the finger-tips, with pale cheeks, but eyes dark and soft, eyes trained to her service, whose flash was an inspiration, whose very droop had set beating the hearts of men less susceptible than the Baron de Grost. Her gown was magnificent, of amber satin, a color daring, but splendid; the outline of her figure, as she leaned slightly back in her seat, might indeed have been traced by the inspired finger of some great sculptor. De Grost, whose reputation as a man of gallantry was well established, felt the whole charm of her presence - felt, too, the subtle indications of preference which she seemed inclined to accord to him. There was nothing which eyes could say which hers were not saying during those few minutes. The Baron, indeed, glanced around a little nervously. His wife had still her moments of unreasonableness; it was just as well that she was engaged with some of her guests at the farther end of the apartments.

"You are trying to turn my head," his beautiful companion whispered. "You flatter me."

"It is not possible," he answered.

Again the fan fluttered for a moment before her face. She sighed.

"Ah. Monsieur!" she continued, dropping her voice until it scarcely rose above a whisper, "there are not many men like you. You speak of my husband and his political gifts. Yet what, after all, do they amount to? What is his position, indeed, if one glanced behind the scenes, compared with yours?"

E. Phillips Oppenheim

The face of the Baron de Grost became like a mask. It was as though suddenly he had felt the thrill of danger close at hand, danger even in that scented atmosphere wherein he sat.

"Alas, Madame!" he answered, "it is you, now, who are pleased to jest. Your husband is a great and powerful ambassador. I, unfortunately, have no career, no place in life save the place which the possession of a few millions gives to a successful financier."

She laughed very softly, and again her eyes spoke to him. "Monsieur," she murmured, "you and I together could make a great alliance, is it not so?"

"Madame," he faltered, doubtfully, "if one dared hope -"

Once more the fire of her eyes, this time not only voluptuous. Was the man stupid, she wondered, or only cautious?

"If that alliance were once concluded," she said, softly, "one might hope for everything."

"If it rests only with me," he began, seriously, "oh, Madame!"

He seemed overcome. Madame was gracious, but was he really stupid or only very much in earnest?

"To be one of the world's money kings," she whispered, "it is wonderful - that. It is power - supreme, absolute power. There is nothing beyond, there is nothing greater."

Then the Baron, who was watching her closely, caught another gleam in her eyes, and he began to understand. He had seen it before among a certain type of her countrywomen - the greed of money. He looked at her jewels and he remembered that, for an ambassador, her husband was reputed to be a poor man. The cloud of misgiving passed away from him; he settled down to the game.

"If money could only buy the desire of one's heart," he murmured. "Alas!"

His eyes seemed to seek out Monsieur de Lamborne among the moving throngs. She laughed softly, and her hand brushed his.

"Money and one other thing, Monsieur le Baron," she whispered in his ear, "can buy the jewels from a crown - can buy, even, the heart of a woman -"

A movement of approaching guests caught them up, and parted them for a time. The Baroness de Grost was at home from ten till one, and her rooms were crowded. The Baron found himself drawn on one side, a few minutes later, by Monsieur de Lamborne himself.

"I have been looking for you, De Grost," the latter declared. "Where can we talk for a moment?"

His host took the ambassador by the arm and led him into a retired corner. Monsieur de Lamborne was a tall, slight man, somewhat cadaverous looking, with large features, hollow eyes, thin but carefully arranged gray hair, and a pointed gray beard. He wore a frilled shirt, and an eye-glass suspended by a broad black ribbon hung down upon his chest. His face, as a rule, was imperturbable enough, but he had the air, just now, of a man greatly disturbed.

"We cannot be overheard here," De Grost remarked. "It must be an affair of a few words only, though."

Monsieur de Lamborne wasted no time in preliminaries. "This afternoon," he said, "I received from my Government papers of immense importance, which I am to hand over to your Foreign Minister at eleven o'clock to-morrow morning."

The Baron nodded.

"Well?"

De Lamborne's thin fingers trembled as they played nervously with the ribbon of his eye-glass.

"Listen," he continued, dropping his voice a little. "Bernadine has undertaken to send a copy of their contents to Berlin by to-morrow night's mail."

"How do you know that?"

The ambassador hesitated.

"We, too, have spies at work," he remarked, grimly. "Bernadine wrote and sent a messenger with the letter to Berlin. The man's body is drifting down the Channel, but the letter is in my pocket."

"The letter from Bernadine?"

"Yes."

"What does he say?"

"Simply that a verbatim copy of the document in question will be despatched to Berlin to-morrow evening, without fail."

"There are no secrets between us," De Grost declared, smoothly. "What is the special importance of this document?"

De Lamborne shrugged his shoulders.

"Since you ask," he said, "I will tell you. You know of the slight coolness which there has been between our respective Governments. Our people have felt that the policy of your ministers in expending all their energies and resources in the building of a great fleet to the utter neglect of your army is a wholly one-sided arrangement, so far as we are concerned. In the event of a simultaneous attack by Germany upon France and England, you would be utterly powerless to render us any measure of assistance. If Germany should attack England alone, it is the wish of your Government that we should be pledged to occupy Alsace-Lorraine. You, on the other hand, could do nothing for us, if Germany's first move were made against France."

The Baron was deeply interested, although the matter was no new one to him.

"Go on," he directed. "I am waiting for you to tell me the specific contents of this document."

"The English Government has asked us two questions: first, how many complete army corps we consider she ought to place at our disposal in this eventuality; and, secondly, at what point should we expect them to be concentrated. The despatch which I received to-night contains the reply to these questions."

"Which Bernadine has promised to forward to Berlin to-morrow night," the Baron remarked, softly.

De Lamborne nodded.

"You perceive," he said, "the immense importance of the affair. The very existence of that document is almost a casus belli."

"At what time did the despatch arrive," the Baron asked, "and what has been its history since?"

"It arrived at six o'clock, and went straight into the inner pocket of my coat; it has not been out of my possession for a single second. Even while I talk to you I can feel it."

"And your plans? How are you intending to dispose of it to-night?"

"On my return to the Embassy I shall place it in the safe, lock

E. Phillips Oppenheim

it up, and remain watching it until morning."

"There doesn't seem to be much chance for Bernadine," the Baron remarked, thoughtfully.

"But there must be no chance - no chance at all," Monsieur de Lamborne asserted, with a note of passion in his thin voice. "It is incredible, preposterous, that he should even make the attempt. I want you to come home with me and share my vigil. You shall be my witness in case anything happens. We will watch together."

De Grost reflected for a moment.

"Bernadine makes few mistakes," he said, thoughtfully. Monsieur de Lamborne passed his hand across his forehead.

"Do I not know it?" he muttered. "In this instance, though, it seems impossible for him to succeed. The time is so short and the conditions so difficult. I may count upon your assistance, Baron?"

The Baron drew from his pocket a crumpled piece of paper.

"I received a telegram from headquarters this after noon," he said, "with instructions to place myself entirely at your disposal."

"You will return with me, then, to the Embassy?" Monsieur de Lamborne asked, eagerly.

The Baron de Grost did not at once reply. He was standing in one of his characteristic attitudes, his hands clasped behind him, his head a little thrust forward, watching with every appearance of courteous interest the roomful of guests, stationary just now, listening to the performance of a famous violinist. It was, perhaps, by accident that his eyes met those of Madame de Lamborne, but she smiled at him subtly, more, perhaps, with her wonderful eyes than her lips themselves. She was the centre of a very brilliant group, a most beautiful woman holding court, as was only right and proper, among her admirers. The Baron sighed.

"No," he said, "I shall not return with you, De Lamborne. I want you to follow my suggestions, if you will."

"But, assuredly!"

"Leave here early and go to your club. Remain there until one, then come to the Embassy. I shall be there awaiting your arrival."

"You mean that you will go there alone? I do not understand," the ambassador protested. "Why should I go to my club? I do not at all understand."

"Nevertheless, do as I say," De Grost insisted. "For the present, excuse me. I must look after my guests."

The music had ceased, there was a movement toward the supper-room. The Baron offered his arm to Madame de Lamborne, who welcomed him with a brilliant smile. Her husband, although, for a Frenchman, he was by no means of a jealous disposition, was conscious of a vague feeling of uneasiness as he watched them pass out of the room together. A few minutes later he made his excuses to his wife and with a reluctance for which he could scarcely account left the house. There was something in the air, he felt, which he did not understand. He would not have admitted it to himself, but he more than half divined the truth. The vacant seat in his wife's carriage was filled that night by the Baron de Grost.

At one o'clock precisely Monsieur de Lamborne returned to his house and heard with well-simulated interest that Monsieur le Baron de Grost awaited his arrival in the library. He found De Grost gazing with obvious respect at the ponderous safe let into the wall.

"A very fine affair - this," he remarked, motioning with his head toward it.

"The best of its kind," Monsieur de Lamborne admitted. "No burglar yet has ever succeeded in opening one of its type. Here is the packet," he added, drawing the document from his pocket. "You shall see me place it in safety myself."

The Baron stretched out his hand and examined the sealed envelope for a moment closely. Then he moved to the writing-table, and, placing it upon the letter scales, made a note of its exact weight. Finally, he watched it deposited in the ponderous safe, suggested the word to which the lock was set, and closed the door. Monsieur de Lamborne heaved a sigh of relief.

"I fancy this time," he said, "that our friends at Berlin will be disappointed. Couch or easy-chair, Baron?"

"The couch, if you please," De Grost replied, "a strong cigar, and a long whiskey and soda. So! Now, for our vigil."

The hours crawled away. Once De Grost sat up and listened.

"Any rats about?" he inquired.

The ambassador was indignant.

"I have never heard one in my life," he answered. "This is quite a modern house."

De Grost dropped his match-box and stooped to pick it up.

"Any lights on anywhere, except in this room?" he asked.

"Certainly not," Monsieur de Lamborne answered. "It is past three o'clock, and every one has gone to bed."

The Baron rose and softly unbolted the door. The passage outside was in darkness. He listened intently, for a moment, and returned, yawning.

"One fancies things," he murmured, apologetically.

"For example?" De Lamborne demanded.

The Baron shook his head.

"One mistakes," he declared. "The nerves become over sensitive."

The dawn broke and the awakening hum of the city grew louder and louder. De Grost rose and stretched himself.

"Your servants are moving about in the house," he remarked. "I think that we might consider our vigil at an end."

Monsieur de Lamborne rose with alacrity.

"My friend," he said, "I feel that I have made false pretenses to you. With the day I have no fear. A thousand pardons for your sleepless night."

"My sleepless night counts for nothing," the Baron assured him, "but, before I go, would it not be as well that we glance together inside the safe?"

De Lamborne shook out his keys.

"I was about to suggest it," he replied.

The ambassador arranged the combination and pressed the lever. Slowly the great door swung back. The two men peered in.

"Untouched!" De Lamborne exclaimed, a little note of triumph in his tone.

De Grost said nothing, but held out his hand.

"Permit me," he interposed.

De Lamborne was conscious of a faint sense of uneasiness. His companion walked across the room and carefully weighed the packet.

"Well?" De Lamborne cried. "Why do you do that? What is wrong?"

The Baron turned and faced him.

"My friend," he said, "this is not the same packet." The ambassador stared at him incredulously.

"You are jesting!" he exclaimed. "Miracles do not happen. The thing is impossible."

"It is the impossible, then, which has happened," De Grost replied, swiftly. "This packet can scarcely have gained two ounces in the night. Besides, the seal is fuller. I have an eye for these details."

De Lamborne leaned against the back of the table. His eyes were a little wild, but he laughed hoarsely.

"We fight, then, against the creatures of another world," he declared. "No human being could have opened that safe last night."

The Baron hesitated.

"Monsieur de Lamborne," he said, "the room adjoining is your wife's."

"It is the salon of Madame," the ambassador admitted.

"What are the electrical appliances doing there?" the Baron demanded. "Don't look at me like that, De Lamborne. Remember that I was here before you arrived."

"My wife takes an electric massage every day," Monsieur de Lamborne answered, in a hard, unnatural voice. "In what way is Monsieur le Baron concerned in my wife's doings?"

"I think that there need be no answer to that question," De Grost said, quietly. "It is a greater tragedy which we have to face."

Quick as lightning, the Frenchman's hand shot out. De Grost barely avoided the blow.

"You shall answer to me for this, sir," De Lamborne cried. "It is the honor of my wife which you assail."

"I maintain only," the Baron answered, "that your safe was entered from that room. A search will prove it."

"There will be no search there," De Lamborne declared, fiercely. "I am the Ambassador of France, and my power under this roof is absolute. I say that you shall not cross that threshold."

De Grost's expression did not change. Only his hands were suddenly outstretched with a curious gesture - the four fingers were raised, the thumbs depressed. Monsieur De Lamborne collapsed.

"I submit," he muttered. "It is you who are the master. Search where you will."

"Monsieur has arrived?" the woman demanded, breathlessly.

The proprietor of the restaurant himself bowed a reply. His client was evidently well-known to him. He answered her in French - French, with a very guttural accent.

"Monsieur has ascended some few minutes ago. Myself, I have not had the pleasure of wishing him bon aperitif, but Fritz

E. Phillips Oppenheim

announced his coming."

The woman drew a little sigh of relief. A vague misgiving had troubled her during the last few hours. She raised her veil as she mounted the narrow staircase which led to the one private room at the Hotel de Lorraine. She entered, without tapping, the room at the head of the stairs, pushing open the ill-varnished door with its white-curtained top. At first she thought that the little apartment was empty.

"Are you there?" she exclaimed, advancing a few steps.

The figure of a man glided from behind the worn screen close by her side, and stood between her and the door.

"Madame!" De Grost said, bowing low.

Even then she scarcely realized that she was trapped. "You?" she cried. "You, Baron? But I do not understand. You have followed me here?"

"On the contrary, Madame," he answered. "I have preceded you."

Her colossal vanity triumphed over her natural astuteness. The man had employed spies to watch her! He had lost his head. It was an awkward matter, this, but it was to be arranged. She held out her hands.

"Monsieur," she said, "let me beg you now to go away. If you care to, come and see me this evening. I will explain everything. It is a little family affair which brings me here."

"A family affair, Madame, with Bernadine, the enemy of France," De Grost declared, gravely.

She collapsed miserably, her fingers grasping at the air, the cry which broke from her lips harsh and unnatural. Before he could tell what was happening, she was on her knees before him.

"Spare me," she begged, trying to seize his hands.

"Madame," De Grost answered, "I am not your judge. You will kindly hand over to me the document which you are carrying."

She took it from the bosom of her dress. De Grost glanced at it, and placed it in his breast-pocket.

"And now?" she faltered.

De Grost sighed - she was a very beautiful woman.

"Madame," he said, "the career of a spy is, as you have doubtless sometimes realized, a dangerous one."

"It is finished," she assured him, breathlessly. "Monsieur le Baron, you will keep my secret? Never again, I swear it, will I sin like this. You, yourself, shall be the trustee of my honor."

Her eyes and arms besought him, but it was surely a changed man - this. There was none of the suaveness, the delicate responsiveness of her late host at Porchester House. The man who faced her now possessed the features of a sphinx. There was not even pity in his face.

"You will not tell my husband?" she gasped.

"Your husband already knows, Madame," was the quiet reply. "Only a few hours ago I proved to him whence had come the leakage of so many of our secrets lately."

She swayed upon her feet.

"He will never forgive me," she cried.

"There are others," De Grost declared, " who forgive more

E. Phillips Oppenheim

rarely, even, than husbands."

A sudden illuminating flash of horror told her the truth. She closed her eyes and tried to run from the room.

"I will not be told," she screamed. "I will not hear. I do not know who you are. I will live a little longer."

"Madame," De Grost said, "the Double-Four wages no war with women, save with spies only. The spy has no sex. For the sake of your family, permit me to send you back to your husband's house."

That night, two receptions and a dinner party were postponed. All London was sympathizing with Monsieur de Lamborne, and a great many women swore never again to take a sleeping draught. Madame de Lamborne lay dead behind the shelter of those drawn blinds, and by her side an empty phial.

CHAPTER IV

THE MAN PROM THE OLD TESTAMENT

Bernadine, sometimes called the Count von Hern, was lunching at the Savoy with the pretty wife of a Cabinet Minister, who was just sufficiently conscious of the impropriety of her action to render the situation interesting.

"I wish you would tell me, Count von Hern," she said, soon after they had settled down in their places, "why my husband seems to object to you so much. I simply dared not tell him that we were going to lunch together, and as a rule he doesn't mind what I do in that way."

Bernadine smiled slowly.

"Ah, well," he remarked, "your husband is a politician and a very cautious man. I dare say he is like some of those others, who believe that, because I am a foreigner and live in London, therefore I am a spy."

"You a spy," she laughed. "What nonsense!"

"Why nonsense?"

She shrugged her shoulders. She was certainly a very pretty woman, and her black gown set off to fullest advantage her deep red hair and fair complexion.

E. Phillips Oppenheim

"I suppose because I can't imagine you anything of the sort," she declared. "You see, you hunt and play polo, and do everything which the ordinary Englishmen do. Then one meets you everywhere. I think, Count von Hern, that you are much too spoilt, for one thing, to take life seriously."

"You do me an injustice," he murmured.

"Of course," she chattered on, "I don't really know what spies do. One reads about them in these silly stories, but I have never felt sure that as live people they exist at all. Tell me, Count, what could a foreign spy do in England?"

Bernadine twirled his fair moustache and shrugged his shoulders.

"Indeed, my dear lady," he admitted, "I scarcely know what a spy could do nowadays. A few years ago, you English people were all so trusting. Your fortifications, your battleships, not to speak of your country itself, were wholly at the disposal of the enterprising foreigner who desired to acquire information. The party who governed Great Britain then seemed to have some strange idea that these things made for peace. To-day, however, all that is changed."

"You seem to know something about it," she remarked.

"I am afraid that mine is really only the superficial point of view," he answered, "but I do know that there is a good deal of information, which seems absolutely insignificant in itself, for which some foreign countries are willing to pay. For instance, there was a Cabinet Council yesterday, I believe, and some one was going to suggest that a secret, but official, visit be paid to your new harbor works up at Rosyth. An announcement will probably be made in the papers during the next few days as to whether the visit is to be undertaken or not. Yet there are countries who are willing to pay for knowing even such an insignificant item of news as that, a few hours before the rest of the world."

Lady Maxwell laughed.

"Well, I could earn that little sum of money," she declared gayly, "for my husband has just made me cancel a dinner-party for next Thursday, because he has to go up to the stupid place."

Bernadine smiled. It was really a very unimportant matter, but he loved to feel, even in his idle moments, that he was not altogether wasting his time.

"I am sorry," he said, "that I am not myself acquainted with one of these mythical personages that I might return you the value of your marvelous information. If I dared think, however, that it would be in any way acceptable, I could offer you the diversion of a restaurant dinner-party for that night. The Duchess of Castleford has kindly offered to act as hostess for me and we are all going on to the Gaiety afterwards."

"Delightful!" Lady Maxwell exclaimed. "I should love to come."

Bernadine bowed.

"You have, then, dear lady, fulfilled your destiny," he said. "You have given secret information to a foreign person of mysterious identity, and accepted payment."

Now, Bernadine was a man of easy manners and unruffled composure. To the natural insouciance of his aristocratic bringing up, he had added the steely reserve of a man moving in the large world, engaged more often than not in some hazardous enterprise. Yet, for once in his life, and in the midst of the idlest of conversations, he gave himself away so utterly that even this woman with whom he was lunching - a very butterfly lady, indeed could not fail to perceive it. She looked at him in something like astonishment. Without the slightest warning his face had become set in a rigid stare, his eyes were filled with the expression of a man who sees into another world. The healthy color faded from his cheeks, he was white even to the parted lips, the wine dripped from his raised glass onto the tablecloth.

"Why, whatever is the matter with you?" she demanded. "Is it a ghost that you see?"

Bernadine's effort was superb, but he was too clever to deny the shock.

"A ghost, indeed," he answered, "the ghost of a man whom every newspaper in Europe has declared to be dead."

Her eyes followed his. The two people who were being ushered to a seat in their immediate vicinity were certainly of somewhat unusual appearance. The man was tall, and thin as a lath, and he wore the clothes of the fashionable world without awkwardness, yet with the air of one who was wholly unaccustomed to them. His cheek-bones were remarkably high, and receded so quickly towards his pointed chin that his cheeks were little more than hollows. His eyes were dry and burning, flashing here and there as though the man himself were continually oppressed by some furtive fear. His thick black hair was short cropped, his forehead high and intellectual. He was a strange figure, indeed, in such a gathering, and his companion only served to accentuate the anachronisms of his appearance. She was, above all things, a woman of the moment - fair, almost florid, a little thick-set, with tightly-laced, yet passable figure. Her eyes were blue, her hair light-colored. She wore magnificent furs, and, as she threw aside her boa, she disclosed a mass of jewelry around her neck and upon her bosom, almost barbaric in its profusion and setting.

"What an extraordinary couple!" Lady Maxwell whispered.

Bernadine smiled.

"The man looks as though he had stepped out of the Old Testament," he murmured.

Lady Maxwell's interest was purely feminine, and was riveted now upon the jewelry worn by the woman. Bernadine, under the mask of his habitual indifference, which had easily reassumed, seemed to be looking away out of the restaurant into the great square of a half-savage city, looking at that marvelous crowd, numbered by their thousands, even by their hundreds of thousands, of men and women whose arms flashed out toward the snow-hung heavens, whose lips were parted in one chorus of rapturous acclamation; looking beyond them to the tall, emaciated form of the bare-headed priest in his long robes, his wind-tossed hair and wild eyes, standing alone before that multitude, in danger of death, or worse, at any moment - their idol, their hero. And again, as the memories came flooding into his brain, the scene passed away, and he saw the bare room with its whitewashed walls and blocked-up windows; he felt the darkness, lit only by those flickering candles. He saw the white, passion-wrung faces of the men who clustered together around the rude table, waiting; he heard their murmurs, he saw the fear born in their eyes. It was the night when their leader did not come.

Bernadine poured himself out a glass of wine and drank it slowly. The mists were clearing away now. He was in London, at the Savoy Restaurant, and within a few yards of him sat the man with whose name all Europe once had rung - the man hailed by some as martyr, and loathed by others as the most fiendish Judas who ever drew breath. Bernadine was not concerned with the moral side of this strange encounter. How best to use his knowledge of this man's identity was the question which beat upon his brain. What use could be made of him, what profit for his country and himself? And then a fear - a sudden, startling fear. Little profit, perhaps, to be made, but the danger - the danger of this man alive with such secrets locked in his bosom! The thought itself was terrifying, and even as he realized it a significant thing happened - he caught the eye of the Baron de Grost, lunching alone at a small table just inside the restaurant.

"You are not at all amusing," his guest declared. "It is nearly five minutes since you have spoken."

"You, too, have been absorbed," he reminded her.

"It is that woman's jewels," she admitted. "I never saw anything more wonderful. The people are not English, of course. I wonder where they come from."

"One of the Eastern countries, without a doubt," he replied, carelessly.

Lady Maxwell sighed.

"He is a peculiar-looking man," she said, "but one could put up with a good deal for jewels like that. What are you doing this afternoon - picture-galleries or your club?"

"Neither, unfortunately," Bernadine answered. "I have promised to go with a friend to look at some polo ponies."

"Do you know," she remarked, "that we have never been to see those Japanese prints yet?"

"The gallery is closed until Monday," he assured her, falsely. "If you will honor me then, I shall be delighted."

She shrugged her shoulders but said nothing. She had an idea that she was being dismissed, but Bernadine, without the least appearance of hurry, gave her no opportunity for any further suggestions. He handed her into the automobile, and returned at once into the restaurant. He touched Baron de Grost upon the shoulder.

"My friend, the enemy!" he exclaimed, smiling.

"At your service in either capacity," the Baron replied. Bernadine made a grimace and accepted the chair which De Grost had indicated.

"If I may, I will take my coffee with you," he said. "I am growing old. It does not amuse me so much to lunch with a pretty woman. One has to entertain, and one forgets the serious business of lunching. I will take my coffee and cigarettes in peace."

De Grost gave an order to the waiter and leaned back in his chair.

"Now," he suggested, "tell me exactly what it is that has brought you back into the restaurant?"

Bernadine shrugged his shoulders.

"Why not the pleasure of this few minutes' conversation with you?" he asked.

The Baron carefully selected a cigar, and lit it.

"That," he said, "goes well, but there are other things."

"As, for instance?"

De Grost leaned back in his chair, and watched the smoke of his cigar curl upwards.

"One talks too much," he remarked. "Before the cards are upon the table, it is not wise."

They chatted upon various matters. De Grost himself seemed in no hurry to depart, nor did his companion show any signs of impatience. It was not until the two people whose entrance had had such a remarkable effect upon Bernadine, rose to leave, that the mask was, for a moment, lifted. De Grost had called for his bill and paid it. The two men strolled out together.

"Baron," Bernadine said, suavely, linking his arm through the other man's as they passed into the foyer, "there are times when candor even among enemies becomes an admirable quality."

"Those times, I imagine," De Grost answered, grimly, "are rare. Besides, who is to tell the real thing from the false?"

"You do less than justice to your perceptions, my friend," Bernadine declared, smiling.

De Grost merely shrugged his shoulders. Bernadine persisted.

"Come," he continued, "since you doubt me, let me be the first to give you a proof that on this occasion, at any rate, I am candor itself. You had a purpose in lunching at the Savoy to-day. That purpose I have discovered by accident. We are both interested in those people." The Baron de Grost shook his head slowly.

"Really," he began -

"Let me finish," Bernadine insisted. "Perhaps when you have heard all that I have to say, you may change your attitude. We are interested in the same people, but in different ways. If we both move from opposite directions, our friend will vanish - he is clever enough at disappearing, as he has proved before. We do not want the same thing from him, I am convinced of that. Let us move together and make sure that he does not evade us."

"Is it an alliance which you are proposing?" De Grost asked, with a quiet smile.

"Why not? Enemies have united before to-day against a common foe."

De Grost looked across the palm court to where the two people who formed the subject of their discussion were sitting in a corner, both smoking, both sipping some red-colored liqueur.

"My dear Bernadine," he said, "I am much too afraid of you to listen any more. You fancy because this man's presence here was an entire surprise to you, and because you find me already on his track, that I know more than you do and that an alliance with me would be to your advantage. You would try to persuade me that your object with him would not be my object. Listen. I am afraid of you - you are too clever for me. I am going to leave you in sole possession."

De Grost's tone was final and his bow valedictory. Bernadine watched him stroll in a leisurely way through the foyer, exchanging greetings here and there with friends, watched him enter the cloakroom, from which he emerged with his hat and overcoat, watched him step into his automobile and leave the restaurant. He turned back with a clouded face, and threw himself into an easy chair.

Ten minutes passed uneventfully. People were passing backwards and forwards all the time, but Bernadine, through his half-closed eyes, did little save watch the couple in whom he was so deeply interested. At last the man rose, and, with a word of farewell to his companion, came out from the lounge, and made his way up the foyer, turning toward the hotel. He walked with quick, nervous strides, glancing now and then restlessly about him. In his eyes, to those who understood, there was the furtive gleam of the hunted man. It was the passing of one who was afraid.

The woman, left to herself, began to look around her with some curiosity. Bernadine, to whom a new idea had occurred, moved his chair nearer to hers, and was rewarded by a glance which certainly betrayed some interest. A swift and unerring judge in such matters, he came to the instant conclusion that she was not unapproachable. He acted immediately and upon impulse. Rising to his feet, he approached her, and bowed easily but respectfully.

"Madame," he said, "it is impossible that I am mistaken. I have had the pleasure, have I not, of meeting you in St. Petersburg?"

Her first reception of his coming was reassuring enough. At his mention of St. Petersburg, however, she frowned.

"I do not think so," she answered, in French. "You are mistaken. I do not know St. Petersburg."

"Then it was in Paris," Bernadine continued, with conviction. "Madame is Parisian, without a doubt."

She shook her head, smiling.

"I do not think that I remember meeting you, Monsieur," she replied, doubtfully, "but perhaps -"

She looked up, and her eyes dropped before his. He was certainly a very personable looking man, and she had spoken to no one for so many months.

"Believe me, Madame, I could not possibly be mistaken," Bernadine assured her, smoothly. "You are staying here for long?"

She shrugged her shoulders.

"Heaven knows!" she declared. "My husband he has, I think, what you call the wander fever. For myself, I am tired of it. In Rome we settle down, we stay five days, all seems pleasant, and suddenly my husband's whim carries us away without an hour's notice. The same thing at Monte Carlo, the same in Paris. Who can tell what will happen here? To tell you the truth, Monsieur," she added, a little archly, "I think that if he were to come back at this moment, we should probably leave England to-night."

"Your husband is very jealous?" Bernadine whispered, softly.

She shrugged her shoulders.

"Partly jealous, and partly, he has the most terrible distaste for acquaintances. He will not speak to strangers himself, or suffer me to do so. It is sometimes - oh! it is sometimes very triste."

"Madame has my sympathy," Bernadine assured her. "It is an impossible life - this. No husband should be so exacting."

She looked at him with her round, blue eyes, a touch of added color in her cheeks.

"If one could but cure him!" she murmured.

"I would ask your permission to sit down," Bernadine remarked, "but I fear to intrude. You are afraid, perhaps, that your husband may return."

She shook her head.

"It will be better that you do not stay," she declared. "For a moment or two he is engaged. He has an appointment in his room with a gentleman, but one never knows how long he may be."

"You have friends in London, then," Bernadine remarked, thoughtfully.

"Of my husband's affairs," the woman said, "there is no one so ignorant as I. Yet since we left our own country, this is the first time I have known him willingly speak to a soul."

"Your own country," Bernadine repeated, softly. "That was Russia, of course. Your husband's nationality is very apparent."

The woman looked a little annoyed with herself. She remained silent.

"May I not hope," Bernadine begged, "that you will give me the pleasure of meeting you again?"

She hesitated for a moment.

"He does not leave me," she replied. "I am not alone for five minutes during the day."

Bernadine scribbled the name by which he was known in that locality, on a card, and passed it to her.

"I have rooms in St. James's Street, quite close to here," he said. "If you could come and have tea with me to-day or to-morrow, it would give me the utmost pleasure."

She took the card, and crumpled it in her hand. All the time, though, she shook her head.

"Monsieur is very kind," she answered. "I am afraid - I do not think that it would be possible. And now, if you please, you must go away. I am terrified lest my husband should return."

Bernadine bent low in a parting salute.

"Madame," he pleaded, "you will come?"

Bernadine was a handsome man, and he knew well enough how to use his soft and extraordinarily musical voice. He knew very well, as he retired, that somehow or other she would accept his invitation. Even then, he felt dissatisfied and ill at ease, as he left the place. He had made a little progress, but, after all, was it worth while? Supposing that the man with whom her husband was even at this moment closeted, was the Baron de Grost! He called a taxicab and drove at once to the Embassy of his country.

Even at that moment, De Grost and the Russian - Paul Hagon he called himself - were standing face to face in the latter's sitting-room. No conventional greetings of any sort had been exchanged. De Grost had scarcely closed the door behind him before Hagon addressed him breathlessly, almost fiercely.

"Who are you, sir," he demanded, "and what do you want with me?"

"You had my letter?" De Grost inquired.

"I had your letter," the other admitted. "It told me nothing. You speak of business. What business have I with any here?"

"My business is soon told," De Grost replied, "but in the first place, I beg that you will not unnecessarily alarm yourself. There is, believe me, no need for it, no need whatever, although, to prevent misunderstandings, I may as well tell you at once that I am perfectly well aware who it is that I am addressing."

Hagon collapsed into a chair. He buried his face in his hands and groaned.

"I am not here necessarily as an enemy," De Grost continued. "You have very excellent reasons, I make no doubt, for remaining unknown in this city, or wherever you may be. As yet, let me assure you that your identity is not even suspected, except by myself and one other. Those few who believe you alive, believe that you are in America. There is no need for any one to know that Father -"

"Stop!" the man begged, piteously. "Stop!"

De Grost bowed.

"I beg your pardon," he said.

"Now tell me," the man demanded, "what is your price? I have had money. There is not much left. Sophia is extravagant and traveling costs a great deal. But why do I weary you with these things?" he added. "Let me know what I have to pay for your silence."

"I am not a blackmailer," De Grost answered, sternly. "I am myself a wealthy man. I ask from you nothing in money - I ask you nothing in that way at all. A few words of information, and a certain paper, which I believe you have in your possession, is all that I require."

"Information," Hagon repeated, shivering.

"What I ask," De Grost declared, "is really a matter of justice. At the time when you were the idol of all Russia and the leader of the great revolutionary party, you received funds from abroad."

"I accounted for them," Hagon muttered. "Up to a certain point I accounted for everything."

"You received funds from the Government of a European power," De Grost continued, "funds to be applied towards developing the revolution. I want the name of that Power, and proof of what I say."

Hagon remained motionless for a moment. He had seated himself at the table, his head resting upon his hand and his face turned away from De Grost.

"You are a politician, then?" he asked, slowly.

"I am a politician," De Grost admitted. "I represent a great secret power which has sprung into existence during the last few years. Our aim, at present, is to bring closer together your country and Great Britain. Russia hesitates because an actual rapprochement with us is equivalent to a permanent estrangement with Germany."

Hagon nodded.

"I understand," he said, in a low tone. "I have finished with politics. I have nothing to say to you."

"I trust," De Grost persisted, suavely, "that you will be better advised."

Hagon turned round and faced him.

"Sir," he demanded, "do you believe that I am afraid of death?"

De Grost looked at him steadfastly.

"No," he answered, "you have proved the contrary."

"If my identity is discovered," Hagon continued, "I have the means of instant death at hand. I do not use it because of my love for the one person who links me to this world. For her sake I live, and for her sake I bear always the memory of the shameful past. Publish my name and whereabouts, if you will. I promise you that I will make the tragedy complete. But for the rest, I refuse to pay your price. A great power trusted me, and whatever its motives may have been, its money came very near indeed to freeing my people. I have nothing more to say to you, sir."

The Baron de Grost was taken aback. He had scarcely contemplated refusal.

"You must understand," he explained, "that this is not a personal matter. Even if I myself would spare you, those who are more powerful than I will strike. The society to which I belong does not tolerate failure. I am empowered even to offer you its protection, if you will give me the information for which I ask."

Hagon rose to his feet, and, before De Grost could foresee his purpose, had rung the bell.

"My decision is unchanging," he said. "You can pull down the roof upon my head, but I carry next my heart an instant and unfailing means of escape."

A waiter stood in the doorway.

"You will take this gentleman to the lift," Hagon directed.

There was once more a touch in his manner of that half divine authority which had thrilled the great multitude of his believers. De Grost was forced to admit defeat.

"Not defeat," he said to himself, as he followed the man to the lift, "only a check."

Nevertheless, it was a serious check. He could not, for the moment, see his way further. Arrived at his house, he followed his usual custom and made his way at once to his wife's rooms. Violet was resting upon a sofa, but laid down her book at his entrance.

"Violet," he declared, "I have come for your advice."

"He refuses, then?" she asked, eagerly.

"Absolutely. What am I to do? Bernadine is already upon the scent. He saw him at the Savoy to-day, and recognized him."

"Has Bernadine approached him yet?" Violet inquired.

"Not yet. He is half afraid to move. I think he realizes, or will very soon, how serious this man's existence may be for Germany."

Violet was thoughtful for several moments, then she looked up quickly.

"Bernadine will try the woman," she asserted. "You say that Hagon is infatuated?"

"Blindly," De Grost replied. "He scarcely lets her out of his sight."

"Your people watch Bernadine?"

"Always."

"Very well, then," Violet went on, "you will find that he will attempt an intrigue with the woman. The rest should be easy for you."

De Grost sighed as he bent over his wife.

"My dear," he said, "there is no subtlety like the subtlety of a woman."

Bernadine's instinct had not deceived him, and the following afternoon his servant, who had already received orders, silently ushered Madame Hagon into his apartments. She was wrapped in magnificent sables and heavily veiled. Bernadine saw at once that she was very nervous and wholly terrified. He welcomed her in as matter-of-fact a manner as possible.

"Madame," he declared, "this is quite charming of you. You must sit in my easy-chair here, and my man shall bring us some tea. I drink mine always after the fashion of your country, with lemon, but I doubt whether we make it so well. Won't you unfasten your jacket? I am afraid that my rooms are rather warm."

Madame had collected herself, but it was quite obvious that she was unused to adventures of this sort. Her hand, when he took it, trembled, and more than once she glanced furtively toward the door.

"Yes, I have come," she murmured. "I do not know why. It is not right for me to come. Yet there are times when I am weary, times when Paul seems fierce and when I am terrified. Sometimes I even wish that I were back -"

"Your husband seems very highly strung," Bernadine remarked. "He has doubtless led an exciting life."

"As to that," she replied, gazing around her now and gradually becoming more at her ease, "I know but little. He was a student professor at Moschaume, when I met him. I think that he was at one of the universities in St. Petersburg."

Bernadine glanced at her covertly. It came to him as an implication that the woman did not know the truth.

"You are from Russia, then, after all," he said, smiling. "I felt sure of it."

"Yes," reluctantly. "Paul is so queer in these things. He will not let me talk of it. He prefers that we are taken for French people. Indeed, it is not I who desire to think too much of Russia. It is not a year since my father was killed in the riots, and two of my brothers were sent to Siberia."

Bernadine was deeply interested.

"They were among the revolutionaries?" he asked.

She nodded.

"Yes," she answered.

"And your husband?"

"He, too, was with them in sympathy. Secretly, too, I believe that he worked among them. Only he had to be careful. You see, his position at the college made it difficult."

Bernadine looked into the woman's eyes and he knew then that she was speaking the truth. This man was, indeed, a great master; he had kept her in ignorance!

"Always," Bernadine said, a few minutes later, as he passed her tea, "I read with the deepest interest of the people's movement in Russia. Tell me, what became eventually of their great leader - the wonderful Father Paul?"

She set down her cup untasted, and her blue eyes flashed with a fire which turned them almost to the color of steel.

"Wonderful indeed!" she exclaimed "Wonderful Judas! It was he who wrecked the cause. It was he who sold the lives and liberty of all of us for gold."

"I heard a rumor of that," Bernadine remarked, "but I never believed it."

"It was true," she declared passionately.

"And where is he now?" Bernadine asked.

"Dead!" she answered fiercely. "Torn to pieces, we believe, one night in a house near Moscow. May it be so!"

She was silent for a moment, as though engaged in prayer. Bernadine spoke no more of these things. He talked to her kindly, keeping up always his role of respectful but hopeful admirer.

"You will come again soon?" he begged, when, at last, she insisted upon going.

She hesitated.

"It is so difficult," she murmured. "If my husband knew -"

Bernadine laughed, and touched her fingers caressingly.

"Need one tell him?" he whispered. "You see, I trust you. I pray that you will come -"

Bernadine was a man rarely moved towards emotion of any sort. Yet even he was conscious of a certain sense of excitement, as he stood looking out upon the Embankment from the windows of Paul Hagon's sitting-room, a few days later. Madame was sitting on the sofa, close at hand. It was for her answer to a certain question that he waited.

"Monsieur," she said at last, turning slowly towards him, "it

E. Phillips Oppenheim

must be no. Indeed, I am sorry, for you have been very charming to me, and without you I should have been dull. But to come to your rooms and dine alone to-night, it is impossible."

"Your husband cannot return before the morning, Bernadine reminded her.

"It makes no difference," she answered. "Paul is sometimes fierce and rough, but he is generous, and all his life he has worshiped me. He behaves strangely at times, but I know that he cares - all the time more, perhaps, than I deserve."

"And there is no one else," Bernadine asked softly, "who can claim even the smallest place in your heart?"

"Monsieur," the woman begged, "you must not ask me that. I think that you had better go away."

Bernadine stood quite still for several moments. It was the climax towards which he had steadfastly guided the course of this mild intrigue.

"Madame," he declared, "you must not send me away. You shall not."

She held out her hand.

"Then you must not ask impossible things," she answered.

Then Bernadine took the plunge. He became suddenly very grave.

"Sophia," he said, "I am keeping a great secret from you and I can do it no longer. When you speak to me of your husband you drive me mad. If I believed that you really loved him, I would go away and leave it to chance whether or not you ever discovered the truth. As it is -"

"Well?" she interposed breathlessly.

"As it is," he continued, "I am going to tell you now. Your husband has deceived you - he is deceiving you every moment."

She looked at him incredulously.

"You mean that there is another woman?"

Bernadine shook his head.

"Worse than that," he answered. "Your husband stole even your love under false pretenses. You think that his life is a strange one, that his nerves have broken down, that he flies from place to place for distraction, for change of scene. It is not so. He left Rome, he left Nice, he left Paris, for one and the same reason. He left because he was in peril of his life. I know little of your history, but I know as much as this. If ever a man deserved the fate from which he flees, your husband deserves it."

"You are mad," she faltered.

"No, I am sane," he went on. "It is you who are mad, not to have understood. Your husband goes ever in fear of his life. His real name is one branded with ignominy throughout the world. The man whom you have married, to whom you are so scrupulously faithful, is the man who sent your father to death and your brothers to Siberia."

"Father Paul!" she screamed.

"You have lived with him, you are his wife," Bernadine declared.

The color had left her cheeks; her eyes, with their penciled brows, were fixed in an almost ghastly stare; her breath was coming in uneven gasps. She looked at him in silent terror.

E. Phillips Oppenheim

"It is not true," she cried at last; "it cannot be true."

"Sophia," he said, "you can prove it for yourself. I know a little of your husband and his doings. Does he not carry always with him a black box which he will not allow out of his sight?"

"Always," she assented. "How did you know? By night his hand rests upon it. By day, if he goes out, it is in my charge."

"Fetch it now," Bernadine directed, "and I will prove my words."

She did not hesitate for a moment. She disappeared into the inner room; and came back, only a few moments absent, carrying in her hand a black leather despatch-box.

"You have the key?" he asked.

"Yes," she answered, looking at him and trembling, "but I dare not - oh, I dare not open it!"

"Sophia," he said, "if my words are not true, I will pass out of your life for always. I challenge you. If you open that box you will know that your husband is, indeed, the greatest scoundrel in Europe."

She drew a key from a gold chain around her neck.

"There are two locks," she told him. "The other is a combination, but I know the word. Who's that?"

She started suddenly. There was a loud tapping at the door. Bernadine threw an antimacassar half over the box, but he was too late. De Grost and Hagon had crossed the threshold. The woman stood like some dumb creature. Hagon, transfixed, stood with his eyes riveted upon Bernadine. His face was distorted with passion, he seemed like a man beside himself with fury. De Grost came slowly forward into the middle of the room.

"Count von Hern," he said, "I think that you had better leave."

The woman found words.

"Not yet," she cried, "not yet! Paul, listen to me. This man has told me a terrible thing."

The breath seemed to come through Hagon's teeth like a hiss.

"He has told you!"

"Listen to me," she continued. "It is the truth which you must tell now. He says that you - you are Father Paul."

Hagon did not hesitate for a second.

"It is true," he admitted.

Then there was a silence - short, but tragical. Hagon seemed suddenly to have collapsed. He was like a man who has just had a stroke. He stood muttering to himself.

"It is the end - this - the end!" he said, in a low tone. "Sophia!"

She shrank away from him. He drew himself up. Once more the great light flashed in his face.

"It was for your sake," he said simply, "for your sake, Sophia. I came to you poor and you would have nothing to say to me. My love for you burned in my veins like fever. It was for you I did it - for your sake I sold my honor, the love of my country, the freedom of my brothers. For your sake I risked an awful death. For your sake I have lived like a hunted man, with the cry of the wolves always in my ears, and the fear of death and of eternal torture with me day by day. No other man since the world was made has done more. Have pity on me!"

She was unmoved; her face had lost all expression. No one

noticed in that rapt moment that Bernadine had crept from the room.

"It was you," she cried, "who killed my father, and sent my brothers into exile."

"God help me!" he moaned.

She turned to De Grost.

"Take him away with you, please," she said. "I have finished with him."

"Sophia!" he pleaded.

She leaned across the table and struck him heavily upon the cheek.

"If you stay here," she muttered, "I shall kill you myself ... "

That night, the body of an unknown foreigner was found in the attic of a cheap lodging-house in Soho. The discovery itself and the verdict at the inquest occupied only a few lines in the morning newspapers. Those few lines were the epitaph of one who was very nearly a Rienzi. The greater part of his papers De Grost mercifully destroyed, but one in particular he preserved. Within a week the much delayed treaty was signed at Paris, London and St. Petersburg.

CHAPTER V

THE FIRST SHOT

De Grost and his wife were dining together at the corner table in a fashionable but somewhat Bohemian restaurant. Both had been in the humor for reminiscences, and they had outstayed most of their neighbors.

"I wonder what people really think of us," Violet remarked pensively. "I told Lady Amershal, when she asked us to go there this evening, that we always dined together alone somewhere once a week, and she absolutely refused to believe me. 'With your own husband, my dear?' She kept on repeating."

"Her Ladyship's tastes are more catholic," the Baron declared dryly. "Yet, after all, Violet, the real philosophy of married life demands something of this sort."

Violet smiled and fingered her pearls for a minute.

"What the real philosophy of married life may be I do not know," she said, "but I am perfectly content with our rendering of it. What a fortunate thing, Peter, with your intensely practical turn of mind, that nature endowed you with so much sentiment."

De Grost gazed reflectively at the cigarette which he had just selected from his case.

"Well," he remarked, "there have been times when I have cursed myself for a fool, but, on the whole, sentiment keeps many fires burning."

She leaned towards him and dropped her voice a little. "Tell me," she begged, "do you ever think of the years we spent together in the country? Do you ever regret?"

He smiled thoughtfully.

"It is a hard question, that," he admitted. "There were days there which I loved, but there were days, too, when the restlessness came, days when I longed to hear the hum of the city and to hear men speak whose words were of life and death and the great passions. I am not sure, Violet, whether, after all, it is well for one who has lived to withdraw absolutely from the thrill of life."

She laughed, Softly but gayly.

"I am with you," she declared, "absolutely. I think that the fairies must have poured into my blood the joy of living for its own sake. I should be an ungrateful woman indeed, if I found anything to complain of, nowadays. Yet there is one thing that troubles me," she went on, after a moment's pause.

"And that?" he asked.

"The danger," she said, slowly. "I do not want to lose you, Peter. There are times when I am afraid."

De Grost flicked the ash from his cigarette.

"The days are passing," he remarked, "when men point revolvers at one another, and hire assassins to gain their ends. Now, it is more a battle of wits. We play chess on the board of Life still, but we play with ivory pieces instead of steel and poison. Our brains direct and not our muscles."

She sighed.

"It is only the one man of whom I am afraid. You have outwitted him so often and he does not forgive."

De Grost smiled. It was an immense compliment - this.

"Bernadine," he murmured, softly, "otherwise, our friend the Count von Hern."

"Bernadine!" she repeated. "All that you say is true, but when one fails with modern weapons, one changes the form of attack. Bernadine at heart is a savage."

"The hate of such a man," De Grost remarked complacently, "is worth having. He has had his own way over here for years. He seems to have found the knack of living in a maze of intrigue and remaining untouchable. There were a dozen things before I came upon the scene which ought to have ruined him. Yet there never appeared to be anything to take hold of. Even the Criminal Department once thought they had a chance. I remember John Dory telling me in disgust that Bernadine was like one of those marvelous criminals one only reads about in fiction, who seem, when they pass along the dangerous places, to walk upon the air, and, leave no trace behind."

"Before you came," she said, "he had never known a failure. Do you think that he is a man likely to forgive?"

"I do not," De Grost answered grimly. "It is a battle, of course, a battle all the time. Yet, Violet, between you and me, if Bernadine were to go, half the savor of life for me would depart with him."

Then there came a curious and wholly unexpected interruption. A man in dark, plain clothes, still wearing his overcoat, and carrying a bowler hat, had been standing in the entrance of the restaurant for a moment or two, looking around the room as though in search of some one. At last he caught the eye of the Baron de Grost and came quickly toward him.

"Charles," the Baron remarked, raising his eyebrows. "I wonder what he wants."

A sudden cloud had fallen upon their little feast. Violet watched the coming of her husband's servant, and the reading of the note which he presented to his master, with an anxiety which she could not wholly conceal. The Baron read the note twice, scrutinizing a certain part of it closely with the aid of the monocle which he seldom used. Then he folded it up and placed it in the breast pocket of his coat.

"At what hour did you receive this, Charles?" he asked.

"A messenger brought it in a taxicab about ten minutes ago, sir," the man replied. "He said that it was of the utmost importance, and that I had better try and find you."

"A district messenger?"

"A man in ordinary clothes," Charles answered. "He looked like a porter in a warehouse, or something of that sort. I forgot to say that you were rung up on the telephone three times previously by Mr. Greening."

The Baron nodded.

"You can go," he said. "There is no reply."

The man bowed and retired. De Grost called for his bill.

"Is it anything serious?" Violet inquired.

"No, not exactly serious," he answered. "I do not understand what has happened, but they have sent for me to go - well, where it was agreed that I should not go except as a matter of urgent necessity."

Violet knew better than to show any signs of disquietude.

"It is in London?" she asked.

"Certainly," her husband replied. "I shall take a taxicab from here. I am sorry, dear, to have one of our evenings disturbed in this manner. I have always done my best to avoid it, but this summons is urgent."

She rose and he wrapped her cloak around her.

"You will drive straight home, won't you?" he begged. "I dare say that I may be back within an hour myself."

"And if not?" she asked, in a low tone.

"If not, there is nothing to be done."

Violet bit her lip, but, as he handed her into the small electric brougham which was waiting, she smiled into his face.

"You will come back, and soon, Peter," she declared, confidently. "Wherever you go I am sure of that. You see, I have faith in my star which watches over you."

He kissed her fingers and turned away. The commissionaire had already called him a taxicab.

"To London Bridge," he ordered, after a moment's hesitation, and drove off.

The traffic citywards had long since finished for the day, and he reached his destination within ten minutes of leaving the restaurant. Here he paid the man, and, entering the station, turned to the refreshment room and ordered a liqueur brandy. While he sipped it, he smoked a cigarette and carefully reread in a strong light the note which he had received. The signature especially he pored over for some time. At last, however, he replaced it in his pocket, paid his bill, and, stepping out once more on to the platform, entered a telephone booth. A few minutes later he left the station, and, turning to the right, walked slowly as far as Tooley Street. He kept on the right-hand side until he arrived at the spot where the great arches, with their scanty lights, make a gloomy thoroughfare into Bermondsey. In the shadow of the first of these he paused, and looked steadfastly across the street. There were few people passing and practically no traffic. In front of him was a row of warehouses, all save one of which was wrapped in complete darkness. It was the one where some lights were still burning which De Grost stood and watched.

The lights, such as they were, seemed to illuminate the ground floor only. From his hidden post he could see the shoulders of a man apparently bending over a ledger, diligently writing. At the next window a youth, seated upon a tall stool, was engaged in presumably the same occupation. There was nothing about the place in the least mysterious or out of the way. Even the blinds of the offices had been left undrawn. The man and the boy, who were alone visible, seemed, in a sense, to be working under protest. Every now and then the former stopped to yawn, and the latter performed a difficult balancing feat upon his stool. De Grost, having satisfied his curiosity, came presently from his shelter, almost running into the arms of a policeman, who looked at him closely. The Baron, who had an unlighted cigarette in his mouth, stopped to ask for a light, and his appearance at once set at rest any suspicions the policeman might have had.

"I have a warehouse myself down in these parts," he remarked, as he struck the match, "but I don't allow my people to work as late as that."

He pointed across the way, and the policeman smiled.

"They are very often late there, sir," he said. "It's a Continental wine business, and there's always one or two of them over time."

"It's bad business, all the same," De Grost declared pleasantly.

"Good night, policeman!"

"Good night, sir!"

De Grost crossed the road diagonally, as though about to take the short cut across London Bridge, but as soon as the policeman was out of sight he retraced his steps to the building which they had been discussing, and turning the battered brass handle of the door, walked calmly in. On his right and left were counting houses framed with glass; in front, the cavernous and ugly depths of a gloomy warehouse. He knocked upon the window-pane on the right and passed forward a step or two, as though to enter the office. The boy, who had been engaged in the left-hand counting house, came gliding from his place, passed silently behind the visitor and turned the key of the outer door. What followed seemed to happen as though by some mysteriously directed force. The figures of men came stealing out from the hidden places. The clerk who had been working so hard at his desk calmly divested himself of a false mustache and wig, and, assuming a more familiar appearance, strolled out into the warehouse. De Grost looked around him with absolutely unruffled composure. He was the centre of a little circle of men, respectably dressed, but every one of them hard-featured, with something in their faces which suggested not the ordinary toiler, but the fighting animal - the man who lives by his wits and knows something of danger. On the outskirts of the circle stood Bernadine.

"Really," De Grost declared, "this is most unexpected. In the matter of dramatic surprises, my friend Bernadine, you are certainly in a class by yourself."

Bernadine smiled.

"You will understand, of course," he said, "that this little entertainment is entirely for your amusement - well stage-managed, perhaps, but my supers are not to be taken seriously.

E. Phillips Oppenheim

Since you are here, Baron, might I ask you to precede me a few steps to the tasting office?

"By all means," De Grost answered cheerfully, "It is this way, I believe."

He walked with unconcerned footsteps down the warehouse, on either side of which were great bins and a wilderness of racking, until he came to a small, glass-enclosed office, built out from the wall. Without hesitation he entered it, and removing his hat, selected the more comfortable of the two chairs. Bernadine alone of the others followed him inside, closing the door behind. De Grost, who appeared exceedingly comfortable, stretched out his hand and took a small black bottle from a tiny mahogany racking fixed against the wall by his side.

"You will excuse me, my dear Bernadine," he said, "but I see my friend Greening has been tasting a few wines. The 'XX' upon the label here signifies approval. With your permission."

He half filled a glass and pushed the bottle toward Bernadine.

"Greening's taste is unimpeachable," De Grost declared, setting down his glass empty. "No use being a director of a city business, you know, unless one interests oneself personally in it. Greening's judgment is simply marvelous. I have never tasted a more beautiful wine. If the boom in sherry does come," he continued complacently, "we shall be in an excellent position to deal with it."

Bernadine laughed softly.

"Oh, my friend - Peter Ruff, or Baron de Grost, or whatever you may choose to call yourself," he said, "I am indeed wise to have come to the conclusion that you and I are too big to occupy the same little spot on earth!"

De Grost nodded approvingly.

"I was beginning to wonder," he remarked, "whether you would not soon arrive at that decision."

"Having arrived at it," Bernadine continued, looking intently at his companion, "the logical sequence naturally occurs to you."

"Precisely, my dear Bernadine," De Grost asserted. "You say to yourself, no doubt, 'One of us two must go!' Being yourself, you would naturally conclude that it must be I. To tell you the truth, I have been expecting some sort of enterprise of this description for a considerable time."

Bernadine shrugged his shoulders.

"Your expectations," he said, "seem scarcely to have provided you with a safe conduct."

De Grost gazed reflectively into his empty glass.

"You see," he explained, "I am such a lucky person. Your arrangements to-night, however, are, I perceive, unusually complete."

"I am glad you appreciate them," Bernadine remarked dryly.

"I would not for a moment," De Grost continued, "ask an impertinent or an unnecessary question, but I must confess that I am rather concerned to know the fate of my manager - the gentleman whom you yourself with the aid, I presume, of Mr. Clarkson, so ably represented."

Bernadine sighed.

"Alas!" he said, "your manager was a very obstinate person."

"And my clerk?"

"Incorruptible, absolutely incorruptible. I congratulate you,

De Grost. Your society is one of the most wonderful upon the face of this earth. I know little about it, but my admiration is very sincere. Their attention to details, and the personnel of their staff, is almost perfect. I may tell you at once that no sum that could be offered, tempted either of these men."

"I am delighted to hear it," De Grost replied, "but I must plead guilty to a little temporary anxiety as to their present whereabouts."

"At this moment," Bernadine remarked, "they are within a few feet of us, but, as you are doubtless aware, access to your delightful river is obtainable from these premises. To be frank with you, my dear Baron, we are waiting for the tide to rise."

"So thoughtful about these trifles," De Grost murmured. "But their present position? They are, I trust, not uncomfortable?"

Bernadine stood up and moved to the further end of the office. He beckoned his companion to his side and, drawing an electric torch from his pocket, flashed the light into a dark corner behind an immense bin. The forms of a man and a youth, bound with ropes and gagged, lay stretched upon the floor. De Grost sighed.

"I am afraid," he said, "that Mr. Greening, at any rate, is most uncomfortable."

Bernadine turned off the light.

"At least, Baron," he declared, "if such extreme measures should become necessary, I can promise you one thing - you shall have a quicker passage into Eternity than they."

De Grost resumed his seat.

"Has it really come to that?" he asked. "Will nothing but so crude a proceeding as my absolute removal satisfy you?"

"Nothing else is, I fear, practicable," Bernadine replied, "unless you decide to listen to reason. Believe me, my dear friend, I shall miss you and our small encounters exceedingly, but, unfortunately, you stand in the way of my career. You are the only man who has persistently balked me. You have driven me to use against you means which I had grown to look upon as absolutely extinct in the upper circles of our profession."

De Grost peered through the glass walls of the office.

"Eight men, not counting yourself," he remarked, "and my poor manager and his faithful clerk lying bound and helpless. It is heavy odds, Bernadine."

"There is no question of odds, I think," Bernadine answered smoothly. "You are much too clever a person to refuse to admit that you are entirely in my power."

"And as regards terms? I really don't feel in the least anxious to make my final bow with so little notice," De Grost said. "To tell you the truth, I have been finding life quite interesting lately."

Bernadine eyed his prisoner keenly. Such absolute composure was in itself disturbing. He was, for the moment, aware of a slight sensation of uneasiness, which his common sense, however, speedily disposed of.

"There are two ways," he announced, "of dealing with an opponent. There is the old-fashioned one - crude, but in a sense eminently satisfactory - which sends him finally to adorn some other sphere."

"I don't like that one," De Grost interrupted. "Get on with the alternative."

"The alternative," Bernadine declared, "is when his capacity for harm can be destroyed."

"That needs a little explanation," De Grost murmured.

"Precisely. For instance, if you were to become absolutely discredited, I think that you would be effectually out of my way. Your people do not forgive."

"Then discredit me, by all means," De Grost begged. "It sounds unpleasant, but I do not like your callous reference to the river."

Bernadine gazed at his ancient opponent for several moments. After all, what was this but the splendid bravado of a beaten man, who is too clever not to recognize defeat?

"I shall require," he said, "your code, the keys of your safe, which contains a great many documents of interest to me, and a free entry into your house."

De Grost drew a bunch of keys reluctantly from his pocket and laid them upon the desk.

"You will find the code bound in green morocco leather," he announced, "on the left-hand side, underneath the duplicate of a proposed Treaty between Italy and some other Power. Between ourselves, Bernadine, I really expect that that is what you are after."

Bernadine's eyes glistened.

"What about the safe conduct into your house?" he asked.

De Grost drew his case from his pocket and wrote few lines on the back of one of his cards.

"This will insure you entrance there," he said, "and access to my study. If you see my wife, please reassure her as to my absence."

"I shall certainly do so," Bernadine agreed, with a faint smile.

"If I may be pardoned for alluding to a purely personal matter," De Grost continued, "what is to become of me?"

"You will be bound and gagged in the same manner as your manager and his clerk," Bernadine replied, smoothly. "I regret the necessity, but you see, I can afford to run no risks. At four o'clock in the morning, you will be released. It must be part of our agreement that you allow the man who stays behind the others for the purpose of setting you free, to depart unmolested. I think I know you better than to imagine you would be guilty of such gaucherie as an appeal to the police."

"That, unfortunately," De Grost declared, with a little sigh, "is, as you well know, out of the question. You are too clever for me, Bernadine. After all, I shall have to go back to my farm."

Bernadine opened the door and called softly to one of his men. In less than five minutes De Grost was bound hand and foot. Bernadine stepped back and eyed his adversary with an air of ill-disguised triumph.

"I trust, Baron," he said, "that you will be as comfortable as possible, under the circumstances."

De Grost lay quite still. He was powerless to move or speak.

"Immediately," Bernadine continued, "I have presented myself at your house, verified your safe conduct, and helped myself to certain papers which I am exceedingly anxious to obtain," he went on, "I shall telephone here to the man whom I leave in charge and you will be set at liberty in due course. If, for any reason, I meet with treachery and I do not telephone, you will join Mr. Greening and his young companion in a little - shall we call it aquatic recreation? I wish you a pleasant hour and success in the future, Baron - as a farmer."

Bernadine withdrew and whispered his orders to his men. Soon the electric light was turned out and the place was in

E. Phillips Oppenheim

darkness. The front door was opened and closed; the group of confederates upon the pavement lit cigarettes and wished one another good night with the brisk air of tired employees, released at last from long labors. Then there was silence.

It was barely eleven when Bernadine reached the west end of London. His clothes had become a trifle disarranged and he called for a few minutes at his rooms in St. James's Street. Afterwards, he walked to Porchester House and rang the bell. To the servant who answered it, he handed his master's card.

"Will you show me the way to the library?" he asked. "I have some papers to collect for the Baron de Grost."

The man hesitated. Even with the card in his hand, it seemed a somewhat unusual proceeding.

"Will you step inside, sir?" he begged. "I should like to show this to the Baroness. The master is exceedingly particular about any one entering his study."

"Do what you like so long as you do not keep me waiting," Bernadine replied. "Your master's instructions are clear enough."

Violet came down the great staircase a few moments later, still in her dinner gown, her face a little pale, her eyes luminous. Bernadine smiled as he accepted her eagerly offered hand. She was evidently anxious. A thrill of triumph warmed his blood. Once she had been less kind to him than she seemed now.

"My husband gave you this!" she exclaimed.

"A few minutes ago," Bernadine answered. "He tried to make his instructions as clear as possible. We are jointly interested in a small matter which needs immediate action."

She led the way to the study.

"It seems strange," she remarked, "that you and he should be working together. I always thought that you were on opposite sides."

"It is a matter of chance," Bernadine told her. "Your husband is a wise man, Baroness. He knows when to listen to reason."

She threw open the door of the study, which was in darkness;

"If you will wait a moment," she said, closing the door, "I will turn on the electric light."

She touched the knobs in the wall and the room was suddenly flooded with illumination. At the further end of the apartment was the great safe. Close to it, in an easy chair, his evening coat changed for a smoking jacket, with a neatly tied black tie replacing his crumpled white cravat, the Baron de Grost sat awaiting his guest. A fierce oath broke from Bernadine's lips. He turned toward the door only in time to hear the key turn. Violet tossed it lightly in the air across to her husband.

"My dear Bernadine," the latter remarked, "on the whole, I do not think that this has been one of your successes. My keys, if you please."

Bernadine stood for a moment, his face dark with passion. He bit his lip till the blood came, and the veins at the back of his clenched hands were swollen and thick. Nevertheless, when he spoke he had recovered in great measure his self-control.

"Your keys are here, Baron de Grost," he said, placing them upon the table. "If a bungling amateur may make such a request of a professor, may I inquire how you escaped from your bonds, passed through the door of a locked warehouse and reached here before me?"

The Baron de Grost smiled as he pushed the cigarettes across to his visitor.

E. Phillips Oppenheim

"Really," he said, "you have only to think for yourself for a moment, my dear Bernadine, and you will understand. In the first place, the letter you sent me signed 'Greening' was clearly a forgery. There was no one else anxious to get me into their power, hence I associated it at once with you. Naturally, I telephoned to the chief of my staff - I, too, am obliged to employ some of these un-uniformed policemen, my dear Bernadine, as you may be aware. It may interest you to know, further, that there are seven entrances to the warehouse in Tooley Street. Through one of these something like twenty of my men passed and were already concealed in the place when I entered. At another of the doors a motor-car waited for me. If I had chosen to lift my finger at any time, your men would have been overpowered and I might have had the pleasure of dictating terms to you in my own office. Such a course did not appeal to me. You and I, as you know, dear Count von Hern, conduct our peculiar business under very delicate conditions, and the least thing we either of us desire is notoriety. I managed things, as I thought, for the best. The moment you left the place my men swarmed in. We kindly, but gently, ejected your guard, released Greening and my clerk, and I passed you myself in Fleet Street, a little more comfortable, I think, in my forty-horsepower motor-car than you in that very disreputable hansom. As to my presence here, I have an entrance from the street there which makes me independent of my servants. The other details are too absurdly simple; one need not enlarge upon them."

Bernadine turned slowly to Violet.

"You knew?" he muttered. "You knew when you brought me here?"

"Naturally," she answered. "We have telephones in every room in the house."

"I am at your service," Bernadine declared, calmly.

De Grost laughed.

"My dear fellow," he said, "need I say that you are free to come or go, to take a whiskey and soda with me, or to depart at once, exactly as you feel inclined? The door was locked only until you restored to me my keys."

He crossed the room, fitted the key in the lock and turned it.

"We do not make war as those others," he remarked, smiling.

Bernadine drew himself up.

"I will not drink with you," he said, "I will not smoke with you. But some day this reckoning shall come."

He turned to the door. De Grost laid his finger upon the bell.

"Show Count von Hern out," he directed the astonished servant who appeared a moment or two later.

E. Phillips Oppenheim

CHAPTER VI

THE SEVEN SUPPERS OF ANDREA KORUST

Peter, Baron de Grost, was enjoying what he had confidently looked forward to as an evening's relaxation, pure and simple. He sat in one of the front rows of the stalls of the Alhambra, his wife by his side and an excellent cigar in his mouth. An hour or so ago he had been in telephonic communication with Paris, had spoken with Sogrange himself, and received his assurance of a calm in political and criminal affairs amounting almost to stagnation. It was out of season, and, though his popularity was as great as ever, neither he nor his wife had any social engagements; hence this evening at a music hall, which Peter, for his part, was finding thoroughly amusing.

The place was packed - some said owing to the engagement of Andrea Korust and his brother, others to the presence of Mademoiselle Sophie Celaire in her wonderful danse des apaches. The violinist that night had a great reception. Three times he was called before the curtain; three times he was obliged to reiterate his grateful but immutable resolve never to yield to the nightly storm which demanded more from a man who has given of his best. Slim, with the worn face and hollow eyes of a genius, he stood and bowed his thanks, but when he thought the time had arrived, he disappeared, and though the house shook for minutes afterwards, nothing could persuade him to reappear.

Afterwards came the turn which, notwithstanding the furore

caused by Andrea Korust's appearance, was generally considered to be equally responsible for the packed house - the apache dance of Mademoiselle Sophie Celaire. Peter sat slightly forward in his chair as the curtain went up. For a time he seemed utterly absorbed by the performance. Violet glanced at him once or twice curiously. It began to occur to her that it was not so much the dance as the dancer in whom her husband was interested.

"You have seen her before - this Mademoiselle Celaire?" she whispered.

"Yes," said Peter, nodding, "I have seen her before."

The dance proceeded. It was like many others of its sort, only a little more daring, a little more finished. Mademoiselle Celaire, in her tight-fitting, shabby black frock, with her wild mass of hair, her flashing eyes, her seductive gestures, was, without doubt, a marvelous person. Peter, Baron de Grost, watched her every movement with absorbed attention. When the curtain went down he forgot to clap. His eyes followed her off the stage. Violet shrugged her shoulders. She was looking very handsome herself in a black velvet dinner gown, and a hat so exceedingly Parisian that no one had had the heart to ask her to remove it.

"My dear Peter," she remarked, reprovingly, "a moderate amount of admiration for that very agile young lady I might, perhaps, be inclined to tolerate; but, having watched you for the last quarter of an hour, I am bound to confess that I am becoming jealous."

"Of Mademoiselle Celaire?" he asked.

"Of Mademoiselle Sophie Celaire."

He leaned a little towards her. His lips were parted; he was about to make a statement or a confession. Just then a tall commissionaire leaned over from behind and touched him on

E. Phillips Oppenheim

the shoulder.

"For Monsieur le Baron de Grost," he announced, handing Peter a note.

Peter glanced towards his wife.

"You permit me?" he murmured, breaking the seal.

Violet shrugged her shoulders, ever so slightly. Her husband was already absorbed in the few lines hastily scrawled across the sheet of notepaper which he held in his hand.

MONSIEUR LE BARON DE GHOST.

Dear Monsieur le Baron,

4 Come to my dressing-room, without 4 fail, as soon as you receive this.

SOPHIE CELAIRE.

Violet looked over his shoulder.

"The hussy!" she exclaimed, indignantly. Her husband raised his eyebrows. With his forefinger he merely tapped the two numerals.

"The Double-Four!" she gasped.

He looked around and nodded. The commissionaire was waiting. Peter took up his silk hat from under the seat.

"If I am detained, dear," he whispered, "you'll make the best of it, won't you? The car will be here and Frederick will be looking out for you."

"Of course," she answered, cheerfully. "I shall be quite all right."

She nodded brightly and Peter took his departure. He passed through a door on which was painted "Private," and through a maze of scenery and stage hands and ballet ladies by a devious route to the region of the dressing-rooms. His guide conducted him to the door of one of these and knocked.

"Entrez, monsieur," a shrill feminine voice replied.

Peter entered and closed the door behind him. The commissionaire remained outside. Mademoiselle Celaire turned to greet her visitor.

"It is a few words I desire with you as quickly as possible, if you please, Monsieur le Baron," she said, advancing towards him. "Listen."

She had brushed out her hair and it hung from her head straight and a little stiff, almost like the hair of an Indian woman. She had washed her face, too, free of all cosmetics and her pallor was almost waxen. She wore a dressing gown of green silk. Her discarded black frock lay upon the floor.

"I am entirely at your service, mademoiselle," Peter answered, bowing. "Continue, if you please."

"You sup with me to-night - you are my guest."

He hesitated.

"I am very much honored," he murmured. "It is an affair of urgency, then? Mademoiselle will remember that I am not alone here."

She threw out her hands scornfully.

"They told me in Paris that you were a genius!" she exclaimed. "Cannot you feel, then, when a thing is urgent? Do you not know it without being told? You must meet me with a carriage at the stage door in forty minutes. We sup in Hamilton Place

E. Phillips Oppenheim

with Andrea Korust and his brother."

"With whom?" Peter asked, surprised.

"With the Korust Brothers," she repeated. "I have just been talking to Andrea. He calls himself a Hungarian. Bah! They are as much Hungarian, those young men, as I am!"

Peter leaned slightly against the table and looked thoughtfully at his companion. He was trying to remember whether he had ever heard anything of these young men.

"Mademoiselle," he said, "the prospect of partaking of any meal in your company is in itself enchanting, but I do not know your friends, the Korust Brothers. Apart from their wonderful music, I do not recollect ever having heard of them before in my life. What excuse have I, then, for accepting their hospitality? Pardon me, too, if I add that you have not as yet spoken as to the urgency of this affair."

She turned from him impatiently and, throwing herself back into the chair from which she had risen at his entrance, she began to exchange the thick woolen stockings which she had been wearing upon the stage for others of fine silk.

"Oh, la, la!" she exclaimed. "You are very slow, Monsieur le Baron. It is, perhaps, my stage name which has misled you. I am Marie Lapouse. Does that convey anything to you?"

"A great deal," Peter admitted, quickly. "You stand very high upon the list of my agents whom I may trust."

"Then stay here no longer," she begged, "for my maid waits outside and I need her services. Go back and make your excuses to your wife. In forty minutes I shall expect you at the stage door."

"An affair of diplomacy, this, or brute force?" he inquired.

"Heaven knows what may happen!" she replied. "To tell you the truth, I do not know myself. Be prepared for anything, but, for Heaven's sake, go now! I can dress no further without my maid, and Andrea Korust may come in at any moment. I do not wish him to find you here."

Peter made his way thoughtfully back to his seat. He explained the situation to his wife so far as he could, and sent her home. Then he waited about until the car returned, smoking a cigarette and trying once more to remember if he had ever heard anything from Sogrange of Andrea Korust or his brother. Punctually at the time stated he was outside the stage door of the music-hall, and a few minutes later Mademoiselle Celaire appeared, a dazzling vision of fur and smiles and jewelry imperfectly concealed. A small crowd pressed around to see the famous Frenchwoman. Peter handed her gravely across the pavement into his waiting car. One or two of the loungers gave vent to a groan of envy at the sight of the diamonds which blazed from her neck and bosom. Peter smiled as he gave the address to his servant and took his place by the side of his companion.

"They see only the externals, this mob," he remarked. "They picture to themselves, perhaps, a little supper for two. Alas!"

Mademoiselle Celaire laughed at him softly.

"You need not trouble to assume that most disconsolate of expressions, my dear Baron," she assured him. "Your reputation as a man of gallantry is beyond question; but remember that I know you also for the most devoted and loyal of husbands. We waste no time in folly, you and I. It is the business of the Double-Four."

Peter was relieved, but his innate politeness forbade his showing it.

"Proceed," he said.

E. Phillips Oppenheim

"The Brothers Korust," she went on, leaning towards him, "have a week's engagement at the Alhambra. Their salary is six hundred pounds. They play very beautifully, of course, but I think that it is as much as they are worth."

Peter agreed with her fervently. He had no soul for music.

"They have taken the furnished house belonging to one of your dukes, in Hamilton Place, for which we are now bound; taken it, too, at a fabulous rent," Mademoiselle Celaire continued. "They, have installed there a chef and a whole retinue of servants. They are here for seven nights; they have issued invitations for seven supper parties."

"Hospitable young men they seem to be," Peter murmured. "I read in one of the stage papers that Andrea is a Count in his own country, and that they perform in public only for the love of their music and for the sake of the excitement and travel."

"A paragraph wholly inspired and utterly false," Mademoiselle Celaire declared, firmly, sitting a little forward in the car, and laying her hand, ablaze with jewels, upon his coat sleeve. "Listen. They call themselves Hungarians. Bah! I know that they are in touch with a great European court, both of them, the court of the country to which they belong. They have plans, plans and schemes connected with their visit here, which I do not understand. I have done my best with Andrea Korust, but he is not a man to be trusted. I know that there is something more in these seven supper parties than idle hospitality. I and others like me, artistes and musicians, are invited, to give the assembly a properly Bohemian tone; but there are to be other guests, attracted there, no doubt, because the papers have spoken of these gatherings."

"You have some idea of what it all means, in your mind?" Peter suggested.

"It is too vague to put into words," she declared, shaking her head. "We must both watch. Afterwards, we will, if you like, compare notes."

The car drew up before the doors of a handsome house in Hamilton Place. A footman received Peter and relieved him of his hat and overcoat. A trim maid performed the same office for Mademoiselle Celaire. They met, a moment or two later, and were ushered into a large drawing-room in which a dozen or two of men and women were already assembled, and from which came a pleasant murmur of voices and laughter. The apartment was hung with pale green satin; the furniture was mostly Chippendale, upholstered in the same shade. A magnificent grand piano stood open in a smaller room, just visible beyond. Only one thing seemed strange to the two newly arrived guests. The room was entirely lit with shaded candles, giving a certain mysterious but not unpleasant air of obscurity to the whole suite of apartments. Through the gloom, the jewels and eyes of the women seemed to shine with a new brilliance. Slight eccentricities of toilette, for a part of the gathering was distinctly Bohemian, were softened and subdued. The whole effect was somewhat weird, but also picturesque.

Andrea Korust advanced from a little group to meet his guests. Off the stage he seemed at first sight frailer and slighter than ever. His dress coat had been exchanged for a velvet dinner jacket, and his white tie for a drooping black bow. He had a habit of blinking nearly all the time, as though his large brown eyes, which he seldom wholly opened, were weaker than they appeared to be. Nevertheless, when he came to within a few paces of his newly arrived visitors, they shone with plenty of expression. Without any change of countenance, however, he held out his hand.

"Dear Andrea," Mademoiselle Celaire exclaimed, "you permit me that I present to you my dear friend, well known in Paris - alas! many years ago - Monsieur le Baron de Grost. Monsieur le Baron was kind enough to pay his respects to me this evening, and I have induced him to become my escort here."

"It was my good fortune," Peter remarked, smiling, "that I saw Mademoiselle Celaire's name upon the bills this evening - my good fortune, since it has procured for me the honor of an acquaintance with a musician so distinguished."

"You are very kind, Monsieur le Baron," Korust replied.

"You stay here, I regret to hear, a very short time?"

"Alas!" Andrea Korust admitted, "it is so. For myself I would that it were longer. I find your London so attractive, the people so friendly. They fall in with my whims so charmingly. I have a hatred, you know, of solitude. I like to make acquaintances wherever I go, to have delightful women and interesting men around, to forget that life is not always gay. If I am too much alone, I am miserable, and when I am miserable I am in a very bad way indeed. I cannot then make music."

Peter smiled gravely and sympathetically.

"And your brother? Does he, too, share your gregarious instincts?"

Korust paused for a moment before replying. His eyes were quite wide open now. If one could judge from his expression, one would certainly have said that the Baron de Grost's attempts to ingratiate himself with his host were distinctly unsuccessful.

"My brother has exactly opposite instincts," he said slowly. "He finds no pleasure in society. At the sound of a woman's voice, he hides."

"He is not here, then?" Peter asked, glancing around.

Andrea Korust shook his head.

"It is doubtful whether he joins us this evening at all," he declared. "My sister, however, is wholly of my disposition.

Monsieur le Baron will permit that I present him."

Peter bowed low before a very handsome young woman with flashing black eyes, and a type of features undoubtedly belonging to one of the countries of eastern Europe. She was picturesquely dressed in a gown of flaming red silk, made as though in one piece, without trimming or flounces, and she seemed inclined to bestow upon her new acquaintance all the attention that he might desire. She took him at once into a corner and seated herself by his side. It was impossible for Peter not to associate the empressement of her manner with the few words which Andrea Korust had whispered into her ear at the moment of their introduction.

"So you," she murmured, "are the wonderful Baron de Grost. I have heard of you so often."

"Wonderful!" Peter repeated, with twinkling eyes. "I have never been called that before. I feel that I have no claims whatever to distinction, especially in a gathering like this."

She shrugged her shoulders and glanced carelessly across the room.

"They are well enough," she admitted, "but one wearies of genius on every side of one. Genius is not the best thing in the world to live with, you know. It has whims and fancies. For instance, look at these rooms - the gloom, the obscurity - and I love so much the light."

Peter smiled.

"It is the privilege of genius," he remarked, "to have whims and to indulge in them."

She sighed.

"To do Andrea justice," she said, "it is, perhaps, scarcely a whim that he chooses to receive his guests in semi-darkness.

He has weak eyes and he is much too vain to wear spectacles. Tell me, you know every one here?"

"No one," Peter declared. "Please enlighten me, if you think it necessary. For myself," he added, dropping his voice a little, "I feel that the happiness of my evening is assured, without making any further acquaintances."

"But you came as the guest of Mademoiselle Celaire," she reminded him, doubtfully, with a faint regretful sigh and a provocative gleam in her eyes.

"I saw Mademoiselle Celaire to-night for the first time for years," Peter replied. "I called to see her in her dressing-room and she claimed me for an escort this evening. I am, alas! a very occasional wanderer in the pleasant paths of Bohemia."

"If that is really true," she murmured, "I suppose I must tell you something about the people, or you will feel that you have wasted your opportunity."

"Mademoiselle," Peter whispered.

She held out her hand and laughed into his face.

"No!" she interrupted. "I shall do my duty. Opposite you is Mademoiselle Trezani, the famous singer at Covent Garden. Do I need to tell you that, I wonder? Rudolf Maesterling, the dramatist, stands behind her there in the corner. He is talking to the wonderful Cleo, whom all the world knows. Monsieur Guyer there, he is manager, I believe, of the Alhambra; and talking to him is Marborg, the great pianist. One of the ladies talking to my brother is Esther Braithwaite, whom, of course, you know by sight; she is leading lady, is she not, at the Hilarity? The other is Miss Ransome; they tell me that she is your only really great English actress."

Peter nodded appreciatively.

"It is all most interesting," he declared. "Now tell me, please, who is the military person with the stiff figure and sallow complexion, standing by the door? He seems quite alone."

The girl made a little grimace.

"I suppose I ought to be looking after him," she admitted, rising reluctantly to her feet. "He is a soldier just back from India - a General Noseworthy, with all sorts of letters after his name. If Mademoiselle Celaire is generous, perhaps we may have a few minutes' conversation later on," she added, with a parting smile.

"Say, rather, if Mademoiselle Korust is kind," De Grost replied, bowing. "It depends upon that only."

He strolled across the room and rejoined Mademoiselle Celaire a few moments later. They stood apart in a corner.

"I should like my supper," Peter declared.

"They wait for one more guest," Mademoiselle Celaire announced.

"One more guest! Do you know who it is?"

"No idea," she answered. "One would imagine that it was some one of importance. Are you any wiser than when you came, dear master?" she added, under her breath.

"Not a whit," he replied, promptly.

She took out her fan and waved it slowly in front of her face.

"Yet you must discover what it all means to-night or not at all," she whispered. "The dear Andrea has intimated to me most delicately that another escort would be more acceptable if I should honor him again."

"That helps," he murmured. "See, our last guest arrives."

A tall, - spare-looking man was just being announced. They heard his name as Andrea presented him to a companion -

"Colonel Mayson!"

Mademoiselle Celaire saw a gleam in her companion's eyes.

"It is coming - the idea?" she whispered.

"Very vaguely," he admitted.

"Who is this Colonel Mayson?"

"Our only military aeronaut," Peter replied.

She raised her eyebrows.

"Aeronaut!" she repeated, doubtfully. "I see nothing in that. Both my own country and Germany are years ahead of poor England in the air. Is it not so?"

Peter smiled and held out his arm.

"See," he said, "supper has been announced. Afterwards, Andrea Korust will play to us, and I think that Colonel Mayson and his distinguished brother officer from India will talk. We shall see."

They passed into a room whose existence had suddenly been revealed by the drawing back of some beautiful brocaded curtains. Supper was a delightful meal, charmingly served. Peter, putting everything else out of his head for the moment, thoroughly enjoyed himself, and, remembering his duty as a guest, contributed in no small degree towards the success of the entertainment. He sat between Mademoiselle Celaire and his hostess, both of whom demanded much from him in the way of attention. But he still found time to tell stories which were listened to by every one, and exchanged sallies with the gayest. Only Andrea Korust, from his place at the head of the table, glanced occasionally towards his popular guest with a curious, half-hidden expression of distaste and suspicion.

The more the Baron de Grost shone, the more uneasy he became. The signal to rise from the meal was given almost abruptly. Mademoiselle Korust hung on to Peter's arm. Her own wishes and her brother's orders seemed absolutely to coincide. She led him towards a retiring corner of the music room. On the way, however, Peter overheard the introduction which he had expected.

"General Noseworthy is just returned from India, Colonel Mayson," Korust said, in his usual quiet, tired tone. "You will, perhaps, find it interesting to talk together a little. As for me, I play because all are polite enough to wish it, but conversation disturbs me not in the least."

Peter passed, smiling, on to the corner pointed out by his companion, which was the darkest and most secluded in the room. He took her fan and gloves, lit her cigarette, and leaned back by her side.

"How does your brother, a stranger to London, find time to make the acquaintance of so many interesting people?" he asked.

"He brought many letters," she replied. "He has friends everywhere."

"I have an idea," Peter remarked, "that an acquaintance of my own, the Count von Hern, spoke to me once about him."

She took her cigarette from her lips and turned her head slightly. Peter's expression was one of amiable reminiscence. His cheeks were a trifle flushed, his appearance was entirely reassuring. She laughed at her brother's caution. She found her companion delightful.

"Yes, the Count von Hern is a friend of my brother's," she admitted, carelessly.

"And of yours?" he whispered, his arm slightly pressed against hers.

She laughed at him silently and their eyes met. Decidedly Peter, Baron de Grost, found it hard to break away from his old weakness! Andrea Korust, from his place near the piano, breathed a sigh of relief as he watched. A moment or two later, however, Mademoiselle Korust was obliged to leave her companion to receive a late but unimportant guest, and almost simultaneously Colonel Mayson passed by on his way to the farther end of the apartment. Andrea Korust was bending over the piano to give some instructions to his accompanist. Peter leaned forward and his face and tone were strangely altered.

"You will find General Noseworthy of the Indian Army a little inquisitive, Colonel," he remarked.

The latter turned sharply round. There was meaning in those few words, without doubt! There was meaning, too, in the still, cold face which seemed to repel his question. He passed on thoughtfully. Mademoiselle Korust, with a gesture of relief, came back and threw herself once more upon the couch.

"We must talk in whispers," she said, gayly. "Andrea always declares that he does not mind conversation, but too much noise is, of course, impossible. Besides, Mademoiselle Celaire will not spare you to me for long."

"There is a whole language," he replied, "which was made for whispers. And as for Mademoiselle Celaire -"

"Well?"

He laughed softly.

"Mademoiselle Celaire is, I think, more your brother's friend than mine," he murmured. "At least, I will be generous. He has given me a delightful evening. I resign my claims upon Mademoiselle Celaire."

"It would break your heart," she declared.

His voice sank even below a whisper. Decidedly, Peter, Baron de Grost, did not improve!

He rose to leave precisely at the right time, neither too early nor too late. He had spent altogether a most amusing evening. There were one or two little comedies which had diverted him extremely. At the moment of parting, the beautiful eyes of Mademoiselle Korust had been raised to his very earnestly.

"You will come again very soon - to-morrow night?" she had whispered. "Is it necessary that you bring Mademoiselle Celaire?"

"It is altogether unnecessary," Peter replied.

"Let me try and entertain you instead, then!"

It was precisely at that instant that Andrea had sent for his sister. Peter watched their brief conversation with much interest and intense amusement. She was being told not to invite him there again and she was rebelling! Without a doubt, he had made a conquest! She returned to him flushed and with a dangerous glitter in her eyes.

"Monsieur le Baron," she said, leading him on one side, "I am ashamed and angry."

"Your brother is annoyed because you have asked me here to-morrow night?" he asked, quickly.

"It is so," she confessed. "Indeed, I thank you that you have spared me the task of putting my brother's discourtesy into words. Andrea takes violent fancies like that sometimes. I am ashamed, but what can I do?"

"Nothing, mademoiselle," he admitted, with a sigh. "I obey, of course. Did your brother mention the source of his aversion to me?"

"He is too absurd sometimes," she declared. "One must treat him like a great baby."

"Nevertheless, there must be a reason," Peter persisted, gently.

"He has heard some foolish thing from Count von Hern," she admitted, reluctantly. "Do not let us think anything more about it. In a few days it will have passed. And meanwhile -"

She paused. He leaned a little towards her. She was looking intently at a ring upon her finger.

"If you would really like to see me," she whispered, "and if you are sure that Mademoiselle Celaire would not object, could you not ask me to tea to-morrow - or the next day?"

"To-morrow," Peter insisted, with a becoming show of eagerness. "Shall we say at the Canton at five?"

She hesitated.

"Isn't that rather a public place?" she objected.

"Anywhere else you like."

She was silent for a moment. She seemed to be waiting for some suggestion from him. None came, however.

"The Carlton at five," she murmured. "I am angry with Andrea. I feel, even, that I could break his wonderful violin in two!"

Peter sighed once more.

"I should like to twist von Hern's neck," he declared. "Lucky for him that he's in St. Petersburg! Let us forget this unpleasant matter, mademoiselle. The evening has been too delightful for such memories."

Mademoiselle Celaire turned to her escort eagerly as soon as they were alone together in the car.

"As an escort, let me tell you, my dear Baron," she exclaimed, with some pique, "that you are a miserable failure! For the rest -"

"For the rest, I will admit that I am puzzled," Peter said. "I need to think. I have the glimmerings of an idea - no more."

"You will act? It is an affair for us - for the Double-Four?"

"Without a doubt - an affair and a serious one," Peter assured her. "I shall act; exactly how I cannot say until after to-morrow."

"To-morrow?" she repeated, inquiringly.

"Mademoiselle Korust takes tea with me," he explained.

In a quiet sort of way, the series of supper parties given by Andrea Korust became the talk of London. The most famous dancer in the world broke through her unvarying rule and night after night thrilled the distinguished little gathering. An opera singer, the "star" of the season, sang, a great genius recited, and Andrea himself gave always of his best. Apart from this wonderful outpouring of talent, Andrea Korust himself seemed to possess the peculiar art of bringing into touch with one another people naturally interested in the same subjects. On the night after the visit of Peter, Baron de Grost, His Grace the Duke of Rosshire was present, the man in whose hands lay the destinies of the British Navy; and, curiously enough, on the same night, a great French writer on naval subjects was present, whom the Duke had never met, and with whom he was delighted to talk for some time apart. On another occasion, the Military Secretary to the French Embassy was able to have a long and instructive chat with a distinguished English general on the subject of the recent maneuvers, and the latter received, in the strictest confidence, some very interesting information concerning the new type of French guns. On the following evening, the greatest of our Colonial statesmen, a red-hot Imperialist, was able to chat about the resources of the Empire with an English politician of similar views whom he chanced never to have previously met. Altogether, these parties seemed to be the means of bringing together a series of most interesting people, interesting not only in themselves, but in their relations to one another. It was noticeable, however, that from this side of his little gatherings Andrea Korust remained wholly apart. He frankly admitted that music and cheerful companionship were the only two things in life he cared for. Politics or matters of world import seemed to leave him unmoved. If a serious subject of conversation were started at supper time, he was frankly bored, and took no particular pains to hide the fact. It is certain that whatever interesting topics were alluded to in his presence, he remained entirely outside any understanding of them. Mademoiselle Celaire, who was present most evenings, although with other escorts, was entirely puzzled. She could see nothing whatever to account for the warning which she had received, and which she had passed on, as was her duty, to the Baron de Grost. She failed, also, to understand the faint but perceptible enlightenment to which Peter himself had admittedly attained after that first evening. Take that important conversation, for instance, between the French military attach, and the English general. Without a doubt it was of interest, and especially so to the country which she was sure claimed his allegiance, but it was equally without doubt that Andrea Korust neither overheard a word of that conversation nor betrayed the slightest curiosity concerning it. Mademoiselle Celaire was a clever woman and she had never felt so hopelessly at fault....

The seventh and last of these famous supper parties was in full swing. Notwithstanding the shaded candles, which left the faces of the guests a little indistinct, the scene was a brilliant one. Mademoiselle Celaire was wearing her famous diamonds, which shone through the gloom like pin-pricks of fire. Garda Desmaines, the wonderful Garda, sat next to her host, her bosom and hair on fire with jewels, yet with the most wonderful light of all glowing in her eyes. A famous actor, who had thrown his proverbial reticence to the winds, kept his immediate neighbors in a state of semi-hysterical mirth. The clink of wine glasses, the laughter of beautiful women, the murmur of cultivated voices, rising and swelling through the faint, mysterious gloom, made a picturesque, a wonderful scene. Pale as a marble statue, with the covert smile of the gracious host, Andrea Korust sat at the head of his table, well pleased with his company, as indeed he had the right to be. By his side was a great American statesman, who was traveling around the world and yet had refused all other invitations of this sort. He had come for the pleasure of meeting the famous Dutch writer and politician, Mr. Van Jool. The two were already talking intimately. It was at this point that tragedy, or something like it, intervened. A impatient voice was heard in the hall outside, a voice which grew louder and louder, more impatient, finally more passionate. People raised their heads to listen. The American statesman, who was, perhaps, the only one to realize exactly what was coming, slipped his hand into his pocket and gripped something cold and hard. Then the door was flung open. An apologetic and much disturbed butler made the announcement which had evidently been demanded of him.

"Mr. Von Tassen!"

A silence followed - breathless - the silence before the bursting of the storm. Mr. Von Tassen was the name of the American statesman, and the man who rose slowly from his place by his host's side was the exact double of the man who stood now upon the threshold, gazing in upon the room. The expression of the two alone was different. The newcomer was furiously angry, and looked it. The sham Mr. Von Tassen was very much at his ease. It was he who broke the silence, and his voice was curiously free from all trace of emotion. He was looking his double over with an air of professional interest.

"On the whole," he said, calmly, "very good. A little stouter, I perceive, and the eyebrows a trifle too regular. Of course, when you make faces at me like that, it is hard to judge of the expression. I can only say that I did the best I could."

"Who the devil are you, masquerading in my name?" the newcomer demanded, with emphasis. "This man is an impostor!" he added, turning to Andrea Korust. "What is he doing at your table?"

Andrea leaned forward and his face was an evil thing to look upon.

"Who are you?" he hissed out.

The sham Mr. Von Tassen turned away for a moment and stooped down. The trick has been done often enough upon the stage, often in less time, but seldom with more effect. The wonderful wig disappeared, the spectacles, the lines in the face, the make-up of diabolical cleverness. With his back to the wall and his fingers playing with something in his pocket, Peter, Baron de Grost, smiled upon his host.

"Since you insist upon knowing - the Baron de Grost, at your service!" he announced.

Andrea Korust was, for the moment, speechless. One of the women shrieked. The real Mr. Von Tassen looked around him helplessly.

"Will some one be good enough to enlighten me as to the meaning of this?" he begged. "Is it a roast? If so, I only want to catch on. Let me get to the joke, if there is one. If not, I should like a few words of explanation from you, sir," he added, addressing Peter.

"Presently," the latter replied. "In the meantime, let me persuade you that I am not the only impostor here."

He seized a glass of water and dashed it in the face of Mr. Van Jool. There was a moment's scuffle, and no more of Mr. Van Jool. What emerged was a good deal like the shy Maurice Korust, who accompanied his brother at the music hall, but whose distaste for these gatherings had been Andrea's continual lament. The Baron de Grost stepped back once more against the wall. His host was certainly looking dangerous. Mademoiselle Celaire was leaning forward, staring through the gloom with distended eyes. Around the table every head was turned towards the centre of the disturbance. It was Peter again who spoke.

"Let me suggest, Andrea Korust," he said, "that you send your guests - those who are not immediately interested in this affair - into the next room. I will offer Mr. Von Tassen then the explanation to which he is entitled."

Andrea Korust staggered to his feet. The nerve had failed. He was shaking all over. He pointed to the music room.

"If you would be so good, ladies and gentlemen?" he begged. "We will follow you immediately."

They went with obvious reluctance. All their eyes seemed focussed upon Peter. He bore their scrutiny with calm cheerfulness. For a moment he had feared Korust, but that moment had passed. A servant, obeying his master's gesture, pulled back the curtains after the departing crowd. The four men were alone.

"Mr. Von Tassen," Peter said, easily, "you are a man who loves adventures. To-night you experience a new sort of one. Over in your great country, such methods are laughed at as the cheap device of sensation mongers. Nevertheless, they exist. To-night is a proof that they exist."

E. Phillips Oppenheim

"Get on to facts, sir," the American admonished. "You've got to explain to me what you mean by passing yourself off as Thomas Von Tassen, before you leave this room."

Peter bowed.

"With much pleasure, Mr. Von Tassen," he declared. "For your information, I might tell you that you are not the only person in whose guise I have figured. In fact, I have had quite a busy week. I have been - let me see - I have been Monsieur le Marquis de Beau Kunel on the night when our shy friend, Maurice Korust, was playing the part of General Henderson. I have also been His Grace the Duke of Rosshire when my friend Maurice here was introduced to me as Francois Defayal, known by name to me as one of the greatest writers on naval matters. A little awkward about the figure I found His Grace, but otherwise I think that I should have passed muster wherever he was known. I have also passed as Sir William Laureston, on the evening when my rival artist here sang the praises of Imperial England."

Andrea Korust leaned forward with venomous eyes.

"You mean that it was you who was here last night in Sir William Laureston's place?" he almost shrieked.

"Most certainly," Peter admitted, "but you must remember that, after all, my performances have been no more difficult than those of your shy but accomplished brother. Whenever I took to myself a strange personality I found him there, equally good as to detail, and with his subject always at his finger tips. We settled that little matter of the canal, didn't we?" Peter remarked, cheerfully, laying his hand upon the shoulder of the young man.

They stared at him, those two white-faced brothers, like tiger-cats about to spring. Mr. Von Tassen was getting impatient.

"Look here," he protested, "you may be clearing matters up so far as regards Mr. Andrea Korust and his brother, but I'm as much in the fog as ever. Where do I come in?"

"Your pardon, sir," Peter replied. "I am getting nearer things now. These two young men - we will not call them hard names - are suffering from an excess of patriotic zeal. They didn't come and sit down on a camp stool and sketch obsolete forts, as those others of their countrymen do when they want to pose as the bland and really exceedingly ignorant foreigner. They went about the matter with some skill. It occurred to them that it might be interesting to their country to know what Sir William Laureston thought about the strength of the Imperial Navy, and to what extent his country was willing to go in maintaining their allegiance to Great Britain. Then there was the Duke of Rosshire. They thought they'd like to know his views as to the development of the Navy during the next ten years. There was that little matter, too, of the French guns. It would certainly be interesting to them to know what Monsieur le Marquis de Beau Kunel had to say about them. These people were all invited to sit at the hospitable board of our host here. I, however, had an inkling on the first night of what was going on, and I was easily able to persuade those in authority to let me play their several parts. You, sir," Peter added, turning to Mr. Von Tassen, "you, sir, floored me. You were not an Englishman, and there was no appeal which I could make. I simply had to risk you. I counted upon your not turning up. Unfortunately, you did. Fortunately, you are the last guest. This is the seventh supper."

Mr. Von Tassen glanced around at the three men and made up his mind.

"What do you call yourself?" he asked Peter.

"The Baron de Grost," Peter replied.

"Then, my friend the Baron de Grost," Von Tassen said, "I think that you and I had better get out of this. So I was to talk about Germany with Mr. Van Jool, eh?"

E. Phillips Oppenheim

"I have already explained your views," Peter declared, with twinkling eyes. "Mr. Van Jool was delighted."

Mr. Von Tassen shook with laughter.

"Say," he exclaimed, "this is a great story! If you're ready, Baron de Grost, lead the way to where we can get a whiskey and soda and a chat."

Mademoiselle Celaire came gliding out to them.

"I am not going to be left here," she whispered, taking Peter's arm.

Peter looked back from the door.

"At any rate, Mr. Andrea Korust," he said, "your first supper was a success. Colonel Mayson was genuine. Our real English military aeronaut was here, and he has disclosed to you, Maurice Korust, all that he ever knew. Henceforth, I presume your great country will dispute with us for the mastery of the air.

"Queer country, this!" Mr. Von Tassen remarked, pausing on the step to light a cigar. "Seems kind of humdrum after New York, but there's no use talking. Things do happen over here, anyway!"

CHAPTER VII

MAJOR KOSUTH'S MISSION

His host, very fussy as he always was on the morning of his big shoot, came bustling towards Peter, Baron de Grost, with a piece of paper in his hand. The party of men had just descended from a large brake and were standing about on the edge of the common, examining cartridges, smoking a last cigarette before the business of the morning, and chatting together over the prospects of the day's sport. In the distance, a cloud of dust indicated the approach of a fast traveling motor-car.

"My dear Baron," Sir William Bounderby said, "I want you to change your stand to-day. I must have a good man at the far corner as the birds go off my hand from there, and Addington was missing them shockingly yesterday. Besides, there is a new man coming on your left and I know nothing of his shooting - nothing at all!"

Peter smiled.

"Anywhere you choose to put me, Sir William," he assented. "They came badly for Addington yesterday, and well for me. However, I'll do my best."

"I wish people wouldn't bring strangers, especially to the one shoot where I'm keen about the bag. I told Portal he could bring his brother-in-law, and he's bringing this foreign fellow

E. Phillips Oppenheim

instead. Don't suppose he can shoot for nuts! Did you ever hear of him, I wonder? The Count von Hern, he calls himself."

The motor-car had come to a standstill by this time. From it descended Mr. Portal himself, a large neighboring land owner, a man of culture and travel. With him was Bernadine, in a very correct shooting suit and Tyrolese hat. On the other side of Mr. Portal was a short, thick set man, with olive complexion, keen black eyes, black mustache and imperial, who was dressed in city clothes. Sir William's eyebrows were slightly raised as he advanced to greet the party. Peter was at once profoundly interested.

Mr. Portal introduced his guests.

"You will forgive me, I am sure, for bringing a spectator, Bounderby," he said. "Major Kosuth, whom I have the honor to present - Major Kosuth, Sir William Bounderby - is high up in the diplomatic service of a country with whom we must feel every sympathy - the young Turks. The Count von Hern, who takes my brother-in-law's place, is probably known to you by name."

Sir William welcomed his visitors cordially.

"You do not shoot, Major Kosuth?" he asked.

"Very seldom," the Turk answered. "I come to-day with my good friend, Count von Hern, as a spectator, if you permit."

"Delighted," Sir William replied. "We will find you a safe place near your friend."

The little party began to move toward the wood. It was just at this moment that Bernadine felt a touch upon his shoulder, and, turning around, found Peter by his side.

"An unexpected pleasure, my dear Count," the latter declared, suavely. "I had no idea that you took interest in such simple sports."

The manners of Count von Hern were universally quoted as being almost too perfect. It is a regrettable fact, however, that at that moment he swore - softly, perhaps, but with distinct vehemence. A moment later he was exchanging the most cordial of greetings with his old friend.

"You have the knack, my dear De Grost," he remarked, "of turning up in the most surprising places. I certainly did not know that among your many accomplishments was included a love for field sports."

Peter smiled quietly. He was a very fine shot, and knew it.

"One must amuse oneself these days," he said. "There is little else to do."

Bernadine bit his lip.

"My absence from this country, I fear, has robbed you of an occupation."

"It has certainly deprived life of some of its savor," Peter admitted, blandly. "By the bye, will you not present me to your friend? I have the utmost sympathy with the intrepid political party of which he is a member."

Von Hern performed the introduction with a reluctance which he wholly failed to conceal. The Turk, however, had been walking on his other side, and his hat was already lifted. Peter had purposely raised his voice.

"It gives me the greatest pleasure, Major Kosuth," Peter said, "to welcome you to this country. In common, I believe, with the majority of my country people, I have the utmost respect and admiration for the movement which you represent."

Major Kosuth smiled slowly. His features were heavy and

E. Phillips Oppenheim

unexpressive. There was something of gloom, however, in the manner of his response.

"You are very kind, Baron," he replied, "and I welcome very much this expression of your interest in my party. I believe that the hearts of your country people are turned towards us in the same manner. I could wish that your country's political sympathies were as easily aroused."

Bernadine intervened promptly.

"Major Kosuth has been here only one day," he remarked, lightly. "I tell him that he is a little too impatient. See, we are approaching the wood. It is as well here to refrain from conversation."

"We will resume it later," Peter said, softly. "I have interests in Turkey, and it would give me great pleasure to have a talk with Major Kosuth."

"Financial interests?" the latter inquired, with some eagerness.

Peter nodded.

"I will explain after the first drive," he said, turning away.

Peter walked rather quickly until he reached a bend in the wood, and overtaking his host, paused for a moment.

"Lend me a loader for half an hour, Sir William," he begged. "I have to send my servant to the village with a telegram."

"With pleasure!" Sir William answered. "There are several to spare. I'll send one to your stand. There's Von Hern going the wrong way!" he exclaimed, in a tone of annoyance.

Peter was just in time to stop the whistle from going to his mouth.

"Do me another favor, Sir William," he pleaded. "Give me time to send off my telegram before the Count sees what I'm doing. He's such an inquisitive person," he went on, noticing his host's look of blank surprise. "Thank you ever so much."

Peter hurried on to his place. It was round the corner of the wood and for the moment out of sight of the rest of the party. He tore a sheet from his pocket-book and scribbled out a telegram. His man had disappeared and a substitute taken his place by the time von Hern arrived. The latter was now all amiability. It was hard to believe, from his smiling salutation, that he and the man to whom he waved his hand in so airy a fashion had ever declared war to the death!

The shooting began a few minutes later. Major Kosuth, from a campstool a few yards behind his friend, watched with some-what languid interest. He gave one, indeed, the impression that his thoughts were far removed from this simple country party, the main object of whose existence for the present seemed to be the slaying of a certain number of inoffensive birds. He watched the indifferent performance of his friend and the remarkably fine shooting of his neighbor on the left, with the same lack-luster eye and want of enthusiasm. The beat was scarcely over before Peter, resigning his smoking guns, lit a cigarette and strolled across to the next stand. He plunged at once into a conversation with Kosuth, notwith-standing Bernadine's ill-concealed annoyance.

"Major Kosuth," he began, "I sympathize with you. It is a hard task for a man whose mind is centered upon great events, to sit still and watch a performance of this sort. Be kind to us all and remember that this represents to us merely a few hours of relaxation. We, too, have our more serious moments."

"You read my thoughts well," Major Kosuth declared. "I do not seek to excuse them. For half a life-time we Turks have toiled and striven, always in danger of our lives, to help forward those things which have now come to pass. I think that our lives have become tinged with somberness and apprehension. Now that the first step is achieved, we go forward, still with trepidation. We need friends, Baron de Grost."

"You cannot seriously doubt but that you will find them in this country," Peter remarked. "There has never been a time when the English nation has not sympathized with the cause of liberty."

"It is not the hearts of your people," Major Kosuth said, "which I fear. It is the antics of your politicians. Sympathy is a great thing, and good to have, but Turkey to-day needs more. The heart of a nation is big, but the number of those in whose hands it remains to give practical expression to its promptings, is few."

Bernadine, who had stood as much as he could, seized forcibly upon his friend.

"You must remember our bargain, Kosuth," he insisted, "no politics to-day. Until to-morrow evening we rest. Now I want to introduce you to a very old friend of mine - the Lord-Lieutenant of the county."

No man was better informed in current political affairs, but Peter, instead of joining the cheerful afternoon tea party at the close of the day, raked out a file of the Times from the library, and studied it carefully in his room. There were one or two items of news concerning which he made pencil notes. He had scarcely finished his task before a servant brought in a dispatch. He opened it with interest and drew pencil and paper towards him. It was from Paris, and in the code which he had learned by heart, no written key of which existed. Carefully he transposed it on to paper and read it through. It was dated from Paris a few hours back.

Kosuth left for England yesterday. Envoy from new Turkish Government. Requiring loan one million pounds. Asked for guarantee that it was not for warlike movement against

Bulgaria, declined to give same. Communicated with English Ambassador and informed Kosuth yesterday that neither government would sanction loan unless undertaking were given that the same was not to be applied for war against Bulgaria. Turkey is under covenant to enter into no financial obligations with any other Power while the interest of former loans remains in abeyance. Kosuth has made two efforts to obtain loan privately, from prominent English financier and French Syndicate. Both have declined to treat on representations from government. Kosuth was expected return direct to Turkey. If, as you say, he is in England with Bernadine, we commend the affair to your utmost vigilance. Germany exceedingly anxious enter into close relations with new government of Turkey. Fear Kosuth's association with Bernadine proof of bad faith. Have had interview with Minister for foreign affairs, who relies upon our help. French Secret Service at your disposal, if necessary.

Peter read the message three times with the greatest care. He was on the point of destroying it when Violet came into the room. She was wearing a long tea jacket of sheeny silk. Her beautiful hair was most becomingly arranged, her figure as light and girlish as ever. She came into the room humming gayly and swinging a gold purse upon her finger.

"Won three rubbers out of four, Peter," she declared, "and a compliment from the Duchess. Am I a pupil to be proud of?"

She stopped short. Her lips formed themselves into the shape of a whistle. She knew very well the signs. Her husband's eyes were kindling, there was a firm set about his lips, the palm of his hand lay flat upon that sheet of paper.

"It was true?" she murmured. "It was Bernadine who was shooting to-day?"

Peter nodded.

"He was on the next stand," he replied.

"Then there is something doing, of course," Violet continued. "My dear Peter, you may be an enigma to other people. To me you have the most expressive countenance I ever saw. You have had a cable which you have just transcribed. If I had been a few minutes later, I think you would have torn up the result. As it is, I think I have come just in time to hear all about it."

Peter smiled, grimly but fondly. He uncovered the sheet of paper and placed it in her hands.

"So far," he said, "there isn't much to tell you. Von Hern turned up this morning with a Major Kosuth, who was one of the leaders of the revolution in Turkey. I wired Paris and this is the reply."

She read the message through thoughtfully and handed it back. Peter lit a match, and standing over the fireplace calmly destroyed it.

"A million pounds is not a great sum of money," Violet remarked. "Why could not Kosuth borrow it for his country from a private individual?"

"A million pounds is not a large sum to talk about," Peter replied, "but it is an exceedingly large sum for any one, even a multi-millionaire, to handle in cash. And Turkey, I gather, wants it at once. Besides, considerations which might be a security from a government, are no security at all as applied to a private individual."

She nodded.

"Do you think that Kosuth means to go behind the existing treaty and borrow from Germany?"

Peter shook his head.

"I can't quite believe that," he said. "It would mean the straining of diplomatic relations with both countries. It is out of the question."

"Then where does Bernadine come in?"

"I do not know," Peter answered.

Violet laughed.

"What is it that you are going to try and find out?" she asked.

"I am trying to discover who it is that Bernadine and Kosuth are waiting to see," Peter replied. "The worst of it is, I daren't leave here. I shall have to trust to the others."

She glanced at the clock.

"Well, go and dress," she said. "I'm afraid I've a little of your blood in me, after all. Life seems more stirring when Bernadine is on the scene."

The shooting party broke up two days later and Peter and his wife returned at once to town. The former found the reports which were awaiting his arrival disappointing. Bernadine and his guest were not in London, or if they were they had carefully avoided all the usual haunts. Peter read his reports over again, smoked a very long cigar alone in his study, and finally drove down to the city and called upon his stockbroker, who was also a personal friend. Things were flat in the city, and the latter was glad enough to welcome an important client. He began talking the usual market shop until his visitor stopped him.

"I have come to you, Edwardes, more for information than anything," Peter declared, "although it may mean that I shall need to sell a lot of stock. Can you tell me of any private financier who could raise a loan of a million pounds in cash within the course of a week?"

The stockbroker looked dubious.

"In cash," he repeated. "Money isn't raised that way, you know. I doubt whether there are many men in the whole city of London who could put up such an amount with only a week's notice."

"But there must be some one," Peter persisted. "Think! It would probably be a firm or a man not obtrusively English. I don't think the Jews would touch it, and a German citizen would be impossible."

"Semi-political, eh?"

Peter nodded.

"It is rather that way," he admitted.

"Would your friend Count von Hern be likely to be concerned in it?"

"Why?" Peter asked, with immovable face.

"Nothing, only I saw him coming out of Heseltine-Wrigge's office the other day," the stockbroker remarked, carelessly.

"And who is Mr. Heseltine-Wrigge?"

"A very wealthy American financier," the stockbroker replied, "not at all an unlikely person for a loan of the sort you mention."

"American citizen?" Peter inquired.

"Without a doubt. Of German descent, I should say, but nothing much left of it in his appearance. He settled over here in a huff because New York society wouldn't receive his wife."

"I remember all about it," Peter declared. "She was a chorus girl, wasn't she? Nothing particular against her, but the fellow had no tact. Do you know him, Edwardes?"

"Slightly," the stockbroker answered.

"Give me a letter to him," Peter said. "Give my credit as good a leg as you can. I shall probably go as a borrower."

Mr. Edwardes wrote a few lines and handed them to his client.

"Office is nearly opposite," he remarked. "Wish you luck, whatever your scheme is."

Peter crossed the street and entered the building which his friend had pointed out. He ascended in the lift to the third floor, knocked at the door which bore Mr. Heseltine-Wrigge's name, and almost ran into the arms of a charmingly dressed little lady, who was being shown out by a broad-shouldered, typical American. Peter hastened to apologize.

"I beg your pardon," he said, raising his hat. "I was rather in a hurry and I quite thought I heard some one say 'Come in.'"

The lady replied pleasantly. Her companion, who was carrying his hat in his hand, paused reluctantly.

"Did you want to see me?" he asked.

"If you are Mr. Heseltine-Wrigge, I did," Peter admitted. "I am the Baron de Grost, and I have a letter of introduction to you from Mr. Edwardes."

Mr. Heseltine-Wrigge tore open the envelope and glanced through the contents of the note. Peter, meanwhile, looked at his wife with genuine but respectfully cloaked admiration. The lady obviously returned his interest.

"Why, if you're the Baron de Grost," she exclaimed, "didn't you marry Vi Brown? She used to be at the Gaiety with me, years ago."

"I certainly did marry Violet Brown," Peter confessed, "and, if you will allow me to say so, Mrs. Heseltine-Wrigge, I should have recognized you anywhere from your photographs."

"Say, isn't that queer?" the little lady remarked, turning to her husband. "I should love to see Vi again."

"If you will give me your address," Peter declared, promptly, "my wife will be delighted to call upon you."

The man looked up from the note.

"Do you want to talk business with me, Baron?" he asked.

"For a few moments only," Peter answered. "I am afraid I am a great nuisance, and if you wish it I will come down to the city again."

"That's all right," Mr. Heseltine-Wrigge replied. "Myra won't mind waiting a minute or two. Come through here."

He turned and led the way into a quiet-looking suite of offices, where one or two clerks were engaged writing at open desks. They all three passed into an inner room.

"Any objections to my wife coming in?" Mr. Heseltine-Wrigge asked. "there's scarcely any place for her out there."

"Delighted," Peter answered.

She glanced at the clock.

"Remember we have to meet the Count von Hern at half past one at Prince's, Charles," she reminded him.

Her husband nodded. There was nothing in Peter's expression to denote that he had already achieved the first object of his visit!

"I shall not detain you," he said. "Your name has been

mentioned to me, Mr. Heseltine-Wrigge, as a financier likely to have a large sum of money at his disposal. I have a scheme which needs money. Providing the security is unexceptionable, are you in a position to do a deal?"

"How much do you want?" Mr. Heseltine-Wrigge asked.

"A million to a million and a half," Peter answered.

"Dollars?

"Pounds."

It was not Mr. Heseltine-Wrigge's pose to appear surprised. Nevertheless, his eyebrows were slightly raised.

"Say, what is this scheme?" he inquired.

"First of all," Peter replied, "I should like to know whether there's any chance of business if I disclose it."

"Not an atom," Mr. Heseltine-Wrigge declared. "I have just committed myself to the biggest financial transaction of my life and it will clean me out."

"Then I won't waste your time," Peter announced, rising.

"Sit down for a moment," Mr. Heseltine-Wrigge invited, biting the end off a cigar and passing the box toward Peter. "That's all right. My wife doesn't mind. Say, it strikes me as rather a curious thing that you should come in here and talk about a million and a half, when that's just the amount concerned in my other little deal."

Peter smiled.

"As a matter of fact, it isn't at all queer," he answered. "I don't want the money. I came to see whether you were really interested in the other affair - the Turkish loan, you know."

Mr. Heseltine-Wrigge withdrew his cigar from his mouth and looked steadily at his visitor.

"Say, Baron," he declared, "you've got a nerve!"

"Not at all," Peter replied. "I'm here as much in your interests as my own."

"Whom do you represent, anyway?" Mr. Heseltine-Wrigge inquired.

"A company you have never heard of," Peter replied. "Our offices are in the underground places of the world, and we don't run to brass plates. I am here because I am curious about that loan. Turkey hasn't a shadow of security to offer you. Everything which she can pledge is pledged, to guarantee the interest on existing loans to France and England. She is prevented by treaty from borrowing in Germany. If you make a loan without security, Mr. Heseltine-Wrigge, I suppose you understand your position. The loan may be repudiated at any moment."

"Kind of a philanthropist, aren't you, Baron?" Mr. Heseltine-Wrigge remarked quietly.

"Not in the least," Peter assured him. "I know there is some tricky work going on and I haven't brains enough to get to the bottom of it. That's why I've come blundering in to you, and why I suppose you'll be telling the whole story to the Count von Hern at luncheon in an hour's time."

Mr. Heseltine-Wrigge smoked in silence for a moment or two.

"This transaction of mine," he said at last, "Isn't one I can talk about. I guess I'm on to what you want to know, but I simply can't tell you. The security is unusual, but it's good enough for me."

"It seems so to you, beyond a doubt," Peter replied. "Still, you have to do with a remarkably clever young man in the Count von Hern. I don't want to ask you any questions you feel I ought not to, but I do wish you'd tell me one thing."

"Go right ahead," Mr. Heseltine-Wrigge invited. "Don't be shy."

"What day are you concluding this affair?"

Mr. Heseltine-Wrigge scratched his chin for a moment thoughtfully and glanced at his diary. "Well, I'll risk that," he decided. "A week to-day I hand over the coin."

Peter drew a little breath of relief. A week was an immense time! He rose to his feet.

"That ends our business, then, for the present," he said. "Now I am going to ask both of you a favor. Perhaps I have no right to, but as a man of honor, Mr. Heseltine-Wrigge, you can take it from me that I ask it in your interests as well as my own. Don't tell the Count von Hern of my visit to you."

Mr. Heseltine-Wrigge held out his hand.

"That's all right," he declared. "You hear, Myra?"

"I'll be dumb, Baron," she promised. "Say, when do you think Vi can come and see me?"

Peter was guilty of snobbery. He considered it quite a justifiable weapon.

"She is at Windsor this afternoon," he remarked.

"What, at the Garden-Party?" Mrs. Heseltine-Wrigge almost shrieked.

Peter nodded.

"I believe there's some fete or other to-morrow," he said, "but we're alone this evening. Why won't you dine with us, say at the Carlton?"

"We'd love to," the lady assented, promptly.

"At eight o'clock," Peter said, taking his leave.

The dinner party was a great success. Mrs. Heseltine-Wrigge found herself among the class of people with whom it was her earnest desire to become acquainted, and her husband was well satisfied to see her keen longing for society likely to be gratified. The subject of Peter's call at the office in the city was studiously ignored. It was not until the very end of the evening, indeed, that the host of this very agreeable party was rewarded by a single hint. It all came about in the most natural manner. They were speaking of foreign capitals.

"I love Paris," Mrs. Heseltine-Wrigge told her host. "Just adore it. Charles is often there on business and I always go along."

Peter smiled. There was just a chance here.

"Your husband does not often have to leave London though," he remarked, carelessly.

She nodded.

"Not often enough," she declared. "I just love getting about. Last week we had a perfectly horrible trip, though. We started off for Belfast quite unexpectedly, and I hated every minute of it."

Peter smiled inwardly, but he said never a word. His companion was already chattering on about something else. Peter crossed the hall a few minutes later, to speak to an acquaintance, slipped out to the telephone booth and spoke to his servant.

"A bag and a change," he ordered, "at Euston Station at twelve o'clock, in time for the Irish mail. Your mistress will be home as usual."

An hour later the dinner party broke up. Early the next morning, Peter crossed the Irish Channel. He returned the following day and crossed again within a few hours. In five days the affair was finished, except for the denouement.

Peter ascended in the lift to Mr. Heseltine-Wrigge's office the following Thursday, calm and unruffled as usual, but nevertheless a little exultant. It was barely half an hour since he had become finally prepared for this interview. He was looking forward to it now with feelings of undiluted satisfaction. Mr. Heseltine-Wrigge was in, he was told, and he was at once admitted to his presence. The financier greeted him with a somewhat curious smile.

"Say, this is very nice of you to look me up again!" he exclaimed. "Still worrying about that loan, eh?"

Peter shook his head.

"No, I'm not worrying about that any more," he answered, accepting one of his host's cigars. "The fact of it is that if it were not for me, you would be the one who would have to do the worrying."

Mr. Heseltine-Wrigge stopped short in the act of lighting his cigar.

"I'm not quite on," he remarked. "What's the trouble?"

"There is no trouble, fortunately," Peter replied. "Only a little disappointment for our friends the Count von Hern and Major Kosuth. I have brought you some information which I think will put an end to that affair of the loan."

Mr. Heseltine-Wrigge sat quite still for a moment. He brows

were knitted, he showed no signs of nervousness.

"Go right on," he said.

"The security upon which you were going to advance a million and a half to the Turkish Government," Peter continued, "consisted of two Dreadnoughts and a cruiser, being built to the order of that country by Messrs. Shepherd & Hargreaves at Belfast."

"Quite right," Mr. Heseltine-Wrigge admitted, quietly. "I have been up and seen the boats. I have seen the shipbuilders, too."

"Did you happen to mention to the latter," Peter inquired, "that you were advancing money upon those vessels?"

"Certainly not," Mr. Heseltine-Wrigge replied. "Kosuth wouldn't hear of such a thing. If the papers got wind of it, there'd be the devil to pay. All the same, I have got an assignment from the Turkish Government."

"Not worth the paper it's written on," Peter declared, blandly.

Mr. Heseltine-Wrigge rose unsteadily to his feet. He was a strong, silent man, but there was a queer look about his mouth.

"What the devil do you mean?" he demanded.

"Briefly, this," Peter explained. "The first payment, when these ships were laid down, was made not by Turkey but by an emissary of the German Government, who arranged the whole affair in Constantinople. The second payment was due ten months ago, and not a penny has been paid. Notice was given to the late government twice and absolutely ignored. According to the charter, therefore, these ships reverted to the shipbuilding companies who retained possession of the first payment as indemnity against loss. The Count von Hern's position was this. He represents the German Government. You were to find a million and a half of money with the ships as security. You also have a contract from the Count von Hern to take those ships off your hands provided the interest on the loan became overdue, a state of affairs which I can assure you would have happened within the next twelve months. Practically, therefore, you were made use of as an independent financier to provide the money with which the Turkish Government, broadly speaking, have sold the ships to Germany. You see, according to the charter of the shipbuilding company, these vessels cannot be sold to any foreign government without the consent of Downing Street. That is the reason why the affair had to be conducted in such a roundabout manner."

"All this is beyond me," Mr. Heseltine-Wrigge said, hoarsely. "I don't care a d-n who has the ships in the end so long as I get my money!"

"But you would not get your money," Peter pointed out, "because there will be no ships. I have had the shrewdest lawyers in the world at work upon the charter, and there is not the slightest doubt that these vessels are, or rather were, the entire property of Messrs. Shepherd & Hargreaves. To-day they belong to me. I have bought them and paid two hundred thousand pounds deposit. I can show you the receipt and all the papers."

Mr. Heseltine-Wrigge, said only one word, but that word was profane.

"I am sorry, of course, that you have lost the business," Peter concluded, "but surely it's better than losing your money?"

Mr. Heseltine-Wrigge struck the table fiercely with his fist. There was a gray and unfamiliar look about his face.

"D-n it, the money's gone!" he declared, hoarsely. "They changed the day. Kosuth had to go back. I paid it twenty-four hours ago."

Peter whistled softly.

"If only you had trusted me a little more!" he murmured. "I tried to warn you."

Mr. Heseltine-Wrigge snatched up his hat.

"They don't leave till the two-twenty," he shouted. "We'll catch them at the Milan. If we don't, I'm ruined! By God, I'm ruined!"

They found Major Kosuth in the hall of the hotel. He was wearing a fur coat and was otherwise attired for traveling. His luggage was already being piled upon a cab. Mr. Heseltine-Wrigge wasted no words upon him.

"You and I have got to have a talk, right here and now," he declared. "Where's the Count?"

Major Kosuth frowned gloomily.

"I do not understand you," he said, shortly. "Our business is concluded and I am leaving by the two-twenty train."

"You are doing nothing of the sort," the American answered, standing before him, grim and threatening.

The Turk showed no sign of terror. He gripped his silver-headed cane firmly.

"I think," he said, "that there is no one here who will prevent me."

Peter, who saw a fracas imminent, hastily intervened. "If you will permit me for a moment," he said, "there is a little explanation I should perhaps make to Major Kosuth."

The Turk took a step towards the door.

"I have no time to listen to explanations from you or any one," he replied. "My cab is waiting. I depart. If Mr. Heseltine-Wrigge is not satisfied with our transaction, I am sorry, but it is too late to alter anything."

For a moment it seemed as though a struggle between the two men was inevitable. Already people were glancing at them curiously, for Mr. Heseltine-Wrigge came of a primitive school, and he had no intention whatever of letting his man escape. Fortunately, at that moment Count von Hern came up and Peter at once appealed to him.

"Count," he said, "may I beg for your good offices? My friend, Mr. Heseltine-Wrigge here, is determined to have a few words with Major Kosuth before he leaves. Surely this is not an unreasonable request when you consider the magnitude of the transaction which has taken place between them! Let me beg of you to persuade Major Kosuth to give us ten minutes. There is plenty of time for the train, and this is not the place for a brawl."

"It will not take us long, Kosuth, to hear what our friend has to say," he remarked. "We shall be quite quiet in the smoking-room. Let us go in there and dispose of the affair."

The Turk turned unwilling ly in the direction indicated. All four men passed through the cafe, up some stairs, and into the small smoking-room. The room was deserted. Peter led the way to the far corner, and standing with his elbow leaning upon the mantelpiece, addressed them.

"The position is this," he said. "Mr. Heseltine-Wrigge has parted with a million and a half of his own money, a loan to the Turkish Government, on security which is not worth a snap of the fingers."

"It is a lie!" Major Kosuth exclaimed.

"My dear Baron, you are woefully misinformed," the

E. Phillips Oppenheim

Count declared.

Peter shook his head slowly.

"No," he said, "I am not misinformed. My friend here has parted with the money on the security of two battleships and a cruiser, now building in Shepherd & Hargreaves' yard at Belfast. The two battleships and cruiser in question belong to me. I have paid two hundred thousand pounds on account of them, and hold the shipbuilder's receipt."

"You are mad!" Bernadine cried, contemptuously.

Peter shook his head and continued.

"The battleships were laid down for the Turkish Government, and the money with which to start them was supplied by the Secret Service of Germany. The second installment was due ten months ago and has not been paid. The time of grace provided for has expired. The shipbuilders, in accordance with their charter, were consequently at liberty to dispose of the vessels as they thought fit. On the statement of the whole of the facts to the head of the firm, he has parted with these ships to me. I need not say that I have a purchaser within a mile from here. It is a fancy of mine, Count von Hern, that those ships will sail better under the British flag."

There was a moment's tense silence. The face of the Turk was black with anger. Bernadine was trembling with rage.

"This is a tissue of lies!" he exclaimed.

Peter shrugged his shoulders.

"The facts are easy enough for you to prove," he said, "and I have here," he added, producing a roll of papers, "copies of the various documents for your inspection. Your scheme, of course, was simple enough. It fell through for this one reason only. A final notice, pressing for the second installment and stating the days of grace, was forwarded to Constantinople about the time of the recent political troubles. The late government ignored it. In fairness to Major Kosuth, we will believe that the present government was ignorant of it. But the fact remains that Messrs. Shepherd & Hargreaves became at liberty to sell those vessels, and that I have bought them. You will have to give up that money, Major Kosuth."

"By God, he shall!" the American muttered.

Bernadine leaned a little towards his enemy.

"You must give us a minute or two," he insisted. "We shall not go away, I promise you. Within five minutes you shall hear our decision."

Peter sat down at the writing-table and commenced a letter. Mr. Heseltine-Wrigge mounted guard over the door and stood there, a grim figure of impatience. Before the five minutes was up, Bernadine crossed the room.

"I congratulate you, Baron," he said, dryly. "You are either an exceedingly lucky person or you are more of a genius than I believe. Kosuth is even now returning his letters of credit to your friend. You are quite right. The loan cannot stand."

"I was sure," Peter answered, "that you would see the matter correctly."

"You and I," Bernadine continued, "know very well that I don't care a fig about Turkey, new or old. The ships I will admit that I intended to have for my own country. As it is, I wish you joy of them. Before they are completed, we may be fighting in the air."

Peter smiled, and, side by side with Bernadine, strolled across to Heseltine-Wrigge, who was buttoning up a pocket-book with trembling fingers.

"Personally," Peter said, "I believe that the days of wars are over."

"That may or may not be," Bernadine answered. "One thing is very certain. Even if the nations remain at peace, there are enmities which strike only deeper as the years pass. I am going to take a drink now with my disappointed friend Kosuth. If I raise my glass 'To the Day!' you will understand."

Peter smiled.

"My friend Mr. Heseltine-Wrigge and I are for the same destination," he replied, pushing open the swing door which led to the bar. "I return your good wishes, Count. I, too, drink 'To the Day!'"

Bernadine and Kosuth left, a few minutes afterwards. Mr. Heseltine-Wrigge, who was feeling himself again, watched them depart with ill-concealed triumph.

"Say, you had those fellows on toast, Baron," he declared, admiringly. "I couldn't follow the whole affair, but I can see that you're in for big things sometimes. Remember this. If money counts at any time, I'm with you."

Peter clasped his hand.

"Money always counts," he said, "and friends!"

CHAPTER VIII

THE MAN BEHIND THE CURTAIN

Peter, Baron de Grost, glanced at the card which his butler had brought in to him, carelessly at first, afterwards with that curious rigidity of attention which usually denotes the setting free of a flood of memories.

"The gentleman would like to see you, sir," the man announced.

"You can show him in at once," Peter replied. The servant withdrew. Peter, during those few minutes of waiting, stood with his back to the room and his face to the window, looking out across the square, in reality seeing nothing, completely immersed in this strange flood of memories. John Dory - Sir John Dory now - his quondam enemy, and he, had met but seldom during these years of their prosperity. The figure of this man, who had once loomed so largely in his life, had gradually shrunk away into the background. Their avoidance of each other arose, perhaps, from a sort of instinct which was certainly no matter of ill-will. Still, the fact remained that they had scarcely exchanged a word for years, and Peter turned to receive his unexpected guest with a curiosity which he did not trouble wholly to conceal.

Sir John Dory - Chief Commissioner now of Scotland Yard, a person of weight and importance - had changed a great deal during the last few years. His hair had become gray, his walk

E. Phillips Oppenheim

more dignified. There was the briskness, however, of his best days in his carriage and in the flash of his brown eyes. He held out his hand to his ancient foe with a smile.

"My dear Baron," he said, "I hope you are going to say that you are glad to see me."

"Unless," Peter replied, with a good-humored grimace, "your visit is official, I am more than glad - I am charmed. Sit down. I was just going to take my morning cigar. You will join me? Good! Now I am ready for the worst that can happen."

The two men seated themselves. John Dory pulled at his cigar appreciatively, sniffed its flavor for a moment, and then leaned forward in his chair.

"My visit, Baron," he announced, "is semi-official. I am here to ask you a favor."

"An official favor?" Peter demanded quickly.

His visitor hesitated as though he found the question hard to answer.

"To tell you the truth," he declared, "this call of mine is wholly an inspiration. It does not in any way concern you personally, or your position in this country. What that may be I do not know, except that I am sure it is above any suspicion."

"Quite so," Peter murmured. "How diplomatic you have become, my dear friend!"

John Dory smiled.

"Perhaps I am fencing about too much," he said. "I know, of course, that you are a member of a very powerful and wealthy French Society, whose object and aims, so far as I know, are entirely harmless."

"I am delighted to be assured that you recognize that fact," Peter admitted.

"I might add," John Dory continued, "that this harmlessness - is of recent date."

"Really, you do seem to know a good deal," Peter confessed.

"I find myself still fencing," Dory declared. "A matter of habit, I suppose. I didn't mean to when I came. I made up my mind to tell you simply that Guillot was in London, and to ask you if you could help me to get rid of him."

Peter looked thoughtfully into his companion's face, but he did not speak. He understood at such moments the value of silence.

"We speak together," Dory continued softly, "as men who understand one another. Guillot is the one criminal in Europe whom we all fear; not I alone, mind you - it is the same in Berlin, in Petersburg, in Vienna. He has never been caught. It is my honest belief that he never will be caught. At the same time, wherever he arrives the thunder-clouds gather. He leaves behind him always a trail of evil deeds."

"Very well put," Peter murmured. "Quite picturesque."

"Can you help me to get rid of him?" Dory inquired. "I have my hands full just now, as you can imagine, what with the political crisis and these constant mass meetings. I want Guillot out of the country. If you can manage this for me, I shall be your eternal debtor."

"Why do you imagine," Peter asked, "that I can help you in this matter?"

There was a brief silence. John Dory knocked the ash from his cigar.

"Times have changed," he said. "The harmlessness of your great Society, my dear Baron, is at present admitted. But there were days -"

"Exactly," Peter interrupted. "As shrewd as ever, I perceive. Do you know anything of the object of his coming?"

"Nothing."

"Anything of his plans?"

"Nothing."

"You know where he is staying?"

"Naturally," Dory answered. "He has taken a second-floor flat in Crayshaw Mansions, Shaftesbury Avenue. As usual, he is above all petty artifices. He has taken it under the name of Monsieur Guillot."

"I really don't know whether there is anything I can do," Peter decided, "but I will look into the matter for you, with pleasure. Perhaps I may be able to bring a little influence to bear - indirectly, of course. If so, it is at your service. Lady Dory is well, I trust?"

"In the best of health," Sir John replied, accepting the hint and rising to his feet. "I shall hear from you soon?"

"Without a doubt," Peter answered. "I must certainly call upon Monsieur Guillot."

Peter certainly wasted no time in paying his promised visit. That same afternoon he rang the bell at the flat in Crayshaw Mansions. A typical French butler showed him into the room where the great man sat. Monsieur Guillot, slight, elegant, pre-eminently a dandy, was lounging upon a sofa, being manicured by a young lady. He threw down his Petit Journal and rose to his feet, however, at his visitor's entrance.

"My dear Baron," he exclaimed, "but this is charming of you! Mademoiselle," he added, turning to the manicurist, "you will do me the favor of retiring for a short time. Permit me."

He opened the door and showed her out. Then he came back to Peter.

"A visit of courtesy, Monsieur le Baron?" he asked.

"Without a doubt," Peter replied.

"It is beyond all measure charming of you," Guillot declared, "but let me ask you a little question. Is it peace or war?"

"It is what you choose to make it," Peter answered.

The man threw out his hands. There was the shadow of a frown upon his pale forehead. It was a matter for protest, this.

"Why do you come?" he demanded. "What have we in common? The Society has expelled me. Very well, I go my own way. Why not? I am free of your control to-day. You have no more right to interfere with my schemes than I with yours."

"We have the ancient right of power," Peter said, grimly. "You were once a prominent member of our organization, the spoilt protege of Madame, a splendid maker, if you will, of criminal history. Those days have passed. We offered you a pension which you have refused. It is now our turn to speak. We require you to leave this city in twenty-four hours."

The face was livid with anger. He was of the fair type of Frenchman, with deep-set eyes, and a straight, cruel mouth only partly concealed by his golden mustache. Just now, notwithstanding the veneer of his too perfect clothes and civilized air, the beast had leaped out. His face was like the face of a snarling animal.

"I refuse!" he cried. "It is I who refuse! I am here on my own affairs. What they may be is no business of yours or of any one else's. That is my answer to you, Baron de Grost, whether you come to me for yourself or on behalf of the Society to which I no longer belong. That is my answer - that and the door," he added, pressing the bell. "If you will, we fight. If you are wise, forget this visit as quickly as you can."

Peter took up his hat. The man-servant was already in the room.

"We shall probably meet again before your return, Monsieur Guillot," he remarked.

Guillot had recovered himself. His smile was wicked, but his bow perfection.

"To the fortunate hour, Monsieur le Baron!" he replied.

Peter drove hack to Berkeley Square, and without a moment's hesitation pressed the levers which set to work the whole underground machinery of the great power which he controlled. Thenceforward, Monsieur Guillot was surrounded with a vague army of silent watchers. They passed in and out of his fiat, their motor cars were as fast as his in the streets, their fancy in restaurants identical with his. Guillot moved through it all like a man wholly unconscious of espionage, showing nothing of the murderous anger which burned in his blood. The reports came to Peter every hour, although there was, indeed, nothing worth chronicling. Monsieur Guillot's visit to London would seem, indeed, to be a visit of gallantry. He spent most of his time with Mademoiselle Louise, the famous dancer. He was prominent at the Empire, to watch her nightly performance, they were a noticeable couple supping together at the Milan afterwards. Monsieur Guillot was indeed a man of gallantry, but he had the reputation of using these affairs to cloak his real purposes. Those who watched him, watched only the more closely. Monsieur Guillot, who stood it very well at first, unfortunately lost his temper. He drove in the great motor car which he had brought with him from

Paris, to Berkeley Square, and confronted Peter.

"My friend," he exclaimed, though indeed the glitter in his eyes knew nothing of friendship, "it is intolerable, this! Do you think that I do not see through these dummy waiters, these obsequious shopmen, these ladies who drop their eyes when I pass, these commissionaires, these would-be acquaintances? I tell you that they irritate me, this incompetent, futile crowd. You pit them against me! Bah! You should know better. When I choose to disappear, I shall disappear, and no one will follow me. When I strike, I shall strike, and no one will discover what my will may be. You are out of date, dear Baron, with your third-rate army of stupid spies. You succeed in one thing only - you succeed in making me angry."

"It is at least an achievement, that," Peter declared.

"Perhaps," Monsieur Guillot admitted, fiercely. "Yet mark now the result. I defy you, you and all of them. Look at your clock. It is five minutes to seven. It goes well, that clock, eh?"

"It is the correct time," Peter said.

"Then by midnight," Guillot continued, shaking his fist in the other's face, "I shall have done that thing which brought me to England and I shall have disappeared. I shall have done it in spite of your watchers, in spite of your spies, in spite, even, of you, Monsieur le Baron de Grost. There is my challenge. Voila. Take it up if you will. At midnight you shall hear me laugh. I have the honor to wish you good-night!"

Peter opened the door with his own hands.

"This is excellent," he declared. "You are now, indeed, the Monsieur Guillot of old. Almost you persuade me to take up your challenge."

Guillot laughed derisively.

E. Phillips Oppenheim

"As you please!" he exclaimed. "By midnight tonight!"

The challenge of Monsieur Guillot was issued precisely at four minutes before seven. On his departure, Peter spent the next half-hour studying certain notes and sending various telephone messages. Afterwards, he changed his clothes at the usual time and sat down to a tete-a-tete dinner with his wife. Three times during the course of the meal he was summoned to the telephone, and from each call he returned more perplexed. Finally, when the servants had left the room, he took his chair around to his wife's side.

"Violet," he said, "you were asking me just now about the telephone. You were quite right. These were not ordinary messages which I have been receiving. I am engaged in a little matter which, I must confess, perplexes me. I want your advice, perhaps your help."

"I am quite ready," she answered, smiling. "It is a long time since you gave me anything to do."

"You have heard of Guillot?"

She reflected for a moment.

"You mean the wonderful Frenchman," she asked, "the head of the criminal department of the Double-Four?"

"The man who was at its head when it existed. The criminal department, as you know, has all been done away with. The Double-Four has now no more concern with those who break the law, save in those few instances where great issues demand it."

"But Monsieur Guillot still exists?"

"He not only exists," answered Peter, "but he is here in London, a rebel and a defiant one. Do you know who came to see me the other morning?"

She shook her head.

"Sir John Dory," Peter continued. "He came here with a request. He begged for my help. Guillot is here, committed to some enterprise which no one can wholly fathom. Dory has enough to do with other things, as you can imagine, just now. Besides, I think he recognizes that Monsieur Guillot is rather a hard nut for the ordinary English detective to crack."

"And you?" she demanded, breathlessly.

"I join forces with Dory," Peter admitted. "Sogrange agrees with me. Guillot was associated with the Double-Four too long for us to have him make scandalous history either here or in Paris."

"You have seen him?"

"I have not only seen him, but declared war against him."

"And he?"

"Guillot is defiant," Peter replied. "He has been here only this evening. He mocks at me. He swears that he will bring off this enterprise, whatever it may be, before midnight to-night, and he has defied me to stop him."

"But you will," she murmured, softly.

Peter smiled. The conviction in his wife's tone was a subtle compliment which he did not fail to appreciate.

"I have hopes," he confessed, "and yet, let me tell you this, Violet. I have never been more puzzled. Ask yourself, now. What enterprise is there worthy of a man like Guillot, in which he could engage himself here in London between now and midnight? Any ordinary theft is beneath him. The purloining of the crown jewels, perhaps, he might consider, but I don't think that anything less in the way of robbery

E. Phillips Oppenheim

would bring him here. He has his code and he is as vain as a peacock. Yet money is at the root of everything he does."

"How does he spend his time here?" Violet asked.

"He has a handsome flat in Shaftesbury Avenue," Peter answered, "where he lives, to all appearance, the life of an idle man of fashion. The whole of his spare time is spent with Mademoiselle Louise, the danseuse at the Empire. You see, it is half-past eight now. I have eleven men altogether at work, and according to my last report he was dining with her in the grill-room at the Milan. They have just ordered their coffee ten minutes ago, and the car is waiting outside to take Mademoiselle to the Empire. Guillot's box is engaged there, as usual. If he proposes to occupy it, he is leaving himself a very narrow margin of time to carry out any enterprise worth speaking of."

Violet was thoughtful for several moments. Then she crossed the room, took up a copy of an illustrated paper, and brought it across to Peter. He smiled as he glanced at the picture to which she pointed, and the few lines underneath.

"It has struck you, too, then!" he exclaimed. "Good! You have answered me exactly as I hoped. Somehow, I scarcely trusted myself. I have both cars waiting outside. We may need them. You won't mind coming to the Empire with me?"

"Mind!" she laughed. "I only hope I may be in at the finish."

"If the finish," Peter remarked, "is of the nature which I anticipate, I shall take particularly good care that you are not."

The curtain was rising upon the first act of the ballet as they entered the most popular music-hall in London and were shown to the box which Peter had engaged. The house was full - crowded, in fact, almost to excess. They had scarcely taken their seats when a roar of applause announced the coming of Mademoiselle Louise. She stood for a moment to receive her nightly ovation, a slim, beautiful creature, looking out upon the great house with that faint, bewitching smile at the corners of her lips, which every photographer in Europe had striven to reproduce. Then she moved away to the music, an exquisite figure, the personification of all that was alluring in her sex. Violet leaned forward to watch her movements as she plunged into the first dance. Peter was occupied looking around the house. Monsieur Guillot was there, sitting insolently forward in his box, sleek and immaculate. He even waved his hand and bowed as he met Peter's eye. Somehow or other, his confidence had its effect. Peter began to feel vaguely troubled. After all, his plans were built upon a surmise. It was so easy for him to be wrong. No man would show his hand so openly, unless he were sure of the game. Then his face cleared a little. In the box adjoining Guillot's, the figure of a solitary man was just visible, a man who had leaned over to applaud Louise, but who was now sitting back in the shadows. Peter recognized him at once, notwithstanding the obscurity. This was so much to the good, at any rate. He took up his hat.

"For a quarter of an hour you will excuse me, Violet," he said. "Watch Guillot. If he leaves his place, knock at the door of your own box, and one of my men, who is outside, will come to you at once. He will know where to find me."

Peter hurried away, pausing for a moment in the promenade, to scribble a line or two at the back of one of his own cards. Presently he knocked at the door of the box adjoining Guillot's and was instantly admitted. Violet continued her watch. She remained alone until the curtain fell upon the first act of the ballet. A few minutes later, Peter returned. She knew at once that things were going well. He sank into a chair by her side.

"I have messages every five minutes," he whispered in her ear, "and I am venturing upon a bold stroke. There is still something about the affair, though, which I cannot understand. You are absolutely sure that Guillot has not moved?"

Violet pointed with her program across the house. "There he

sits," she remarked. "He left his chair as the curtain went down, but he could scarcely have gone out of the box, for he was back within ten seconds."

Peter looked steadily across at the opposite box. Guillot was sitting a little further back now, as though he no longer courted observation. Something about his attitude puzzled the man who watched him. With a sudden quick movement he caught up the glasses which stood by his wife's side. The curtain was going up for the second act, and Guillot had turned his head. Peter held the glasses only for a moment to his eyes, and then glanced down at the stage.

"My God!" he muttered. "The man's a genius! Violet, the small motor is coming for you."

He was out of the box in a single step. Violet looked after him, looked down upon the stage and across at Guillot's box. It was hard to understand.

The curtain had scarcely rung up upon the second act of the ballet when a young lady who met from all the loungers, and even from the doorkeeper himself, the most respectful attention, issued from the stage-door at the Empire and stepped into the large motor car which was waiting, drawn up against the curb. The door was opened from inside and closed at once. She held out her hands, as yet ungloved, to the man who sat back in the corner.

"At last!" she murmured. "And I thought, indeed, that you had forsaken me."

He took her hands and held them tightly, but he answered only in a whisper. He wore a sombre black cloak and a broad-brimmed black hat. A muffler concealed the lower part of his face. She put her finger upon the electric light, but he stopped her.

"I must not be recognized," he said thickly. "Forgive me,

Louise, if I seem strange at first, but there is more in it than I can tell you. No one must know that I am in London to-night. When we reach this place to which you are taking me, and we are really alone, then we can talk. I have so much to say."

She looked at him doubtfully. It was indeed a moment of indecision with her. Then she began to laugh softly.

"Dear one, but you have changed!" she exclaimed, compassionately. "After all, why not? I must not forget that things have gone so hardly with you. It seems odd, indeed, to see you sitting there, muffled up like an old man, afraid to show yourself. You know how foolish you are? With your black cape and that queer hat, you are so different from all the others. If you seek to remain unrecognized, why do you not dress as all the men do? Any one who was suspicious would recognize you from your clothes."

"It is true," he muttered. "I did not think of it."

She leaned towards him.

"You will not even kiss me?" she murmured.

"Not yet," he answered.

She made a little grimace.

"But you are cold!"

"You do not understand," he answered. "They are watching me - even to-night they are watching me. Oh, if you only knew, Louise, how I have longed for this hour that is to come!"

Her vanity was assuaged. She patted his hand but came no nearer.

"You are a foolish man," she said, "very foolish."

"It is not for you to say that," he replied. "If I have been foolish, were not you often the cause of my folly?" Again she laughed.

"Oh, la, la! It is always the same! It is always you men who accuse! For that presently I shall reprove you. But now - as for now, behold, we have arrived!"

"It is a crowded thoroughfare," the man remarked, nervously, looking up and down Shaftesbury Avenue.

"Stupid!" she cried, stepping out. "I do not recognize you to-night, little one. Even your voice is different. Follow me quickly across the pavement and up the stairs. There is only one flight. The flat I have borrowed is on the second floor. I do not care very much that people should recognize me either, under the circumstances. There is nothing they love so much," she added, with a toss of the head, "as finding an excuse to have my picture in the paper."

He followed her down the dim hall and up the broad, flat stairs, keeping always some distance behind. On the first landing she drew a key from her pocket and opened a door. It was the door of Monsieur Guillot's sitting-room. A round table in the middle was laid for supper. One light alone, and that heavily shaded, was burning.

"Oh, la, la!" she exclaimed. "How I hate this darkness! Wait till I can turn on the lights, dear friend, and then you must embrace me. It is from outside, I believe. No, do not follow. I can find the switch for myself. Remain where you are. I return instantly."

She left him alone in the room, closing the door softly. In the passage she reeled for a moment and caught at her side. She was very pale. Guillot, coming swiftly up the steps, frowned as he saw her.

"He is there?" he demanded, harshly.

"He is there," Louise replied, "but, indeed, I am angry with myself. See, I am faint. It is a terrible thing, this, which I have done. He did me no harm, that young man, except that he was stupid and heavy, and that I never loved him. Who could love him, indeed! But, Guillot -"

He passed on, scarcely heeding her words, but she clung to his arm.

"Dear one," she begged, "promise that you will not really hurt him. Promise me that, or I will shriek out and call the people from the streets here. You would not make an assassin of me? Promise!"

Guillot turned suddenly towards her and there were strange things in his face. He pointed down the stairs.

"Go back, Louise," he ordered, "back to your rooms, for your own sake. Remember that you have left the theatre too ill to finish your performance. You have had plenty of time already to get home. Quick! Leave me to deal with this young man. I tell you to go."

She retreated down the stairs, dumb, her knees shaking with fear. Guillot entered the room, closing the door behind him. Even as he bowed to that dark figure standing in the corner, his left hand shot forward the bolt.

"Monsieur," he said -

"What is the meaning of this?" the visitor interrupted, haughtily. "I am expecting Mademoiselle Louise. I did not understand that strangers had the right of entry into this room."

Guillot bowed low.

"Monsieur," he said once more, "it is a matter for my eternal regret that I am forced to intrude even for a moment upon an

E. Phillips Oppenheim

assignation so romantic. But there is a little matter which must first be settled. I have some friends here who have a thing to say to you."

He walked softly, with catlike tread, along by the wall to where the thick curtains shut out the inner apartment. He caught at the thick velvet, dragged it back, and the two rooms were suddenly flooded with light. In the recently discovered one, two stalwart-looking men in plain clothes, but of very unmistakable appearance, were standing waiting. Guillot staggered back. They were strangers to him. He was like a man who looks upon a nightmare. His eyes protruded. The words which he tried to utter, failed him. Then, with a swift, nervous presentiment, he turned quickly around towards the man who had been standing in the shadows. Here, too, the unexpected had happened. It was Peter, Baron de Grost, who threw his muffler and broad-brimmed hat upon the table.

"Five minutes to eleven, I believe, Monsieur Guillot," Peter declared. "I win by an hour and five minutes."

Guillot said nothing for several seconds. After all, though, he had great gifts. He recovered alike his power of speech and his composure.

"These gentlemen," he said, pointing with his left hand towards the inner room - "I do not understand their presence in my apartments."

Peter shrugged his shoulders.

"They represent, I am afraid, the obvious end of things," he explained. "You have given me a run for my money, I confess. A Monsieur Guillot who is remarkably like you, still occupies your box at the Empire, and Mademoiselle Jeanne Lemere, the accomplished understudy of the lady who has just left us, is sufficiently like the incomparable Louise to escape, perhaps, detection for the first few minutes. But you gave the game away a little, my dear Guillot, when you allowed your quarry to come and gaze even from the shadows of his box at the woman he adored."

"Where is - he?" Guillot faltered.

"He is on his way back to his country home," Peter replied. "I think that he will be cured of his infatuation for Mademoiselle. The assassins whom you planted in that room are by this time in Bow Street. The price which others beside you knew, my dear Guillot, was placed upon that unfortunate young head, will not pass this time into your pocket. For the rest -"

"The rest is of no consequence," Guillot interrupted, bowing. "I admit that I am vanquished. As for those gentlemen there," he added, waving his hand towards the two men who had taken a step forward, "I have a little oath which is sacred to me concerning them. I take the liberty, therefore, to admit myself defeated, Monsieur le Baron, and to take my leave."

No one was quick enough to interfere. They had only a glimpse of him as he stood there with the revolver pressed to his temple, an impression of a sharp report, of Guillot staggering back as the revolver slipped from his fingers on to the floor. Even his death cry was stifled. They carried him away without any fuss, and Peter was just in time, after all, to see the finish of the second act of the ballet. The sham Monsieur Guillot still smirked at the sham Louise, but the box by his side was empty.

"It is over?" Violet asked, breathlessly.

"It is over," Peter answered.

It was, after all, an unrecorded tragedy. In an obscure corner of the morning papers one learned the next day that a Frenchman, who had apparently come to the end of his means, had committed suicide in a furnished flat of Shaftesbury Avenue. Two foreigners were deported without having been brought up for trial, for being suspected persons. A little languid interest was aroused at the inquest when one of the witnesses deposed to the deceased's having been a famous French criminal. Nothing further transpired, however, and the readers of the halfpenny press for once were deprived of their sensation. For the rest, Peter received, with much satisfaction, a remarkably handsome signet ring, bearing some famous arms, and a telegram from Sogrange: "Well done, Baron! May the successful termination of your enterprise nerve you for the greater undertaking which is close at hand. I leave for London by the night train. Sogrange."

CHAPTER IX

THE GHOSTS OF HAVANA HARBOR

"We may now," Sogrange remarked, buttoning up his ulster, and stretching himself out to the full extent of his steamer chair, "consider ourselves at sea. I trust, my friend, that you are feeling quite comfortable."

Peter, lying at his ease upon a neighboring chair, with a pillow behind his head, a huge fur coat around his body, and a rug over his feet, had all the appearance of being very comfortable indeed. His reply, however, was a little short - almost peevish.

"I am comfortable enough for the present, thank you. Heaven knows how long it will last!"

Sogrange waved his arms towards the great uneasy plain of blue sea, the showers of foam leaping into the sunlight, away beyond the disappearing coast of France.

"Last!" he repeated. "For eight days, I hope. Consider, my dear Baron! What could be more refreshing, more stimulating to our jaded nerves than this? Think of the December fogs you have left behind, the cold, driving rain, the puddles in the street, the gray skies - London, in short, at her ugliest and worst."

"That is all very well," Peter protested, "but I have left several other things behind, too."

E. Phillips Oppenheim

"As, for instance?" Sogrange inquired, genially.

"My wife," Peter informed him. "Violet objects very much to these abrupt separations. This week, too, I was shooting at Saxthorpe, and I had also several other engagements of a pleasant nature. Besides, I have reached that age when I find it disconcerting to be called out of bed in the middle of the night to answer a long distance telephone call, and told to embark on a White Star liner leaving Liverpool early the next morning. It may be your idea of a pleasure trip. It isn't mine."

Sogrange was amused. His smile, however, was hidden. Only the tip of his cigarette was visible.

"Anything else?"

"Nothing much, except that I am always seasick," Peter replied deliberately. "I can feel it coming on now. I wish that fellow would keep away with his beastly mutton broth. The whole ship seems to smell of it."

Sogrange laughed, softly but without disguise.

"Who said anything about a pleasure trip?" he demanded.

Peter turned his head.

"You did. You told me when you came on at Cherbourg that you had to go to New York to look after some property there, that things were very quiet in London, and that you hated traveling alone. Therefore, you sent for me at a few hours' notice."

"Is that what I told you?" Sogrange murmured.

"Yes! Wasn't it true?" Peter asked, suddenly alert.

"Not a word of it," Sogrange admitted. "It is quite amazing that you should have believed it for a moment."

"I was a fool," Peter confessed. "You see, I was tired and a little cross. Besides, somehow or other, I never associated a trip to America with -"

Sogrange interrupted him quietly, but ruthlessly.

"Lift up the label attached to the chair next to yours. Read it out to me."

Peter took it into his hand and turned it over. A quick exclamation escaped him.

"Great Heavens! The Count von Hern - Bernadine!"

"Just so," Sogrange assented. "Nice clear writing, isn't it?"

Peter sat bolt upright in his chair.

"Do you mean to say that Bernadine is on board?" Sogrange shook his head.

"By the exercise, my dear Baron," he said, "of a superlative amount of ingenuity, I was able to prevent that misfortune. Now lean over and read the label on the next chair."

Peter obeyed. His manner had acquired a new briskness. "La Duchesse della Nermino," he announced.

Sogrange nodded.

"Everything just as it should be," he declared. "Change those labels, my friend, as quickly as you can."

Peter's fingers were nimble and the thing was done in a few seconds.

"So I am to sit next the Spanish lady," he remarked, feeling for his tie.

"Not only that, but you are to make friends with her," Sogrange replied. "You are to be your captivating self, Baron. The Duchesse is to forget her weakness for hot rooms. She is to develop a taste for sea air and your society."

"Is she," Peter asked, anxiously, "old or young?"

Sogrange showed a disposition to fence with the question. "Not old," he answered; "certainly not old. Fifteen years ago she was considered to be one of the most beautiful women in the world."

"The ladies of Spain," Peter remarked, with a sigh, "are inclined to mature early."

"In some cases," Sogrange assured him, "there are no women in the world who preserve their good looks longer. You shall judge, my friend. Madame comes! How about that sea-sickness now?"

"Gone," Peter declared, briskly. "Absolutely a fancy of mine. Never felt better in my life."

An imposing little procession approached along the deck. There was the deck steward leading the way; a very smart French maid carrying a wonderful collection of wraps, cushions and books; a black-browed, pallid man-servant, holding a hot water bottle in his hand, and leading a tiny Pekinese spaniel, wrapped in a sealskin coat; and finally Madame la Duchesse. It was so obviously a procession intended to impress, that neither Peter nor Sogrange thought it worth while to conceal their interest.

The Duchesse, save that she was tall and wrapped in magnificent furs, presented a somewhat mysterious appearance. Her features were entirely obscured by an unusually thick veil of black lace, and the voluminous nature of her outer garments only permitted a suspicion as to her figure, which was, at that time, at once the despair and the triumph of her corsetiere.

With both hands she was holding her fur-lined skirts from contact with the deck, disclosing at the same time remarkably shapely feet encased in trim patent shoes with plain silver buckles, and a little more black silk stocking than seemed absolutely necessary. The deck steward, after a half-puzzled scrutiny of the labels, let down the chair next to the two men. The Duchesse contemplated her prospective neighbors with some curiosity, mingled with a certain amount of hesitation. It was at that moment that Sogrange, shaking away his rug, rose to his feet.

"Madame la Duchesse permits me to remind her of my existence?" he said, bowing low. "It is some years since we met, but I had the honor of a dance at the Palace in Madrid."

She held out her hand at once, yet somehow Peter felt sure that she was thankful for her veil. Her voice was pleasant, and her air the air of a great lady. She spoke French with the soft, sibilant intonation of the Spaniard.

"I remember the occasion perfectly, Marquis," she admitted. "Your sister and I once shared a villa in Mentone."

"I am flattered by your recollection, Duchesse," Sogrange murmured.

"It is a great surprise to meet with you here, though," she continued. "I did not see you at Cherbourg or on the train."

"I motored from Paris," Sogrange explained, "and arrived, contrary to my custom, I must confess, somewhat early. Will you permit that I introduce an acquaintance, whom I have been fortunate enough to find on board - Monsieur le Baron de Grost - Madame la Duchesse della Nermino."

Peter was graciously received and the conversation dealt, for a few moments, with the usual banalities of the voyage. Then followed the business of settling the Duchesse in her place. When she was really installed, and surrounded with all the paraphernalia of a great and fanciful lady, including a handful of long cigarettes, she raised for the first time her veil. Peter, who was at the moment engaged in conversation with her, was a little shocked by the result. Her features were worn, her face dead-white, with many signs of the ravages wrought by the constant use of cosmetics. Only her eyes had retained something of their former splendor. These latter were almost violet in color, deep-set, with dark rims, and were sufficient almost in themselves to make one forget for a moment the less prepossessing details of her appearance. A small library of books was by her side, but after a while she no longer pretended any interest in them. She was a born conversationalist, a creature of her country entirely and absolutely feminine, to whom the subtle and flattering deference of the other sex was the breath of life itself. Peter burned his homage upon her altar with a craft which amounted to genius. In less than half an hour, Madame la Duchesse was looking many years younger. The vague look of apprehension had passed from her face. Their voices had sunk to a confidential undertone, punctuated often by the music of her laughter. Sogrange, with a murmured word of apology, had slipped away long ago. Decidedly, for an Englishman, Peter was something of a marvel!

Madame la Duchesse moved her head towards the empty chair.

"He is a great friend of yours - the Marquis de Sogrange?" she asked, with a certain inflection in her tone which Peter was not slow to notice.

"Indeed no!" he answered. "A few years ago I was frequently in Paris. I made his acquaintance then, but we have met very seldom since."

"You are not traveling together, then?"

"By no means. I recognized him only as he boarded the steamer at Cherbourg."

"He is not a popular man in our world," she remarked. "One speaks of him as a schemer."

"Is there anything left to scheme for in France?" Peter asked, carelessly. "He is, perhaps, a monarchist?"

"His ancestry alone would compel a devoted allegiance to royalism," the Duchesse declared, "but I do not think that he is interested in any of these futile plots to reinstate the House of Orleans. I, Monsieur le Baron, am Spanish."

"I have scarcely lived so far out of the world as to have heard nothing of the Duchesse della Nermino," Peter replied with empressement. "The last time I saw you, Duchesse, you were in the suite of the Infanta."

"Like all Englishmen, I see you possess a memory," she said, smiling.

"Duchesse," Peter answered, lowering his voice, "without the memories which one is fortunate enough to collect as one passes along, life would be a dreary place. The most beautiful things in the world cannot remain always with us. It is well, then, that the shadow of them can be recalled to us in the shape of dreams."

Her eyes rewarded him for his gallantry. Peter felt that he was doing very well indeed. He indulged himself in a brief silence. Presently she returned to the subject of Sogrange.

"I think," she remarked, "that of all the men in the world I expected least to see the Marquis de Sogrange on board a steamer bound for New York. What can a man of his type find to amuse him in the New World?"

"One wonders, indeed," Peter assented. "As a matter of fact, I did read in a newspaper a few days ago that he was going to Mexico in connection with some excavations there. He spoke to me of it just now. They seem to have discovered a ruined temple of the Incas, or something of the sort."

The Duchesse breathed what sounded very much like a sigh of relief.

"I had forgotten," she admitted, "that New York itself need not necessarily be his destination."

"For my own part," Peter continued, "it is quite amazing, the interest which the evening papers always take in the movements of one connected ever so slightly with their world. I think that a dozen newspapers have told their readers the exact amount of money I am going to lend or borrow in New York, the stocks I am going to bull or bear, the mines I am going to purchase. My presence on an American steamer is accounted for by the journalists a dozen times over. Yours, Duchesse, if one might say so without appearing over curious, seems the most inexplicable. What attraction can America possibly have for you?"

She glanced at him covertly from under her sleepy eyelids. Peter's face was like the face of a child.

"You do not, perhaps, know," she said, "that I was born in Cuba. I lived there, in fact, for many years. I still have estates in the country."

"Indeed?" he answered. "Are you interested, then, in this reported salvage of the Maine?"

There was a short silence. Peter, who had not been looking at her when he had asked his question, turned his head, surprised at her lack of response. His heart gave a little jump. The Duchesse had all the appearance of a woman on the point of fainting. One hand was holding a scent bottle to her nose; the other, thin and white, ablaze with emeralds and diamonds, was gripping the side of her chair. Her expression was one of blank terror. Peter felt a shiver chill his own blood at the things he saw in her face. He himself was confused, apologetic, yet absolutely without understanding. His thoughts reverted at first to his own commonplace malady.

"You are ill, Duchesse!" he exclaimed. "You will allow me to call the deck steward? Or perhaps you would prefer your own maid? I have some brandy in this flask."

He had thrown off his rug, but her imperious gesture kept him seated. She was looking at him with an intentness which was almost tragical.

"What made you ask me that question?" she demanded.

His innocence was entirely apparent. Not even Peter could have dissembled so naturally.

"That question?" he repeated, vaguely. "You mean about the Maine? It was the idlest chance, Duchesse, I assure you. I saw something about it in the paper yesterday and it seemed interesting. But if I had had the slightest idea that the subject was distasteful to you, I would not have dreamed of mentioning it. Even now - I do not understand -"

She interrupted him. All the time he had been speaking she had shown signs of recovery. She was smiling now, faintly and with obvious effort, but still smiling.

"It is altogether my own fault, Baron," she admitted, graciously. "Please forgive my little fit of emotion. The subject is a very sore one among my countrypeople, and your sudden mention of it upset me. It was very foolish."

"Duchesse, I was a clumsy idiot!" Peter declared, penitently. "I deserve that you should be unkind to me for the rest of the voyage."

"I could not afford that," she answered, forcing another smile. "I am relying too much upon you for companionship. Ah! could I trouble you?" she added. "For the moment I need my

E. Phillips Oppenheim

maid. She passes there."

Peter sprang up and called the young woman, who was slowly pacing the dock. He himself did not at once return to his place. He went instead in search of Sogrange, and found him in his stateroom. Sogrange was lying upon a couch, in a silk smoking suit, with a French novel in his hand and an air of contentment which was almost fatuous. He laid down the volume at Peter's entrance.

"Dear Baron," he murmured, "why this haste! No one is ever in a hurry upon a steamer. Remember that we can't possibly get anywhere in less than eight days, and there is no task in the world, nowadays, which cannot be accomplished in that time. To hurry is a needless waste of tissue, and, to a person of my nervous temperament, exceedingly unpleasant."

Peter sat down on the edge of the bunk.

"I presume you have quite finished?" he said. "If so, listen to me. I am moving in the dark. Is it my fault that I blunder? By the merest accident I have already committed a hideous faux pas. You ought to have warned me."

"What do you mean?"

"I have spoken to the Duchesse of the Maine disaster."

The eyes of Sogrange gleamed for a moment, but he lay perfectly still.

"Why not?" he asked. "A good many people are talking about it. It is one of the strangest things I have ever heard of, that after all these years they should be trying to salve the wreck."

"It seems worse than strange," Peter declared. "What can be the use of trying to stir up bitter feelings between two nations who have fought their battles and buried the hatchet? I call it an act of insanity."

A bugle rang. Sogrange yawned and sat up.

"Would you mind touching the bell for my servant, Baron," he asked. "Dinner will be served in half an hour. Afterwards, we will talk, you and I."

Peter turned away, not wholly pleased.

"The sooner, the better," he grumbled, "or I shall be putting my foot into it again." . . .

After dinner, the two men walked on deck together. The night was dark but fine, with a strong wind blowing from the northwest. The deck steward called their attention to a long line of lights, stealing up from the horizon on their starboard side.

"That's the Lusitania, sir. She'll be up to us in half an hour."

They leaned over the rail. Soon the blue fires began to play about their mast head. Sogrange watched them thoughtfully.

"If one could only read those messages," he remarked, with a sigh, "it might help us."

Peter knocked the ash from his cigar and was silent for a time. He was beginning to understand the situation.

"My friend," he said at last, "I have been doing you an injustice. I have come to the conclusion that you are not keeping me in ignorance of the vital facts connected with our visit to America, willfully. At the present moment you know just a little more, but a very little more than I do."

"What perception!" Sogrange murmured. "My dear Baron, sometimes you amaze me. You are absolutely right. I have some pieces and I am convinced that they would form a puzzle the solution of which would be interesting to us, but how or

E. Phillips Oppenheim

where they fit in, I frankly don't know. You have the facts so far."

"Certainly," Peter replied.

"You have heard of Sirdeller?"

"You mean the Sirdeller?" Peter asked.

"Naturally. I mean the man whose very movements sway the money markets of the world, the man who could, if he chose, ruin any nation, make war impossible; who could if he had ten more years of life and was allowed to live, draw to himself and his own following the entire wealth of the universe."

"Very eloquent," Peter remarked. "We'll take the rest for granted."

"Then," Sogrange continued, "you have probably also heard of Don Pedro, Prince of Marsine, one time Pretender to the Throne of Spain?"

"Quite a striking figure in European politics," Peter assented, quickly. "He is suspected of radical proclivities, and is still, it is rumored, an active plotter against the existing monarchy."

"Very well," Sogrange said. "Now listen carefully. Four months ago, Sirdeller was living at the Golden Villa, near Nice. He was visited more than once by Marsine, introduced by the Count von Hern. The result of those visits was a long series of cablegrams to certain great engineering firms in America. Almost immediately, the salvage of the Maine was started. It is a matter of common report that the entire cost of these works is being undertaken by Sirdeller."

"Now," Peter murmured, "you are really beginning to interest me."

"This week," Sogrange went on, "it is expected that the result of the salvage works will be made known. That is to say, it is highly possible that the question of whether the Maine was blown up from outside or inside, will be settled once and for all. This week, mind, Baron. Now see what happens. Sirdeller returns to America. The Count von Hern and Prince Marsine come to America. The Duchesse della Nermino comes to America. The Duchesse, Sirdeller and Marsine are upon this steamer. The Count von Hern travels by the Lusitania only because it was reported that Sirdeller at the last minute changed his mind and was traveling by that boat. Mix these things up in your brain - the conjurer's hat, let us call it," Sogrange concluded, laying his hand upon Peter's arm, "Sirdeller, the Duchesse, Von Hern, Marsine, the raising of the Maine - mix them up and what sort of an omelette appears?"

Peter whistled softly.

"No wonder," he said, "that you couldn't make the pieces of the puzzle fit. Tell me more about the Duchesse?"

Sogrange considered for a moment.

"The principal thing about her which links her with the present situation," he explained, "is that she was living in Cuba at the time of the Maine disaster, married to a rich Cuban."

The affair was suddenly illuminated by the searchlight of romance. Peter, for the first time, saw not the light, but the possibility of it.

"Marsine has been living in Germany, has he not?" he asked.

"He is a personal friend of the Kaiser," Sogrange replied.

They both looked up and listened to the crackling of the electricity above their heads.

"I expect Bernadine is a little annoyed," Peter remarked.

"It isn't pleasant to be out of the party," Sogrange agreed. "Nearly everybody, however, believed at the last moment that Sirdeller had transferred his passage to the Lusitania."

"It's going to cost him an awful lot in marconigrams," Peter said. "By the bye, wouldn't it have been better for us to have traveled separately, and incognito?"

Sogrange shrugged his shoulders slightly.

"Von Hern has at least one man on board," he replied. "I do not think that we could possibly have escaped observation. Besides, I rather imagine that any move we are able to make in this matter must come before we reach Fire Island."

"Have you any theory at all?" Peter asked.

"Not the ghost of a one," Sogrange admitted. "One more fact, though, I forgot to mention. You may find it important. The Duchesse comes entirely against Von Hern's wishes. They have been on intimate terms for years, but for some reason or other he was exceedingly anxious that she should not take this voyage. She, on the other hand, seemed to have some equally strong reason for coming. The most useful piece of advice I could give you would be to cultivate her acquaintance."

"The Duchesse -"

Peter never finished his sentence. His companion drew him suddenly back into the shadow of a lifeboat.

"Look!"

A door had opened from lower down the deck, and a curious little procession was coming towards them. A man, burly and broad-shouldered, who had the air of a professional bully, walked by himself ahead. Two others of similar build walked a few steps behind. And between them a thin, insignificant figure, wrapped in an immense fur coat and using a strong walking stick, came slowly along the deck. It was like a procession of prison warders guarding a murderer, or perhaps a nerve-racked royal personage moving the end of his days in the midst of enemies. With halting steps the little old man came shambling along. He looked neither to the left nor to the right. His eyes were fixed and yet unseeing, his features were pale and bony. There was no gleam of life, not even in the stone-cold eyes. Like some machine-made man of a new and physically degenerate age, he took his exercise under the eye of his doctor, a strange and miserable-looking object.

"There goes Sirdeller," Sogrange whispered. "Look at him - the man whose might is greater than any emperor's. There is no haven in the universe to which he does not hold the key. Look at him - master of the world!"

Peter shivered. There was something depressing in the sight of that mournful procession.

"He neither smokes nor drinks," Sogrange continued. "Women, as a sex, do not exist for him. His religion is a doubting Calvinism. He has a doctor and a clergyman always by his side to inject life and hope if they can. Look at him well, my friend. He represents a great moral lesson."

"Thanks!" Peter replied. "I am going to take the taste of him out of my mouth with a whiskey and soda. Afterwards, I'm for the Duchesse."

But the Duchesse, apparently, was not for Peter. He found her in the music-room with several of the little Marconi missives spread out before her, and she cut him dead. Peter, however, was a brave man, and skilled at the game of bluff. So he stopped by her side and without any preamble addressed her.

"Duchesse," he said, "you are a woman of perceptions. Which do you believe, then, in your heart to be the more trustworthy - the Count von Hern or I?"

She simply stared at him. He continued promptly.

"You have received your warning, I see."

"From whom?"

"From the Count von Hern. Why believe what he says? He may be a friend of yours - he may be a dear friend - but in your heart you know that he is both unscrupulous and selfish. Why accept his word and distrust me? I, at least, am honest."

She raised her eyebrows.

"Honest?" she repeated. "Whose word have I for that save your own? And what concern is it of mine if you possess every one of the bourgeois qualities in the world? You are presuming, sir."

"My friend Sogrange will tell you that I am to be trusted," Peter persisted.

"I see no reason why I should trouble myself about your personal characteristics," she replied, coldly. "They do not interest me."

"On the contrary, Duchesse," Peter continued, fencing wildly, "you have never in your life been more in need of any one's services than you are of mine."

The conflict was uneven. The Duchesse was a nervous, highly strung woman. The calm assurance of Peter's manner oppressed her with a sense of his mastery. She sank back upon the couch from which she had arisen.

"I wish you would tell me what you mean," she said. "You have no right to talk to me in this fashion. What have you to do with my affairs?"

"I have as much to do with them as the Count von Hem,"

Peter insisted, boldly.

"I have known the Count von Hern," she answered, "for very many years. You have been a shipboard acquaintance of mine for a few hours."

"If you have known the Count von Hern for many years," Peter asserted, "you have found out by this time that he is an absolutely untrustworthy person."

"Supposing he is," she said, "will you tell me what concern it is of yours? Do you suppose for one moment that I am likely to discuss my private affairs with a perfect stranger?"

"You have no private affairs," Peter declared, sternly. "They are the affairs of a nation."

She glanced at him with a little shiver.

From that moment he felt that he was gaining ground. She looked around the room. It was still filled, but in their corner they were almost unobserved.

"How much do you know?" she asked in a low tone which shook with passion.

Peter smiled enigmatically.

"Perhaps more, even, than you, Duchesse," he replied. "I should like to be your friend. You need one - you know that."

She rose abruptly to her feet.

"For to-night it is enough," she declared, wrapping her fur cloak around her. "You may talk to me to-morrow, Baron. I must think. If you desire really to be my friend, there is, perhaps, one service which I may require of you. But to-night, no!"

Peter stood aside and allowed her to step past him. He was perfectly content with the progress he had made. Her farewell salute was by no means ungracious. As soon as she was out of sight, he returned to the couch where she had been sitting. She had taken away the marconigrams, but she had left upon the floor several copies of the New York Herald. He took them up and read them carefully through. The last one he found particularly interesting, so much so that he folded it up, placed it in his coat pocket, and went off to look for Sogrange, whom he found at last in the saloon, watching a noisy game of "Up Jenkins!" Peter sank upon the cushioned seat by his side.

"You were right," he remarked. "Bernadine has been busy."

Sogrange smiled.

"I trust," he said, "that the Duchesse is not proving faithless?"

"So far," Peter replied, "I have kept my end up. Tomorrow will be the test. Bernadine had filled her with caution. She thinks that I know everything - whatever everything may be. Unless I can discover a little more than I do now, to-morrow is going to be an exceedingly awkward day for me."

"There is every prospect of your acquiring a great deal of valuable information before then," Sogrange declared. "Sit tight, my friend. Something is going to happen."

On the threshold of the saloon, ushered in by one of the stewards, a tall, powerful-looking man, with a square, well-trimmed black beard, was standing looking around as though in search of some one. The steward pointed out, with an unmistakable movement of his head, Peter and Sogrange. The man approached and took the next table.

"Steward," he directed, "bring me a glass of Vermouth and some dominoes."

Peter's eyes were suddenly bright. Sogrange touched his foot under the table and whispered a word of warning. The dominoes were brought. The newcomer arranged them as though for a game. Then he calmly withdrew the double-four and laid it before Sogrange.

"It has been my misfortune, Marquis," he said, "never to have made your acquaintance, although our mutual friends are many, and I think I may say that I have the right to claim a certain amount of consideration from you and your associates. You know me?"

"Certainly, Prince," Sogrange replied. "I am charmed. Permit me to present my friend, the Baron de Grost."

The newcomer bowed and glanced a little nervously around.

"You will permit me," he begged. "I travel incognito. I have lived so long in England that I have permitted myself the name of an Englishman. I am traveling under the name of Mr. James Fanshawe."

"Mr. Fanshawe, by all means," Sogrange agreed. "In the meantime -"

"I claim my rights as a corresponding member of the Double-Four," the newcomer declared. "My friend the Count von Hern finds menace to certain plans of ours in your presence upon this steamer. Unknown to him, I come to you openly. I claim your aid, not your enmity."

"Let us understand one another clearly," Sogrange said. "You claim our aid in what?"

Mr. Fanshawe glanced around the saloon and lowered his voice.

"I claim your aid towards the overthrowing of the usurping House of Brangaza and the restoration to power in Spain of my own line."

　　　　E. Phillips Oppenheim

Sograwere was silent for several moments. Peter was leaning forward in his place, deeply interested. Decidedly, this American trip seemed destined to lead towards events!

"Our active aid towards such an end," Sograre said at last, "is impossible. The Society of the Double-Four does not interfere in the domestic policy of other nations for the sake of individual members."

"Then let me ask you why I find you upon this steamer?" Mr. Fanshawe demanded, in a tone of suppressed excitement. "Is it for the sea voyage that you and your friend the Baron de Grost cross the Atlantic this particular week, on the same steamer as myself, as Mr. Sirdeller, and - and the Duchesse? One does not believe in such coincidences! One is driven to conclude that it is your intention to interfere."

"The affair almost demands our interference," Sograre replied, smoothly. "With every due respect to you, Prince, there are great interests involved in this move of yours."

The Prince was a big man, but for all his large features and bearded face his expression was the expression of a peevish and passionate child. He controlled himself with an effort.

"Marquis," he said, "this is necessary - I say that it is necessary that we conclude an alliance."

Sograre nodded approvingly.

"It is well spoken," he said, "but remember - the Baron de Grost represents England and the English interests of our Society."

The Prince of Marsine's face was not pleasant to look upon.

"Forgive me if you are an Englishman by birth, Baron," he said, turning towards him, "but a more interfering nation in other people's affairs than England has never existed in the pages of history. She must have a finger in every pie. Bah!"

Peter leaned over from his place.

"What about Germany - Mr. Fanshawe?" he asked, with emphasis.

The Prince tugged at his beard. He was a little nonplussed.

"The Count von Hern," he confessed, "has been a good friend to me. The rulers of his country have always been hospitable and favorably inclined towards my family. The whole affair is of his design. I myself could scarcely have moved in it alone. One must reward one's helpers. There is no reason, however," he added, with a meaning glance at Peter, "why other helpers should not be admitted."

"The reward which you offer to the Count von Hern," Peter remarked, "is of itself absolutely inimical to the interests of my country."

"Listen!" the Prince demanded, tapping the table before him. "It is true that within a year I am pledged to reward the Count von Hern in certain fashion. It is not possible that you know the terms of our compact, but from your words it is possible that you have guessed. Very well. Accept this from me. Remain neutral now, allow this matter to proceed to its natural conclusion, let your government address representations to me when the time comes, adopting a bold front, and I promise that I will obey them. It will not be my fault that I am compelled to disappoint the Count von Hern. My seaboard would be at the mercy of your fleet. Superior force must be obeyed."

"It is a matter, this," Sogrange said, "for discussion between my friend and me. I think that you will find that we are neither of us unreasonable. In short, Prince, I see no insuperable reason why we should not come to terms."

"You encourage me," the Prince declared, in a gratified tone. "Do not believe, Marquis, that I am actuated in this matter wholly by motives of personal ambition. No, it is not so. A great desire has burned always in my heart, but it is not that alone which moves me. I assure you that of my certain knowledge Spain is honeycombed - is rotten with treason. A revolution is a certainty. How much better that that revolution should be conducted in a dignified manner; that I, with my reputation for democracy which I have carefully kept before the eyes of my people, should be elected President of the new Spanish Republic, even if it is the gold of the American which places me there. In a year or two, what may happen who can say? This craving for a republic is but a passing dream. Spain, at heart, is monarchial. She will be led back to the light. It is but a short step from the president's chair to the throne."

Sogrange and his companion sat quite still. They avoided looking at each other.

"There is one thing more," the Prince continued, dropping his voice, as if, even at that distance, he feared the man of whom he spoke. "I shall not inform the Count von Hern of our conversation. It is not necessary, and, between ourselves, the Count is jealous. He sends me message after message that I remain in my stateroom, that I seek no interview with Sirdeller, that I watch only. He is too much of the spy - the Count von Hern. He does not understand that code of honor, relying upon which I open my heart to you."

"You have done your cause no harm," Sogrange assured him, with subtle sarcasm. "We come now to the Duchesse."

The Prince leaned towards him. It was just at this moment that a steward entered with a marconigram, which he presented to the Prince. The latter tore it open, glanced it through, and gave vent to a little exclamation. The fingers which held the missive trembled. His eyes blazed with excitement. He was absolutely unable to control his feelings.

"My two friends," he cried, in a tone broken with emotion, "it is you first who shall hear the news! This message has just arrived. Sirdeller will have received its duplicate. The final report of the works in Havana Harbor will await us on our arrival in New York, but the substance of it is this. The Maine was sunk by a torpedo, discharged at close quarters underneath her magazine. Gentlemen, the House of Brangaza is ruined!"

There was a breathless silence.

"Your information is genuine?" Sogrange asked, softly.

"Without a doubt," the Prince replied. "I have been expecting this message. I shall cable to Von Hern. We are still in communication. He may not have heard."

"We were about to speak of the Duchesse," Peter reminded him.

The Prince shook his head.

"Another time," he declared. "Another time."

He hurried away. It was already half past ten and the saloon was almost empty. The steward came up to them.

"The saloon is being closed for the night, sir," he announced.

"Let us go on deck," Peter suggested.

They found their way up on to the windward side of the promenade, which was absolutely deserted. Far away in front of them now were the disappearing lights of the Lusitania. The wind roared by as the great steamer rose and fell on the black stretch of waters. Peter stood very near to his companion.

"Listen, Sogrange," he said, "the affair is clear now save for one thing."

"You mean Sirdeller's motives?"

"Not at all," Peter answered. "An hour ago, I came across the explanation of these. The one thing I will tell you afterwards. Now listen. Sirdeller came abroad last year for twelve months' travel. He took a great house in San Sebastian."

"Where did you hear this?" Sogrange asked.

"I read the story in the New York Herald," Peter continued. "It is grossly exaggerated, of course, but this is the substance of it. Sirdeller and his suite were stopped upon the Spanish frontier and treated in an abominable fashion by the customs officers. He was forced to pay a very large sum, unjustly I should think. He paid under protest, appealed to the authorities, with no result. At San Sebastian he was robbed right and left, his privacy intruded upon. In short, he took a violent dislike and hatred to the country and every one concerned in it. He moved with his entire suite to Nice, to the Golden Villa. There he expressed himself freely concerning Spain and her Government. Count von Hern heard of it and presented Marsine. The plot was, without doubt, Bernadine's. Can't you imagine how he would put it? 'A revolution,' he would tell Sirdeller, 'is imminent in Spain. Here is the new President of the Republic. Money is no more to you than water. You are a patriotic American. Have you forgotten that a warship of your country with six hundred of her devoted citizens was sent to the bottom by the treachery of one of this effete race? The war was an inefficient revenge. The country still flourishes. It is for you to avenge America. With money Marsine can establish a republic in Spain within twenty-four hours.' Sirdeller hesitates. He would point out that it had never been proved that the destruction of the Maine was really due to Spanish treachery. It is the idea of a business man which followed. He, at his own expense, would raise the Maine. If it were true that the explosion occurred from outside, he would find the money. You see, the message has arrived. After all these years the sea has given up its secret. Marsine will return to Spain with an unlimited credit behind him. The House of

Brangaza will crumble up like a pack of cards."

Sogrange looked out into the darkness. Perhaps he saw in that great black gulf the pictures of these happenings which his companion had prophesied. Perhaps, for a moment, he saw the panorama of a city in flames, the passing of a great country under the thrall of these new ideas. At any rate, he turned abruptly away from the side of the vessel, and taking Peter's arm, walked slowly down the deck.

"You have solved the puzzle, Baron," he said, gravely. "Now tell me the one thing. Your story seems to dovetail everywhere."

"The one thing," Peter said, "is connected with the Duchesse. It was she, of her own will, who decided to come to America. I believe that, but for her coming, Bernadine and the Prince would have waited in their own country. Money can flash from America to England over the wires. It does not need to be fetched. They have still one fear. It is connected with the Duchesse. Let me think."

They walked up and down the deck. The lights were extinguished one by one, except in the smoking-room. A strange breed of sailors from the lower deck came up with mops and buckets. The wind changed its quarter and the great ship began to roll. Peter stopped abruptly.

"I find this motion most unpleasant," he said. "I am going to bed. To-night I cannot think. To-morrow, I promise you, we will solve this. Hush!"

He held out his hand and drew his companion back into the shadow of a lifeboat. A tall figure was approaching them along the deck. As he passed the little ray of light thrown out from the smoking-room, the man's features were clearly visible. It was the Prince. He was walking like one absorbed in thought. His eyes were set like a sleep-walker's. With one hand he gesticulated. The fingers of the other were twitching all the time. His head was lifted to the skies. There was something in his face which redeemed it from its disfiguring petulance.

"It is the man who dreams of power," Peter whispered. "It is one of his best moments, this. He forgets the vulgar means by which he intends to rise. He thinks only of himself, the dictator, king, perhaps emperor. He is of the breed of egoists."

Again and again the Prince passed, manifestly unconscious even of his whereabouts. Peter and Sogrange crept away unseen to their staterooms.

In many respects the room resembled a miniature court of justice. The principal sitting-room of the royal suite, which was the chief glory of the Adriatic, had been stripped of every superfluous article of furniture or embellishment. Curtains had been removed, all evidences of luxury disposed of. Temporarily the apartment had been transformed into a bare, cheerless place. Seated on a high chair, with his back to the wall, was Sirdeller. At his right hand was a small table, on which stood a glass of milk, a phial, a stethoscope. Behind his doctor. At his left hand a smooth-faced, silent young man - his secretary. Before him stood the Duchesse, Peter and Sogrange. Guarding the door was one of the watchmen, who, from his great physique, might well have been a policeman out of livery. Sirdeller himself, in the clear light which streamed through the large window, seemed more aged and shrunken than ever. His eyes were deep set. No tinge of color was visible in his cheeks. His chin protruded, his shaggy gray eyebrows gave him an unkempt appearance. He wore a black velvet gown, a strangely cut black morning coat and trousers, felt slippers, and his hands were clasped upon a stout ash walking-stick. He eyed the newcomers keenly but without expression.

"The lady may sit," he said.

He spoke almost in an undertone, as though anxious to avoid the fatigue of words. The guardian of the door placed a chair, into which the Duchesse subsided. Sirdeller held his right hand towards his doctor, who felt his pulse. All the time Sirdeller watched him, his lips a little parted, a world of hungry excitement in his eyes. The doctor closed his watch with a snap and whispered something in Sirdeller's ear, apparently reassuring.

"I will hear this story," Sirdeller announced. "In two minutes every one must leave. If it takes longer, it must remain unfinished."

Peter spoke up briskly.

"The story is this," he began. "You have promised to assist the Prince of Marsine to transform Spain into a republic, providing the salvage operations on the Maine prove that that ship was destroyed from outside. The salvage operations have been conducted at your expense and finished. It has been proved that the Maine was destroyed by a mine or torpedo from the outside. Therefore, on the assumption that it was the treacherous deed of a Spaniard or Cuban imagining himself to be a patriot, you are prepared to carry out your undertaking and supply the Prince of Marsine with means to overthrow the Kingdom of Spain."

Peter paused. The figure on the chair remained motionless. No flicker of intelligence or interest disturbed the calm of his features. It was a silence almost unnatural. "I have brought the Duchesse here," Peter continued, "to tell you the truth as to the Maine disaster."

Not even then was there the slightest alteration in those ashen gray features. The Duchesse looked up. She had the air of one only too eager to speak and finish.

"In those days," she said, "I was the wife of a rich Cuban gentleman, whose name I withhold. The American officers on board the Maine used to visit at our house. My husband was jealous; perhaps he had cause."

The Duchesse paused. Even though the light of tragedy and romance side by side seemed suddenly to creep into the room, Sirdeller listened as one come back from a dead world.

"One night," the Duchesse went on, "my husband's suspicions were changed into knowledge. He came home unexpectedly. The American - the officer - I loved him - he was there on the balcony with me. My husband said nothing. The officer returned to the ship. That night my husband came into my room. He bent over my bed. 'It is not you,' he whispered, 'whom I shall destroy, for the pain of death is short. Anguish of mind may live. To-night six hundred ghosts may hang about your pillow!'"

Her voice broke. There was something grim and unnatural in that curious stillness. Even the secretary was at last breathing a little faster. The watchman at the door was leaning forward. Sirdeller simply moved his hand to the doctor, who held up his finger while he felt the pulse. The beat of his watch seemed to sound through the unnatural silence. In a minute he spoke.

"The lady may proceed," he announced.

"My husband," the Duchesse continued, "was an officer in charge of the Mines and Ordnance Department. He went out that night in a small boat, after a visit to the strong house. No soul has ever seen or heard of him since, or his boat. It is only I who know!"

Her voice died away. Sirdeller stretched out his hand and very deliberately drank a tablespoonful or two of his milk.

"I believe the lady's story," he declared. "The Marsine affair is finished. Let no one be admitted to have speech with me again upon this subject."

He had half turned towards his secretary. The young man bowed. The doctor pointed towards the door. The Duchesse, Peter and Sogrange filed slowly out. In the bright sunlight the

Duchesse burst into a peal of hysterical laughter. Even Peter felt, for a moment, unnerved. Suddenly he, too, laughed.

"I think," he said, "that you and I had better get out of the way, Sogrange, when the Count von Hern meets us at New York!"

CHAPTER X

THE AFFAIR or AN ALIEN SOCIETY

Sograngе and Peter, Baron de Grost, standing upon the threshold of their hotel, gazed out upon New York and liked the look of it. They had landed from the steamer a few hours before, had already enjoyed the luxury of a bath, a visit to an American barber's, and a genuine cocktail.

"I see no reason," Sograngе declared, "why we should not take a week's holiday."

Peter, glancing up into the blue sky and down into the faces of the well-dressed and beautiful women who were streaming up Fifth Avenue, was wholly of the same mind.

"If we return by this afternoon's steamer," he remarked, "we shall have Bernadine for a fellow passenger. Bernadine is annoyed with us just now. I must confess that I should feel more at my ease with a few thousand miles of the Atlantic between us."

"Let it be so," Sograngе assented. "We will explore this marvelous city. Never," he added, taking his companion's arm, "did I expect to see such women save in my own, the mistress of all cities. So chic, my dear Baron, and such a carriage! We will lunch at one of the fashionable restaurants and drive in the Park afterwards. First of all, however, we must take a stroll along this wonderful Fifth Avenue."

The two men spent a morning after their own hearts. They lunched astonishingly well at Sherry's and drove afterwards in Central Park. When they returned to the hotel, Sogrange was in excellent spirits.

"I feel, my friend," he announced, "that we are going to have a very pleasant and, in some respects, a unique week. To meet friends and acquaintances, everywhere, as one must do in every capital in Europe, is, of course, pleasant, but there is a monotony about it from which one is glad sometimes to escape. We lunch here and we promenade in the places frequented by those of a similar station to our own, and behold! we know no one. We are lookers on. Perhaps for a long time it might gall. For a brief period there is a restfulness about it which pleases me."

"I should have liked," Peter murmured, "an introduction to the lady in the blue hat."

"You are a gregarious animal," Sogrange declared. "You do not understand the pleasures of a little comparative isolation with an intellectual companion such as myself . . . What the devil is the meaning of this!"

They had reached their sitting-room and upon a small round table stood a great collection of cards and notes. Sogrange took them up helplessly, one after the other, reading the names aloud and letting them fall through his fingers. Some were known to him, some were not. He began to open the notes. In effect they were all the same - what evening would the Marquis de Sogrange and his distinguished friend care to dine, lunch, yacht, golf, shoot, go to the opera, join a theatre party? Of what clubs would they care to become members? What kind of hospitality would be most acceptable?

Sogrange sank into a chair.

"My friend," he exclaimed, "they all have to be answered - that collection there! The visits have to be returned. It is

E. Phillips Oppenheim

magnificent, this hospitality, but what can one do?"

Peter looked at the pile of correspondence upon which Sogrange's inroad, indeed, seemed to have had but little effect.

"One could engage a secretary, of course," he suggested, doubtfully. "But the visits! Our week's holiday is gone."

"Not at all," Sogrange replied. "I have an idea."

The telephone bell rang. Peter took up the receiver and listened for a moment. He turned to Sogrange, still holding it in his hand.

"You will be pleased, also, to hear," he announced, "that there are half a dozen reporters downstairs waiting to interview [Transcriber's note: word missing]."

Sogrange received the information with interest.

"Have them sent up at once," he directed, "every one of them."

"What, all at the same time?" Peter asked.

"All at the same time it must be," Sogrange answered. "Give them to understand that it is an affair of five minutes only."

They came trooping in. Sogrange welcomed them cordially.

"My friend, the Baron de Grost," he explained, indicating Peter. "I am the Marquis de Sogrange. Let us know what we can do to serve you."

One of the men stepped forward.

"Very glad to meet you, Marquis, and you, Baron," he said. "I won't bother you with any introductions, but I and the company here represent the Press of New York. We should like some information for our papers as to the object of your visit here and the probable length of your stay."

Sogrange extended his hands.

"My dear friend," he exclaimed, "the object of our visit was, I thought, already well known. We are on our way to Mexico. We leave to-night. My friend the Baron is, as you know, a financier. I, too, have a little money to invest. We are going out to meet some business acquaintances with a view to inspecting some mining properties. That is absolutely all I can tell you. You can understand, of course, that fuller information would be impossible."

"Why, that's quite natural, Marquis," the spokesman of the reporters replied. "We don't like the idea of your hustling out of New York like this, though?"

Sogrange glanced at the clock.

"It is unavoidable," he declared. "We are relying upon you, gentlemen, to publish the fact, because you will see," he added, pointing to the table, "that we have been the recipients of a great many civilities, which it is impossible for us to acknowledge properly. If it will give you any pleasure to see us upon our return, you will be very welcome. In the meantime, you will understand our haste."

There were a few more civilities and the representatives of the Press took their departure. Peter looked at his companion doubtfully, as Sogrange returned from showing them out.

"I suppose this means that we have to catch to-day's steamer, after all?" he remarked.

"Not necessarily," Sogrange answered. "I have a plan. We will leave for the Southern depot, wherever it may be. Afterwards, you shall use that wonderful skill of yours, of which I have heard so much, to effect some slight change in our appearance.

We will then go to another hotel, in another quarter of New York, and take our week's holiday incognito. What do you think of that for an idea?"

"Not much," Peter replied. "It isn't so easy to **dodge** the newspapers and the Press in this country. Besides, although I could manage myself very well, you would be an exceedingly awkward subject. Your tall and elegant figure, your aquiline nose, the shapeliness of your hands and feet, give you a distinction which I should find it hard to conceal."

Sogrange smiled.

"You are a remarkably observant fellow, Baron. I quite appreciate your difficulty. Still, with a club foot, eh, and spectacles instead of my eyeglass -"

"Oh, no doubt, something could be managed," Peter interrupted. "You're really in earnest about this, are you?"

"Absolutely," Sogrange declared. "Come here!"

He drew Peter to the window. They were on the twelfth story, and to a European there was something magnificent in that tangled mass of buildings threaded by the elevated railway, with its screaming trains, the clearness of the atmosphere, and in the white streets below, like polished belts through which the swarms of people streamed like insects.

"Imagine it all lit up!" Sogrange exclaimed. "The sky-signs all ablaze, the flashing of fire from those cable wires, the lights glittering from those tall buildings! This is a wonderful place, Baron. We must see it. Ring for the bill. Order one of those magnificent omnibuses. Press the button, too, for the personage whom they call the valet. Perhaps, with a little gentle persuasion, he could be induced to pack our clothes."

With his finger upon the bell, Peter hesitated. He, too, loved adventures, but the gloom of a presentiment had momentarily depressed him.

"We are marked men, remember, Sogrange," he said. "An escapade of this sort means a certain amount of risk, even in New York."

Sogrange laughed.

"Bernadine caught the midday steamer! We have no enemies here that I know of."

Peter pressed the button. An hour or so later, the Marquis de Sogrange and Peter, Baron de Grost, took their leave of New York.

They chose a hotel on Broadway, within a stone's throw of Rector's. Peter, with whitened hair, gold-rimmed spectacles, a slouch hat and a fur coat, passed easily enough for an English maker of electrical instruments; while Sogrange, shabbier, and in ready-made American clothes, was transformed into a Canadian having some connection with the theatrical business. They plunged into the heart of New York life, and found the whole thing like a tonic. The intense vitality of the people, the pandemonium of Broadway at midnight, with its flaming illuminations, its eager crowd, its inimitable restlessness, fascinated them both. Sogrange, indeed, remembering the decadent languor of the crowds of pleasure seekers thronging his own boulevards, was never weary of watching these men and women. They passed from the streets to the restaurants, from the restaurants to the theatre, out into the streets again, back to the restaurants, and once more into the streets. Sogrange was like a glutton. The mention of bed was hateful to him. For three days they existed without a moment's boredom.

On the fourth evening, Peter found Sogrange deep in conversation with the head porter. In a few minutes he led Peter away to one of the bars where they usually took their cocktail.

E. Phillips Oppenheim

"My friend," he announced, "to-night I have a treat for you. So far we have looked on at the external night life of New York. Wonderful and thrilling it has been, too. But there is the underneath, also. Why not? There is a vast polyglot population here, full of energy said life. A criminal class exists as a matter of course. To-night we make our bow to it."

"And by what means?" Peter inquired.

"Our friend the hall-porter," Sogrange continued, "has given me the card of an ex-detective who will be our escort. He calls for usto-night, or rather to-morrow morning, at one o'clock. Then behold! the wand is waved, the land of adventures opens before us."

Peter grunted.

"I don't want to damp your enthusiasm, my Canadian friend," he said, "but the sort of adventures you may meet with to-night are scarcely likely to fire your romantic nature. I know a little about what they call this underneath world in New York. It will probably resolve itself into a visit to Chinatown, where we shall find the usual dummies taking opium and quite prepared to talk about it for the usual tip. After that we shall visit a few low dancing halls, be shown the scene of several murders, and the thing is done."

"You are a cynic," Sogrange declared. "You would throw cold water upon any enterprise. Anyway, our detective is coming. We must make use of him, for I have engaged to pay him twenty-five dollars."

"We'll go where you like," Peter assented, "so long as we dine on a roof garden. This beastly fur coat keeps me in a state of chronic perspiration."

"Never mind," Sogrange said, consolingly, "it's most effective. A roof garden, by all means."

"And recollect," Peter insisted, "I bar Chinatown. We've both of us seen the real thing, and there's nothing real about what they show you here."

"Chinatown is erased from our program," Sogrange agreed. "We go now to dine. Remind me, Baron, that I inquire for those strange dishes of which one hears Terrapin, Canvas-backed Duck, Green Corn, Strawberry Shortcake."

Peter smiled grimly.

"How like a Frenchman," he exclaimed, "to take no account of seasons! Never mind, Marquis, you shall give your order and I will sketch the waiter's face. By the bye, if you're in earnest about this expedition to-night, put your revolver into your pocket."

"But we 're going with an ex-detective," Sogrange replied.

"One never knows," Peter said, carelessly.

They dined close to the stone palisading of one of New York's most famous roof gardens. Sogrange ordered an immense dinner but spent most of his time gazing downwards. They were higher up than at the hotel and they could see across the tangled maze of lights even to the river, across which the great ferry-boats were speeding all the while - huge creatures of streaming fire and whistling sirens. The air where they sat was pure and crisp. There was no fog, no smoke, to cloud the almost crystalline clearness of the night.

"Baron," Sogrange declared, "if I had lived in this city I should have been a different man. No wonder the people are all conquering."

"Too much electricity in the air for me," Peter answered. "I like a little repose. I can't think where these people find it."

"One hopes," Sogrange murmured, "that before they progress

E. Phillips Oppenheim

any further in utilitarianism, they will find some artist, one of themselves, to express all this."

"In the meantime," Peter interrupted, "the waiter would like to know what we are going to drink. I've eaten such a confounded jumble of things of your ordering that I should like some champagne."

"Who shall say that I am not generous!" Sogrange replied, taking up the wine carte. "Champagne it shall be. We need something to nerve us for our adventures."

Peter leaned across the table.

"Sogrange," he whispered, "for the last twenty-four hours I have had some doubts as to the success of our little enterprise. It has occurred to me more than once that we are being shadowed."

Sogrange frowned.

"I sometimes wonder," he remarked, "how a man of your suspicious nature ever acquired the reputation you undoubtedly enjoy."

"Perhaps it is because of my suspicious nature," Peter said. "There is a man staying in our hotel whom we are beginning to see quite a great deal of. He was talking to the head porter a few minutes before you this afternoon. He supped at the same restaurant last night. He is dining now three places behind you to the right, with a young lady who has been making flagrant attempts at flirtation with me, notwithstanding my gray hairs."

"Your reputation, my dear Peter," Sogrange murmured -

"As a decoy," Peter interrupted, "the young lady's methods are too vigorous. She pretends to be terribly afraid of her companion, but it is entirely obvious that she is acting on his instructions. Of course, this may be a ruse of the reporters. On the other hand, I think it would be wise to abandon our little expedition to-night."

Sogrange shook his head.

"So far as I am concerned," he said, "I am committed to it."

"In which case," Peter replied, "I am certainly committed to being your companion. The only question is whether one shall fall to the decoy and suffer oneself to be led in the direction her companion desires, or whether we shall go blundering into trouble on our own account with your friend the ex-detective."

Sogrange glanced over his shoulder, leaned back in his chair for a moment, as though to look at the stars, and finally lit a cigarette.

"There is a lack of subtlety about that young person, Baron," he declared, "which stifles one's suspicions. I suspect her to be merely one more victim to your undoubted charms. In the interests of Madame your wife, I shall take you away. The decoy shall weave her spells in vain."

They paid their bill and departed a few minutes later. The man and the girl were also in the act of leaving. The former seemed to be having some dispute about the bill. The girl, standing with her back to him, scribbled a line upon a piece of paper, and, as Peter went by, pushed it into his hand with a little warning gesture. In the lift he opened it. The few penciled words contained nothing but an address: Number 15, 100th Street, East.

"Lucky man!" Sogrange sighed.

Peter made no remark, but he was thoughtful for the next hour or so.

The ex-detective proved to be an individual of fairly obvious appearance, whose complexion and thirst indicated a very possible reason for his life of leisure. He heard with surprise that his patrons were not inclined to visit Chinatown, but he showed a laudable desire to fall in with their schemes, provided always that they included a reasonable number of visits to places where refreshment could be obtained. From first to last, the expedition was a disappointment. They visited various smoke-hung dancing halls, decorated for the most part with oleographs and cracked mirrors, in which sickly-Looking young men of unwholesome aspect were dancing with their feminine counterparts. The attitude of their guide was alone amusing.

"Say, you want to be careful in here!" he would declare, in an awed tone, on entering one of these tawdry palaces. "Guess this is one of the toughest spots in New York City. You stick close to me and I'll make things all right."

His method of making things all right was the same in every case. He would form a circle of disreputable-looking youths, for whose drinks Sograngé was called upon to pay. The attitude of these young men was more dejected than positively vicious. They showed not the slightest signs of any desire to make themselves unpleasant. Only once, when Sograngé incautiously displayed a gold watch, did the eyes of one or two of their number glisten. The ex-detective changed his place and whispered hoarsely in his patron's ear.

"Say, don't you flash anything of that sort about here! That young cove right opposite to you is one of the best known sneak-thieves in the city. You're asking for trouble that way."

"If he or any other of them want my watch," Sograngé answered calmly, "let them come and fetch it. However," he added, buttoning up his coat, "no doubt you are right. Is there anywhere else to take us?"

The man hesitated.

"There ain't much that you haven't seen," he remarked.

Sograngc laughed softly as he rose to his feet.

"A sell, my dear friend," he said to Peter. "This terrible city keeps its real criminal class somewhere else rather than in the show places."

A man who had been standing in the doorway, looking in for several moments, strolled up to them. Peter recognized him at once and touched Sogrange on the arm. The newcomer accosted them pleasantly.

"Say, you'll excuse my butting in," he began, "but I can see you're kind of disappointed. These suckers" - indicating the ex-detective - "talk a lot about what they're going to show you, and when they get you round it all amounts to nothing. This is the sort of thing they bring you to, as representing the wickedness of New York! That's so, Rastall, isn't it?"

The ex-detective looked a little sheepish.

"Yes, there ain't much more to be seen," he admitted. "Perhaps you'll take the job on if you think there is."

"Well, I'd show the gentlemen something of a sight more interesting that this," the newcomer continued. "They don't want to sit down and drink with the scum of the earth."

"Perhaps," Sogrange suggested, "this gentleman has something in his mind which he thinks would appeal to us. We have a motor car outside and we are out for adventures."

"What sort of adventures?" the newcomer asked, bluntly.

Sogrange shrugged his shoulders lightly.

"We are lookers-on merely," he explained. "My friend and I have traveled a good deal. We have seen something of criminal life in Paris and London, Vienna and Budapest. I shall not break any confidence if I tell you that my friend is a writer, and material such as this is useful."

The newcomer smiled.

"Well," he exclaimed, "in a way, it's fortunate for you that I happened along! You come right with me and I'll show you something that very few other people in this city know of. Guess you'd better pay this fellow off," he added, indicating the ex-detective. "He's no more use to you."

Sogrange and Peter exchanged questioning glances.

"It is very kind of you, sir," Peter decided, "but for my part I have had enough for one evening."

"Just as you like, of course," the other remarked, with studied unconcern.

"What sort of place would it be?" Sogrange asked.

The newcomer drew them on one side, although, as a matter of fact, every one else had already melted away.

"Have you ever heard of the Secret Societies of New York?" he inquired. "Well, I guess you haven't, any way - not to know anything about them. Well, then, listen. There's a Society meets within a few steps of here, which has more to do with regulating the criminal classes of the city than any police establishment. There'll be a man there within an hour or so, who, to my knowledge, has committed seven murders. The police can't get him. They never will. He's under our protection."

"May we visit such a place as you describe without danger?" Peter asked, calmly.

"No!" the man answered. "There's danger in going anywhere, it seems to me, if it's worth while. So long as you keep a still tongue in your head and don't look about you too much, there's nothing will happen to you. If you get gassing a lot, you might tumble in for almost anything. Don't come unless you like. It's a chance for your friend, as he's a writer, but you'd best keep out of it if you're in any way nervous."

"You said it was quite close?" Sogrange inquired.

"Within a yard or two," the man replied. "It's right this way."

They left the hall with their new escort. When they looked for their motor car, they found it had gone.

"It don't do to keep them things waiting about round here," their new friend remarked, carelessly. "I guess I'll send you back to your hotel all right. Step this way."

"By the bye, what street is this we are in?" Peter asked.

"100th Street," the man answered.

Peter shook his head.

"I'm a little superstitious about that number," he declared. "Is that an elevated railway there? I think we've had enough, Sogrange."

Sogrange hesitated. They were standing now in front of a tall gloomy house, unkempt, with broken gate - a large but miserable-looking abode. The passers-by in the street were few. The whole character of the surroundings was squalid. The man pushed open the broken gate.

"You cross the street right there to the elevated," he directed. "If you ain't coming, I'll bid you good-night."

Once more they hesitated. Peter, perhaps, saw more than his companion. He saw the dark shapes lurking under the railway arch. He knew instinctively that they were in some sort of danger. And yet the love of adventure was on fire in his blood.

His belief in himself was immense. He whispered to Sogrange.

"I do not trust our guide," he said. "If you care to risk it, I am with you."

"Mind the broken pavement," the man called out. "This ain't exactly an abode of luxury."

They climbed some broken steps. Their guide opened a door with a Yale key. The door swung to, after them, and they found themselves in darkness. There had been no light in the windows; there was no light, apparently, in the house. Their companion produced an electric torch from his pocket.

"You had best follow me," he advised. "Our quarters face out the other way. We keep this end looking a little deserted."

They passed through a swing door and everything was at once changed. A multitude of lamps hung from the ceiling, the floor was carpeted, the walls clean.

"We don't go in for electric light," their guide explained, "as we try not to give the place away. We manage to keep it fairly comfortable, though."

He pushed open the door and entered a somewhat gorgeously furnished salon. There were signs here of feminine occupation, an open piano, and the smell of cigarettes. Once more Peter hesitated.

"Your friends seem to be in hiding," he remarked. "Personally, I am losing my curiosity."

"Guess you won't have to wait very long," the man replied, with meaning.

The room was suddenly invaded on all sides. Four doors, which were quite hidden by the pattern of the wall, had opened almost simultaneously, and at least a dozen men had entered. This time both Sogrange and Peter knew that they were face to face with the real thing. These were men who came silently in, no cigarette-stunted youths. Two of them were in evening dress; three or four had the appearance of prize fighters. In their countenances was one expression common to all - an air of quiet and conscious strength.

A fair-headed man, in dinner jacket and black tie, became at once their spokesman. He was possessed of a very slight American accent, and he beamed at them through a pair of gold-rimmed spectacles.

"Gentlemen," he said, "I am glad to meet you both."

"Very kind of you, I'm sure," Sogrange answered. "Our friend here," he added, indicating their guide, "found us trying to gain a little insight into the more interesting part of New York life. He was kind enough to express a wish to introduce us to you."

The man smiled. He looked very much like some studious clerk, except that his voice seemed to ring with some latent power.

"I am afraid," he said, "that your friend's interest in you was not entirely unselfish. For three days he has carried in his pocket an order instructing him to produce you here."

"I knew it!" Peter whispered, under his breath.

"You interest me," Sogrange replied. "May I know whom I have the honor of addressing?"

"You can call me Burr," the man announced, "Philip Burr. Your names it is not our wish to know."

"I am afraid I do not quite understand," Sogrange said.

"It was scarcely to be expected that you should," Mr. Philip

E. Phillips Oppenheim

Burr admitted. "All I can tell you is that, in cases like yours, I ically prefer not to know with whom I have to deal."

"You speak as though you had business with us," Peter remarked.

"Without doubt, I have," the other replied, grimly. "It is my business to see that you do not leave these premises alive."

Sogrange drew up a chair against which he had been leaning, and sat down.

"Really," he said, "that would be most inconvenient." Peter, too, shook his head, sitting upon the end of a sofa and folding his arms. Something told him that the moment for fighting was not yet.

"Inconvenient or not," Mr. Philip Burr continued, "I have orders to carry out which I can assure you have never yet been disobeyed since the formation of our Society. From what I can see of you, you appear to be very amiable gentlemen, and if it would interest you to choose the method - say, of your release - why, I can assure you we'll do all we can to meet your views."

"I am beginning," Sogrange remarked, "to feel quite at home."

"You see, we've been through this sort of thing before," Peter added, blandly.

Mr. Philip Burr took a cigar from his case and lit it. At a motion of his hand, one of the company passed the box to his two guests.

"You're not counting upon a visit from the police, or anything of that sort, I hope?" Mr. Philip Burr asked.

Sogrange shook his head.

"Certainly not," he replied. "I may say that much of the earlier portion of my life was spent in frustrating the well-meant but impossible schemes of that body of men."

"If only we had a little more time," Mr. Burr declared, "it seems to me I should like to make the acquaintance of you two gentlemen."

"The matter is entirely in your own hands," Peter reminded him. "We are in no hurry."

Mr. Burr smiled genially.

"You make me think better of humanity," he confessed. "A month ago we had a man here - got him along somehow or another - and I had to tell him that he was up against it like you two are. My! the fuss he made! Kind of saddened me to think a man should be such a coward."

"Some people like that," Sogrange remarked. "By the bye, Mr. Burr, you'll pardon my curiosity. Whom have we to thank for our introduction here to-night?"

"I don't know as there's any particular harm in telling you," Mr. Burr replied -

"Nor any particular good," a man who was standing by his side interrupted. "Say, Phil, you drag these things out too much. Are there any questions you've got to ask 'em, or any property to collect?"

"Nothing of the sort," Mr. Burr admitted.

"Then let the gang get to work," the other declared.

The two men were suddenly conscious that they were being surrounded. Peter's hand stole on to the butt of his revolver. Sogrange rose slowly to his feet. His hands were thrust out in front of him with the thumbs turned down. The four fingers of each hand flashed for a minute through the air. Mr. Philip

E. Phillips Oppenheim

Burr lost all his self-control.

"Say, where the devil did you learn that trick?" he cried.

Sogrange laughed scornfully.

"Trick!" he exclaimed. "Philip Burr, you are unworthy of your position. I am the Marquis de Sogrange, and my friend here is the Baron de Grost."

Mr. Philip Burr had no words. His cigar had dropped on to the carpet. He was simply staring.

"If you need proof," Sogrange continued, "further than any I have given you, I have in my pocket, at the present moment, a letter, signed by you yourself, pleading for formal reinstatement. This is how you would qualify for it! You make use of your power to run a common decoy house, to do away with men for money. What fool gave you our names, pray?"

Mr. Philip Burr was only the wreck of a man. He could not even control his voice.

"It was some German or Belgian nobleman," he faltered. "He brought us excellent letters, and he made a large contribution. It was the Count von Hern."

The anger of Sogrange seemed suddenly to fade away. He threw himself into a chair by the side of his companion.

"My dear Baron," he exclaimed, "Bernadine has scored, indeed! Your friend has a sense of humor which overwhelms me. Imagine it. He has delivered the two heads of our great Society into the hands of one of its cast-off branches! Bernadine is a genius, indeed!"

Mr. Philip Burr began slowly to recover himself. He waved his hand. Nine out of the twelve men left the room.

"Marquis," he said, "for ten years there has been no one whom I have desired to meet so much as you. I came to Europe but you declined to receive me. I know very well we can't keep our end up like you over there, because we haven't politics and that sort of things to play with, but we've done our best. We've encouraged only criminology of the highest order. We've tried all we can to keep the profession select. The jail-bird, pure and simple, we have cast out. The men who have suffered at our hands have been men who have met with their deserts."

"What about us?" Peter demanded. "It seems to me that you had most unpleasant plans for our future."

Philip Burr held up his hands.

"As I live," he declared, "this is the first time that any money consideration has induced me to break away from our principles. That Count von Hern, he had powerful friends who were our friends, and he gave me the word, straight, that you two had an appointment down below which was considerably overdue. I don't know, even now, why I consented. I guess it isn't much use apologizing."

Sogrange rose to his feet.

"Well," he said, "I am not inclined to bear malice, but you must understand this from me, Philip Burr. As a Society, I dissolve you. I deprive you of your title and of your signs. Call yourself what you will, but never again mention the name of the 'Double-Four.' With us in Europe, another era has dawned. We are on the side of law and order. We protect only criminals of a certain class, in whose operations we have faith. There is no future for such a society in this country. Therefore, as I say, I dissolve it. Now, if you are ready, perhaps you will be so good as to provide us with the means of reaching our hotel."

Philip Burr led them into a back street, where his own handsome automobile was placed at their service.

"This kind of breaks me all up," he declared, as he gave the instructions to the chauffeur. "If there were two men on the face of this earth whom I'd have been proud to meet in a friendly sort of way, it's you two."

"We bear no malice, Mr. Burr," Sogrange assured him. "You can, if you will do us the honor, lunch with us to-morrow at one o'clock at Rector's. My friend here is quite interested in the Count von Hern, and he would probably like to hear exactly how this affair was arranged."

"I'll be there, sure," Philip Burr promised, with a farewell wave of the hand.

Sogrange and Peter drove back towards their hotel in silence. It was only when they emerged into the civilized part of the city that Sogrange began to laugh softly.

"My friend," he murmured, "you bluffed fairly well, but you were afraid. Oh, how I smiled to see your fingers close round the butt of that revolver!"

"What about you?" Peter asked, gruffly. "You don't suppose you took me in, do you?"

Sogrange smiled.

"I had two reasons for coming to New York," he said. "One we accomplished upon the steamer. The other was -"

"Well?"

"To reply personally to this letter of Mr. Philip Burr," Sogrange replied, "which letter, by the bye, was dated from 15, 100th Street, New York. An ordinary visit there would have been useless to me. Something of this sort was necessary."

"Then you knew!" Peter gasped. "Notwithstanding all your bravado, you knew!"

"I had a very fair idea," Sogrange admitted. "Don't be annoyed with me, my friend. You have had a little experience. It is all useful. It isn't the first time you've looked death in the face. Adventures come to some men unasked. You, I think, were born with the habit of them."

Peter smiled. They had reached the hotel courtyard and he raised himself stiffly.

"There's a little fable about the pitcher that went once too often to the well," he remarked. "I have had my share of luck - more than my share. The end must come sometime, you know."

"Is this superstition?" Sogrange asked.

"Superstition, pure and simple," Peter confessed, taking his key from the office. "It doesn't alter anything. I am fatalist enough to shrug my shoulders and move on. But I tell you, Sogrange," he added, after a moment's pause, "I wouldn't admit it to any one else in the world, but I am afraid of Bernadine. I have had the best of it so often. It can't last. In all we've had twelve encounters. The next will be the thirteenth."

Sogrange shrugged his shoulders slightly as he rang for the lift.

"I'd propose you for the Thirteen Club, only there's some uncomfortable clause about yearly suicides which might not suit you," he remarked. "Good-night, and don't dream of Bernadine and your thirteenth encounter."

"I only hope," Peter murmured, "that I may be in a position to dream after it."

CHAPTER XI

THE THIRTEENTH ENCOUNTER

The Marquis de Sogrange arrived in Berkeley Square with the gray dawn of an October morning, showing in his appearance and dress few enough signs of his night journey. Yet he had traveled without stopping from Paris, by fast motor car and the mail boat.

"They telephoned me from Charing Cross," Peter said, "that you could not possibly arrive until midday. The clerk assured me that no train had yet reached Calais."

"They had reason in what they told you," Sogrange remarked, as he leaned back in a chair and sipped the coffee which had been waiting for him in the Baron de Grost's study. "The train itself never got more than a mile away from the Gare du Nord. The engine driver was shot through the head and the metals were torn from the way. Paris is within a year now of a second and more terrible revolution."

"You really believe this?" Peter asked, gravely.

"It is a certainty," Sogrange replied. "Not I alone but many others can see this clearly. Everywhere the Socialists have wormed themselves into places of trust. They are to be met with in every rank of life, under every form of disguise. The post-office strike has already shown us what deplorable disasters even a skirmish can bring about. To-day the railway strike has paralyzed France. To-day our country lies absolutely at the mercy of any invader. As it happens, none is, for the moment, prepared. Who can tell how it may be next time?"

"This is had news," Peter declared. "If this is really the position of affairs, the matter is much more serious than the newspapers would have us believe."

"The newspapers," Sogrange muttered, "ignore what lies behind. Some of them, I think, are paid to do it. As for the rest, our Press had always an ostrich-like tendency. The Frenchman of the cafe does not buy his journal to be made sad."

"You believe, then," Peter asked, "that these strikes have some definite tendency?"

Sogrange set down his cup and smiled bitterly. In the early sunlight, still a little cold and unloving, Peter could see that there was a change in the man. He was no longer the debonair aristocrat of the race-courses and the boulevards. The shadows under his eyes were deeper, his cheeks more sunken. He had lost something of the sprightliness of his bearing. His attitude, indeed, was almost dejected. He was like a man who sees into the future and finds there strange and gruesome things.

"I do more than believe that," he declared. "I know it. It has fallen to my lot to make a very definite discovery concerning them. Listen, my friend. For more than six months the government has been trying to discover the source of this stream of vile socialistic literature which has contaminated the French working classes. The pamphlets have been distributed with devilish ingenuity among all national operatives, the army and the navy. The government has failed. The Double-Four has succeeded."

"You have really discovered their source?" Peter exclaimed.

"Without a doubt," Sogrange assented. "The government

appealed to us first some months ago when I was in America. For a time we had no success. Then a clue, and the rest was easy. The navy, the army, the post-office employees, the telegraph and telephone operators and the railway men, have been the chief recipients of this incessant stream of foul literature. To-day one cannot tell how much mischief has been actually done. The strikes which have already occurred are only the mutterings of the coming storm. But mark you, wherever those pamphlets have gone, trouble has followed. What men may do the government is doing, but all the time the poison is at work, the seed has been sown. Two millions of money have been spent to corrupt that very class which should be the backbone of France. Through the fingers of one man has come this shower of gold, one man alone has stood at the head of the great organization which has disseminated this loathsome disease. Behind him - well, we know."

"The man?"

"It is fitting that you should ask that question," Sogrange replied. "The name of that man is Bernadine, Count von Hern."

Peter remained speechless. There was something almost terrible in the slow preciseness with which Sogrange had uttered the name of his enemy, something unspeakably threatening in the cold glitter of his angry eyes.

"Up to the present," Sogrange continued, "I have watched - sympathetically, of course, but with a certain amount of amusement - the duel between you and Bernadine. It has been against your country and your country's welfare that most of his efforts have been directed, which perhaps accounts for the equanimity with which I have been contented to remain a looker-on. It is apparent, my dear Baron, that in most of your encounters the honors have remained with you. Yet, as it has chanced, never once has Bernadine been struck a real and crushing blow. The time has come when this and more must happen. It is no longer a matter of polite exchanges. It is a duel a outrance."

"You mean," Peter began -

"I mean that Bernadine must die," Sogrange declared.

There was a brief silence. Outside, the early morning street noises were increasing in volume as the great army of workers, streaming towards the heart of the city from a hundred suburbs, passed on to their tasks. A streak of sunshine had found its way into the room, lay across the carpet and touched Sogrange's still, waxen features. Peter glanced half fearfully at his friend and visitor. He himself was no coward, no shrinker from the great issues. He, too, had dealt in life and death. Yet there was something in the deliberate preciseness of Sogrange's words, as he sat there only a few feet away, unspeakably thrilling. It was like a death sentence pronounced in all solemnity upon some shivering criminal. There was something inevitable and tragical about the whole affair. A pronouncement had been made from which there was no appeal - Bernadine was to die!

"Isn't this a little exceeding the usual exercise of our powers?" Peter asked, slowly.

"No such occasion as this has ever yet arisen," Sogrange reminded him. "Bernadine has fled to this country with barely an hour to spare. His offense is extraditable by a law of the last century which has never been repealed. He is guilty of treason against the Republic of France. Yet they do not want him back, they do not want a trial. I have papers upon my person which, if I took them into an English court, would procure for me a warrant for Bernadine's arrest. It is not this we desire. Bernadine must die. No fate could be too terrible for a man who has striven to corrupt the soul of a nation. It is not war, this. It is not honest conspiracy. Is it war, I ask you, to seek to poison the drinking water of an enemy, to send stalking into their midst some loathsome disease? Such things belong to the ages of barbarity. Bernadine has striven to revive them and

Bernadine shall die."

"It is justice," Peter admitted.

"The question remains," Sogrange continued, "by whose hand - yours or mine?"

Peter started uneasily.

"Is that necessary?" he asked.

"I fear that it is," Sogrange replied. "We had a brief meeting of the executive council last night, and it was decided, for certain reasons, to entrust this task into no other hands. You will smile when I tell you that these accursed pamphlets have found their way into the possession of many of the rank and file of our own order. There is a marked disinclination on the part of those who have been our slaves, to accept orders from any one. Espionage we can still command - the best, perhaps, in Europe - because here we use a different class of material. But of those underneath, we are, for the moment, doubtful. Paris is all in a ferment. Under its outward seemliness a million throats are ready to take up the brazen cry of revolution. One trusts nobody. One fears all the time."

"You or I!" Peter repeated, slowly. "It will not be sufficient, then, that we find Bernadine and deliver him over to your country's laws?"

"It will not be sufficient," Sogrange answered, sternly. "From those he may escape. For him there must be no escape."

"Sogrange," Peter said, speaking in a low tone, "I have never yet killed a human being."

"Nor I," Sogrange admitted. "Nor have I yet set my heel upon its head and stamped the life from a rat upon the pavement. But one lives and one moves on. Bernadine is the enemy of your country and mine. He makes war after the fashion of vermin. No ordinary cut-throat would succeed against him. It must be you or I."

"How shall we decide?" Peter asked.

"The spin of a coin," Sogrange replied. "It is best that way. It is best, too, done quickly."

Peter produced a sovereign from his pocket and balanced it on the palm of his hand.

"Let it be understood," Sogrange continued, "that this is a dual undertaking. We toss only for the final honor - for the last stroke. If the choice falls upon me, I shall count upon you to help me to the end. If it falls upon you, I shall be at your right hand even when you strike the blow."

"It is agreed," Peter said. "See, it is for you to call."

He threw the coin high into the air.

"I call heads," Sogrange decided.

It fell upon the table. Peter covered it with his hand and then slowly withdrew the fingers. A little shiver ran through his veins. The harmless head that looked up at him was like the figure of death. It was for him to strike the blow!

"Where is Bernadine now?" he asked.

"Get me a morning paper and I will tell you," Sogrange declared, rising. "He was in the train which was stopped outside the Gare du Nord, on his way to England. What became of the passengers I have not heard. I knew what was likely to happen, and I left an hour before in a 100 H. P. Charron."

Peter rang the bell and ordered the servant who answered it to procure the Daily Telegraph. As soon as it arrived, he spread it open upon the table and Sogrange looked over his shoulder. These are the headings which they saw in large black characters:

RENEWED RIOTS IN PARIS

THE GARE DU NORD IN FLAMES

TERRIBLE ACCIDENT TO THE CALAIS-DOUVRES EXPRESS

MANY DEATHS

Peter's forefinger traveled down the page swiftly. It paused at the following paragraph:

The 8.55 train from the Gare du Nord, carrying many passengers for London, after being detained within a mile of Paris for over an hour owing to the murder of the engine-driver, made an attempt last night to proceed, with terrible results. Near Chantilly, whilst travelling at over fifty miles an hour, the switches were tampered with and the express dashed into a goods train laden with minerals. Very few particulars are yet to hand, but the express was completely wrecked and many lives have been lost.

Among the dead are the following:

One by one Peter read out the names. Then he stopped short. A little exclamation broke from Sogrange's lips. The thirteenth name upon that list of dead was that of Bernadine, Count von Hern.

"Bernadine!" Peter faltered. "Bernadine is dead!"

"Killed by the strikers!" Sogrange echoed! "It is a just thing, this."

The two men looked down at the paper and then up at one

another. A strange silence seemed to have found its way into the room. The shadow of death lay between them. Peter touched his forehead and found it wet.

"It is a just thing, indeed," he repeated, "but justice and death are alike terrible." . . .

Late in the afternoon of the same day, a motor car, splashed with mud, drew up before the door of the house in Berkeley Square. Sogrange, who was standing talking to Peter before the library window, suddenly broke off in the middle of a sentence. He stepped back into the room and gripped his friend's shoulder.

"It is the Baroness!" he exclaimed, quickly. "What does she want here?"

"The Baroness who? Peter demanded.

"The Baroness von Ratten. You must have heard of her - she is the friend of Bernadine."

The two men had been out to lunch at the Ritz with Violet and had walked across the Park home. Sogrange had been drawing on his gloves in the act of starting out for a call at the Embassy.

"Does your wife know this woman?" he asked. Peter shook his head.

"I think not," he replied.

"Then she has come to see you," Sogrange continued. "What does it mean, I wonder?"

Peter shrugged his shoulders.

"We shall know in a minute."

There was a knock at the door and his servant entered, bearing a card.

"This lady would like to see you, sir, on important business," he said.

"You can show her in here," Peter directed.

There was a very short delay. The two men had no time to exchange a word. They heard the rustling of a woman's gown, and immediately afterwards the perfume of violets seemed to fill the room.

"The Baroness von Ratten!" the butler announced.

The door was closed behind her. The servant had disappeared. Peter advanced to meet his guest. She was a little above medium height, very slim, with extraordinarily fair hair, colorless face, and strange eyes. She was not strictly beautiful and yet there was no man upon whom her presence was without its effect. Her voice was like her movements, slow and with a grace of its own.

"You do not mind that I have come to see you?" she asked, raising her eyes to Peter's. "I believe before I go that you will think terrible things of me, but you must not begin before I have told you my errand. It has been a great struggle with me before I made up my mind to come here."

"Won't you sit down, Baroness?" Peter invited.

She saw Sogrange and hesitated.

"You are not alone," she said, softly. "I wish to speak with you alone."

"Permit me to present to you the Marquis de Sogrange," Peter begged.

"He is my oldest friend, Baroness. I think that whatever you might have to say to me you might very well say before him."

"It is - of a private nature," she murmured.

"The Marquis and I have no secrets," Peter declared, "either political or private."

She sat down and motioned Peter to take a place by her side upon the sofa.

"You will forgive me if I am a little incoherent," she implored. "To-day I have had a shock. You, too, have read the news? You must know that the Count von Hern is dead - killed in the railway accident last night?"

"We read it in the Daily Telegraph," Peter replied.

"It is in all the papers," she continued. "You know that he was a very dear friend of mine?"

"I have heard so," Peter admitted.

"Yet there was one subject," she insisted, earnestly, "upon which we never agreed. He hated England. I have always loved it. England was kind to me when my own country drove me out. I have always felt grateful. It has been a sorrow to me that in so many of his schemes, in so much of his work, Bernadine should consider his own country at the expense of yours."

Sograinge drew a little nearer. It began to be interesting, this.

"I heard the news early this morning by telegram," she went on. "For a long time I was prostrated. Then early this afternoon I began to think - one must always think. Bernadine was a dear friend, but things between us lately have been different, a little strained. Was it his fault or mine - who can say? Does one tire with the years, I wonder? I wonder!"

Her eyes were lifted to his and Peter was conscious of the fact that she wished him to know that they were beautiful. She looked slowly away again.

"This afternoon, as I sat alone," she proceeded, "I remembered that in my keeping were many boxes of papers and many letters which have recently arrived, all belonging to Bernadine. I reflected that there were certainly some who were in his confidence, and that very soon they would come from his country and take them all away. And then I remembered what I owed to England, and how opposed I always was to Bernadine's schemes, and I thought that the best thing I could do to show my gratitude would be to place his papers all in the hands of some Englishman, so that they might do no more harm to the country which has been kind to me. So I came to you."

Again her eyes were lifted to his and Peter was very sure indeed that they were wonderfully beautiful. He began to realize the fascination of this woman, of whom he had heard so much. Her very absence of coloring was a charm.

"You mean that you have brought me these papers?" he asked.

She shook her head slowly.

"No," she said, "I could not do that. There were too many of them - they are too heavy, and there are piles of pamphlets - revolutionary pamphlets, I am afraid - all in French, which I do not understand. No, I could not bring them to you. But I ordered my motor car and I drove up here to tell you that if you like to come down to the house in the country where I have been living, to which Bernadine was to have come to-night - yes, and bring your friend, too, if you will - you shall look through them before any one else can arrive."

"You are very kind," Peter murmured. "Tell me where it is that you live."

"It is beyond Hitchin," she told him, "up the Great North Road. I tell you at once, it is a horrible house in a horrible lonely spot. Within a day or two I shall leave it myself forever. I hate it - it gets on my nerves. I dream of all the terrible things which perhaps have taken place there. Who can tell? It was Bernadine's long before I came to England."

"When are we to come?" Peter asked.

"You must come back with me now, at once," the Baroness insisted. "I cannot tell how soon some one in his confidence may arrive."

"I will order my car," Peter declared.

She laid her hand upon his arm.

"Do you mind coming in mine?" she begged. "It is of no consequence, if you object, but every servant in Bernadine's house is a German and a spy. There are no women except my own maid. Your car is likely enough known to them and there might be trouble. If you will come with me now, you and your friend, if you like, I will send you to the station to-night in time to catch the train home. I feel that I must have this thing off my mind. You will come? Yes?"

Peter rang the bell and ordered his coat.

"Without a doubt," he answered. "May we not offer you some tea first?"

She shook her head.

"To-day I cannot think of eating or drinking," she replied. "Bernadine and I were no longer what we had been, but the shock of his death seems none the less terrible. I feel like a traitor to him for coming here, yet I believe that I am doing what is right," she added, softly.

"If you will excuse me for one moment," Peter said, "while I take leave of my wife, I will rejoin you presently."

Peter was absent for only a few minutes. Sogrange and the Baroness exchanged the merest commonplaces. As they all passed down the hall, Sogrange lingered behind.

"If you will take the Baroness out to the car," he suggested, "I will telephone to the Embassy and tell them not to expect me."

Peter offered his arm to his companion. She seemed, indeed, to need support. Her fingers clutched at his coat-sleeve as they passed on to the pavement.

"I am so glad to be no longer quite alone," she whispered. "Almost I wish that your friend were not coming. I know that Bernadine and you were enemies, but then you were enemies not personally, but politically. After all, it is you who stand for the things which have become so dear to me."

"It is true that Bernadine and I were bitter antagonists," Peter admitted, gravely. "Death, however, ends all that. I wish him no further harm."

She sighed.

"As for me," she said, "I am growing used to being friendless. I was friendless before Bernadine came, and latterly we have been nothing to one another. Now, I suppose, I shall know what it is to be an outcast once more. Did you ever hear my history, I wonder?"

Peter shook his head.

"Never, Baroness," he replied. "I understood, I believe, that your marriage -"

"My husband divorced me," she confessed, simply. "He was quite within his rights. He was impossible. I was very young and very sentimental. They say that Englishwomen are cold," she added. "Perhaps that is so. People think that I look cold. Do you?"

Sogrange suddenly opened the door of the car in which they were already seated. She leaned back and half closed her eyes.

"It is rather a long ride," she said, "and I am worn out. I hope you will not mind, but for myself I cannot talk when motoring. Smoke, if it pleases you."

"Might one inquire as to our exact destination?" Sogrange asked.

"We go beyond Hitchin, up the Great North Road," she told him again. "The house is called the High House. It stands in the middle of a heath and I think it is the loneliest and most miserable place that was ever built. I hate it and I am frightened in it. For some reason or other, it suited Bernadine, but that is all over now."

The little party of three relapsed into silence. The car, driven carefully enough through the busy streets, gradually increased its pace as they drew clear of the suburbs. Peter leaned back in his place, thinking. Bernadine was dead! Nothing else would have convinced him so utterly of the fact as that simple sentence in the Daily Telegraph, which had been followed up by a confirmation and a brief obituary notice in all the evening papers. Curiously enough, the fact seemed to have drawn a certain spice out of even this adventure; to point, indeed, to a certain monotony in the future. Their present enterprise, important though it might turn out to be, was nothing to be proud of. A woman, greedy for gold, was selling her lover's secrets before the breath was out of his body. Peter turned in his cushioned seat to look at her. Without doubt, she was beautiful to one who understood, beautiful in a strange, colorless, feline fashion, the beauty of soft limbs, soft movements, a caressing voice, with always the promise beyond of more than the actual words. Her eyes now were closed, her face was a little weary. Did she really rest, Peter wondered? He watched the rising and falling of her bosom, the quivering now and then of her eyelids. She had indeed the appearance of a woman who had suffered

The car rushed on into the darkness. Behind them lay that restless phantasmagoria of lights streaming to the sky. In front, blank space. Peter, through half-closed eyes, watched the woman by his side. From the moment of her entrance into his library, he had summed her up in his mind with a single word. She was, beyond a doubt, an adventuress. No woman could have proposed the things which she had proposed, who was not of that ilk. Yet for that reason it behooved them to have a care in their dealings with her. At her instigation they had set out upon this adventure, which might well turn out according to any fashion that she chose. Yet without Bernadine what could she do? She was not the woman to carry on the work which he had left behind, for the love of him. Her words had been frank, her action shameful but natural. Bernadine was dead and she had realized quickly enough the best market for his secrets. In a few days' time his friends would have come and she would have received nothing. He told himself that he was foolish to doubt her. There was not a flaw in the sequence of events, no possible reason for the suspicions which yet lingered at the back of his brain. Intrigue, it was certain, was to her as the breath of her body. He was perfectly willing to believe that the death of Bernadine would have affected her little more than the sweeping aside of a fly. His very common sense bade him accept her story.

By degrees he became drowsy. Suddenly he was startled into a very wide-awake state. Through half-closed eyes he had seen Sogrange draw a sheet of paper from his pocket, a gold pencil from his chain, and commence to write. In the middle of a sentence, his eyes were abruptly lifted. He was looking at the Baroness. Peter, too, turned his head; he, also, looked at the Baroness. Without a doubt, she had been watching both of them. Sogrange's pencil continued its task, only he traced no more characters. Instead, he seemed to be sketching a face, which presently he tore carefully up into small pieces and destroyed. He did not even glance towards Peter, but Peter understood very well what had happened. He had been about to send him a message, but had found the Baroness watching. Peter was fully awake now. His faint sense of suspicion had deepened into a positive foreboding. He had a reckless desire to stop the car, to descend upon the road and let the secrets of Bernadine go where they would. Then his natural love of adventure blazed up once more. His moment of weakness had passed. The thrill was in his blood, his nerves were tightened. He was ready for what might come, seemingly still half asleep, yet, indeed, with every sense of intuition and observation keenly alert.

Sogrange leaned over from his place.

"It is a lonely country, this, into which we are coming, madame," he remarked.

She shrugged her shoulders.

"Indeed, it is not so lonely here as you will think it when we arrive at our destination," she replied. "There are houses here, but they are hidden by the trees. There are no houses near us."

She rubbed the pane with her hand.

"We are, I believe, very nearly there," she said. "This is the nearest village. Afterwards, we just climb a hill and about half a mile along the top of it is the High House."

"And the name of the village," Sogrange inquired.

"St Mary's," she told him, "In the summer people call it beautiful around here. To me it is the most melancholy spot I ever saw. There is so much rain, and one hears the drip, drip in the trees all the day long. Alone I could not bear it. To-morrow or the next day I shall pack up my belongings and come to London. I am, unfortunately," she added, with a little sigh, "very, very poor, but it is my hope that you may find the papers, of which I have spoken to you, valuable."

Sogranse smiled faintly. Peter and he could scarcely forbear to exchange a single glance. The woman's candor was almost brutal. She read their thoughts.

"We ascend the hill," she continued. "We draw now very near to the end of our journey. There is still one thing I would say to you. Do not think too badly of me for what I am about to do. To Bernadine, while he lived, I was faithful. Many a time I could have told you of his plans and demanded a great sum of money, and you would have given it me willingly, but my lips were sealed because, in a way, I loved him. While he lived I gave him what I owed. To-day he is dead, and, whatever I do, it cannot concern him any more. To-day I am a free woman and I take the side I choose."

"Dear madame," he replied, "what you have proposed to us is, after all, quite natural and very gracious. If one has a fear at all about the matter, it is as to the importance of these documents you speak of. Bernadine, I know, has dealt in great affairs; but he was a diplomat by instinct, experienced and calculating. One does not keep incriminating papers."

She leaned a little forward. The car had swung round a corner now and was making its way up an avenue as dark as pitch.

"The wisest of us, Monsieur le Marquis," she whispered, "reckon sometimes without that one element of sudden death. What should you say, I wonder, to a list of agents in France pledged to circulate in certain places literature of an infamous sort? What should you say, monsieur, to a copy of a secret report of your late maneuvers, franked with the name of one of your own staff officers? What should you say," she went on, "to a list of Socialist deputies with amounts against their name, amounts paid in hard cash? Are these of no importance to you?"

"Madame," Sogrange answered, simply, "for such information, if it were genuine, it would be hard to mention a price which we should not be prepared to pay."

The car came to a sudden standstill. The first impression of the two men was that the Baroness had exaggerated the loneliness and desolation of the place. There was nothing mysterious or forbidding about the plain, brownstone house before which they had stopped. The windows were streaming with light; the hall door, already thrown open, disclosed a very comfortable hall, brilliantly illuminated. A man-servant assisted his mistress to alight, another ushered them in. In the background were other servants. The Baroness glanced at the clock.

"About dinner, Carl?" she asked.

"It waits for madame," the man answered.

She nodded.

"Take care of these gentlemen till I descend," she ordered. "You will not mind?" she added, turning pleadingly to Sogrange. "To-day I have eaten nothing. I am faint with hunger. Afterwards, it will be a matter but of half an hour. You can be in London again by ten o'clock."

"As you will, madame," Sogrange replied. "We are greatly indebted to you for your hospitality. But for costume, you understand that we are as we are?"

"It is perfectly understood," she assured him. "For myself, I rejoin you in ten minutes. A loose gown, that is all."

Sogrange and Peter were shown into a modern bathroom by a servant who was so anxious to wait upon them that they had difficulty in sending him away. As soon as he was gone and the door closed behind him, Peter put his foot against it and turned the key.

E. Phillips Oppenheim

"You were going to write something to me in the car?"

Sogrange nodded.

"There was a moment," he admitted, "when I had a suspicion. It has passed. This woman is no Roman. She sells the secrets of Bernadine as she would sell herself. Nevertheless, it is well always to be prepared. There were probably others beside Bernadine who had the entree here."

"The only suspicious circumstance which I have noticed," Peter remarked, "is the number of men-servants. I have seen five already."

"It is only fair to remember," Sogrange reminded him, "that the Baroness herself told us that there were no other save men-servants here and that they were all spies. Without a master, I cannot see that they are dangerous. One needs, however, to watch all the time."

"If you see anything suspicious," Peter said, "tap the table with your forefinger. Personally, I will admit that I have had my doubts of the Baroness, but on the whole I have come to the conclusion that they were groundless. She is not the sort of woman to take up a vendetta, especially an unprofitable one."

"She is an exceedingly dangerous person for an impressionable man like myself," Sogrange remarked, arranging his tie.

The butler fetched them in a very few moments and showed them into a pleasantly-furnished library, where he mixed cocktails for them from a collection of bottles upon the sideboard. He was quite friendly and inclined to be loquacious, although he spoke with a slight foreign accent. The house belonged to an English gentleman from whom the honored Count had taken it, furnished. They were two miles from a station and a mile from the village. It was a lonely part, but there were always people coming or going. With one's work one scarcely noticed it. He was gratified that the gentlemen found his cocktails so excellent. Perhaps he might be permitted the high honor of mixing them another? It was a day, this, of deep sadness and gloom. One needed to drink something, indeed, to forget the terrible thing which had happened. The Count had been a good master, a little impatient sometimes, but kind-hearted. The news had been a shock to them all.

Then, before they had expected her, the Baroness reappeared. She wore a wonderful gray gown which seemed to be made in a single piece, a gown which fitted her tightly, and yet gave her the curious appearance of a woman walking without the burden of clothes. Sogrange, Parisian to the finger-tips, watched her with admiring approval. She laid her fingers upon his arm, although it was towards Peter that her eyes traveled.

"Will you take me in, Marquis?" she begged. "It is the only formality we will allow ourselves."

They entered a long, low dining-room, paneled with oak, and with the family portraits of the owner of the house still left upon the wall. Dinner was served upon a round table and was laid for four. There was a profusion of silver, very beautiful glass, and a wonderful cluster of orchids. The Marquis, as he handed his hostess to her chair, glanced towards the vacant place.

"It is for my companion, an Austrian lady," she explained. "To-night, however, I think that she will not come. She was a distant connection of Bernadine's and she is much upset. We leave her place and see. You will sit on my other side, Baron."

The fingers which touched Peter's arm brushed his hand, and were withdrawn as though with reluctance. She sank into her chair with a little sigh.

"It is charming of you two, this," she declared, softly. "You help me through this night of solitude and sadness. What I should do if I were alone, I cannot tell. You must drink with me a toast, if you will. Will you make it to our better acquaintance?"

No soup had been offered and champagne was served with the hors d'oeuvre. Peter raised his glass and looked into the eyes of the woman who was leaning so closely towards him that her soft breath fell upon his cheek. She whispered something in his ear. For a moment, perhaps, he was carried away, but for a moment only. Then Sogrange's voice and the beat of his forefinger upon the table stiffened him into sudden alertness. They heard a motor car draw up outside.

"Who can it be?" the Baroness exclaimed, setting her glass down abruptly.

"It is, perhaps, our fourth guest who arrives," Sogrange remarked.

They all three listened, Peter and Sogrange with their glasses still suspended in the air.

"Our fourth guest?" the Baroness repeated. "Madame von Estenier is upstairs, lying down. I cannot tell who this may be."

Her lips were parted. The lines of her forehead had suddenly appeared. Her eyes were turned toward the door, hard and bright. Then the glass which she had nervously picked up again and was holding between her fingers, fell on to the tablecloth with a little crash, and the yellow wine ran bubbling on to her plate. Her scream echoed to the roof and rang through the room. It was Bernadine who stood there in the doorway, Bernadine in a long traveling ulster and the air of one newly arrived from a journey. They all three looked at him, but there was not one who spoke. The Baroness, after her one wild cry, was dumb.

"I am indeed fortunate," Bernadine said. "You have as yet, I see, scarcely commenced. You probably expected me. I am charmed to find so agreeable a party awaiting my arrival."

He divested himself of his ulster and threw it across the arm of the butler, who stood behind him.

"Come," he continued; "for a man who has just been killed in a railway accident, I find myself with an appetite. A glass of wine, Carl. I do not know what that toast was, the drinking of which my coming interrupted, but let us all drink it together. Aimee, my love to you, dear. Let me congratulate you upon the fortitude and courage with which you ignored those lying reports of my death. I had fears that I might find you alone in a darkened room, with tear-stained eyes and sal volatile by your side. This is infinitely better. Gentlemen, you are welcome."

Sograge lifted his glass and bowed courteously. Peter followed suit.

"Really," Sograge murmured, "the Press nowadays becomes more unreliable every day. It is apparent, my dear Von Hern, that this account of your death was, to say the least of it, exaggerated."

Peter said nothing. His eyes were fixed upon the Baroness. She sat in her chair quite motionless, but her face had become like the face of some graven image. She looked at Bernadine, but her eyes said nothing. Every glint of expression seemed to have left her features. Since that one wild shriek she had remained voiceless. Encompassed by danger though he knew they now must be, Peter found himself possessed by one thought only. Was this a trap into which they had fallen, or was the woman, too, deceived?

"You bring later news from Paris than I myself," Sograge proceeded, helping himself to one of the dishes which a footman was passing round. "How did you reach the coast? The evening papers stated distinctly that since the accident no attempt had been made to run trains."

"By motor car from Chantilly," Bernadine replied. "I had the misfortune to lose my servant, who was wearing my coat, and who, I gather from the newspaper reports, was mistaken for me. I myself was unhurt. I hired a motor car and drove to

Boulogne - not the best of journeys, let me tell you, for we broke down three times. There was no steamer there, but I hired a fishing boat, which brought me across the Channel in something under eight hours. From the coast I motored direct here. I was so anxious," he added, raising his eyes, "to see how my dear friend - my dear Aimee - was bearing the terrible news."

She fluttered for a moment like a bird in a trap. Peter drew a little sigh of relief. His self-respect was reinstated. He had decided that she was innocent. Upon them, at least, would not fall the ignominy of having been led into the simplest of traps by this white-faced Delilah. The butler had brought her another glass, which she raised to her lips. She drained its contents, but the ghastliness of her appearance remained unchanged. Peter, watching her, knew the signs. She was sick with terror.

"The conditions throughout France are indeed awful," Sogrange remarked. "They say, too, that this railway strike is only the beginning of worse things."

Bernadine smiled.

"Your country, dear Marquis," he said, "is on its last legs. No one knows better than I that it is, at the present moment, honeycombed with sedition and anarchical impulses. The people are rotten. For years the whole tone of France has been decadent. Its fall must even now be close at hand."

"You take a gloomy view of my country's future," Sogrange declared.

"Why should one refuse to face facts?" Bernadine replied. "One does not often talk so frankly, but we three are met together this evening under somewhat peculiar circumstances. The days of the glory of France are past. England has laid out her neck for the yoke of the conqueror. Both are doomed to fall. Both are ripe for the great humiliation. You two gentlemen whom I have the honor to receive as my guests," he concluded, filling his glass and bowing towards them, "in your present unfortunate predicament represent precisely the position of your two countries."

"Ave Caesar!" Peter muttered grimly, raising his glass to his lips.

Bernadine accepted the challenge.

"It is not I, alas! who may call myself Caesar," he replied, "although it is certainly you who are about to die."

Sogrange turned to the man who stood behind his chair.

"If I might trouble you for a little dry toast?" he inquired. "A modern but very uncomfortable ailment," he added, with a sigh. "One's digestion must march with the years, I suppose."

Bernadine smiled.

"Your toast you shall have, with pleasure, Marquis," he said, "but as for your indigestion, do not let that trouble you any longer. I think that I can promise you immunity from that annoying complaint for the rest of your life."

"You are doing your best," Peter declared, leaning back in his chair, "to take away my appetite."

Bernadine looked searchingly from one to the other of his two guests.

"Yes," he admitted, "you are brave men. I do not know why I should ever have doubted it. Your pose is excellent. I have no wish, however, to see you buoyed up by a baseless optimism. A somewhat remarkable chance has delivered you into my hands. You are my prisoners. You, Peter, Baron de Grost, I have hated all my days. You have stood between me and the achievement of some of my most dearly-cherished tasks. Always I have said

E. Phillips Oppenheim

to myself that the day of reckoning must come. It has arrived. As for you, Marquis de Sogrange, if my personal feelings towards you are less violent, you still represent the things absolutely inimical to me and my interests. The departure of you two men was the one thing necessary for the successful completion of certain tasks which I have in hand at the present moment."

Peter pushed away his plate.

"You have succeeded in destroying my appetite, Count," he declared. "Now that you have gone so far in expounding your amiable resolutions towards us, perhaps you will go a little further and explain exactly how, in this eminently respectable house, situated, I understand, in an eminently respectable neighborhood, with a police station within a mile, and a dozen or so witnesses as to our present whereabouts, you intend to expedite our removal?"

Bernadine pointed toward the woman who sat facing him.

"Ask the Baroness how these things are arranged."

They turned towards her. She fell back in her chair with a little gasp. She had fainted. Bernadine shrugged his shoulders. The butler and one of the footmen, who during the whole of the conversation had stolidly proceeded with their duties, in obedience to a gesture from their master took her up in their arms and carried her from the room.

"The fear has come to her, too," Bernadine murmured, softly. "It may come to you, my brave friends, before morning."

"It is possible," Peter answered, his hand stealing around to his hip pocket, "but in the meantime, what is to prevent -"

The hip pocket was empty. Peter's sentence ended abruptly. Bernadine mocked him.

"To prevent your shooting me in cold blood, I suppose," he remarked. "Nothing except that my servants are too clever. No one save myself is allowed to remain under this roof with arms in their possession. Your pocket was probably picked before you had been in the place five minutes. No, my dear Baron, let me assure you that escape will not be so easy! You were always just a little inclined to be led away by the fair sex. The best men in the world, you know, have shared that failing, and the Baroness, alone and unprotected, had her attractions, eh?"

Then something happened to Peter which had happened to him barely a dozen times in his life. He lost his temper and lost it rather badly. Without an instant's hesitation, he caught up the decanter which stood by his side and flung it in his host's face. Bernadine only partly avoided it by thrusting out his arms. The neck caught his forehead and the blood came streaming over his tie and collar. Peter had followed the decanter with a sudden spring. His fingers were upon Bernadine's throat and he thrust his head back. Sogrange sprang to the door to lock it, but he was too late. The room seemed full of men-servants. Peter was dragged away, still struggling fiercely.

"Tie them up!" Bernadine gasped, swaying in his chair. "Tie them up, do you hear? Carl, give me brandy."

He swallowed half a wineglassful of the raw spirit. His eyes were red with fury.

"Take them to the gun room," he ordered, "three of you to each of them, mind. I'll shoot the man who lets either escape."

But Peter and Sogrange were both of them too wise to expend any more of their strength in a useless struggle. They suffered themselves to be conducted without resistance across the white stone hall, down a long passage, and into a room at the end, the window and fireplace of which were both blocked up. The floor was of red flags and the walls whitewashed. The only furniture was a couple of kitchen chairs and a long table. The door was of stout oak and fitted with a double lock. The sole outlet, so far as they could see, was a small round hole at the top of the roof. The door was locked behind them. They were alone.

"The odd trick to Bernadine!" Peter exclaimed hoarsely, wiping a spot of blood from his forehead. "My dear Marquis, I scarcely know how to apologize. It is not often that I lose my temper so completely."

"The matter seems to be of very little consequence," Sogrange answered. "This was probably our intended destination in any case. Seems to be rather an unfortunate expedition of ours, I am afraid."

"One cannot reckon upon men coming back from the dead," Peter declared. "It isn't often that you find every morning and every evening paper mistaken. As for the woman, I believe in her. She honestly meant to sell us those papers of Bernadine's. I believe that she, too, will have to face a day of reckoning."

Sogrange strolled around the room, subjecting it everywhere to a close scrutiny. The result was hopeless. There was no method of escape save through the door.

"There is certainly something strange about this apartment," Peter remarked. "It is, to say the least of it, unusual to have windows in the roof and a door of such proportions. All the same, I think that those threats of Bernadine's were a little strained. One cannot get rid of one's enemies, nowadays, in the old-fashioned, melodramatic way. Bernadine must know quite well that you and I are not the sort of men to walk into a trap of any one's setting, just as I am quite sure that he is not the man to risk even a scandal by breaking the law openly."

"You interest me," Sogrange said. "I begin to suspect that you, too, have made some plans."

"But naturally," Peter replied. "Once before Bernadine set a trap for me and he nearly had a chance of sending me for a swim in the Thames. Since then one takes precautions as a matter of course. We were followed down here, and by this time I should imagine that the alarm is given. If all was well, I was to have telephoned an hour ago."

"You are really," Sogrange declared, "quite an agreeable companion, my dear Baron. You think of everything."

The door was suddenly opened. Bernadine stood upon the threshold and behind him several of the servants.

"You will oblige me by stepping back into the study, my friends," he ordered.

"With great pleasure," Sogrange answered, with alacrity. "We have no fancy for this room, I can assure you."

Once more they crossed the stone hall and entered the room into which they had first been shown. On the threshold, Peter stoped short and listened. It seemed to him that from somewhere upstairs he could hear the sound of a woman's sobs. He turned to Bernadine.

"The Baroness is not unwell, I trust?" he asked.

"The Baroness is as well as she is likely to be for some time," Bernadine replied, grimly.

They were all in the study now. Upon a table stood a telephone instrument. Bernadine drew a small revolver from his pocket.

"Baron de Grost," he said, "I find that you are not quite such a fool as I thought you. Some one is ringing up for you on the telephone. You will reply that you are well and safe and that you will be home as soon as your business here is finished. Your wife is at the other end. If you breathe a single word to her of your approaching end, she shall hear through the telephone the sound of the revolver shot that sends you to Hell."

"Dear me," Peter protested, "I find this most unpleasant. If you will excuse me, I don't think I'll answer the call at all."

"You will answer it as I have directed," Bernadine insisted. "Only remember this - if you speak a single ill-advised word, the end will be as I have said."

Peter picked up the receiver and held it to his ear.

"Who is there?" he asked.

It was Violet whose voice he heard. He listened for a moment to her anxious flood of questions.

"There is not the slightest cause to be alarmed, dear," he said. "Yes, I am down at the High House, near St. Mary's. Bernadine is here. It seems that those reports of his death were absolutely unfounded. . . . Danger? Unprotected? Why, my dear Violet, you know how careful I always am. Simply because Bernadine used once to live here, and because the Baroness was his friend, I spoke to Sir John Dory over the telephone before we left, and an escort of half-a-dozen police followed us. They are about the place now, I have no doubt, but their presence is quite unnecessary. I shall be home before long, dear. . . . Yes, perhaps it would be as well to send the car down. Any one will direct him to the house - the High House, St. Mary's, remember. Good-by!"

Peter replaced the receiver and turned slowly round. Bernadine was smiling.

"You did well to reassure your wife, even though it was a pack of lies you told her," he remarked.

Peter shrugged his shoulders contemptuously.

"My dear Bernadine," he said, "up till now I have tried to take you seriously. You are really passing the limit. I must positively ask you to reflect a little. Do men who live the life that you and I live, trust any one? Am I - is the Marquis de Sogrange here - after a lifetime of experience, likely to leave the safety of our homes in company with a lady of whom we knew nothing except that she was your companion, without precautions? I do you the justice to believe you a person of commonsense. I know that we are as safe in this house as we should be in our own. War cannot be made in this fashion in an over-policed country like England."

"Do not be too sure," Bernadine replied. "There are secrets about this house which have not yet been disclosed to you. There are means, my dear Baron, of transporting you into a world where you are likely to do much less harm than here, means ready at hand, and which would leave no more trace behind than those crumbling ashes can tell of the coal mine from which they came."

Peter preserved his attitude of bland incredulity.

"Listen," he said, drawing a whistle from his pocket, "it is just possible that you are in earnest. I will bet you, then, if you like, a hundred pounds, that if I blow this whistle you will either have to open your door within five minutes or find your house invaded by the police."

No one spoke for several moments. The veins were standing out upon Bernadine's forehead.

"We have had enough of this folly," he cried. "If you refuse to realize your position, so much the worse for you. Blow your whistle, if you will. I am content."

Peter waited for no second bidding. He raised the whistle to his lips and blew it, loudly and persistently. Again there was silence. Bernadine mocked him.

"Try once more, dear Baron," he advised. "Your friends are perhaps a little hard of hearing. Try once more, and when you have finished, you and I and the Marquis de Sogrange will find our way once more to the gun room and conclude that trifling matter of business which brought you here."

Again Peter blew his whistle and again the silence was broken only by Bernadine's laugh. Suddenly, however, that laugh was checked. Every one had turned toward the door, listening. A bell was ringing throughout the house.

"It is the front door!" one of the servants exclaimed.

No one moved. As though to put the matter beyond doubt, there was a steady knocking to be heard from the same direction.

"It is a telegram or some late caller," Bernadine declared, hoarsely. "Answer it, Carl. If any one would speak with the Baroness, she is indisposed and unable to receive. If any one desires me, I am here."

The man left the room. They heard him withdraw the chain from the door. Bernadine wiped the sweat from his forehead as he listened. He still gripped the revolver in his hand. Peter had changed his position a little and was standing now behind a high-backed chair. They heard the door creak open, a voice outside, and presently the tramp of heavy footsteps. Peter nodded understandingly.

"It is exactly as I told you," he said. "You were wise not to bet, my friend."

Again the tramp of feet in the hall. There was something unmistakable about the sound, something final and terrifying. Bernadine saw his triumph slipping away. Once more this man who had defied him so persistently, was to taste the sweets of victory. With a roar of fury he sprang across the room. He fired his revolver twice before Sogrange, with a terrible blow, knocked his arm upwards and sent the weapon spinning to the ceiling. Peter struck his assailant in the mouth, but the blow seemed scarcely to check him. They rolled on the floor together, their arms around one another's necks. It was an affair, that, but of a moment. Peter, as lithe as a cat, was on his feet again almost at once, with a torn collar and an ugly mark on his face. There were strangers in the room now and the servants had mostly slipped away during the confusion. It was Sir John Dory himself who locked the door. Bernadine struggled slowly to his feet. He was face to face with half a dozen police constables in plain clothes.

"You have a charge against this man, Baron?" the police commissioner asked.

Peter shook his head.

"The quarrel between us," he replied, "is not for the police courts, although I will confess, Sir John, that your intervention was opportune."

"I, on the other hand," Sogrange put in, "demand the arrest of the Count von Hern and the seizure of all papers in this house. I am the bearer of an autograph letter from the President of France in connection with this matter. The Count von Hern has committed extraditable offenses against my country. I am prepared to swear an information to that effect."

The police commissioner turned to Peter.

"Your friend's name?" he demanded.

"The Marquis de Sogrange," Peter told him.

"He is a person of authority?"

"To my certain knowledge," Peter replied, "he has the implicit confidence of the French Government."

Sir John Dory made a sign. In another moment Bernadine would have been arrested. It seemed, indeed, as though nothing could save him now from this crowning humiliation. He himself, white and furious, was at a loss how to deal with an unexpected situation. Suddenly a thing happened stranger than any one of them there had ever dreamed of, so strange that even men such as Peter, Sogrange and Dory, whose nerves were of iron, faced one another, doubting and amazed. The floor beneath them rocked and billowed like the waves of a canvas sea. The windows were filled with flashes of red light, a great fissure parted the wall, the pictures and book-cases came crashing down beneath a shower of masonry. It was the affair of a second. Above them shone the stars and around them a noise like thunder. Bernadine, who alone understood, was the first to recover himself. He stood in the midst of them, his hands above his head, laughing as he looked around at the strange storm, laughing like a madman.

"The wonderful Carl," he cried. "Oh, matchless servant. Arrest me now, if you will, you dogs of the police. Rout out my secrets, dear Baron de Grost. Tuck them under your arm and hurry to Downing Street. This is the hospitality of the High House, my friends. It loves you so well that only your ashes shall leave it."

His mouth was open for another sentence when he was struck. A whole pillar of marble from one of the rooms above came crashing through and buried him underneath a falling shower of masonry. Peter escaped by a few inches. Those who were left unhurt sprang through the yawning wall out into the garden. Sir John, Sogrange and Peter, three of the men - one limping badly, came to a standstill in the middle of the lawn. Before them, the house was crumbling like a pack of cards, and louder even than the thunder of the falling structure was the roar of the red flames.

"The Baroness!" Peter cried, and took one leap forward.

"I am here," she sobbed, running to them from out of the

shadows. "I have lost everything - my jewels, my clothes, all except what I have on. They gave me but a moment's warning."

"Is there any one else in the house?" Peter demanded.

"No one but you who were in that room," she answered.

"Your companion!"

She shook her head.

"There was no companion," she faltered. "I thought it sounded better to speak of her. I had her place laid at table, but she never even existed."

Peter tore off his coat.

"There are the others in the room!" he exclaimed. "We must go back."

Sogrange caught him by the shoulder and pointed to a shadowy group some distance away.

"We are all out but Bernadine," he said. "For him were is no hope. Quick!"

They sprang back only just in time. The outside wall of the house fell with a terrible crash. The room which they had quitted was blotted now out of existence. From right and left, in all directions along the country road, came the flashing of lights and little knots of hurrying people.

"It is the end!" Peter muttered. "Yesterday I should have regretted the passing of a brave enemy. To-day I hail with joy the death of a brute."

The Baroness, who had been sitting upon a garden seat, sobbing, came softly up to them. She laid her fingers upon

Peter's arm imploringly.

"You will not leave me friendless?" she begged. "The papers I promised you are destroyed, but many of his secrets are here."

She tapped her forehead.

"Madame," Peter answered, "I have no wish to know them. Years ago I swore that the passing of Bernadine should mark my own retirement from the world in which we both lived. I shall keep my word. To-night Bernadine is dead. To-night, Sogrange, my work is finished." The Baroness began to sob again.

"And I thought that you were a man," she moaned, "so gallant, so honorable -"

"Madame," Sogrange intervened, "I shall commend you to the pension list of the Double-Four."

She dried her eyes.

"It is not money only I want," she whispered, her eyes following Peter.

Sogrange shook his head.

"You have never seen the Baroness de Grost?" he asked her.

"But no!"

"Ah!" Sogrange murmured. . . . "Our escort, madame, is at your service - as far as London."

ABOUT THE AUTHOR

Edward Phillips Oppenheim (1866–1946), self-styled "prince of storytellers," was an English novelist, a major and successful writer of genre fiction including thrillers. He composed during his lifetime more than a hundred novels, mostly of the suspense and international intrigue nature, as well as romances, comedies, and parables of everyday life. The sole biography of Oppenheim is Robert Standish's (pseudonym of Digby George Gerahty) Prince of Storytellers: The Life of E. Phillips Oppenheim; London: Peter Davies 1957.

Oppenheim's work possesses a unique charm all its own, featuring protagonists who delight in Epicurean meals, surroundings of intense luxury, and the relaxed pursuit of criminal practice, on either side of the law. Perhaps Oppenheim's most enduring creation is General Besserley, the protagonist of General Besserley's Puzzle Box and General Besserley's New Puzzle Box (this last volume, written in 1939, was one of Oppenheim's last works).

For most of his life, Oppenheim maintained a regular schedule of work and productivity of an almost monastic nature, despite his fondness for Monte Carlo and his love of good food and wine. Troubled in his last years by intense prostate problems, Oppenheim persevered in the creation of a series of charming, escapist novels which still hold the reader's attention today.

Choose from Thousands of 1stWorldLibrary Classics By

A. M. Barnard
Ada Leverson
Adolphus William Ward
Aesop
Agatha Christie
Alexander Aaronsohn
Alexander Kielland
Alexandre Dumas
Alfred Gatty
Alfred Ollivant
Alice Duer Miller
Alice Turner Curtis
Alice Dunbar
Allen Chapman
Alleyne Ireland
Ambrose Bierce
Amelia E. Barr
Amory H. Bradford
Andrew Lang
Andrew McFarland Davis
Andy Adams
Angela Brazil
Anna Alice Chapin
Anna Sewell
Annie Besant
Annie Hamilton Donnell
Annie Payson Call
Annie Roe Carr
Annonaymous
Anton Chekhov
Archibald Lee Fletcher
Arnold Bennett
Arthur C. Benson
Arthur Conan Doyle
Arthur M. Winfield
Arthur Ransome
Arthur Schnitzler
Arthur Train
Atticus
B.H. Baden-Powell
B. M. Bower
B. C. Chatterjee
Baroness Emmuska Orczy
Baroness Orczy
Basil King
Bayard Taylor
Ben Macomber
Bertha Muzzy Bower
Bjornstjerne Bjornson

Booth Tarkington
Boyd Cable
Bram Stoker
C. Collodi
C. E. Orr
C. M. Ingleby
Carolyn Wells
Catherine Parr Traill
Charles A. Eastman
Charles Amory Beach
Charles Dickens
Charles Dudley Warner
Charles Farrar Browne
Charles Ives
Charles Kingsley
Charles Klein
Charles Hanson Towne
Charles Lathrop Pack
Charles Romyn Dake
Charles Whibley
Charles Willing Beale
Charlotte M. Braeme
Charlotte M. Yonge
Charlotte Perkins Stetson
Clair W. Hayes
Clarence Day Jr.
Clarence E. Mulford
Clemence Housman
Confucius
Coningsby Dawson
Cornelis DeWitt Wilcox
Cyril Burleigh
D. H. Lawrence
Daniel Defoe
David Garnett
Dinah Craik
Don Carlos Janes
Donald Keyhoe
Dorothy Kilner
Dougan Clark
Douglas Fairbanks
E. Nesbit
E. P. Roe
E. Phillips Oppenheim
E. S. Brooks
Earl Barnes
Edgar Rice Burroughs
Edith Van Dyne
Edith Wharton

Edward Everett Hale
Edward J. O'Biren
Edward S. Ellis
Edwin L. Arnold
Eleanor Atkins
Eleanor Hallowell Abbott
Eliot Gregory
Elizabeth Gaskell
Elizabeth McCracken
Elizabeth Von Arnim
Ellem Key
Emerson Hough
Emilie F. Carlen
Emily Bronte
Emily Dickinson
Enid Bagnold
Enilor Macartney Lane
Erasmus W. Jones
Ernie Howard Pie
Ethel May Dell
Ethel Turner
Ethel Watts Mumford
Eugene Sue
Eugenie Foa
Eugene Wood
Eustace Hale Ball
Evelyn Everett-green
Everard Cotes
F. H. Cheley
F. J. Cross
F. Marion Crawford
Fannie E. Newberry
Federick Austin Ogg
Ferdinand Ossendowski
Fergus Hume
Florence A. Kilpatrick
Fremont B. Deering
Francis Bacon
Francis Darwin
Frances Hodgson Burnett
Frances Parkinson Keyes
Frank Gee Patchin
Frank Harris
Frank Jewett Mather
Frank L. Packard
Frank V. Webster
Frederic Stewart Isham
Frederick Trevor Hill
Frederick Winslow Taylor

Friedrich Kerst
Friedrich Nietzsche
Fyodor Dostoyevsky
G.A. Henty
G.K. Chesterton
Gabrielle E. Jackson
Garrett P. Serviss
Gaston Leroux
George A. Warren
George Ade
Geroge Bernard Shaw
George Cary Eggleston
George Durston
George Ebers
George Eliot
George Gissing
George MacDonald
George Meredith
George Orwell
George Sylvester Viereck
George Tucker
George W. Cable
George Wharton James
Gertrude Atherton
Gordon Casserly
Grace E. King
Grace Gallatin
Grace Greenwood
Grant Allen
Guillermo A. Sherwell
Gulielma Zollinger
Gustav Flaubert
H. A. Cody
H. B. Irving
H.C. Bailey
H. G. Wells
H. H. Munro
H. Irving Hancock
H. R. Naylor
H. Rider Haggard
H. W. C. Davis
Haldeman Julius
Hall Caine
Hamilton Wright Mabie
Hans Christian Andersen
Harold Avery
Harold McGrath
Harriet Beecher Stowe
Harry Castlemon
Harry Coghill
Harry Houidini

Hayden Carruth
Helent Hunt Jackson
Helen Nicolay
Hendrik Conscience
Hendy David Thoreau
Henri Barbusse
Henrik Ibsen
Henry Adams
Henry Ford
Henry Frost
Henry James
Henry Jones Ford
Henry Seton Merriman
Henry W Longfellow
Herbert A. Giles
Herbert Carter
Herbert N. Casson
Herman Hesse
Hildegard G. Frey
Homer
Honore De Balzac
Horace B. Day
Horace Walpole
Horatio Alger Jr.
Howard Pyle
Howard R. Garis
Hugh Lofting
Hugh Walpole
Humphry Ward
Ian Maclaren
Inez Haynes Gillmore
Irving Bacheller
Isabel Cecilia Williams
Isabel Hornibrook
Israel Abrahams
Ivan Turgenev
J.G.Austin
J. Henri Fabre
J. M. Barrie
J. M. Walsh
J. Macdonald Oxley
J. R. Miller
J. S. Fletcher
J. S. Knowles
J. Storer Clouston
J. W. Duffield
Jack London
Jacob Abbott
James Allen
James Andrews
James Baldwin

James Branch Cabell
James DeMille
James Joyce
James Lane Allen
James Lane Allen
James Oliver Curwood
James Oppenheim
James Otis
James R. Driscoll
Jane Abbott
Jane Austen
Jane L. Stewart
Janet Aldridge
Jens Peter Jacobsen
Jerome K. Jerome
Jessie Graham Flower
John Buchan
John Burroughs
John Cournos
John F. Kennedy
John Gay
John Glasworthy
John Habberton
John Joy Bell
John Kendrick Bangs
John Milton
John Philip Sousa
John Taintor Foote
Jonas Lauritz Idemil Lie
Jonathan Swift
Joseph A. Altsheler
Joseph Carey
Joseph Conrad
Joseph E. Badger Jr
Joseph Hergesheimer
Joseph Jacobs
Jules Vernes
Julian Hawthrone
Julie A Lippmann
Justin Huntly McCarthy
Kakuzo Okakura
Karle Wilson Baker
Kate Chopin
Kenneth Grahame
Kenneth McGaffey
Kate Langley Bosher
Kate Langley Bosher
Katherine Cecil Thurston
Katherine Stokes
L. A. Abbot
L. T. Meade

L. Frank Baum
Latta Griswold
Laura Dent Crane
Laura Lee Hope
Laurence Housman
Lawrence Beasley
Leo Tolstoy
Leonid Andreyev
Lewis Carroll
Lewis Sperry Chafer
Lilian Bell
Lloyd Osbourne
Louis Hughes
Louis Joseph Vance
Louis Tracy
Louisa May Alcott
Lucy Fitch Perkins
Lucy Maud Montgomery
Luther Benson
Lydia Miller Middleton
Lyndon Orr
M. Corvus
M. H. Adams
Margaret E. Sangster
Margret Howth
Margaret Vandercook
Margaret W. Hungerford
Margret Penrose
Maria Edgeworth
Maria Thompson Daviess
Mariano Azuela
Marion Polk Angellotti
Mark Overton
Mark Twain
Mary Austin
Mary Catherine Crowley
Mary Cole
Mary Hastings Bradley
Mary Roberts Rinehart
Mary Rowlandson
M. Wollstonecraft Shelley
Maud Lindsay
Max Beerbohm
Myra Kelly
Nathaniel Hawthrone
Nicolo Machiavelli
O. F. Walton
Oscar Wilde
Owen Johnson
P.G. Wodehouse
Paul and Mabel Thorne
Paul G. Tomlinson
Paul Severing
Percy Brebner
Percy Keese Fitzhugh
Peter B. Kyne
Plato
Quincy Allen
R. Derby Holmes
R. L. Stevenson
R. S. Ball
Rabindranath Tagore
Rahul Alvares
Ralph Bonehill
Ralph Henry Barbour
Ralph Victor
Ralph Waldo Emmerson
Rene Descartes
Ray Cummings
Rex Beach
Rex E. Beach
Richard Harding Davis
Richard Jefferies
Richard Le Gallienne
Robert Barr
Robert Frost
Robert Gordon Anderson
Robert L. Drake
Robert Lansing
Robert Lynd
Robert Michael Ballantyne
Robert W. Chambers
Rosa Nouchette Carey
Rudyard Kipling
Saint Augustine
Samuel B. Allison
Samuel Hopkins Adams
Sarah Bernhardt
Sarah C. Hallowell
Selma Lagerlof
Sherwood Anderson
Sigmund Freud
Standish O'Grady
Stanley Weyman
Stella Benson
Stella M. Francis
Stephen Crane
Stewart Edward White
Stijn Streuvels
Swami Abhedananda
Swami Parmananda
T. S. Ackland
T. S. Arthur
The Princess Der Ling
Thomas A. Janvier
Thomas A Kempis
Thomas Anderton
Thomas Bailey Aldrich
Thomas Bulfinch
Thomas De Quincey
Thomas Dixon
Thomas H. Huxley
Thomas Hardy
Thomas More
Thornton W. Burgess
U. S. Grant
Upton Sinclair
Valentine Williams
Various Authors
Vaughan Kester
Victor Appleton
Victor G. Durham
Victoria Cross
Virginia Woolf
Wadsworth Camp
Walter Camp
Walter Scott
Washington Irving
Wilbur Lawton
Wilkie Collins
Willa Cather
Willard F. Baker
William Dean Howells
William le Queux
W. Makepeace Thackeray
William W. Walter
William Shakespeare
Winston Churchill
Yei Theodora Ozaki
Yogi Ramacharaka
Young E. Allison
Zane Grey

www.ingramcontent.com/pod-product-compliance
Lightning Source LLC
Chambersburg PA
CBHW020828030726
47496CB00001B/135